Readers Love Amy Lane

The Mastermind

"There are heartache and heartbreak and heartwarming moments galore in this story. And there's a long complex con that's ingenious in its execution."

—Rainbow Book Reviews

Fish Out of Water

"*Fish Out of Water* is a fast-paced, tightly plotted, steamy romantic thriller that grabbed me from the very first moments, didn't let me go until the end and left me wanting more."

—All About Romance Reviews

Riding Shotgun

"Overall, it's a quick, fun story with lots of action and some hot sex, and a HEA that satisfies. Recommended."

—Sparkling Book Reviews

Shades of Henry

"The story of Henry's past is hard to deal with, but Lance gives Henry a reason to trust. Henry gives Lance all he needs to trust back. I just love it when a plan comes together!! Can't wait for more."

—Paranormal Romance Guild

Bonfires

"This book is for everybody, for the gay and the straight, for the open minded and the close minded for the brave and for those who are afraid! Everybody…"

—OptimuMM Book Reviews

By Amy Lane

An Amy Lane Christmas
Behind the Curtain
Bewitched by Bella's Brother
Bolt-hole
Bowling for Turkeys
ChrisMyths
Christmas Kitsch
Christmas with Danny Fit
Clear Water
Do-over
Food for Thought
Freckles
Gambling Men
Going Up
Hammer & Air
Hiding the Moon
With Andrew Grey: Holiday Cheer Anthology
Homebird
If I Must
Immortal
It's Not Shakespeare
Karma Kitty Christmas
Late for Christmas
Left on St. Truth-be-Well
The Locker Room
Mourning Heaven
Phonebook
Puppy, Car, and Snow
Racing for the Sun
Raising the Stakes
Regret Me Not
Shiny!
Shirt
Sidecar
Slow Pitch
String Boys
A Solid Core of Alpha
Swipe Left, Power Down, Look Up
Three Fates
Truth in the Dark
Turkey in the Snow
The 12 Kittens of Christmas
Under the Rushes
Weirdos
Wishing on a Blue Star Anthology

BENEATH THE STAIN
Beneath the Stain
Paint It Black

BONFIRES
Bonfires
Crocus
Sunset
Torch Songs

CANDY MAN
Candy Man
Bitter Taffy
Lollipop
Tart and Sweet

COVERT
Under Cover

Published by Dreamspinner Press
www.dreamspinnerpress.com

By Amy Lane (cont'd)

DREAMSPUN BEYOND
HEDGE WITCHES
LONELY HEARTS CLUB
Shortbread and Shadows
Portals and Puppy Dogs
Pentacles and Pelting Plants
Heartbeats in a Haunted House

DREAMSPUN DESIRES
THE MANNIES
The Virgin Manny
Manny Get Your Guy
Stand by Your Manny
A Fool and His Manny

SEARCH AND RESCUE
Warm Heart
Silent Heart
Safe Heart
Hidden Heart

FISH OUT OF WATER
Fish Out of Water
Red Fish, Dead Fish
A Few Good Fish
Hiding the Moon
Fish on a Bicycle
School of Fish
Fish in a Barrel
A Perfectly Sonny Daye
Only Fish
Devil and the Deep Blue Fish
Assassin Fish

FAMILIAR LOVE
Familiar Angel
Familiar Demon

FLOPHOUSE
Shades of Henry
Constantly Cotton
Sean's Sunshine

GRANBY KNITTING
The Winter Courtship Rituals of Fur-Bearing Critters
How to Raise an Honest Rabbit
Knitter in His Natural Habitat
Blackbird Knitting in a Bunny's Lair
Weddings, Christmas, and Such
The Granby Knitting Menagerie Anthology

JOHNNIES
Chase in Shadow
Dex in Blue
Ethan in Gold
Black John
Bobby Green
Super Sock Man

KEEPING PROMISE ROCK
Keeping Promise Rock
Making Promises
Living Promises
Forever Promised

Published by Dreamspinner Press
www.dreamspinnerpress.com

By AMY LANE (cont'd)

LONG CON ADVENTURES
The Mastermind
The Muscle
The Driver
The Suit
The Tech
The Face Man
The Grifter

LUCK MECHANICS
The Rising Tide
A Salt Bitter Sea

PRINCETON ROYALS
Riding Shotgun
Running Scared

TALKER
Talker
Talker's Redemption
Talker's Graduation
The Talker Collection
Anthology

WINTER BALL
Winter Ball
Summer Lessons
Fall Through Spring

Published by DSP Publications

ALL THAT HEAVEN
WILL ALLOW
All the Rules of Heaven

GREEN'S HILL
The Green's Hill Novellas

LITTLE GODDESS
Vulnerable
Wounded, Vol. 1
Wounded, Vol. 2
Bound, Vol. 1
Bound, Vol. 2
Rampant, Vol. 1
Rampant, Vol. 2
Quickening, Vol. 1
Quickening, Vol. 2
Green's Hill Werewolves, Vol. 1
Green's Hill Werewolves, Vol. 2

Published by Harmony Ink Press

BITTER MOON SAGA
Triane's Son Rising
Triane's Son Learning
Triane's Son Fighting
Triane's Son Reigning

Published by DREAMSPINNER PRESS
www.dreamspinnerpress.com

The Grifter

AMY LANE

DREAMSPINNER
PRESS

Published by
DREAMSPINNER PRESS

8219 Woodville Hwy #1245
Woodville, FL 32362 USA
www.dreamspinnerpress.com

Trade Paperback ISBN: 9781641088954
Digital ISBN: 9781641088961
Trade Paperback published March 2026
v. 1.0

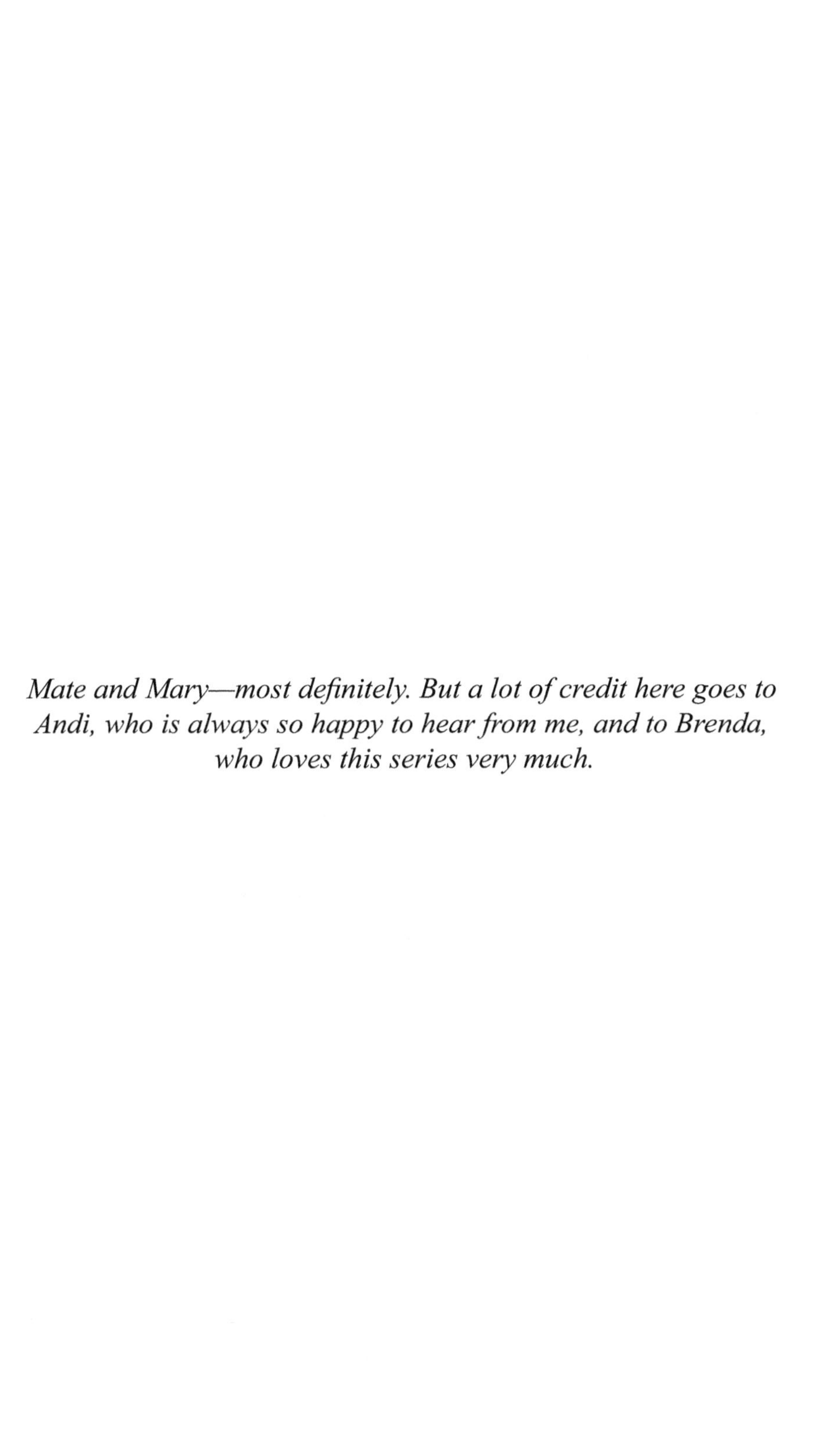

Mate and Mary—most definitely. But a lot of credit here goes to Andi, who is always so happy to hear from me, and to Brenda, who loves this series very much.

Author's Note

Supposed to be a fantasy; however, there was a rather spectacular robbery at the Louvre AFTER I wrote that scene, and I had to add the jewels in at the end as a tribute to the mother of all heists.

Long Way Down

JOSH SALINGER peered over the edge of the fifteenth-floor balcony and hissed. He was low enough that the high-rise forest of Chicago obscured his view of even the most vestigial sky, and his heart hammered with a combination of fear and claustrophobia.

He didn't feel ready for this jump, and it pissed him off.

In his ear, his comms piece buzzed, and his best friend, Dylan Li—aka Grace—said, "You gonna make this, Recovery Boy, or do we need a Plan B?"

Josh glanced behind him where the darkened "thief-proof" room sat, looking pristine and unmolested as it teased the city beyond its outstretched arms with the treasures contained within.

Thief proof Josh's still-scrawny ass. He and his team had spent *weeks* planning this job. Hacking the temperature control had stumped them for a while, until Stirling had pointed out that instead of trying to pump up the temp to ninety-eight degrees so a human could walk in the room (which would put many of the priceless works inside at risk), all they had to do was account for what the temperature was when disturbed by one human.

And putting the human in a dry suit to contain some of his heat put that difficulty in the bounds of acceptable risk.

Josh had gotten access as an up-and-coming art dealer, his bona fides backed up by Stirling's excellent hacking and his Uncle Danny's references. Uncle Danny's day job was being an art docent for the Chicago Art Institute, so that hadn't been hard, and Josh had grown up around art, both in America and abroad. He knew his shit, so actually *doing* the job of an art dealer wasn't a stretch. Which was good because he had to be doing *something* to keep his cover up. Besides, he and his family liked art. With his family's help, he'd spotted a couple of new talents and gotten them coveted places in nearby shows, even offering to showcase paintings and one sculpture at his parents' home. His father, Felix Salinger, owned a Chicago-based cable network that had gone national. Without his ever asking a broker's fee, a *lot* of art had been sold because somebody had seen it on the wall in the Salinger dining room. His mother had planned the entire room around doing that.

So yeah. The side gig that was supposed to be his real gig had been satisfying, but what it *really* had done was give him unlimited access to the private collection of Celeste Buenaventura, heiress, party girl, jet-setter, and, in his mother's words, "porcutwat." Looked pretty and sexy, had a thousand ways to make any interaction unnecessarily painful.

Sadly, along with her mother's billions, the girl had also inherited her father's ruthlessness and recklessness in business. She ran his enterprises deftly, cheated unions and vendors alike, bought art in quantity and quality to hoard and lord over the masses, and slept with anything that slithered.

She was that rare bird—a person with no moral center but wielding enough imagination to love and appreciate art, even the weird stuff like Otto Dix that made people both queasy and tearful with the horrific nature of mankind at war.

Much of her private collection was stolen; she had a fondness for stuff that had disappeared during WWII after having been confiscated from their victims by the Nazis.

Again, a real porcutwat.

She said it was for "historical significance," but the majority of recovered art that had been stolen by the Third Reich had been restored to the original owners, or more recently their descendants. With the exception of the United States government, most of the world still regarded the ideals of the Nazis with contempt.

No, Celeste Buenaventura liked to keep stolen art because it made her feel powerful over the poor and unlucky, which made her the perfect person to set up for this caper, which was why Josh had spent the last four weeks pretending to be her art dealer—and keeping one step away from her entitled octopus hands.

Ugh. As. If.

But her much-examined history had shown that Josh, of all the men in the crew, was Celeste's type, which was unfortunate, because he was also the guy planning the heist and the guy who needed to be *back* downstairs at the party to give coy, shy smiles and dodge neatly out of the way from Celeste's wandering hands like a champion twat tease.

However, that's what put him on this ledge right now, attaching the paracord to his carabiner and getting ready to leap three stories, catch his weight on the cord, and then rappel three more floors down to the men's room he'd excused himself into fifteen minutes ago.

"Josh? Recovery Boy? You ready to go? That's one hell of a jump."

Josh blinked. The voice was different—no longer the staccato patter of his best friend, the thief who *should* have been doing this if he'd been at all able to people enough to pull a grift. Instead it was the deeper, more gravelly bass of Grace's boyfriend, Hunter.

"How long's it been?" Josh asked hoarsely. His bones felt fragile, his muscles weak. Oh God. He was about to blow this caper because he'd pushed himself too far, too fast, and now he was about to prove everybody who loved him right by wimping out at the last possible moment.

Jesus, boy-o, what in the hell are you trying to prove?

Liam's voice, during their last heated conversation, reverberated through his head.

Josh had scowled and walked away, leaving Liam, curly hair in stunning disarray, freckled face blotched, usually smiling mouth compressed in anger, and, Josh knew in his fragile bones, hurt.

Josh had owed him an explanation, and now, before making a jump that would have been easy fifteen months ago, before the cancer had sucked out his strength and his stamina, he hoped he'd have the chance to give it to him.

God, Liam, I don't want you to see me as wounded. Is that too much to fucking ask?

But he hadn't asked, had he? He'd simply gone about and planned the damned op, politely asking his Uncle Danny—who'd been the one to bring Interpol Officer Liam Craig into their painfully intimate circle of grifters, thieves, and muscle—to pass along their planning to "anybody who might need to know."

Danny had given him a distinctly disapproving look but had done as Josh asked, probably figuring—as most parental figures did when their children hit adulthood—he would eventually pull his head out of his ass and fix this thing with Liam, who didn't seem to have a petty or bitter bone in his body.

I want to see him again, Josh thought. *I need to tell him I'm sorry. I need to tell him why.*

"Josh?" Hunter asked tentatively.

"Yee-fucking-haw," Josh said grimly… and made the jump.

The first descent was terrifying—and exhilarating—and for a whole heartbeat Josh remembered why he'd done this for fun before. And then a gust of wind came out of fucking nowhere from off the fucking lake, and Josh was slammed sideways and into the building. He let out a grunt of pain, and his left arm went numb.

Oh fuck. He had to be three stories lower and to the left and ready to party in less than three minutes.

"Josh?" Hunter asked, his voice taking on the restrained tension of someone trying not to panic.

"Arm," Josh gasped. "Shoulder. Have Grace ready to pull me in when I hit the balcony."

Hunter muttered something to somebody else, and Josh concentrated on not throwing up. God, he'd hardly ever thrown up as a kid, but since the big C and chemo and recovery and special foods and protein drinks, throwing up was his go-to for any sort of discomfort.

Fiercely, he concentrated on working the rope, the pulley, gloved hands and slippered feet finding purchase on the hundred-year-old stone of the stately apartment building. Oh thank you, Celeste Buenaventura and your great taste in art and living quarters, even if you are a shitty human being!

He'd forgotten how pain could dog even the most fluid movement, could make his breath come short, could… oh God, foot, foot, foot—he was so close. If only he could extend his arm to pull himself closer.

Pain blinded him, and he almost lost his grip on the rope. He fought the urge to throw up and was trying to pull his shit together enough to actually slide onto the balcony when he felt an arm around his waist and a hand at his belt, while a familiar voice, accented with London's East End, conferred with Grace.

"He right bloody bollixed it," Liam hissed. "God. Out of socket, you think?"

"Here," Grace said, sounding flat and unemotional, which meant he was *really* panicked. "Liam, you steady him, I'll hold his arm. Hunter—"

The crack his shoulder made when it slid back into its socket was what pushed him over the edge.

"Gonna puke," he rasped, and before he could even position himself, he felt strong hands on his waist and another under his chin, and somebody—probably Grace—was holding the puke bag.

The stomach spasm was mercifully swift, and Grace—ethereally graceful and beautiful like the stars even with such an awful chore—disappeared with the offending receptacle. Someone—Hunter, Grace's decked, stoic boyfriend—wiped Josh down and thrust a breath mint into his mouth, and Liam…?

Definitely Liam… simply held him upright, whispering into his hair.

"Goddammit, boy-o, you had to do all this without me? Can I come help now? Please?"

Oh God. "Dammit, Liam," Josh rasped, trying to put his weight on his feet. "I missed you so bad. Do you really have to see me like this?"

"I'll take you anyway I can get you, lad. Just don't leave me behind."

And then Grace was back, lint roller in one hand for Josh's all-black suit, bottle of water so Josh could rinse and spit the breath freshener, and a comb for a quick touch-up. Grace—whose real name was Dylan Li—was often described as a firefly in a tornado. Off-the-charts brilliant, a stunning dancer, so much natural beauty most people claimed it was like a slug to the gut. The catch to all this might have been called ADHD on steroids with a nuclear chaser: Grace was lucky he lived through most days, either because his own recklessness and lack of focus would get him killed or because the people around him wanted to kill him before the gods took their share.

But nobody who believed that had seen Grace over this last year, working his ass off to keep Josh alive.

"Thanks, Dylan," Josh said softly, catching Grace's hands as he went for one more swipe of Josh's suit. "I'm fine."

"You are not fine, and I need at least twenty minutes to tell you why you're *fucked* and a fucking asshole, so let me—" He literally spit on his hand, wiped a scuff of dirt from Josh's check, and then flounced off.

"Oh dear," Josh murmured. "Everybody's pissed off, and I've got to go get my ass grabbed."

"Good news is," Hunter said, shining a light in Josh's eyes to make sure he wasn't concussed, "a bigwig entered right when she would have been searching for you. She's been kissing up to him for the last fifteen minutes."

Josh perked up. "Our target?"

"No," Hunter said. "Leon di Rossi, the European shipping tycoon, with his newest belle, Julia Salinger."

Josh groaned. "They didn't—"

"They were on standby, my boy," came a new voice, and Josh hoped the balcony would break off the side of the building so he could die right there.

"Uncle Danny… this was supposed to be—"

"Oh, son," Danny—who was not Josh's real uncle, but Josh had always considered him a second father—said. "This is a big enterprise, but we're a big crew. We've all had a hand in this. You wouldn't want to cut us out now, would you?"

Josh gave him a weak smile. "No," he said softly. "Sorry, Uncle Danny."

Danny gave him a tender kiss on the forehead. "Plenty of people will yell at you—you don't need me. Give your prize to Liam and then go back in there and put on your show. This little caper has had some glitches, but they all do. If you and your mother and Uncle Leon can get out of there without notice, this will all be worth it. Trust me."

Josh felt some strength infusing him. Worth it? Well, then—let the con go on!

At his side, Liam gave a nod to Danny, who nodded back, and with that, Hunter, Danny, and Grace all faded away—probably to scale back down the dark side of the building to the waiting van—and only Liam was left.

"Liam…," Josh said plaintively, hating that his voice was still a little thready with fear and hurt.

"Stop," Liam said harshly. "No. Not from you. You asked me to stay away until you were up to full strength, and here you are. Jumping out of buildings and risking your life. You're up to full strength, and here I am."

Josh grunted. "Not so full strength if I'm fucking up this early in the game, am—"

The self-deprecation died aborning.

Liam Craig had been by his side for so much of his illness. He'd caught Josh when he'd stumbled, carried him to bed when Josh had overdone it, entertained him for hours while Josh's family went out on capers much like this one and Josh had to stay behind.

Secret by painful secret they'd peeled the veils from each other's hearts until Josh felt as naked with Liam as he'd ever felt with another human being, including the few lovers he'd taken in his short span on the planet.

It was a painful sort of intimacy, a frightening sort of need, but Josh had been sick, leukemia ravaging his slender body, threatening to destroy every plan and every hope and every dream he'd ever had.

For all that Liam was to his heart, for all that he'd been devastated when Josh had begged him to stay away these last five months, not once—not ever—had they kissed.

Until now.

Liam's mouth crashed onto Josh's with absolute fury, and Josh's breath caught in his chest as he fought for the strength to keep up.

I Don't Think I'll Make it On My Own

Six months earlier

"NOW THAT'S a ship," Liam said, mostly to himself as he approached the yacht in San Juan harbor. Liam had come quite a ways from his mother's East End flat and the five younger siblings he'd worked hard to feed from the time he'd hit fourteen.

Even as a copper, his income hadn't increased that much from what he'd received as a strong back loading freight on the docks. He'd continued to live in the flat until his brothers and sisters got old enough to help their mum, and then while spending his days as a bobby, he'd done a remarkable thing.

A series of small art thefts had occurred in the local museums about his neighborhood. Nothing too large—nothing that would bankrupt the places—but small things, almost whimsical items. A button from a uniform worn by a general rumored to be Oscar Wilde's first lover. The tiara from a cottage maid who'd lived happily with the Archduke of Somebody, giving him many children while he was ostensibly married to his cousin.

Nothing too spendy. Nothing too spectacular.

And nothing to be related to the following month or two, wherein something *fabulous*—a Monet thought to be destroyed when the Nazis invaded Paris, for instance—would suddenly resurface, hung on full display for the world to see where no painting or sculpture had been before.

The events were… sporadic. There was no rhyme or reason to them. No pattern, except that when one small thing disappeared, one large thing took its place. Liam had been… intrigued. In his spare hours, sitting cross-legged on his twin bed in the room he still shared with his younger brother, he'd mapped out the museums that had been hit, the things taken, the things returned.

And had come to an odd conclusion.

Money wasn't involved in either the thefts or the returns. The thefts were *so* small, but they all had to do with, of all things, love affairs ending badly—or held in secret. The returns had to do with righting a terrible wrong.

One day, his day off, he was wandering a small museum—one of the ones that had been hit already—when he came upon a miniature that, Liam could *swear* it, had been painted by Francis Bacon upon the suicide of his lover, George Dyer. He stared at the six-inch painting, heartsickened by the image, trying desperately to remember if the artist ever worked this small. This seemed a sketch, framed, not a fully realized painting, and while Liam wasn't really a fan of the work—Bacon hurt his heart and his senses—he could appreciate the skill and the passion.

"Lovely sketch, that," said a man passing by. He was cute—a good ten years older than Liam but puckish, with curly brown hair and slightly crooked teeth. Slender in build, with a vulpine face, the man shouldn't have been remarkable, but somehow he had Liam's complete attention.

"Tragic," Liam said, giving the man a slight smile. Then, quite seriously, he said, "But this sketch doesn't belong here—these are all nineteenth-century expressionist. I have no idea what a modern-art sketch is doing with this lot."

"You know your art, then?" the man asked, cocking his head. Liam got a faint whiff of expensive scotch and tried not to recoil. It could be as innocent as a businessman having a drink with lunch, but Liam's father had died young of too much drink—and too much driving near country bridges—and Liam had no fond memories of scotch.

"I know my crime," Liam murmured, frowning at the sketch. "Have you seen the art docent nearby? I want to ask him about—"

But the man was gone.

And while there was nothing to suggest it overtly—Liam knew his own freckled features with the slight gap in his front teeth were neither elite nor particularly stunning—he had the feeling it wasn't because the man had found his company unpleasant.

In fact, he was pretty sure it was because he'd spoken to the thief/art restorer himself.

And after a brief, frantic consultation with the docent, who had *never* seen that Francis Bacon sketch before—this, goddammit, *wasn't* that sort of museum!—Liam was quite sure of it.

And after writing a detailed report and sending it to his local Interpol office, he had his guess confirmed and was invited to a one-on-one meeting with Detective Chief Inspector Alec Lawson.

Lawson was about fifteen years Liam's senior, with prematurely silver hair, tired eyes—wandering eyes, as Liam would discover—and a kind, distracted smile.

And two file boxes on a thief he and half of Europe called "Lightfingers."

"You talked to him?" Lawson asked excitedly, like a much younger man asking about a pop star.

"I suspect so," Liam said. "He… he said the sketch was a good one when it clearly didn't belong there."

"What was he like?"

Liam thought carefully over the seconds-long exchange. "Sad," he said after a moment. "That painting. It really… it meant something."

Lawson's face fell. "That's too bad," he said. "In the past he's been… whimsical. Happy paintings, pretty families." He brightened. "He once substituted a child's sculpture of a cartoon character for the sculpture he stole from a private collector who had the original illegally."

"He kept the original?" Liam asked.

Lawson shook his head. "No, no—it found its way back to the French museum where it had been stolen." That soft expression again. "No fatalities," he said. "No big break-ins through glass ceilings. Ninety percent of the time the thefts are to return something where it belongs. I swear to God, he's like king of the goddamned fairies."

Liam—who'd once been given that moniker in school and had to bloody a lot of noses before losing it—grimaced.

Alec caught the expression and misinterpreted it. "I don't know if he's that kind of fairy too, but so what?" That last was said challengingly, and Liam gave a startled chuckle.

"I thought that was my name," he said, and Lawson's sad eyes turned speculative.

"I could have sworn it was mine."

The dalliance lasted only six months, but it was long enough for Liam to get promoted to Detective Inspector and Interpol liaison—and for Lawson to rekindle his romance with the wife he'd never told Liam about.

Disappointed and more than ready to move out of his mother's flat, Liam took an assignment from Interpol that involved a more frightening kind of criminal. Andres Kadjic was a Jack-of-all-trades. Guns, drugs, girls—he trafficked them all, and surprisingly, he spent much of his ill-gotten gains on *art*.

Before Lawson retired into politics, he'd put Liam on a task force trailing Kadjic through North Africa and Eastern Europe.

Liam had been but a tiny cog in a big bureaucratic wheel at the time, but he'd gotten to travel, gotten to see Morocco and Prague, St. Petersburg and Istanbul, and everywhere he went, he'd catch a whisper, a scent, of Lightfingers, the man who sometimes stole for profit (but usually from the filthy rich) and often stole to even the scales. (He was the tinier museums' best friend.)

The hard-core law and order folk at Interpol would loudly decry that a thief was a thief, but the younger generation would file their reports on the crimes—still with that element of whimsy—and say to themselves that they'd be very disappointed if this man was caught.

"Seriously, we've got the likes of Kadjic literally polluting the world with misery, and this guy swaps out the portrait of some noble's wife for a privately commissioned one of his mistress, and we're supposed to go after him, guns blazing? It's a *joke*, for God's sake."

For his part, Liam kept to himself that memory of the puckish, boozy man who had chuckled to himself about the painting being hung in the wrong place. He felt as though he'd been allowed a privileged glimpse of an endangered species in its natural habitat. The gentleman thief was, after all, a rare bird indeed.

And then Liam tracked a pair of forged passports to Morocco. The carriers of the documents were a father and his son—both artists—but Liam had noted that they seemed to be running from wherever Kadjic was. Which made him think that if he could find *them* before Kadjic did, he could make one of those arrests that young up-and-coming officers only dreamed about—and maybe earn the rank that Alec Lawson had bestowed upon him out of guilt.

He was literally wandering the streets one evening when he heard the chatter of excited children. He walked through that back alley and saw a dozen kids, each with their own set of thick crayons, all of them scribbling on the outside wall of one of the most unpleasant vendors in the square—a man who sold Khubz, and who sold it dearly and would rather feed the crusts to the pigs or chickens than to give even a scrap to the hungry children.

The children were not drawing graffiti, though; they were drawing pictures. Yes, some of them were of the baker, and none too flattering, but some of them were of hawks from the world-famous aerie nearby, and some were of horses, and some were of sparrows.

Liam approached a little girl drawing a dragonfly and offered her a dirham. "Yes?" he asked.

She nodded, her eyes fastened hungrily on the coin.

"Who gave you the crayons?" he asked in passable French.

Her response sounded like "Dwyleje," and it took him a moment to translate.

Doigts Le'gers.

Light fingers.

"Only crayons?" he asked her.

"Khubz," she replied happily, and only then did he notice the paper-wrapped bread in the pocket of every child there.

Lightfingers bringing food and art to street children.

Idly, he wondered which item would be reported stolen next.

In any event, it wasn't his circus—nor his particular monkey—and he had business to attend to in Casino de Monte Carlo, where the current pit boss was trying very hard not to turn on Liam's big fish, who also happened to be the casino's biggest client.

Ayoub Fassi was a muscular man with a stout face and a constantly sour expression. He seemed to have a hatred for everybody—not only Liam, but anybody foreign or who spoke English as opposed to French was on his hit list.

When Liam, wearing a white linen suit and a straw hat in deference to the sun, walked into the man's office and gave his most charming smile, Ayoub had merely wrinkled his nose and launched into a diatribe against anybody with freckles, curly hair and….

Liam had to look up the word the man kept using, and then his eyebrows went up.

"Really, mate," he said in his broadest East End accent. "We're not good enough friends for you to comment on that!"

Fassi gave a hiss, as though knowing damned well he had gone too far. "It is this Kadjic," he spat. "He's one. He and his…." The word that came next was best translated as "concubine," but it had a distinctly male flavor. "He drags the man in, and neither of them are decent. Swilling scotch, laughing—he dresses like a cartoon character. Is insulting."

"Cartoon character?" Liam asked, at a loss.

"Aladdin," Fassi said succinctly. "So insulting."

Well, yes, there was some cultural appropriation involved, but a lot of kids loved that cartoon. Liam wasn't going to dissect the implications *now*.

"So Kadjic and his boyfriend are here?" he asked. "In the city? When did you last see them?"

Fassi shrugged. "An hour ago? 'Aladdin' was trying to get him to forget something… something about a painter. I don't know." He sighed. "If I did not hate that cartoon so much, I might find the young man charming."

Liam blinked. The word was… evocative somehow.

"Do you know where they went?" Liam asked.

"The market district," Fassi said unequivocally. "Kadjic had found somebody there he'd been searching for."

Liam felt his face pale. Fassi might not know this, because apparently Kadjic spent his money prodigiously at this establishment, but "finding somebody" Kadjic had been hunting for did not bode well for anybody.

Without another word, Liam bolted, pulling his comms out and rushing to find a cab that would take him to the market district where he'd just been.

On a burst of breath, he told the other two people he'd managed to drag with him to Morocco chasing the painter lead—oh shit, oh hell, *a painter* that Kadjic had *found*—and told them to search the market district, close to the bazaar where a father and his son might slip in to what was left of the afternoon crowd.

The cab let him out before the streets became pedestrian traffic only, and the absolute stillness of the evening told him something was happening that only the people who lived there would know.

He paused for a moment after the cab roared off, and he listened. He heard a man plead. And a child's scream. And then another man yell… and chaos erupt.

He rounded the corner of the alley, weapon out, badge extended, screaming, "Interpol, put your weapons down!" in time to see a midsize man wearing a very sharp European suit and black leather shoes disappear around the corner. Liam would later hear that he'd allowed his target to escape, but he couldn't regret it.

In front of him was a scene from a nightmare. A man with pale skin and light blue open eyes—poor, with a battered knapsack in his hands and wearing the most threadbare of traditional garments—slumped against the wall, his head tilted to the side, halfway separated from his neck. His mouth was open, blood still oozing from his throat like a dying river.

On the ground next to him was a thug—no other word for it—a thickly muscled man in another sharp black suit (in this heat, for fuck's sake!) He had black hair, white, white skin, and his hands were coated in blood. As was the weapon in his fist. The thug groaned slightly, and a third man on the ground a few feet from him let out a sob.

"Is the…," he gasped. "Is the boy okay?"

At that moment one of Liam's fellow agents rounded the corner, and Liam gestured at the groaning armed man.

"Cuff him," he said imperiously, as though he knew exactly what had happened when all he knew for sure was that the thug with the knife was bad news. When that guy had been secured, he bent next to the bleeding man on the ground, and almost cried to recognize his phantom thief, the giver of crayons and bread.

"Hello, my friend," he said softly, wincing at the mess of blood on the man's midsection. "What happened to you here?"

"Kadjic," gasped the man. "Didn't like it when I jumped on Yuri's back. Said he'd teach me manners. Good thing he forgot how to spell."

"Spell?" Liam glanced up at Carter, his counterpart.

Carter shrugged and spoke into his comms, asking for medical assistance while the boozy, youngish man with the curly hair and the charm—and the blue velveteen harem pants and vest of an expensively dressed Aladdin—tried to talk.

"His name. My flesh. I think he forgot the d."

Liam stared at him in horror, squatting to take his hand regardless of protocol. "Weren't you his boyfriend?" he asked baldly, and that earned him a blood-flecked smile. *Nicked lung*, Liam thought, and prayed the medics would arrive soon.

"Right up until—" The man gasped. "—I stopped Yuri from killing Antoine Couvier's son." He squeezed his eyes closed. "I didn't know he'd kill Antoine. Poor Antoine… seemed like such a gentle man. Fucking booze. I should have known."

Liam smoothed his hand over the man's brow, wanting to give comfort, until it hit him. "His son!" he gasped. "Did he get away?"

Aladdin nodded. "Nicked the paint in his bag. You can see it. Green. Like grass." He let out a little sob. "Like home."

Liam could see the man losing consciousness and thought, *I should arrest him for art theft. He must be Lightfingers—he must be!* But Andre Kadjic had just tried to carve his initials in the man's ribs—after he'd choked out the thug who'd killed Antoine Couvier and gone after his son.

That was a lot of valor in their little thief, Liam thought. Arresting him now would be a poor way to repay him.

At that moment the medics arrived in a small, old white-painted van with a red cross on the front. Liam moved out of the way to let them work, getting the location of the hospital from the driver before he went to talk to Carter.

"What'd he say?" the man asked, stepping aside so a medic could treat the still-groaning mob muscle on the ground.

"Said Kadjic ordered his man to kill Antoine Couvier and then the man's son. L… little guy couldn't stop Couvier's death, but he did manage to choke out the hired help while the kid got away." Liam glanced around at the dark that had fallen dreadfully fast. "Poor kid," he muttered. "Must be scared to death."

Carter, a fortyish veteran with the hide of a Komodo dragon, gave a snort. "Not for long. If Kadjic finds him, he'll be dead!"

Liam's heart started pounding in his ears. He may have moved out of his mother's flat, but that didn't mean he didn't miss the whole stinking lot of them. How old would the boy be? He'd been what? Six? Seven? When his father had first gone on the run after tipping the authorities off to one of Kadjic's operations via a clever flaw in their forged documents. That would make Etienne twelve now. Liam could see his own little brother, Caleb, with spidery arms and legs, thin wrists and ankles, and that sort of perpetually super-excited/super-confused expression that a lot of boys that age seemed to have.

"We need to find him," he said, trying not to let his panic show.

Carter looked around as though there were listening devices on the dirt streets, the clay walls, the colorful canopies set up to temper the brutal daytime sun that only blocked the stars now.

"If we do find him," he said softly, "he needs to *disappear*, you hear me? So he doesn't *disappear*."

Liam blinked. "Any ideas where he should *disappear* to?" he asked, realizing that Carter had just suggested waggling their fingers and making a material witness go away to save the boy's life. It was an unexpectedly human move from the seemingly implacable Carter, but maybe Carter had memories of children he loved too.

"Talk to your Aladdin friend," Carter said. "He seems to feel some obligation to the boy. But first let's find him."

It took them all night.

The green paint helped, but the boy had been wily—and fast. Over, around, through—he must have hit every street in Morocco before finally crawling into a back alley and curling up, head on his knees, to sleep.

The eyes the boy turned to Liam when he approached were unutterably weary… but grateful.

Liam stashed the boy in his own small flat to sleep, bathe, recover, while he went to see how their Aladdin friend was doing. Tienne—as he gave his own name—seemed to be in a sort of fugue state. Liam didn't think he'd run, but he had Carter come over to keep him company anyway. Carter promised to sleep on the couch all day and maybe get them food, which for Carter was a declaration of responsibility.

Aladdin was waking up from surgery when Liam showed up in his room in the early afternoon, but that didn't mean he wasn't trying to cadge some scrubs from the attending orderly so he could slip out the back door.

"Oh-ho, now!" Liam said cheerfully. "That's no way to repay the man who rescued you, is it?"

He got a sour look in return. "Rescue me? Are you serious? After trying to drink myself to death for a year, I finally found a shortcut. You *cheated* me is what you did. I could have been happy and dead by now."

Liam gasped as though slapped, and remembered the Francis Bacon painting. Aladdin of the velveteen pantaloons was apparently in a dark place.

Well, Liam could go there with him. "That's a shitty thing to do to the people around you, isn't it? There's got to be somebody out there who would miss you."

Aladdin sagged into the bed and rubbed the back of his neck. "I… wow, copper, you don't know it, but you hit me where I don't live anymore." He took the deep shuddering breath of a man who was trying not to cry, because men *weren't* supposed to cry, and kept his face averted. "What are you doing here?"

"I wanted to tell you that the boy—Tienne—is okay. I'd say fine, but—"

Aladdin swallowed. "He just saw his father practically beheaded in a back alley. No. Not fine. Poor kid."

Listening to him now, Liam could hear the British accent he'd affected—fairly successfully—slipping. What remained was subtly American, although Liam wasn't yet great at gauging from where. If it wasn't a moviesque New York or Southern accent, he was at a loss.

"He thinks you're a hero, you know." Liam softened his own tone and, trying to appear non-threatening, sat down in the chair across from the reluctant patient and got a good look at his face.

He was breathing hard—Liam had heard he'd nicked a lung, although there'd been no pneumothorax, thanks to the quick treatment. But the flesh of his rib cage and concave stomach had been *carved* upon—literally a *K*, *A*, *D* and the beginnings of a *J*.

Liam could see blood seeping out through the bandages and thought with a sudden cold sweat that if he'd managed to get some scrubs and slip out the window—and it was obvious he'd been eyeing it the entire time as an exit—the young man might truly fulfill his wish and die. Quickly or slowly, it wouldn't matter.

With a swallow, Aladdin dashed at his eyes with the palm of his hand. "He doesn't know, though, does he?" he mumbled, almost to himself. "What a real waste of oxygen I am."

"You saved his life," Liam said. "And now we need your help."

Surprised, the man glanced up, his eyes red-rimmed and shadowed with pain and exhaustion. The hand he moved to wipe more tears was shaking, and Liam had a sudden flash of insight. The boozy humor in the museum, the announcement of "trying to drink himself to death."

He apparently almost *had* drunk himself to death. Now that he was coming down from the anesthetic, he was detoxing.

"I'm a wreck," the man said, laughing bitterly at himself. "I'm not sure what I can do."

"Do you know the boy?" Liam asked.

A shake of the head. "No. First time I saw him was in that alley. I tried not to pay attention when Kadjic was working."

As long as the booze was good—the words remained unspoken, but the recrimination hung in the air.

"Well, we've got two options. One is to take him into custody as a material witness—"

"And sign the boy's death warrant?"

Those puckish features suddenly sharpened, and Liam could feel it roaring out of the man: Protectiveness for a boy he'd never met.

"Or find someone willing to shelter him," Liam said. *Besides me mum, who would do it, too, but that's a fine way to thank her.*

"Shit," Aladdin muttered. "Shit, shit, shit-shit-shit-shit-shit. Fuck. Goddammit. *Fuck*."

Liam found himself chuckling in spite of the direness of the situation. "That was impressive."

There was a roll of the eyes. "Is my bag of stuff still here?" Aladdin asked. Liam found it on the side of the bed and handed it over. Inside was a cell phone—but not a smart phone. This was a dinosaur, a Nokia, the tiny coffin-shaped one that needed shortcut keys and a degree in cryptography to text.

The charge was dying on the thing, but there was a cord—as ancient as the phone—and an adapter in the bag too.

And enough cash to rent a flat for a year.

And a small silver flask. Liam checked it for an inscription.

Danny, to grand adventures. Love forever, Felix.

Liam swallowed, and then watched as Danny—it had to be his flask—plugged in the phone and hit a number. Not a preset, from memory.

"Dearest?" he said in a voice one might use for a beloved sister. "No, no—don't give him the phone. Don't tell Josh either. Just… goddammit, I had no idea you'd all be eating breakfast. Get up, apologize to Fox, and hide in the office for a minute. I've got…." His voice fractured. "Julia, I have a huge favor to ask you, but it's important."

There was a pause as Danny waited for the woman to do what he asked. Then after a brief, tearful entreaty on the other end of the line, Danny replied in an equally fractured voice, "Sweetheart, I'm a mess. I can't come home like this. Do you think I want the boy to see me like this? I can't… I can't come back to Fox when I'm looking up to see rock bottom. I… a man has his pride."

He broke on the word "pride," and Liam had a terrible sense of how much this conversation was costing him.

That tearful voice again, but with an edge of control. They were both pulling themselves together.

"There's a boy," Danny said. "Our boy's age. He's… he's seen terrible things. He needs shelter. I… I have no idea if he understands family like we do. He may prefer boarding school—" Danny paused. "Art, I think. He and his father make—made—beautiful art. That is the only thing I know about him. But he needs home. Someplace that is home. You… I may not be able to come back, but he's got no sins to repent. He needs somebody, and I- I can't be that somebody. Not now."

There was a digestive silence, and then the voice, calmer now, in charge.

"I'll give the phone to my young copper friend—" A sudden look of disgust. "No, I didn't get nicked. My God, woman, cut a man when he's down. He is…." Danny gave Liam a beseeching glance. "He is a friend. And he's doing this boy a big favor shipping him to you. He'll need another name and ID. I'll…." Danny let out a breathy sigh and seemed to sag even more against the bed.

Gently, Liam took the phone from his fingers and gestured for him to lie down to rest. This man had just come out of surgery—and, as he'd told the woman on the phone, he had to look up to see rock bottom.

"Hello?" Liam said softly. "This is Agent Liam Craig, Interpol. Your friend here—"

"Danny?" she said, and while her voice was thick, it was also begging for confirmation.

"Danny," he confirmed when the figure in the bed nodded. "He's been helping us in an investigation, and the boy… he's at risk. I don't know if you're equipped to deal with someone who needs a new identity—"

"Oh, you leave that part to us," she said, so dryly Liam had to wonder at her background with Danny Lightfingers, the thief. "But Danny—"

"Please," Danny said, shivering in what was probably his first shock of the DTs. "Please don't tell her."

"He needs to dry out," Liam said. "Don't worry. I can find him a place."

"Tell her not to tell Felix," Danny whispered. "Not anything. Just shelter the boy."

"He…." Liam swallowed, realizing that here was when he put himself between two lovers. "He requests that you don't tell Felix."

"Fucking aces," Julia said acidly. "Tell him…." Her venom only lasted four words. "Tell him he can come home anytime."

"I'll do that," Liam said. "Here's my number." He rattled it off. "I'll call you with travel information—"

"What does the boy have?" she asked. "Does he need anything?"

"He needs everything," Liam told her, thinking of the backpack, which had been sliced by the murderer's knife and had bled its contents, including the green paint, all over the streets of Morocco. "I don't think he's got a spare pair of skivvies to call his own."

"Poor baby," she said, and her compassion was real. "Contact me in an hour with a place to send money, and I'll see that you get him kitted out and on a plane to Chicago. I've got to get my son off to school and speak to my husband, but we'll get this sorted."

It was on the tip of his tongue to warn her again not to speak to Felix, whoever he was to her, but she signed off, and the line went dead.

He handed the phone back to Lightfingers, who unconsciously cradled it to his chest.

"She's… formidable," he said and was amused by Lightfingers's adamant nod.

"She is." He closed his eyes. "I hate to turn the boy loose, but if anybody can offer him shelter, she and Fox can."

"Is she your sister?" he asked. Something about their familiarity, their pained separation, spoke deeply of family.

Danny Lightfingers let out a fractured laugh. "Lover's wife," he said, with a bitter smile at Liam's surprise. "It's not as sordid as you're thinking. She…." He shuddered. "She needed to escape. She was pregnant, and her father would have beaten her to death if he'd found out. So we married her off to Felix." And then, to Liam's everlasting wonder, he saw Danny Lightfingers smile. He was huddling in the bed, in pain and detoxing, and he smiled.

He looked like a fallen angel.

"And she had the baby, and we were a family. And it was really wonderful." Then a tear escaped from eyes he'd squeezed shut. "The boy… he's ten now. Just went to his party. Snuck in, hugged him, left him a gift, snuck out. So smart. Kind. Light of my life."

"Why'd you leave?" Liam asked, his heart hurting.

"'Cause that's all I ever was to them," Danny whispered, and he was *Danny* now, whatever his last name. He was young—Liam would find out later he was barely thirty—and he was sad and lonely and in pain. "I was the thing that crept in their windows, made love to Fox, played games with the boy, hugged my sister… crept out. It's cold in the shadows, young copper. Pretty soon I needed the scotch to warm my heart so it would beat. None of it was any way to live."

Liam's eyes were burning. He didn't know the whole of the story, but he knew enough now. He'd had a dalliance with a man who had lied about being married. It had hurt, but the thought of being in love, not only with a man but with a *family*, and being the dirty secret—the ache that would cause….

Chilled Liam to the bone, and he was just sitting by the man's bed.

"What next?" he asked, settling down in the chair again, this time so Danny could see him sitting.

"I have no idea," Danny mumbled.

"I do," Liam said. "You know, Interpol agents have a thing for scotch."

He got a crooked smile. "Oh really?"

"Or coke or gin." Liam had seen enough of it—Carter was headed for a treatment program if he didn't stop taking a snort in the morning to wake himself up. Either that or a cardiac infarction.

"There's a center—a good place. Not an awful place. It's in Ireland. I can get you a bed there, Lightfingers."

"So I could wake up in prison? No thank you." Danny managed to open his eyes for that one, and Liam had to laugh.

"Well, you get me a name I can give them that *isn't* an international art thief, and I'll get you there," Liam said, meaning it.

Danny closed his eyes. "This is a nice fantasy," he mumbled. "But it's never going to work—"

"That boy," Liam said harshly. "You're going to just leave him?"

"Tienne?" The reply was puzzled. "I thought we were hashing that out!"

"The other one," Liam said. "Josh. The one you snuck in to see. He'll want to see you again. And again. My father was a drunk. And, you know, he died early, and he left us poor, but you know what? We miss him. You keep going like you are, I won't be in the next alleyway to bail you out."

"Oh God," Danny groaned. "You're young, copper, but I think I hate you."

Liam reached out and took one of those fine-boned, trembling hands in his own. He felt a kinship for this man.

"You," Danny said, "are far too young for me."

"My last lover was ten years your senior," Liam told him dryly. "But that's the last time I sleep with a married man, and your heart is obviously already taken by this Fox fellow. No, this is a simple human touch, my friend." His dryness faded. "Please. My father was a sweet man with a weakness. I'd give anything to have him back. You… you just saved a boy at your worst moment. I think you've got the strength to fight this thing. That boy you love—he's waiting to see you again. Think about how he'd feel if you crawled off to die."

There was a deadly quiet then, and Liam could hear, barely, the changes in Danny's breathing as the tears slipped through in spite of his best efforts.

Finally, "I'll need a sedative," he murmured. "Enough to kill the DTs while I go find my cache."

Liam cocked his head. "I'm in *Interpol*—"

"Nothing stolen!" Danny retorted, voice wounded. "My God, you people—you and Julia—with the insults. Just my ID, my computer. Did you think I left that with *Kadjic*? Not enough booze in the *world*."

My God, he was sharp. Liam wondered what sort of menace he'd be when he was fully sober.

And suddenly resolved to find out.

Liam wasn't in love with Danny Lightfingers—and Lightfingers didn't seem to be in love with him. But Liam thought of his father, of his siblings, of this man who was loved so much that his lover's *wife* begged him to come home.

He seemed like a man worth knowing.

Kadjic had left Morocco, but Liam still got points for getting so close to him in the first place when his entire detail thought Liam was mad for searching there. He was reassigned to the UK to take on a ring of car thieves, which proved to be exciting. And it gave him opportunities to visit Lightfingers in rehab, where he stayed for three months. While he was there, Liam helped him set up a dead drop in New York so he could send mail to Josh without being traced and witnessed firsthand the brilliance of the man when unhampered with booze or despair.

Toward the end of Danny's stay, Liam arrived with a gift. A trunk-sized suitcase to hold the things Danny had gathered in Ireland, since he'd left Morocco with barely the clothes on his back.

Danny had greeted him warmly, but as he did so, he gave a tall young Viking about his own age a gentle "this is private" glance, and the man nodded and ambled off in a dignified manner.

"A conquest?" Liam asked, laughing. Not handsome or beautiful, no. In fact, perfectly ordinary—but there was that puckish appeal that was, apparently, irresistible.

"A… dalliance," Danny said, inclining his head. He sobered. "I'm going to have to leave him soon. He knows it."

Liam nodded. "I'm going to ask—is Felix, perhaps, tall and blond?"

Danny grimaced. "You mean because Carl is tall and blond?"

"Yes, and Kadjic is—"

"Not," Danny finished blandly. "Yes. Kadjic was a petty little tyrant. He was cruel and violent, and I felt like deserved that." He blew out a breath. "You know, they have a perfectly adequate therapy program here. I'm sure I've covered this."

Liam nodded and sighed. "All I'm saying, Danny, is that… it sounds like your family was doing the best it could. Maybe don't try so hard to forget him is all."

Danny rolled his eyes. "I can hardly forget him if I'm going to be going back to Chicago to see Josh and Tienne while *dodging* him at the same time, can I?"

Liam gave him a flat look. "That's mature."

"I'll take my little revenges where I can." Danny sniffed. Then, soberly, he said, "But this next trip isn't to see them, so avoiding the whole fam damily should be easy."

Liam cocked his head. "What are you going to do?"

He would start to identify that special little lip curl Danny made when he was planning to do something DCI Liam Craig, currently assigned to Interpol, could not condone.

"An old friend of the family died," he said, and Liam heard the lie. Whoever had died, Danny wasn't sorry in the least to hear he was dead. "And I must pay my respects. Don't worry your pretty little head about it," he added with a rakish smile, and Liam, who had come to trust Lightfingers on some base level, didn't. He wasn't going after Kadjic. If he stole something, it was something the victims could afford or probably deserved to have stolen. And as for being caught? Even if Liam decided to bring him in for suspected crimes, what did he have to convict? A boozy smile and an impish wink at a not-really-a-crime scene?

And so it went.

They would meet every so often, usually because Danny was nearby (he managed to keep tabs on Liam although Liam had no idea where *Danny* would be), and they would catch up. Liam's love life (usually dismal) and Danny's (he had a parade of lovers whom he left on good terms) were discussed, and then the heart of the meeting.

Pictures. Usually candids: Josh, his friend Grace, Tienne. Even Felix and Julia, taken in secret, who did not disappoint.

By the time Danny and Felix reunited—in a suitably spectacular and public fashion—and Danny contacted Liam about making an arrest for a *very* bad person, Liam felt like they were a second family. He would visit his mum and his siblings, and if the visit was long enough, they would usually ask him, "Hey, how's Lightfingers? Any new stories?"

Always. Always with Danny there were stories.

And as the boys grew, many of the stories centered around them. Liam watched with interest as the pictures on Danny's phone grew from children to teenagers to adults—well and truly. Tienne, so shy and blond as to be nearly transparent, even when smiling for the camera. Josh's friend Grace, vibrant and pulsating, *demanding* attention for his beauty, his intelligence, his wildness. Stirling and Molly, Josh and Grace's friends since middle school—Stirling compact and intense, Molly exuberant, with a glorious cascade of red ringlets and a muscular grace and beauty that could conquer any obstacle.

And Josh himself, who while not related to Danny by blood, seemed to have inherited everything—his build, his fierce intelligence, his impish sense of humor—from the man who had stolen parenthood from thin air and lavished it on him.

After the reunion, Danny and his new "crew" seemed to be getting on swimmingly doing the same thing Danny had done on his own—but on a larger scale. Evening the odds. Liam enjoyed their exchanges even more now that Danny was officially "Benjamin Morgan." Having a home, a family, people to care for, young adults to mentor, seemed to bring out the greatness Liam had seen from the very first, obscured as it was by alcohol and despair.

But still… he had not been prepared for that first meeting with Josh.

He'd arrived in the middle of a firefight, and then along with the rest of the crew, had waited with bated breath as a bruiser named Chuck had disconnected a bomb from the electronics-filled van where Stirling and Josh had been trapped.

When it was time to open the van's doors, Liam had stepped up, because that's what you did when you were law enforcement, right? You stepped up?

And Josh Salinger, sick from his first round of chemo, had all but fainted into his arms.

But not before gazing into Liam's eyes with a fiercely intelligent, kind, and clever expression, his dark brown eyes limpid with pain and avid with curiosity.

Liam had held him until they'd secured a vehicle and, under the guise of solicitous concern, had managed to hover over the boy for the rest of the night.

The next six months had been… odd.

Josh wasn't merely *sick*, he was all but dying. Danny had called Liam one night in early November, because he didn't have a sponsor to call, to confess that after a long, terrible week when the rest of the crew was off chasing murder birds, Josh had been in the hospital, literally fighting for his life.

Only Danny and Felix knew. Josh had begged them to send his mother away, and they had, but the burden of being Felix's strength, of being Josh's, was almost enough to make Danny break a then ten-year-old vow to never drink again.

And Liam had stayed in touch, calling Danny, calling Felix, being included in the crew's adventures and almost coyly insinuating himself into Josh Salinger's life.

On the one hand it felt deceitful. Josh had no way of knowing that Liam felt connected to his family after years of association with Danny.

But on the other hand… if all Liam ever had was that moment, that one moment, of Josh Salinger in his arms, scowling with embarrassment, still trying to run the op as his entire family lost their mind over his health, then he still would have known that the boy was extraordinary.

He still would have wanted to know the man whom Lightfingers had helped to raise.

And Josh seemed to realize there was something… a connection, a plucked and vibrant string, binding them together.

His emails to Liam were oddly formal when the language of his crew was almost free-flowing performance art.

The times Liam sat for dinner with the crew were the only times Liam ever saw him discomfited.

And now…? Now they would be stuck together on a yacht for three weeks of vacation and mystery solving, investigating the deaths of Stirling and Molly's parents. Stirling and Molly were two of Josh's oldest friends, foster siblings who'd been adopted by a couple of sweet middle-aged zillionaires, a breed Liam could have sworn was born in myth.

But leave it to Felix and Julia to know two unicorns, and leave it to Josh and his friends to want to avenge their untimely demise.

Liam wanted in. He'd benefited from some of their capers, had gotten some promotions from the leads they'd let him in on.

He wanted in on this one.

But mostly he wanted the in to Josh. He wanted the right to sit at the boy's table. To hear him talk, to learn the language of the crew so he spoke it like his own.

That string that had plucked in his heart when he'd first seen the boy smile—that sound, that chord—had grown cacophonously louder in his ears since that close day in July. It only stilled when Josh glanced at him or, hell, texted him a detail or wrote an email.

He felt ridiculous on the one hand. He was past thirty; Josh had turned twenty-one in January. What sort of addled, daft, lecherous… oh dear God!

As Liam approached the yacht again—he'd made friends with the captain the day before while waiting for the others to arrive—one of the younger crew came dashing down the dock.

Liam knew them by now. Stirling, of course, was the crew's computer specialist—their hacker—and Liam had seen firsthand that the boy was sort of a prodigy. Compact, midsize, Black, with hair kept precision short, Stirling wasn't always great with people, but he *was* practical to the bone, and he seemed a bit rattled now.

"Heya, Stirling," Liam said, concerned. "Did you get lost?"

"I was looking for Julia or Danny or Felix," he said unhappily, peering back to where Grace, Josh, Hunter, and Tienne were grouped. "I know this is supposed to be Leon's yacht, but Josh can't really wait—"

At the mention of Josh's name, Liam's head came up like a prized pointer's—he couldn't seem to help himself. "Is he not feeling well?"

"Recovery lasts a long time," Stirling said, which was something Liam had been trying to drill down into his own head for the past six months.

"I know it," Liam muttered. "Here, I introduced myself to the captain while I was waiting and—oop! Shit!"

While they'd been talking, the object of their concern turned cloud white and fell immediately into Hunter's arms.

The one thing Liam could think as he and Stirling hustled down the dock was that the only person who got to carry Josh Salinger was him.

Hunter gave over, though, and in no time at all, Josh was in his arms, cranky and exasperated and tired enough to actually *mention* their polite dance around each other on group email and texts.

"You've got to let me in, boy-o," Liam murmured into his hair. "I don't go where I'm not wanted."

"Dick," Josh muttered, and Liam was grateful. The boy with his blood up was so much less worrisome than "Recovery Boy," as Josh's friend Grace called him.

But Recovery Boy *was* worrisome—enough so that Liam stashed him in his own air-conditioned cabin, watched over first by Stirling and then by Julia while he went to find a shipboard doctor.

After Josh had been checked out (showing great patience, Liam thought, for all the family's fussing), the boy was asleep on Liam's bed, covered in a cotton throw, and his mother—stunningly elegant woman, barely forty, with the grace and poise of a young Grace Kelly—turned to him and said, "If you like, you can use his room in the upper deck until he awakes—"

Liam shrugged. "I've got my book," he said, indicating his phone and meaning his audiobook, since his dyslexia made reading onerous but he *loved* adventure stories. "I can keep him company while the rest of you get situated."

Julia nodded gratefully, her gaze resting on her sleeping son with a mother's trouble. "He's so over this cancer thing," she said with a short laugh. "Which is unfair, I know. He's got a good six months before he's even close to where he was before he got sick, and at least three years before we can truly breathe a sigh of relief. But he's always been precocious. Since the cradle, really. Has wanted to be out in the world, doing, planning, *being* a part of it. And he knows—he knows how lucky he is. I don't think…." Her voice caught. "I don't think he knows how lucky *we* are—"

He saw her swallow and take a deep breath. And then, showing the strength she'd exhibited all those years ago when told she'd be taking in a stranger for the sake of a man she loved like a brother, she cleaned up her mascara with the tip of her third finger and smiled again.

"Let us know if you need anything. I'll have somebody run you both a tray for dinner if he's not ready to join us by then. I'll tell the staff that you're welcome to sleep in Josh's cabin if he doesn't feel like moving. You've been so much help, Liam. I cannot thank you enough."

And with that she left, and Liam was free to kick off his shoes and move to the window side of the bed, where he could gaze out at the lovely city above San Juan harbor and enjoy the sudden quiet.

He'd just placed his earbuds in and was settling back on the pillow when Josh murmured, "What did you mean by that?"

"By what, my boy?"

"Stop," Josh muttered, "with the boy-o, the my boy, the lad. Call me by my name and tell me what you meant when you were carrying me in."

Liam swallowed. Oh, this was embarrassing.

"You… you were upset, because I was keeping my distance," he said softly. "This fall. Bo—Josh, you've got to understand. I'm a friend of your *father's*, and you are ten years younger than me and were very, very sick. Of course I felt it last summer. You fell into my arms—that doesn't happen every day." He gave a slight smile that Josh couldn't see. He'd been curled on his side facing the door since Liam had laid him on the bed. "Certainly not as much as you complain about it."

Josh grunted. "I had the biggest… *thing* for this other policeman," he murmured. "So bad. Hurt my chest. He was married with a baby—like I was going to come between *that*, you know?"

Liam *did* know, mostly because Danny told him, keeping him ever so subtly apprised of Josh's life, of his activities, while Liam ever so subtly asked. Both of them knew the tenor of those exchanges had changed the moment Liam had felt that slight weight, tempered by steel, in his arms.

"So your Uncle Danny tells me," he confessed, and Josh let out a humorless laugh.

"Nick Denning… he wanted me," Josh confessed quietly. "But I'd already fallen into your arms, smelled you. Did you know you smell good?"

Liam had to smile at that one. "I had no idea," he said, pleased. Then he sobered. "Funny, you know. How some moments… some moments take over your life." He was thinking about that moment Danny had spoken to him in the museum. Or the moment he'd found Tienne, covered in his father's blood and crouched in an alleyway.

Or the moment Josh had stumbled coming out of the electronics van, and Liam had caught him, thinking he was being a Good Samaritan.

He hadn't realized he was catching his own destiny in a resentful bundle, but here in this quiet cabin, listening to the sounds of the sea—and the voices echoing up and down the corridor—he could think of nothing but the man beside him, talking as though he knew exactly what had been in Liam's heart since that one moment.

Funny, that. Until this heartbeat, right here, it hadn't occurred to Liam that it had taken over both their lives, together, and that they'd been bound the entire time, no matter how hard they thought they'd fought it.

Quietly, without fuss, Liam reached out and put his hand on Josh's shoulder.

Josh reached across his body and laced their fingers together. In a few heartbeats, Liam heard his breath even out in sleep, and he turned his audiobook back on.

Clive Cussler, one of his favorite authors. For an hour he sat there, the book running, and didn't hear a word.

All he could hear was the regular in-and-out sound of Josh Salinger's life force, growing a little bit stronger with every beat of his heart.

I Think I'm Falling

And back on the balcony…

JOSH HAD been kissed a few times in his life—once by a guy he thought he could really love. But he'd had to pull away and remind Nick Denning that he had a *family*, for sweet fuck's sake, and Josh was *not* that guy.

But he'd never been kissed like this. All those hours he'd spent in the yacht with Liam, playing cribbage, discussing books, *baring their souls*, and there'd been hugs, falling sleep with his head on Liam's shoulder, holding hands—subtly, ever so subtly. While Josh's friends had gone out and played, leaving Josh behind, he and Liam had become quietly close, until Liam's scent was as familiar to Josh as his own.

There'd been nuzzles on the temple, chaste kisses on the forehead, Liam's hands on his cheeks, his hair, rubbing soft circles on his back as he tried to get to sleep with the pain of healing still in his bones.

There had never been a passionate siege of Josh's senses, a sensual warfare, Liam's mouth plundering his own as his knees buckled and he fought to be closer, closer, merged forever with this funny, bright, kind, and decent man.

Until now.

Liam tore his mouth away, and Josh fought for breath, to orient himself to the here and now on this darkened balcony when his caper, his identity, hell, his *life* was at risk if he didn't pull his brains back into his ears.

"Dear God," Josh whispered.

"I'll be here when you're done," Liam told him harshly. "And you and me, boy-o, we're having this out. No more polite emails. No more telling me not to worry my pretty little head about things. I told you in January, I'm all in. Did you think that didn't mean you?"

Josh closed his eyes and felt the burn behind them, so discombobulated in this instance he was shocked into telling the truth.

"I missed you," he said.

Liam's hand cupping his cheek—*that* was familiar. "My God, so did I." This next kiss was soft, almost chaste after that carnal apocalypse Liam had wreaked on Josh's senses. "Now go do what you've got to, boy—"

Josh grunted. They had a *deal*, dammit.

"Josh," Liam said, one corner of his mouth quirking, just enough for Josh to see his slightly overlapping teeth. His wildly curly dark brown hair was slicked back tonight, and he was wearing close-fitted trousers and a black turtleneck—not quite thieves' clothes, but with a brightly colored turquoise scarf as a belt, he fit right into the art scene. "I'll be out in the main room, making small talk with your mother. You go keep your ass away from Ms. Octopus Hands, and we'll all keep our eyes out for you-know-who."

They didn't need to say his name—that felt almost like summoning a genie from a bottle—but there was no mistaking who Liam meant.

Andres Kadjic was going to show up at Celeste Buenaventura's for an audience with the painting Josh had just stolen, a heretofore hidden piece called *Crown of Roses*, a lost work of the surrealist, Gertrude Abercrombie.

And in its place he was going to see one of Tienne's most excellent forgeries—with a surprise worked into the signature.

Josh and the crew had worked for *weeks* to get to this point. It was the whole reason Josh had taken the job, although fake ID or not, he risked exposure in his hometown. Andres Kadjic, the man who had tried to kill Danny Lightfingers, whose guns had been the reason Stirling and Molly's parents were killed, and who had ordered the death of Tienne's father—*that* Andres Kadjic—had found Danny in January. Fortunately, he only knew that Danny was *alive*. Stirling's computer system had been *very* secure, and they were pretty sure they'd left Kadjic searching Helsinki for the famed Lightfingers. To solidify that impression, they'd dispatched Grace, Hunter, and Carl there for two weeks, with strict instructions for Grace to go on a wild stealing spree, all in the name of Lightfingers.

The three of them had returned exhausted and exhilarated. Carl's day job was as an investigator for an insurance company, and by making sure at least half the art they'd brought home was insured by Serpentus, he'd been able to stick it to his unscrupulous employers in really delightful ways.

And for Grace it had been a necessary way to blow off steam after the months of worrying about Josh's health. For the first time in a long while, Grace was able to worry about *Grace*, and about *Hunter*, whom Grace loved with all his soul. The young man who'd returned to Chicago had been both smug and sober and determined to treat his best gifts—dancing, caring for people, kindness—with as much respect as he treated his gift of kleptomania.

And the trip had done more than just get them two original prints by David McKeown, a photographer who could capture his country's beauty with simple, enduring elegance and charm. It had, according to Liam's sources, thrown Kadjic enough off the scent to have him haunting Helsinki, throwing his weight around art galleries and brothels alike, trying to get hold of the elusive Lightfingers.

Which had given Josh and his parents and friends some time to come up with a plan to lure Kadjic to Chicago and find a way to bring him down.

The job with Celeste Buenaventura had been step one.

Josh stepped away and held his core iron-tight, the better to support his back and the shoulder that felt bruised and tender, albeit serviceable.

"See you out there," he said, pulling his game face on.

"You'd better believe it, boy-o."

And before Josh could protest the name, Liam was back off the balcony, and Danny slithered out to give him another once-over.

"It's about time for you to make your entrance, my boy," Danny said softly. "But… here." Out of nowhere the man who had been Josh's second father—who had made it to every birthday, Christmas, and performance whether he and Felix were speaking or not, who had replied to every letter Josh had written, and who had listened thoughtfully as angsty adolescent Josh had poured out all of his fears and hopes and plans and joys—produced a handkerchief and cleaned the spit marks from around Josh's mouth.

"Oh God," Josh muttered, embarrassed beyond belief.

"It's fine," Danny said, giving his nose a brief boop, as he had when Josh had been a child. "I get the feeling that kiss has been a long time coming."

Josh gave him a smile that even *Josh* knew was besotted. "I've been waiting for that man to kiss me for a *year*," he confided.

"Excellent, excellent. Nothing like two glaciers in courtship. Exciting. We can buy frozen popcorn and watch."

Josh laughed at the absurdity, which was one of Danny's best gifts—the ability to make people smile, relax, and feel comfortable in their own skins.

"No offense, Uncle Danny, but there are some things glaciers like to do that are *private*."

"No-no-no-no," Danny said, shaking his head. "I'm your *father*, young man. I don't want to hear about your privates."

Josh laughed and then sobered. "Thanks, Uncle Danny. But, uhm, you know."

"Yes, son. It's time."

And then even Danny faded into the shadows, and Josh made his way into the apartment and through the bathroom, his features schooled into a mask of polite efficiency, which was how he'd gotten through nearly two months as a member of Celeste's staff, her art dealer, with only his ass fondled.

Celeste's party was bursting with Studio 54 energy. Artists, actors—everybody hip, now, and happening. Celeste was a recent Los Angeles transplant, which made her perfect for this caper, because while she came from old money—and old prejudice—she wasn't au courant with the big names in Chicago. Julia Dormer-Salinger she recognized because she and her ex-husband still ran their cable network together. But their son, Josh Salinger, wouldn't be on her radar, particularly since he'd been ill in the last year and hadn't appeared at any events with the two of them. Just in case, Josh had used Danny's alias, Morgan, and the first name J.D. It wasn't Teflon, but he could always say he hadn't wanted to trade on his parents' influence to get his job, and most people would buy that. So Josh could wander in and out of the big names at the party with ease, introducing himself as an art dealer—the one, in fact, who had arranged to buy Celeste's newest painting.

The painting had been a windfall. Danny had discovered it at an estate sale of a man reputed to be Gertrude's lover after her first marriage, and he and Tienne had spent weeks authenticating it. Most of Gertrude's works had been donated to a collective for Midwestern painters, and to find one in the wild? Serendipity. The picture had her signature elements—an austere woman in a flowing dress, displaced shadows, forms from nowhere, items of sorcery, owls, and a cat—in this case, arranged around a crown of roses, the thorns of which dripped stylized blood.

Josh had always thought the paintings (like much of Gertrude Abercrombie's work) had been lonely and haunted, and that the cat had represented emotional connection of any kind, and this one was no exception. Tienne had grimaced when he'd seen it and had remarked that while she was talented, it would be one of his easiest forgeries.

It was important that the forgery be perfect down to every last detail so the false signature would be so much more jarring.

Besides being made to be forged, the painting was also perfect because Abercrombie had a connection with Dizzy Gillespie, the jazz musician, and Kadjic had a weakness for jazz.

Throwing a giant reception in Celeste's quarters and then taking everybody upstairs to premier the new painting in her collection should be the perfect bait to pull Kadjic from his foxhunt in Finland and into the Salinger hunting fields.

He'd spilled enough of their blood, had been the boogeyman in enough of their stories. It was time they made *him* the fox and ran him to ground.

But the timing had been tricky. *Celeste* had to be the last person to see the painting in its special display alcove, with her security consultant, Harvey Merritt, in her company. Stirling could disable and loop the cameras, Josh could fool the temperature sensors, and Grace could (and did) loosen all the screws in the frame and hide the forgery so Josh could have easy access, but the security really started at the door to the twentieth floor, where Celeste's four floors of apartments began. Hunter and Molly could get away with being on the catering team, and Julia and Josh's uncle, Leon di Rossi, could crash the party on reputation alone, but nobody else on the team would have any reason to be upstairs while the party was in full swing and before the presentation of the painting.

Except Josh.

So Josh had retired to the restroom, scaled the wall, replaced the painting, and leaped back down to the balcony outside the bathroom, and now he had to mingle with the elite, the moneyed, and the beautiful as though nothing had happened.

It was a good thing he'd grown up doing this.

When he was a child, Felix, Julia, and Danny—tired of putting on a show for the elite in Chicago—had taken Josh on a tour of Europe. For Josh's mother, the freedom had been *exhilarating*. Never in her life had she been able to get up in the morning, take a walk down by the river, and flirt with a handsome man while buying baguettes and cheese for breakfast. And Danny and Felix had been such fun companions. They bantered to amuse themselves, and Julia, so relieved to live without her father's constant efforts to control her life, had reveled in their foolery. Josh had been along for the ride, and the four of them had lied, stolen, and grifted their way across the continent, learning the languages they didn't know and practicing the languages they'd learned, and all of them giving money to the poor and righting the wrongs nobody else would, simply because they could.

Josh wasn't afraid of crowds or of getting caught with a false name. He knew how to brazen out a lie, and while he'd never meant for it to be his livelihood, he'd been on the professional stage for much of his adolescence and young adulthood.

And of course Danny had taught him everything he knew.

So he could smile charmingly at a matron, flirt harmlessly with her daughter, and offer a firm handshake to the sugar daddy who bankrolled them, making a good impression—but hopefully not a memorable one. He knew he was pretty, but he was a lackey for this production. An art dealer should never be in the forefront; the art should be the star.

He'd immersed himself back into the role effortlessly, was in fact enjoying one of the canapes Hunter had offered him, with a chaser of sparkling water so Josh could knock back the ibuprofen hidden in the flap of prosciutto, when he sensed a disturbance at the door.

"Remember," Hunter murmured, "one of us needs to be next to him for the count of twenty."

Josh didn't even nod. He knew that part of the plan. It had been his idea.

He glanced over casually and then returned his eyes to the modern, arresting painting by Armani Howard he'd procured for Celeste before the Abercrombie had fallen into their laps. Titled *Rapture*, the work featured electric humanoids rising to an apocalyptic sky from a bucolic earth, and Josh rather mourned that he hadn't been able to get it for his parents' display of artwork, because he loved it.

But that one casual glance had been all he'd needed to see that their trap had sprung.

Celeste's tasteful (and oh my God *vast*) display apartment space was entered by private elevator. Her living quarters and dining room were on the floors between the gallery and this cavernous living room, and while her party was *very* well attended, it was easy to spot the newcomers.

The man crossing the space, his hard-soled shoes ringing on the tile along with the shoes of the giant bodyguards on his flanks, was not "brutally handsome" like Josh's Uncle Leon. Instead his looks were simply "brutal." At fifty, his flushed skin was coarsened—apparently by drink and sun and scowling—and his wiry hair was slicked back from a deeply receded widow's peak. The crevasses between his eyebrows and the bridge of his nose did not appear to be cleaned, harboring flakes of skin that Josh was going to have to *not* stare at, and his blue eyes were practically hidden by his brows and his cheeks, which were sagging into jowls.

He walked like he was sex on legs and knew it, and once, perhaps twenty years ago, Andres Kadjic *had been* brutally handsome. Now Josh had to control his revulsion, particularly that this man had ever touched his Uncle Danny.

Josh knew enough to not let his eyes linger, to pick up the details on one casual swoop as though looking for somebody behind his target and not the target himself. Personally, Josh was dressed to disappear in a black suit, chic but conservatively cut, with a black pocket square—

As he glanced down automatically, Josh's eyes widened. Rather than the black square he'd chosen originally, a turquoise bit of silk now poked from his vest pocket, and he had to fight not to yank it out and hide it in his pants pocket instead.

Liam!

Josh had caught him, too, in his sweep of the room, having a casual interaction with Hunter, probably to ask if Josh had gotten the painkiller for his shoulder. That turquoise scarf hanging at Liam's waist like a pirate's sash still looked dashing, and Josh had to take a deep breath not to stalk across the room and start a wholly irrational argument with him.

You want to play romance games when I'm in the middle of a job?

But then Liam met his eyes, and there was no play in him. Then Josh got it. The pocket square wasn't some sort of bullshit power play—it was a reminder.

No matter what happened, Josh wasn't alone.

Josh turned his attention back to the painting, the internal shaking he'd been fighting since he'd smacked into the wall on the descent finally easing up.

Not alone.

In his ear, Grace murmured, "You see him yet?"

"Yup."

"And…?"

"Ugly as sin."

"Step on him," Grace said, and Josh smiled softly, immersing himself in the painting once more.

In fact he was so immersed in his job that he was surprised by an authoritative tap on his sore shoulder.

He held back a wince and turned to find himself face-to-face with the enemy.

"Is nice," Kadjic said dismissively of the painting. "But not what we are here for."

Josh gave him a deliberate glance and then turned back once again. "I like this artist," he said. "I'd like to work with him some more."

"Too… how you say? Ethnic."

Josh refused to look at him—or rise to the bait. "As is much of Chicago," he said. "An African and Thai American background gives him amazing choices of history to choose from." He offered his own casual, dismissive glance. "European heritage is not the end-all and be-all of art."

He heard it—the sucking in of breath—and regretted his words. He wasn't supposed to catch Kadjic's attention.

"You are?" The question was low and obviously intrigued.

"J.D. Morgan," Josh responded without offering a hand. "I'm Celeste's art dealer."

Some of the innuendo fell away. "Oh! You're the one who found the Abercrombie?"

Josh nodded, able to tell the truth. "A friend of mine did. It was at an estate sale. Hidden treasure."

"What sort of friend?"

Real reactions are the best reactions, son. Don't give away any piece of your soul to this man. He's dangerous, so we'll trap him—but he's nobody we need to play up to.

His other father, Felix Salinger, had said that, and his mother had seconded it.

"A friend who doesn't need to be harassed," Josh retorted. "He called me, and I made the sale. Does it matter?"

To his surprise, Kadjic affected an ingratiating sort of smile, and Josh realized with a shock that the man was playing up to *him*.

"I want to make sure I am not… imposing," he said, and Josh's stomach roiled.

"Only on me," he said mildly, although that bright, whimsical little pocket square seemed to spread a web of protective warmth over his body.

In his ear Grace was saying, "He's not close enough for the clone, dammit. But don't move any closer—he'll take it wrong."

At that moment, Celeste, wearing a bright red satin version of what Yzma wore in the children's cartoon *Emperor's New Groove*, stood on top of her wood-and-steel staircase to the next level and called out, "We should be ready! Everybody put down your canapes and drinks and come up to the exhibition level. My art dealer and I have been *very* busy preparing our little display for you, and we're so proud for you to see our newest selection!"

"Oh thank God," Grace said in his ear. "No lie, you've got Chuck and Carl out here ready to rush in there and defend your virtue."

Josh didn't respond—he couldn't without arousing Kadjic's suspicions—but he did allow his lips to curl into a smile.

"Will you accompany me?" Kadjic asked. "Ms. Buenaventura asked me here specifically to see this painting. The least you can do is escort me up."

"Don't let him," Grace hissed. "With that staircase, all he has to do is hip-check you off and you're toast."

The staircase *was* frightening—no guardrail from bottom to top, and Josh had been forced to use the elevator more than once. But Celeste had wanted her guests to "tour" the grounds, and that involved the three flights of stairs through her kitchen and sleeping quarter levels.

"Mr. Morgan," purred a female voice behind Josh, "if you remember, you promised to escort me and my date to see the new painting."

Josh turned gratefully to find his mother and his uncle Leon, his biological father's brother, so actually the only person in his life who could technically be called his uncle, which was an irony for another day. Tonight "Uncle Leon," who had been located and contacted and dragged into Josh's life for the express purpose of donating his bone marrow so Josh might live, was playing Josh's mother's besotted swain—a role that was damned close to real life.

"Of course, Ms. Dormer-Salinger," he said with a nod. "Mr. Di Rossi. I haven't forgotten my promise."

He gave Kadjic an apologetic smile and led the couple toward the staircase. Behind him he heard his mother say, sotto voce, "Dear God that man gives me the creeps."

"I do *not* like the way he was staring at you," Leon said, definitely to Josh. "I was pretty sure none of our plans involved laying a honey trap."

Josh chuffed air and made a production of showing the two of them the planned beauty of Celeste's sitting room, laid out below them like a living work of art. As he did, he saw that Kadjic had lingered at the bottom of the staircase, waiting for his two goons, and he gave a sigh of relief.

"They didn't," he blew out on a hiss. "I almost threw up again—"

"When did you throw up?" his mother asked, and he grimaced to himself as he remembered she hadn't been out on the balcony.

"Unimportant," he said with dignity. "The point is, I don't think I'm as forgettable as I'd hoped I'd be."

"Hahahahahaha," Grace laughed crassly in his ear. "Oh my God, Joshy-Sue, are all the boys chasing you?"

Josh grunted, and behind him his mother said, "Grace, I can hear you, and you're being an ass."

"But I'm right, Mrs. Josh's Mom," Grace said with the innocence of a choir boy. "And that's what's important. Liam's following the mark." He said that last with absolute professionalism. "And Kadjic is looking to catch up to you by the time you reach the top. Mrs. Josh's Mom, Uncle Leon, you guys need to make room for him—I don't think he's pleased."

"Shit," Julia murmured.

"The bathroom," Josh said, loud enough to carry, "is on the next landing. Would you like me to wait for you so I can present the art myself, or…."

"Oh, bless you," Julia said, almost on a giggle. "Leon and I can find our way up. But thank you. One too many glasses of champagne in a tight dress, you know."

That had been for Kadjic, as they'd known their voices would echo, and it would keep the man from making a dangerous play for Josh on the damned slat-stairs.

"I told you not to wear the stilettos," Josh murmured for his mother's ears alone.

"I'll be damned if I let this Nazi cow show me up in Manolo Blahniks," Julia muttered, and Josh's smile was real this time.

"You could take her out wearing those shoes or with those shoes," Leon said, and in Josh's ear, Grace murmured, "Nice work, Mr. Rich Tycoon Man. We'll keep you."

Leon's pleased grunt let Josh know that he was mic'd too, and that made him smile. Going begging for bone marrow hadn't been Josh's idea, and he'd spent some time being resentful of Leon di Rossi and the sudden need for the biological father Josh had never missed. But Leon—a shipping magnate on paper but an ex-smuggler in real time—had fit right into Josh's little Robin Hood syndicate. Part if it was, Josh thought, that the crew had solved the mystery of what had happened to Leon's brother, Josh's father, who had been killed in a terrible accident for trying to do the right thing. But part of it was that, like Josh's mother and Grace, he'd discovered that a rich family did not necessarily buy a rich life. He appreciated the family banter, and he loved that they set out to help even the odds for people who otherwise might not have anywhere to turn.

It could just be that he really loved that they let him in.

And, Josh was starting to suspect, love was a weak, all-purpose, worn-thin word when it came to what Leon felt for Josh's mother. For her part, once Josh's illness had gone into remission, Julia Dormer-Salinger had begun to glow, radiant as a star. Josh—who was not used to thinking of his mother as a person so much as a warm, maternal, glorious force of nature—had been thinking more and more often that his mother had never really had a chance to fall in love… until now.

Josh's father had been a weeklong dalliance—dangerous for both of them since they both had powerful, violent fathers who would not have approved of the match.

And Felix and Danny had been in love long before they'd gotten embroiled with Julia and the danger growing in her womb at an extraordinary rate. When they'd concocted the plan for Julia and Felix to marry and for the three of them to raise Josh like a family, they'd been younger than Josh was now, and as he watched his mother finally meet an equal, somebody as fierce and brilliant as she was, somebody who could love her like she deserved, the last of his reservations about "Uncle Leon" melted away.

If he could make Julia Dormer-Salinger happy, Josh would welcome him into the family with a whole heart.

And Leon was getting to be damned helpful on the job too.

Although he tried to hide it, Leon also worried for every member of the family when something dangerous was afoot—especially for Josh. The glance he gave Josh as he escorted Julia to the powder room at the next landing was parent code for "be careful," and Josh nodded in acknowledgment as he continued up the stairs.

This next bit was going to be tricky. It was everything they'd engineered to this point, but it needed their full attention nonetheless.

Kadjic wasn't supposed to be able to pick Josh out of a crowd, but he'd zeroed in on Josh from the very beginning.

He likes them young, Josh could hear Danny saying in preparation. *He may try to flirt with you, to pick up on you, but he usually likes his toys weak and pretty and pliable. Be yourself and don't lead him on. Being his lover is dangerous. Pretending to be his lover is a death sentence.*

"Okay, we've got an exfil if this goes bad," Grace said in Josh's ear.

"Exfil?" Josh was surprised enough to vocalize.

"Trust us," Grace said smugly. "You import Mr. Interpol Officer with the power of your tiny saggy ass and you expect no exfil?"

Josh wanted to groan. He'd wanted Liam left out of this.

The memory of that kiss suffused him.

Did you really?

I don't need to be rescued.

No, but maybe he wants to be by your side.

And like that Josh found a tiny smile working its way through his game face.

"My ass is *not* saggy," he murmured, barely loud enough for Grace to hear.

"Bony as a box of tossed chicken, boy-o," came Liam's voice, and he scowled to himself but, mindful that the procession of art goers trooping up the stairs could hear odd bits of conversation as they moved about in the space vault that was Celeste's four converted floors of apartment, kept his retort locked firmly behind his lips.

Liam laughed softly, and Josh could hear the sound in echo and resisted the urge to glance wildly around. For one thing, his balance wasn't what it had been before the cancer, and a wild glance around the loft could end up with him falling down the stairs and going splat. If it hadn't been for his damnable pride, he could have asked to be in the party that took the elevator up, but Celeste didn't know who Josh Salinger was, and she certainly didn't know J.D. Morgan had only been in full remission for a couple of months.

He marched grimly on up the last set of stairs, and as he came to the landing where Celeste was holding court, he was aware that while Liam may have been somewhere in the procession to see the new painting, Andres Kadjic really *had* shouldered his way to arrive on Josh's heels, practically panting on the back of his neck.

Josh was very careful to take several steps forward, close enough for Celeste to point him out as she made her opening remarks as the "genius" who had unearthed a real Gertrude Abercrombie from the "pit of forgotten despair."

Of course Celeste would think of an estate sale as the "pit of forgotten despair." She probably planned to sit on her treasures like a vampire, until her firm thirty-fiveish skin shriveled like dampened crepe paper adhering to her skeletal frame.

Tall, willfully emaciated, with any extra body fat relocated to her lips, Celeste could have been a great beauty if she'd simply accepted that she was a human being and not a stick figure. Her hair had been dyed fire-engine red so many times, Josh had actually seen strands of it break and float down into the air like tiny feathered corpses to match the boa that trimmed her garish dress. For all that, the woman had been kind to Josh to the point of obsequy; he absolutely couldn't be bitchy to her. He knew what her policy was—knew what her politics were—but until she was crass enough to use innuendo as opposed to her paycheck, sniping at her would get him kicked out of her circle, and this moment wouldn't happen.

"Have you seen the picture?" Kadjic asked, up against Josh's shoulder again.

Josh barely peered behind him. "Yes, this morning, when it was mounted."

"Mounting can be an exciting moment," Kadjic purred, and Josh was disgusted enough to glance over his shoulder and wrinkle his nose.

"Ew," he said, meaning it with every fiber in his being.

Kadjic cackled, showing yellow teeth, as Celeste said, "And now, I present to you, the forgotten work of one of Chicago's most famous native artists, *Crown of Roses*."

And with a grand gesture (and a few woebegone feathers floating to the floor in sympathy), Celeste indicated the curtain hanging over the modern wood frame, mounted on the center load-bearing wall of the gallery level.

With the press of a button, Harvey, the head of security, unveiled the prize.

Josh turned from Kadjic to smile at it, taking in Tienne's masterfully imitated brush strokes, the way he'd broken down the painting into visual and material component with perfect spacing, perfect color choice, a perfect eye. Nobody—*nobody*—not even Celeste's authenticator, who was very good, would have been able to tell the painting was forged if they hadn't seen the original and had known for a fact that the tiny letters, K, A, D and part of a J, were incorporated into the signature with a fine brush and a faint bit of white paint where no such device was part of the original.

"Remarkable," said Kadjic by Josh's shoulder. Everybody else had oohed and aahed and then stepped back to take in the painting, leaving Josh stuck here with the one guy he didn't want to be near when the depth of the deception hit.

"Do you think so?" Josh asked blandly. "I've always thought she was… sad. Cats and owls could be so much more joyous, but here they seem to be a part of the artist's emotional disconnection."

"I like the shadows," Kadjic said ruminatively. "I like how they appear where no shadows should be, and the forms that cast them, or the light that creates them, are lost somewhere in the past… the past…."

Kadjic squinted and leaned forward, eyes narrowed. "What… what in the hell…?"

And Josh found his character. "Sir, you need to back away from the frame or the alarm will go—"

With a squeal the alarm—light and sound—began to glare from around the painting, because Kadjic *had* set it off with his proximity, but the furious man didn't seem to notice.

"What is this?" he shouted at Celeste. "What is this! Who did this?"

"Who did what?" she asked, gesturing frantically at Harvey to still the alarm. Harvey was so busy playing with the remote that he didn't catch that Kadjic had drawn a small fixed-blade knife from his sleeve and was prodding at the plexiglass plate held a half-inch from the painting by the mounting screws.

The alarm went off again, and Kadjic gestured with the blade. "Do you see that?" he demanded, frothing from the mouth. "Do you see that?"

"I see *you* getting bloody close to my painting!" Celeste shouted back, her own spittle flying. "What do you think you're doing, sir—"

"When?" Kadjic asked, gesturing with the knife again. "When did you last see this painting? Who was alone with it last?"

Celeste and Harvey exchanged glances. "We were," she said. "Tonight. Right before we opened the doors for canapes. *What* is the problem?"

"Was this there?" he demanded, and using the dagger point, he made scratches in the Plexiglas around where the anomaly was.

There was no alarm sound this time, and Josh took a step back, ready to fade into the startled crowd if he could only get one… more….

"No," Celeste said softly, glancing closer. "J.D., come here."

Shit. Well, they'd thought it could happen. "What do you see?" he asked, sounding legitimately puzzled. "I was here this morning, and everything was fine."

"Yes," she said, "and it looks almost the same—right down to that one—remember, we couldn't figure out if it was a brush stroke or a dead fly?"

Tienne had pronounced it a dead fly with a grimace, and the entire mansion had set about trying to capture a fly that exact size and color. A lot of flies had died that week, Molly had said direly, but apparently not in vain.

"Well, it's still there," Josh said with a smile. "But what…?" And oh yes. He could pretend to see it now. "Oh. That's odd. How… how did we not see that before?"

"Was it there before?" Celeste asked, and Josh made a mental note to tell Tienne he'd done a top-rate job.

"The authenticator would have noted it," Josh said confidently. "I don't think that particular letter combination—or even any words—were an Abercrombie device. Where did that…?" A gasp of horror here. "Did somebody *deface* your painting?" he asked. "Why? What do those letters even *mean*?"

The grasp of his shoulder was unexpected and brutal. "You tell *me*!" Kadjic ground out, while Josh's puke reflex ramped up on cue. "*You* discovered the painting!"

"And I don't know how this got on it!" Josh gasped, knowing his face was pale as the pain that had faded with the ibuprofen Hunter had slipped him came roaring back. "Sir, you are *hurting* me!"

"That painting," Kadjic hissed, "is a *forgery*—a personal message to *me*. Who sent it, boy—"

"Ouch!" Josh cried out, not dissembling in the least. "It wasn't there before. The painting I found was an authentic Gertude Abercrombie, and I'm going to puke on your shoes!"

Another vicious twist of the thumb, but before Josh could lose control and follow up on his promise, the pressure disappeared, and Kadjic gave a grunt of pain before dropping the knife on the floor with a clatter.

"You. Will. Not. Touch. Him."

Josh put a trembling hand to his stomach and stared as Liam Craig, smiling Interpol guy, the nice young man who had kept him company and made him laugh during some of the saddest moments of his illness, now metamorphized into an avenging angel.

His hair was still slicked back, and his eyes were still that merry blue, but his face was flushed with fury, and his jaw clenched so hard his cheekbones stood out in stark relief as he grasped Kadjic's wrist, putting pressure on his ulnar nerve, which had been why he'd dropped his knife.

Liam gave a little twist with his fingers, and Kadjic cried out. "That painting is a message to me!" he said. "It's a ghost of the past!" He sounded almost afraid.

"And what's it saying, mate?" Liam asked, his lower East End coming out in a guttural burst. "Can you share with the crowd?"

"Lightfingers," Kadjic gasped. "Lightfingers was here."

Celeste gasped. "Lightfingers is a *myth*," she said.

"But I understand this is something he'd do," Leon said, emerging from the crowd with Julia on his arm. "Even in Italy we've heard of Lightfingers."

"You may let go now," Kadjic muttered. He cast a baleful glare at Josh, who was in too much pain to so much as shake out his arm. "I hurt you?" He sounded puzzled. Then, suspiciously, "I *hurt* you? Or you were already hurt?"

Oh no. "Would you like to see the bruises, asshole?" Josh spat, using the obscenity on purpose to make himself sound young and callow.

He wanted to make eye contact with Liam so badly, but he couldn't. They couldn't establish that they knew each other. Josh *couldn't* fall into Liam's arms when they were so close to free and clear.

And for fuck's sake, Josh couldn't throw up on *anybody's* shoes.

"Celeste," Josh gasped, his act of pulling his shit together by sheer force of will purely authentic. "I will go call Jones to come reauthenticate. Too many people have been up here, wandering around, touching—this bozo just got his prints all over the place. We need to call the FBI art division to see if security has been tampered with. I don't give a fuck *who* this guy is"—and he barely refrained from spitting on Kadjic's shoes since he wasn't going to puke—"but if this painting has been tampered with or replaced, your insurance people need to know. I'll call Serpentus to make doubly sure."

"You know who did this," Kadjic roared. "You, boy—you *know* who did this! I will find him. I will find Lightfingers, and I will find *you*!"

Josh turned from what had been going to be a glorious and dignified swanning out of Celeste's gallery toward the elevators and her office. "This entire gallery heard you threaten me, whoever the hell you are. I'd better not get a *hangnail* before this is over, or Celeste here is going to sue you for your shitty suit."

And before Celeste could turn pale and stammer—as Josh knew she would because no way could she pretend not to know that Josh had just sneered at one of the most powerful mobsters in the world—he hit the elevator, surprised to see that Liam was at his shoulder as the door closed.

Josh's knees wobbled, and Liam's arms came around him, holding him firmly until Liam hit the button and the car started its descent.

"What are you doing here?" Josh mumbled against his chest.

"Leon picked up Kadjic's knife, and your security man finally stepped up to block him."

"Thank you," Josh said, still shaking. "But what are *you* doing here?"

Liam chuckled, the sound strained. With a soft movement he kissed Josh's temple and whispered, "I've told you before, boy-o, nobody catches you but me."

BETWEEN JOSH and Liam, they'd managed to contact the authenticator and the FBI stolen art department before the elevator touched the ground.

Carl was waiting in front of the elevators on the ground floor to represent Serpentus—capers like this were the whole reason Carl hadn't quit his day job as a claims investigator for stolen art.

"Heya," Josh managed. "Nice suit." He tried to stand up straight, but Liam kept him anchored to his side, and Josh let him, his knees wobbling, his body done for the night.

But Carl had recently been talked out of wearing boxy American suits in brown, had actually tried a European cut suit in dark blue with a dark brown tie. The result was devastatingly handsome, and Josh didn't want old habits to settle in.

"Thank you," Carl said dryly. "Your mother gave it to me. My boyfriend ratted out my birthday, and here we are. Anyway—your 'ride,'" and oh, that subtle emphasis did not bode well, "is right outside, pissing off the bellman."

"Wait!" Josh said rather desperately—he'd planned this whole damned caper, dammit, and he wouldn't leave any threads dangling. "Why are you here? I mean, it was an elevator ride and a stop in the office for my stuff. You wouldn't be here that fast—"

Carl rolled his eyes. "My boyfriend and I were at a classic car show at the convention center a few blocks away. Besides, Josh, most rich people expect you to teleport—"

Josh swallowed and tried to warn his friend. "This is Kadjic," he said softly. "He's damned quick, and he's mean."

Carl's eyes went dark. "So we heard. Go let Felix and Danny take you to the ER. You won't hear the end of it until a doctor says you're good."

Josh swallowed, and Carl shook his head. "C'mon, kid, you did good. Trust your crew. You staying in the city?"

"Danny's old digs," Liam said, and Josh glanced at him in surprise. He'd thought he was in for a long haul back to Glencoe, but apparently not.

"Good. Serpentus will interview you in the morning. I'll tell them I made you go get any bruises photographed, so that'll keep everybody on their best behavior." Carl made little shooing motions with his fingers. "Now go."

And Josh had no choice but to do what he asked. Carl, or "Soderburgh," as they called him, because when they'd all first met him he'd been using that as a cover identity, was actually a skilled insurance investigator, which only made him a better con man. He'd seen the best and worst in insurance fraud. He knew the desperate from the crooked and the grifter from the truly in need, and he knew how to catch both and let one slip away and the other twist in the wind.

That's really all Josh's people wanted from the world.

"Well," Liam said as they got outside, "let's get you settled."

He opened the back door to the luxury SUV Josh's father had pulled in front of the building and hit the button for the side step. Josh wanted to bitch—the nerf bar? Really? But his arms trembled, and so did his knees as he used the thing to boost himself up into his seat.

Liam shut the door and trotted around to the other door, and Josh's two dads turned around from the front seat to get a good look at him. Danny had an eyebrow quirked up, and Josh grimaced, because that was his "Felix is on a rampage" warning expression, which meant his other dad, Felix Salinger—Julia's ex-husband and the man who was, in public and in Josh's heart, his actual father—was not pleased.

Liam climbed in, shut the door, and pulled his belt on as Josh tried to do the same. He twisted his shoulder then and let out an involuntary sound of pain, and shit. There it was.

"So," Felix said grimly, "are you ready for a postmortem of the situation, or would that be me interfering?"

Josh let out a sigh and conceded to the inevitable. "Can we save the postmortem for the den in Glencoe tomorrow?" he begged and swallowed down his nausea. "And who's got the barf bags? I make no promises between here and the ER."

"Sure, son," Felix said, and some of the irritation and worry seemed to seep out of his stiff back as he turned to pay attention to traffic. "And while I'm not excited about the trip to the ER, I've got to say, you were right about everything else. Do you have the phone?"

Josh breathed out. "Liam, could you dig it out of my back pocket—the smaller one." Liam's hands were warm and familiar, and Josh felt a bit of resentment that they weren't groping him for real.

"Give it to Danny?" Liam double-checked.

"Yes."

"Danny?" Felix asked.

"Phone fully cloned," Danny said. "I'll hand it off to Stirling later tonight."

"Well, then," Felix said, sounding pleased. "Achievement unlocked. It's time to get to the real work, right?"

Josh leaned back against his seat and smiled to himself, thinking he might make it without throwing up after all. His father was right. The first part of their plan was in place.

Kadjic was right there, exposed and ripe for the plucking.

Lightfingers was *back*.

Serpent in the Garden

CARL KNEW how to keep his face absolutely impassive. The son of a middle-class businessman and a chain-smoking harpy, Carl had found his center long before he'd become his company's most highly sought after insurance investigator. Yes, he'd had to spend a month in rehab to figure out what it was, and another month in Danny Mitchell's bed, but even at the time he'd known that for what it was. Danny had been using him to get through rehab and missing Felix, and Carl had been using Danny to reassure himself that his life and his profession weren't a waste.

Long before he'd been part of the Salinger crew, he'd been solving cases that exposed the bad guys and protected the ones who were just trying not to get screwed by their company. He did it with a fountain pen, some misdirection, and a lot of damned hard work. He'd never considered himself a grifter or a con man, but after more than a year with Danny's crew, he was proud to call himself both.

And he had more than enough confidence to walk into Celeste Buenaventura's loft gallery and shoulder his way through the crowd. Neither Julia nor Leon let on by so much as a whisker that they knew him, but Carl detected something—was it a slight tremble in Julia's lip or a certain grim set to Leon's jaw?—that told him things were not going well.

"Ms. Buenaventura?" he inquired politely, although Celeste's garish outfit pretty much announced her the bright red zinnia in the garden of black orchids. "I'm Carl Kohlcroft, your insurance investigator. I was nearby when your young art dealer, Mr. Morgan?" His company provided him with pseudonyms and backstopped IDs, but this was one that had been provided for him by Felix and Tienne, who, like his father, forged not only paintings but also some excellent identification papers. If anybody queried Serpentus, he'd say he'd heard Kadjic was there and had wanted extra-deep cover.

Which was pretty much the God's honest truth—Carl Soderburgh had been forced to disappear after an incident on an island off the coast of Barbados the summer before.

And his delivery must have been flawless. Celeste nodded, some of the tension from her shoulders relaxing.

"Yes," Carl said. "He called our office, and they asked if I could get here ASAP. Is the FBI investigator here yet?"

"Not yet," said the ruddy middle-aged man standing rather awkwardly by Celeste. "I'm Harvey Merritt, head of security—"

"And I'm Andres Kadjic, the man who must bear this insult," snarled the man himself.

Carl didn't allow himself so much as an eyebrow raise for the man's rudeness. "Kadjic," he murmured. "Have I heard that name before?"

Kadjic's crusty eyebrows shot up, and Carl could see the exact instant it occurred to the man that he should have kept silent.

"No," he muttered, giving the two goons flanking him the side-eye so they'd stand down. "I am a businessman is all."

"Then why would you suspect this—was this a theft? Was it fraud? I'm afraid my dispatcher was sketchy on the details."

Celeste appeared absolutely baffled. "It was just so odd," she said, almost to herself. "I… I could swear it's the same painting we mounted and examined this morning, with J.D. And Harvey and I gave it one last peek this evening before the party. If it wasn't for that one little—"

"It was my *name*," Kadjic snapped, obviously forgetting his resolution to not make waves. "And it was Lightfingers!"

Carl gave a soft, fond laugh. "Oh, we do like to hear about Lightfingers," he said, in such a way as to make it sound like he enjoyed a good fairy tale or scary campfire story. "But here. You three stand over here, and allow me to get the names and numbers of your guests for the FBI when they arrive, and then we can start our investigation."

Carl was quick and good at his job, and while the plan had been to save Leon and Julia for last, appearing to get their statements in an official capacity when they all knew those statements would be conveniently lost when it came time to talk to the other authorities, he could tell that, while normally poised and able to stand for hours, Julia's night was taking a toll. In fact, her pallor became more and more pronounced, and he turned from the group of people he'd just spoken to and gone to the couple's side.

"I'm sorry," he said, in character, "is Ms....?"

"Dormer-Salinger," Julia said tightly.

"Are you all right, Ms. Dormer-Salinger?"

Julia swallowed, her face turning the same color Josh's had been before Liam had hustled him out. "Not really," she mumbled. "I didn't get dinner, and...."

Leon was there to catch her as she actually *swooned* into his arms.

Carl stared, nonplussed for the first time all night. With a clearing of his throat, he shook himself and asked Leon for a business card so they could be interviewed later, and then he pretended to take one from him so Leon didn't have to root through his wallet. As he was doing that, he murmured, "Are you okay?"

"Next time," Julia said, and he could tell she was struggling for tartness, "I'll eat dinner before I attend. You never know when art theft is going to derail your evening."

Carl nodded and gestured for Leon to take the elevator, Julia still nestled in his arms. As he turned back toward the last of the people waiting to give their information, he shuddered hard and glanced up.

Andres Kadjic was glaring at him, an expression so ugly on his craggy face that Carl had to work to keep his naturally stoic expression up and running.

In his ear, Grace and Hunter were going off in panic.

"She fainted? Mrs. Josh's Mom fainted? I can't do this again, Mr. Insurance Asshole Man, I can't—"

"Calm down, Grace."

"But she *fainted*. Oh my God—"

"Hush," Carl said, his back to Kadjic as he moved across the room. "We've got bigger problems than Julia fainting."

"How could it get worse!" Grace's voice was high enough to short out the earwig.

"Kadjic suspects," Carl told them both softly. "Now shut up and let me get through this night, and have Stirling hack *all his comms* to see who he talks to and what he says."

And with that, they clicked off, and Carl began his night in earnest.

Tasks Pleasant and Less So

"UGH," JOSH muttered as Felix pulled up in front of the ER entrance of the hospital. "I wasn't supposed to be back here for another six weeks."

"And yet here we are," Felix told him, voice weighted with meaning. "Danny, you take him in and deal with the doctors. Young Liam and I will join you after I park."

"Oh, but I—"

"Would love a nice walk in the brisk evening air," Danny filled in dryly, giving Liam an apologetic glance, and Liam got it then—there would be conversation while Josh got his shoulder checked out.

"It's fine," Josh said on a yawn. "We can talk at the apartment tonight when I'm done."

Danny helped him down from the vehicle and closed both doors, leaving Felix free to find a spot in the lot.

"Good thought about the apartment," Felix said as he pulled into a space and killed the engine. "Glencoe's a slog if you're not feeling well."

"Is this the part, sir, where you ask about my intentions?" Liam asked doubtfully. He'd *thought* his intentions had been perfectly clear since that vacation in January, and these people didn't seem stupid.

Felix's bark of laughter reassured him. "Oh my God, no. My son's virtue is his own, to give or keep as he wants," he said, unbuckling his belt. "Come—I know for a fact neither of you have eaten. There's a woman in the cafeteria who makes five-star sandwiches. Let's go see if we can get some of those."

It was a summer night by a lake—the air was crisp enough for long sleeves, but the wind was a wholly pleasant break from the humidity of the day. The two men walked shoulder to shoulder for a moment until Felix broke the silence again.

"Now, I don't want to alarm either of you—I take it you both killed your comm links?"

"While we were calling the proper authorities," Liam confirmed. "Why?"

"Well, when Carl went up, Josh's mother—who much like Josh likes to skip meals when she's focused on something—had a little bit of a moment. She fainted, Leon swept her out of there, and they too are going to come to the hospital to get checked out. Now I'm going to ask a favor of you, a large one, and that's to—"

"Not tell Josh until tomorrow?" Liam said, crossing his fingers for luck. He had *plans* for tonight. Not necessarily carnal ones (not after the whole injury bollix) but *personal* plans. He wanted this thing hashed out with Josh before their plan to bring Kadjic down got any further. Dammit, he'd waited. He'd understood Josh's reluctance in a way; nobody wanted to be loved because they were helpless.

That wasn't why Liam had been drawn to the boy, not from the first and certainly not now. But Josh and his friends were entering into uncharted, *dangerous* waters here, and *dammit*, Liam wanted to be part of that journey. He felt like he'd been there from the very beginning, from that first whimsical encounter with Lightfingers to that terrible moment in the alley. The whole time he'd been heading for three weeks in a small berth on a big yacht, talking to a young man of extraordinary grace and humor.

Liam would give anything—his job, his savings, his reputation, *anything*—for the right to be by his side when things got frightening.

That's what this night was about—and as much as he loved and respected Julia, oh God, he'd waited all these months, and he really didn't want another crisis to interfere with his plans.

"Exactly," Felix said. "Not tell Josh until tomorrow. In fact I'm sure we'll all address it at the meeting tomorrow night. So whatever you and Josh are doing virtue-wise, you have until a family dinner at six tomorrow to get it resolved."

"Oh, I think we're going to need years to get it resolved," Liam said. "But we'll be there tomorrow for family dinner, ready to work."

Felix's reply was a gentle laugh. "It's good you feel so strongly about it. I… I love my son very much, but although he's got no claim by blood or legality, I think we can all say that he resembles Danny the most of anybody in this family."

Liam grunted. He'd thought it before, but he could definitely see it now. The size, yes—Felix was tall, broad shouldered, blond, and blue-eyed, whereas Lightfingers was smaller, dark-haired and dark-eyed, but more than that. While not trained—and not overtly elegant—Danny Lightfingers moved with a dancer's grace, a thief's quickness, and an ability to fade into the background when needed, or capture the world's attention when he was on what he thought of as a stage.

Josh had these qualities in spades, and while he had his mother's elegance and poise, and a powerful intelligence probably engendered by all three, including his biological father, Liam understood what Felix was saying.

Danny's gifts could easily lead him in too many directions at a time. Liam could see how Josh's could too.

"There's a reason he bends toward coppers, you think?" Liam asked, his uncertainty making his accent broad.

Felix gave him a sweet smile. "I was not always the force of order you see before you," he said. "But yes. I tilted that way, and… and I think Danny was drawn to that. And…." Now it was Felix's turn to be uncertain. "You know, we gave Josh everything we could. We gave him love, we gave him kindness, a sense of play, a sense of right and wrong. The only thing we could not give him was respect for the law. Our very existence broke it, and we have no apologies. So maybe you… you are his hope that the laws that govern man can be the same laws that govern his heart."

"Kindness," Liam murmured. "Love. Play. Right and wrong." His own heart ached when he heard the list, but not with pain. With a sort of hopeful joy.

Oh, he wanted this evening to go well. But that meant he had to tell a lie of omission, and he wasn't sure he could do it.

"You're sure Julia will be all right?" he asked.

Felix's expression was indefinable, but it also wasn't sad or worried. In fact it was the sort of thing Liam had seen on his next oldest brother's face, right before Liam had walked their oldest sister down the aisle.

Which made Liam curious but not alarmed.

And not willing to sacrifice something that both he and Josh needed, he figured.

"All right, then," he said. "Let's start this relationship off with a lie. In this crew, I'm in good company."

Felix grimaced. "And there you go, hitting me where I live."

"Well, how about I just tell him and reassure him she's fine. Maybe it'll make *him* remember to eat for once."

Felix's irritated sniff sounded like agreement, so Liam decided to take it for that, and they walked into the hospital together.

The cafeteria was, well, a cafeteria, but the beloved sandwich maker was there. And she knew all of the Salinger crew by sight, apparently. All Felix had to do was rattle off names, and she laughed and clapped her hands together and got to work, pointing out the bread pudding and the fresh fruit cups and generally spoiling Felix, who flirted with her gently and told her, finger to lips, that they wouldn't mention the little thing Hunter and Chuck had done for her nephew *or* her son.

By the time Liam sat—with Felix and two trays full of dinner—he felt as though he'd learned a great deal about how Josh's family had dealt with his illness, and a lot of it had to do with being kind to the people at the hospital who had taken such good care of their child.

Leon joined them almost as they sat down, grateful for the sandwich and pleased to take one to Julia when she was done with her checkup.

"If it's okay," Felix said carefully, "I'd like to take it to her. Don't worry, I'm sure she's fine. And if you two could wait here, Danny will be by in a moment to help you pass the time."

It was so skillfully done, Liam noted, that Leon didn't seem put out in the least, and Liam settled down for his sandwich and his fruit cup and, after months of waiting, resigned himself to a whole other hour.

And that's when his phone started to buzz—and Leon's too.

After a good thirty minutes of doing nothing but texting, the two of them looked at each other, turned their phones facedown, and invested in bites of their sandwiches.

"Oh my God," Leon said on a sigh. "I love these people, but they're *intense*."

He sounded much younger than his late-forties, man of the world demeanor, and Liam had to smile, because he thought maybe the Salingers had to do with that too.

"They're certainly not going to let this go, are they?" Liam asked with a smile.

"It's good," Leon said, smoothing his beard in an unconscious gesture. "I… my children had gotten to that point where talking to their parents was… passé. You understand?"

"I'm the oldest of six," Liam said. "Oh yes. Suddenly this little person whose nappies you used to change is the most grown-up of grown-up little arseholes on the planet, and fuck you for changing their nappies in the first place."

Leon chuckled. "You *do* understand." They both took bites of their sandwiches and chewed, and when they were done, Leon continued. "Getting to know my brother's son, his family—it gave me the language of being young again. Not the slang so much, but the… the freedom of not thinking any idea was stupid, of looking at the world afresh. Suddenly I have a sister and brothers of all ages who can give me advice, or even give me an amusing anecdote so my children know that I wasn't born old, I *sound* that way because I'm trying to keep them safe."

Liam nodded. "I…." And he hadn't confessed this to anybody but Josh. "I would like very much for my family to meet the crew. Lightfingers at the least, but all of them. They've grown up on my stories of this family, you know? And part of it was the job." He grimaced. "One of my brothers and two of my sisters are already married. And there they are, starting families and lives, and all I had was Danny's stories to share with them. But part of it is… the joy of it. We find the same joy." He shrugged. He didn't want to talk about Danny's drinking or his own father's—not with Leon anyway—but they were both outsiders there. Being here at the hospital was like being in the inner sanctum, and it felt right to share.

Leon chuckled. "It must be magical," he said, wiping his mouth. "Because I am sitting at a table with a member of Interpol, and I've got to tell you, in my family that's practically a crime."

Liam gave a grin, tickled at that, and then they were interrupted by Danny, escorting a beleaguered-looking Josh, who now wore a sling.

"Bone bruise," Josh muttered. "Go ahead, text it. Tell everybody I'm fine. Some anti-inflammatories, two weeks in the sling, and don't forget my vitamins. Then log off and talk to me while I eat. Leon, you're a nice guy, and I love you, but Danny thought maybe I didn't have to know about my mom fainting, and I'm telling you, that doesn't work for me."

Danny shook his head. "Well, you made it work for your mom in November. I thought perhaps you owed us a little willful ignorance."

The two of them took their places, Danny next to Leon, grabbing the sandwich with his name on a Post-it on top and a stack of napkins, while Josh slid in next to Liam. Liam snagged Josh's sandwich and a plastic knife and started cutting it into pieces and setting the pieces on the tray.

"This is romantic," Josh said, his tone absolutely arid.

"Would you like me to change your nappy and do your pigtails?" Liam retorted. "Because that could be arranged. Or maybe you could just eat and not be such a pain in my arse—"

Josh held up his hand, forestalling the "boy-o" they both saw coming. "I'll eat. Leon talks. It's been a long night, and it's only eight o'clock."

Leon's story was short—and the salient point seemed to be that Julia had fainted when Kadjic had gotten suspicious of her, and Carl had filled in admirably—but still a little worrisome.

"She said it was hunger," Leon told them, brow furrowed. "Which is understandable. She was wearing this ice-blue dress that all but cracked her ribs."

"Very elegant," Danny said proudly. "There were only two dresses of color tonight, Julia's ice blue and that terrible scarlet macaw thing that Celeste had going on."

Josh grimaced and swallowed his first bite of sandwich. "I tried to tell her that didn't work like she thought it did."

"Did you mention *The Emperor's New Groove* thing?" Liam asked seriously. "Because all I could think was, 'Yzma?'"

Josh had to put his hand over his mouth so he wouldn't sputter crumbs. "No," he said behind his hand. "Because I put my age as twenty-nine on my résumé, and I didn't want to sound ten!"

"Twenty-nine?" Liam asked, eyeballing him up and down. "And she *bought* that?"

Josh scowled at him. "She did. She seemed to think I was the perfect age." He shuddered. "My God, people should keep their hands off other people's asses unless they have a sign and an arrow and a contract that says 'I give consent.'"

"I'll remember that," Liam murmured, and Josh shot him a glance.

"We signed that contract on the balcony," he said, and Liam's eyebrows went up in surprise.

"Look who is clearly all out of fucks," he said.

Josh flushed and turned back toward his tray. "I'm sorry," he muttered. "I'm just… it's been a night."

"It has indeed," Felix said, arriving just in time. "And if it's okay, I'm going to call an audible. Leon, can our young Interpol friend here have your keys?"

"It's the red Porsche," Leon said. "It's parked near Felix's SUV."

Liam extended his hand and tried not to drool.

"You know how to drive that?" Felix asked, probably because he'd loaned it to Leon while he was in Chicago.

"I do," Liam said. "I once tracked down a gang of car thieves—nicked 'em right after your friend Chuck left the crew, 'cause they were violent sadists, and Chuck wanted no part of that."

"Did you drive their cars?" Felix asked pointedly.

"Oh aye. Even wrecked one, but I don't recommend it."

Josh snickered weakly. "Dad, give it up. He's a grown-assed man, and he has letters behind his name. Give him the keys."

"Do we have to have the yelling tonight?" Felix asked pointedly. "Do we? Just because I was at the car show with Carl for plausible deniability doesn't mean I wasn't on comms."

Josh winced, and Liam could suddenly see pain etched in the corners of his eyes. "No, Dad," he murmured. "No yelling tonight. Just, you know, trust him. He'll get me to the apartment in one piece, and we'll be home tomorrow."

Felix sighed and bent to give his son a gentle kiss on the top of the head. "No yelling tomorrow either," he said. "I'm not sure if anybody's told you, but the job went really well. Yes, there were glitches, but I seem to remember that thing in January that turned into a WWF melee, and this went considerably better."

There were pained chuckles around the table; *everybody* had visited the hospital after that one, Chuck, Carl, and Hunter included, and they were the team's bruisers.

"Seconded," Danny said with a smile.

"Thirded?" Leon added. And his smile was considerably broader. "Although I could be biased because I got to be part of this one."

"A pivotal part, as it were," Felix said, and Liam tilted his head, taking in Felix's expression. There was something in there… something Felix wasn't telling them, and Liam had to trust, once again, that Felix would tell them if something was seriously wrong with Julia.

Leon's phone buzzed again, and he turned it over with exasperation before his expression lightened. "Oh! Julia says I can come pick her up now."

"And I'm about done," Josh said. "Let me go hug my mom and we can leave."

FELIX STOOD back and watched them exit, lingering for a moment so he could wrap his arm around Danny's shoulders and take a breath.

"So?" Danny asked, sounding excited.

Felix turned to him with a grin. "Oh yeah, you pegged it. She's so knocked up."

"I *knew it*!" Danny chortled. "So tell me, how'd it go?"

Felix paused for a moment, remembering the pure relief on Julia's face when Felix had entered her exam room with a smuggled sandwich.

"Hungry are we?" he'd needled gently.

"Stupid of me," she'd replied, taking the sandwich greedily.

"So…." He'd given her a sideways glance, urging her to tell him so he didn't have to intrude.

She'd smacked his arm. "You've guessed already," she muttered, and her hands, cradling the sandwich she'd begun to devour, dropped into her lap. "Of course you have."

"Danny guessed first," Felix said, because Danny had always been smarter. "He remembered when you and I first arrived here. Remember the train station?"

He'd sat next to her, as familiar as a brother, and she'd hidden her face against his shoulder. "Oh God, yes. How could I forget?"

The plan—Danny's plan—had been for the two of them to elope to America. They'd made appointments with a justice of the peace by phone from Rome. Escaping had been fraught—truly fraught—because Julia's father *would* have killed her for defying him, and for being pregnant in the first place, and for depriving him of the match he'd hoped to make with one of his many mob contacts so he could solidify his holdings. Felix left the house that morning, claiming the relatives he'd purportedly been supposed to visit had called to give him access to their villa. Knowing that Hiram Dormer took Julia to the marketplace every day (the better to parade her in front of his cronies and their sons), Felix had stolen some small tchotchkes for Danny to sell for tickets.

As far as they all knew, Dormer had never missed the tchotchkes, and it had taken him half an hour to realize that his daughter—who had asked to be allowed to shop and try on clothes—had escaped out the back of one of her favorite boutiques.

By the time Julia's father had realized she was missing, she and Felix were on the way to the airport.

By the time he realized she was no longer in Rome, they were married, and she was drawing on her mother's trust to buy the mansion and send wedding announcements to every news outlet in Chicago.

Danny remained behind, leaving false trails and paying people to claim they'd seen Julia Dormer when they hadn't. He and Felix kept in touch with burner phones, so Danny had been there when Felix had called him, panicked and tearful, because Julia had passed out at the train station and been taken to the hospital. Felix—who had been establishing his false credentials as a businessman, the better to impress Dormer when he arrived to find his daughter's marriage a fait accompli—had been called as her first contact, and suddenly it had occurred to him what he, Danny, and Julia were doing.

"I'm the father, Danny! I'm the goddamned father, and this girl passed out and—"

"Felix, pinch yourself."

"What?"

"Pinch your wrist. Really fucking hard."

Felix had done so—the bruise had remained for days.

"Why did I do that?" he asked when his breathing had stopped hitching.

"You are the father. However this plays out, we promised her we'd be there. Don't you get it, Felix? You and me—we're what she's got. You can't go bye-bye on her now. You just fucking can't. We've all had bye-bye parents—all three of us. There is a baby waiting to be born who thinks the world is a place to be trusted. Well, we have got to make it that place. So you start with the girl. You show up at the hospital, tell her I said to eat a goddamned sandwich in the morning and another one in the afternoon and to fuck all the salads, and you make sure she doesn't pass out again. You can't be her lover, but by God we will take care of her, do you under-fucking-stand?"

And Felix had. After he hung up and the train had gotten him to the hospital, he'd gone to visit Julia—much like he was now—with a sandwich and a chocolate milk and a gentle smile.

And the gut punch of a realization that he and Danny hadn't just "helped out a girl," they had irrevocably changed the course of their lives.

And now as he sat next to her on the bed, she touched his arm with delicate fingers, rubbing the place on his wrist that had blossomed with bruises over twenty years ago.

"You two," she whispered. "You gave up so much for me."

He wrapped his arm around her shoulders. "But look what we got in return," he said, and they both knew he wasn't talking about the money or the mansion or even the prestige they all enjoyed.

"I'm so afraid," she confessed, leaning her head on his shoulder. "How do I do this without you?"

Felix snorted, genuinely shocked. "Without us?" he asked.

"Well, yes," she said, staring at him. "I mean, Leon loves children. He's going to want to be part of this child's life, and—"

"So let him," Felix muttered. "But you have an entire wing of a mansion, dearest. Were you planning to kick us out? I mean, you *could*—" And for a moment he fought off hurt.

"Of course not!" she sputtered, absolutely indignant. "No! That's our home! Everybody's home! The whole crew. I *love* having it filled with people!"

"Well, we love living there!" He laughed, hugging her tighter. "And I'll tell you this. The people in your life now will be as involved as you want us to be in this child's life. But when it comes to the core parenting team, Danny and I will be absolutely ready to walk the floors, clean the barf, and take junior to the park. Just like we were before." His voice softened. "Except this time Danny won't have to tell people he's the manny. And I can watch him play and…." His voice was catching as he remembered moments—so many moments—when he'd watched Danny playing with Josh, teaching him to dance, to fence, to swing, to twirl, and had wanted to kiss the man he'd loved but couldn't—and how he'd seen that in Danny's eyes at the same time.

"This time, you both can parent," she said softly. "In front of the world."

Felix shook his head and looked away. "It's unfair of me to put that expectation on you," he said, trying to be noble. "This is your body, your child, your choices, but don't assume Danny and I will run screaming for the hills because you had the good sense to get knocked up by a good man who understands your life and your past and your family. I… I saw you"—and goddamn his voice; he was supposed to be an adult!—"when Danny returned. You were so happy—"

"And so was he," she said, and she was crying shamelessly. "He had every right to be furious with me. So much of why you and I didn't divorce was my fear of my father—"

"Your legitimate fear of your father," Felix reminded her. "It was a mess. The three of us made it, and Danny did what he thought he had to do to fix it. But God, dearest, I will be as hands-on or hands-off as Uncle Felix as you want, but please, please don't kick us out of your life."

"Not in a thousand years," she wailed against his neck, and he managed to save her sandwich before she threw her arms around him.

They'd had a good cry—cathartic and bonding—but now, standing by Danny's side as he pumped his fist in the triumph of a lucky guess, his heart ached once more.

"She wants us to be part of it again," he said softly, and his reward was a smile like a sunbeam on his beloved's face.

"Really?" Danny asked, his voice shaking with such joy that Felix almost wept all over again.

"Yes," Felix told him, wrapping his arm around his shoulders. "And this time—"

"No hiding," Danny said, leaning his head against Felix's shoulder, much like Julia had, but with an intimate promise that Felix would never take for granted, not after their separation, not after their reunion, not after everything they'd survived.

"No hiding," Felix whispered. Across the hallway, they heard Leon in Julia's room, his resonant voice taking on the squeaky timbre of an excited young man.

"Really?" he asked. "Really? Ours?"

There was a quieter reply from Julia, and then a thunderous laugh, the sound a grown man makes when he understands what true family is.

"Well, *all* of ours," he said. "Of course, beloved." His voice sank lower, but they could still hear the last part. "I bet Danny is amazing with children."

"He's the very best," Julia said, her voice breaking again. "Oh, Leon, you should see them play."

The Hardest Part

JOSH WAS falling asleep by the time Liam pulled the Porsche (oh Lordy, what a sweet ride!) up to the building where Danny kept his pied á terre. Originally he'd purchased the apartment so he could have a place to stay when he snuck into Glencoe to visit Josh, but after the reunion last year, he'd kept it because the mansion had filled up with hackers, thieves, grifters, and muscle, and it was always nice to have a place for Felix's business contacts to stay. It was like offering them hospitality without taking the risk that they'd recognize anybody from their extracurricular activities.

The building was sleek and modern—which was not what Liam associated with the Salingers at all, given everybody's penchant for classic art—but inside, the place had been refurbished, claimed, *loved*.

A flowered Persian rug sat in the living room, surrounded by comfortable furniture such as stuffed couches with tapestry upholstery and a cherrywood coffee table that would have felt at home in a mansion much like Leon di Rossi's, which Liam'd had the privilege of visiting.

The kitchen had once been black wood and white marble, but it had been redone too, with bright backsplashes behind the sink and stove and new cream countertops with flecks of matching colors in them. There were two bedrooms with solid furniture and entertainment systems, and a small dining room, as well as stools surrounding the kitchen itself, which stood as an island in the apartment space.

The layout was ugly—Liam couldn't argue—but every effort had been made to create something warm and welcoming, including the glorious art on the walls.

"New piece," Josh mumbled, nodding at a spectacular series of tropical fish, each segment placed on a different wall around the living space.

"One of Tienne's?" Liam asked. That poor fragile child he'd discovered in an alleyway had fulfilled every promise to become an amazing artist. He was still quiet and shy, but he and Stirling had formed a relationship of introverts that Liam thought of as a hidden glass ball full of wonders. Only those who loved the two young men knew where to look for them, but knowing them was so worth the effort.

"From the trip to Barbados," Josh confirmed, yawning. With an effort, he stood up straight and looked to Liam for direction. "Are we talking now?"

Liam, who had been poking into the two bedrooms, turned and laughed. "No. Which room do you stay in when you're here?"

"The one on the corner," Josh said. "I've got clothes in the drawers, stuff in the bathroom, whatever."

"Good," Liam said. "That's where I've parked my bag." His voice dropped. "Nothing dire tonight. I just…." Carefully, he moved into that stoic, wounded space and framed Josh's slim waist with his hands. "I just really want to hold you. Is that so bad?"

Josh's smile was like sunshine through clouds. "No," he said, raising his face shyly for a kiss.

Liam answered, and for a moment, a blessedly quiet, *private* moment, it was the two of them, the feel of Josh in his arms, his taste, even his *smell*. Nothing overt—a subdued hint of aftershave, something airy, not earthbound, and sweat.

It was the latter that pulled Liam back, not because it was unpleasant but because they both smelled of it, and he wanted them to be comfortable.

"Have you had your pain med yet?" he asked.

Josh grimaced. "No, and that ibuprofen you had Hunter sneak me is wearing off."

Liam chuckled. "The ibuprofen was Hunter's idea. Something tells me that bloke knows a great deal about pain management."

"Well, he is sleeping with Grace," Josh said grimly, and Liam chuckled again. Grace's mercurial temper was a good match for Hunter's solid dependability, but it was a match nobody had seen coming and few had thought would last. Josh had, though.

Grace is like Peter Pan, Josh had told him when they'd been stuck in that cabin. *Hunter doesn't need him to grow up, Hunter just needs him to exist. As long as Hunter treats him like spun glass, I'm okay with them, you know?*

But don't you want your friend to be stronger? Liam remembered saying.

Oh he is. Liam could see him so clearly, lying on his side, fathomless brown eyes earnest with a love for his friend that Liam could only remember feeling for Danny. Not a lover, but someone to be made family from sheer act of will. *Someday you will love Grace just like I do, if for no other reason than he kept me alive.*

Liam hadn't said then that it was done. For more moments like that one—Josh staring into his eyes, the light like spun gold through their porthole weaving magic between them—Liam would protect the spun-up, toe-shoed disaster like his own brother from that moment on.

He had that same feeling now, Josh in his arms, raising his face for another kiss, and Liam had to step back.

"Another painkiller," he said, no-nonsense. "And a shower. And then bed. I'll even let you bring snacks."

Josh gave one of those smiles again, devastating because Josh was never shy, not with anybody else. He was brilliant and confident and determined and damned intense, but never shy. Not with Danny Lightfingers, Felix the Fox, and Lady Julia as his parents he wasn't.

But he was with Liam.

"Perfect," Josh said. Then with a coy little tilt of his head, "And more kissing?"

Liam brushed his lips, his stomach tightening with yearning. "God yes," he breathed, and then he practically ran to the kitchen to get some water and some ibuprofen to get Josh to take his meds.

A HALF HOUR later, they were seated on the bed, a bag of crisps between them, watching, of all things, an animated feature called *Bad Guys*.

"I can't even believe we're watching this," Liam muttered.

"For the twelfth time," Josh said happily, munching. "Grace and I quote dialog."

"Why? What even *is* that creature with all the teeth?"

"The shark or the piranha?"

"The *wolf*!" Liam said, eating another crisp in exasperation. "Why—"

"Because," Josh said with the patience of a third-grade teacher, "they're *bad guys*, but they're really *good guys*. The police want to catch them, but they're trying to be *good*. Do I have to explain the parallels here?"

Liam gave him a sour look. "Can I say my profession is not well represented here?"

Josh chuckled. "You haven't even seen the end of the movie, when you guys look *really* bad."

Liam laughed, but in his head he was remembering what Felix had said outside the hospital.

"What?" Josh asked, wiping some orange crisp dust from his lips with his one good hand.

Liam leaned forward and licked it off, grinning when he was done because Josh's eyes were crossed, much like a child's would be with an unruly pet.

"You didn't answer my question," Josh mumbled, licking his own lips between words. "And that tickled."

Liam chuckled and leaned back against the pillows, grateful for this quiet between them. Too often around Josh, life was crazy, people were cattywampus, the stakes were dire, and a moment's delay could mean catastrophe.

Liam wanted to be there for the quiet moments—the ones where no catastrophe would materialize if they took a breath and laughed together.

But that meant honesty. He moved the crisps and turned to his side, resting his head on his fist while Josh paused the movie.

"Felix thought that maybe you liked us law-and-order people because it was something your parents—all three of them—could never give you."

Josh grunted. "We never did have the body count conversation, did we," he stated, and Liam shook his head.

"I don't need a number—"

"Three," Josh said, "if you include the first guy I dated in high school."

Liam clutched his chest. "You're going to kill this old man before he has a chance to count your body!"

Josh booped his nose. "Look at those freckles," he said happily. "How could I resist?"

Liam grinned at him, loving his sense of play, but stuck to the subject. "Yeah, so three. One was a copper—"

And Josh grimaced. "Two. I counted Nick Denning there."

Liam's heart thudded in his stomach as the implications hit him. "But you and Nick were never a thing," he said. Josh had told him this, and Josh hadn't lied to him, not once. Sure, he could put on a show for a mark, but the people in his life were inviolate. No grifting his friends.

"Well, no," Josh said softly. "But… but I thought I really loved the guy. It was very tragic and star-crossed, since, you know, he was married and I wouldn't. But…." Josh booped his nose again, but this time it felt more like a caress. "And then I fell into your arms, and Nick started to fade." He shrugged. "Like the red from Van Gogh's poppies."

"I had no idea they used to be red," Liam said, still stunned. "But Josh—"

Josh swallowed but kept eye contact.

"That leaves Sean."

"Who was in the closet," Josh said. "So not a lot of, you know, actual experience under my belt." This grin wasn't as confident. "A lot like running ops, you know? Lots of observation, but the rest of it is figuring out how things work."

Liam couldn't smile. He wanted to ask "Why me?" but they'd already established Josh had a bent for law enforcement. He wanted to say "Don't play with my heart," but the one thing he knew about these people—knew about *Josh*—was that when it came to the important stuff, nobody played to hurt.

Josh took in his silence, and his expression changed subtly, and Liam could feel Felix's calm strength radiating from his son.

"You don't know what to do with that, do you," Josh stated softly.

Liam swallowed and closed his eyes. "I…." *East Ender, boy. I'm a flatfoot who slept his way to a job I don't deserve and have been riding your Uncle Danny's coattails ever since.*

"I'm careful," Josh said, and this time it wasn't Liam's imagination. His touch on Liam's cheek *was* a caress. "I watched the dads fall apart—not because they didn't love each other, or me, or even my mom, but because sometimes love just hurts."

Liam opened his eyes and took in Josh's expression. Of all their conversations on that ship, this was the first time Josh had said anything—*anything*—about the hurt the family schism had caused *him*.

"It does," Liam said gruffly. "My da—my father wasn't a bad man. So much disappointment. Jobs he didn't get, things he wanted for my mother, things he wanted for us. It fell to shit, and he fell to drink. And people think, you know, you have to stop loving somebody when they disappoint you like that. But the love stays, and the disappointment…."

"Hurts worse," Josh whispered. "Danny… he must have told me a thousand times that he left so he could heal, so he could be his best for me. And even though I know that's true, the time he was gone—half my life—feels like he ripped it out of my heart. I… I'm so glad to have him back. But it makes you… careful," he said at last. "It's given me lots of things. A sense of how to be fair to other people, because when you hurt them, it hurts everybody. Forgiveness. People ask how I can be friends with Grace, but I know that he's so hard on himself, he needs someone in his life who will forgive him for anything. But… maybe that's why I go for law enforcement." He smiled bitterly—too bitterly for somebody so young. "Because I'm hoping somebody entrusted with public safety will know how to be careful with my heart."

And Liam had no choice. "I… I watched you grow up in Lightfinger's pictures, you know."

"Creepy," Josh said, waggling his eyebrows. But they were so close right now, in breath and in heart, and Liam couldn't make light of this.

"I thought, 'If we ever meet, he'll be like my little brother, or a nephew.' I honestly thought that, until… until I caught you. And you were in my arms. And you… you weren't anything like a little brother or a nephew." His eyes burned. "And you were so sick…. I prayed, you know?"

"You never told me that," Josh whispered.

"I said, 'Please, God—I'll give anything you want, just let him get better. Let us know what we can be.' And you did. And then you pushed me away."

It was Josh's turn to close his eyes with pain. "I'm careful," he said again. "I couldn't have stood it if you felt sorry for me. I spent so much of that trip in that wretched berth, and my bright spot—besides the op that almost went to hell—was that you would come visit me. I could trust you to watch out for my family when I couldn't. And I came to feel so much for you. I just… I *needed* you to love me for who I am, not… not what illness made me."

Liam brushed Josh's lips with his own but didn't deepen the kiss. He pulled back and said, "You… you've always been extraordinary." He chuffed out a breath. "Do you have any idea how ordinary I am?"

Josh blinked owlishly at him. "To quote Grace, 'Why are you talking stupid, Mr. Interpol Man?'"

And Liam felt this in his bones. "Do you know how I got the appointment to work Interpol?" he asked bitterly.

"You were awesome at your job as a detective inspector?" Josh hazarded, and Liam snorted.

"I was *decent* at my job as PC. A constable. It's the beginning rank, if you didn't know," he said, and Josh stared at him, his eyes lit up in fascination.

"I did," Josh said. "I *did* know, and I have no idea how a public constable got to be in Interpol. You weren't even a detective?"

"I was aiming for it," Liam said. "And there was a case—you might recognize it—where somebody was stealing art from people who hadn't purchased it, or had stolen it from a museum and not returned it, and in the same go, rearranging the museums, putting odd returned bits in different places—"

"Oh my God," Josh said in surprise. "Danny?"

"Oh yes. So I take this to my DI's attention, and he sends me to the DCI liaison with the art division in Interpol."

"This makes sense…."

Josh was still eyeing him like he knew where this was going, but Liam couldn't help it. He kept blurting the entire stupid, sorry story out so Josh would know exactly what a fraud he was—nominally—in bed with.

He finished up with, “And so there I was, six months later, holding my broken heart in my hands with three giant promotions to show for it and… and…. God, I was so fucking embarrassed I took the first Interpol assignment out of fucking London I could find. Which was how I ended up….” He was stretched out on his stomach, his weight on his elbows so he couldn’t even flail his hands.

“In that terrible alleyway,” Josh said softly. “Where Tienne’s father died and Danny almost did the same.”

“Yes,” Liam said, some of his urgency fading. “So you see….”

“You,” Josh said softly. “I see you. You’re anything but incompetent, Liam. You’re *compassionate*, which not all rule-following law enforcement *is*, or my family wouldn’t be doing what it does.”

“I *slept my way* into my job,” Liam said, laughing a little with bitterness and embarrassment.

Josh’s grin was one of the sexiest things Liam had ever seen. “You,” he said with another one of those sensual *boops*, “are as bent as the rest of my family.”

He said it with a sort of predatory gleam in his eyes, and Liam swallowed, suddenly knowing what it was like to have Josh Salinger’s full and adult attention on him.

“What is it about my nose?” he asked, suddenly as shy as Josh had been in the beginning.

“Freckles,” Josh said immediately. “I told you I adore them.”

Liam hid his face on the pillow between them. “Those weeks on the damned ship, you said nothing about loving freckles.”

“More and more kept popping out,” Josh said, sounding like a baffled yet delighted child. “It was *amazing*. I was afraid you’d start covering your face completely in zinc oxide to scare them away.”

Liam glanced up and smiled. “That’s you,” he said, his voice gruff. “It’s your entire family, really, but you’re the one who makes me feel it right here.” He rubbed his chest through the sleep shirt he’d put on after they’d showered.

“Feel what?” Josh asked, and he cupped Liam’s face again, his thumb brushing Liam’s lips.

“Worthy,” Liam murmured.

“You are,” Josh confirmed, inching closer. “Did you tell me that story, the one about sleeping with your married boss, to make sure?”

"Sure of what?" Liam asked.

"Sure I wouldn't reject you. That if I knew the worst thing about you and still wanted to be here, you could trust me?"

There was no lying here. "Yes," Liam whispered.

"I'm still here," Josh murmured, and moved closer, until their lips brushed, their breath mingled, and the air between them was full of the last year of unspoken promises.

Josh had promised to get better.

Liam had promised to be there when he did.

And now here they were, alone and—

This time as Josh's mouth found his, Josh took the initiative, plundering with his tongue. Josh's injured shoulder was between them, so Liam pushed up on his own elbow, covering Josh's body so Josh could use his uninjured arm to shove under his T-shirt, to palm his skin, to squeeze his shoulders, his biceps, then lower, lower—

"Ah!" Liam sighed, thrusting up against the bed, his cock hard, the kiss still raging between them.

Josh pulled back and grimaced. "Gah! Stupid shoulder," he muttered, and Liam took over the kiss for a moment, kissing him until he was slack and pliant, which didn't happen often with Josh Salinger, Liam was starting to realize.

Liam felt the urgency in his loins again and pulled back, noting Josh's scowl.

"If you're pulling away to go jerk off in the bathroom, so help me—"

Another hard kiss on that playful, swollen mouth, and Liam lifted his head and grinned. "Would you trust me? I *was* seduced by an older, more experienced man, you know. I've got tricks up my sleeve."

And again that scowl, but this time Liam resisted it as he wiggled down the bed and thrust his own hands up under Josh's T-shirt.

"There was no older, more experienced man," Josh sighed, gasping as Liam's thumbs, then his lips, found his nipples. Dear Lord, they were delicious, and Liam tugged and pulled and nibbled on them until Josh's fingers tangled in his curly hair and a surprisingly strong grip pulled him off. "I am going to come from that," he breathed. "And that would be a shame, because after that kiss on the balcony tonight, I *really* want to see you naked."

"Same," Liam panted, kissing his way down a concave tummy. It was flat and soft now, but Liam knew Josh was working for muscle tone, eating protein when he could stomach it, dancing and running as much as his healing body would allow.

Liam was done waiting for a perfect body. He didn't care if there were love handles or he could count ribs (fuck, he could *almost* count ribs). This young man was more than his body, more than his abilities. His heart—that playful, exasperated warrior's heart—had been the thing Liam remembered from that first night, catching Josh in his arms. Even illness hadn't dimmed the fire in him, and now Liam wanted that fire for his own.

With some maneuvering, Liam tugged at the flannel sleep shorts and gazed at the sexy black briefs underneath. He glanced up Josh's body and grinned, gaze flicking to the briefs.

"Prepared, are we?"

Josh rolled his eyes. "I wear thieves' clothes a lot," he said.

"And…?" Liam placed little kisses at the waistband of the tight briefs.

"And I hoped somebody would finally see my underwear," Josh said on a breathy moan.

"But only me, right?" Liam cocked his head.

"You heard my body count," Josh muttered.

"I'm not sure if any of those bodies hit the floor," Liam prodded. Josh was hard already, leaking through his briefs, and Liam shivered as anticipation washed through him, followed by a sort of need he didn't think he possessed.

"Not the way you're thinking," Josh admitted, thrusting his hips up. "I was waiting for the right older man to come along and seduce me."

Liam gave a rather broken laugh, and before he could think too much about all those things that had occupied him for the six months of being pushed away, locked out of *his* boy's life, he stripped off the briefs and took Josh's cock in his mouth.

Josh moaned. "My God, it took you long enough."

Liam was busy trying to fit the thing into the back of his throat. He *had* more practice than Josh; he'd had an active sex life since his affair with Alec Lawson. But Josh was… impressive.

"Hey…," Josh murmured, his fingertips brushing Liam's cheeks. "It's okay—easy."

Liam closed his eyes and tried to let go of some of the need. He slurped his way up to the head and played delicately with it, appreciating Josh's responsiveness, the way his breath caught, the small noises he made as Liam ran his lips along his skin.

For a moment, Liam balanced Josh's head on the tip of his tongue, appreciating the wideness of it, the tenderness of the frenulum, and Josh ran his fingers through Liam's hair again, pulling at the tangles that curls made.

"What do you want?" Josh whispered.

"Oh, I want all of you," Liam said, wrapping his hand around the shaft and fisting it slowly. "I want all of you, and I want to fit inside you so perfect you never let me go."

Josh tilted his head back and shuddered, and a burst of precome slid over the head. "That sounds *awesome*," he said. "Don't hold back. I've thought of nobody but you, practically since I fell out of that van."

Liam had thought he was evil, depraved, seducing a younger man of twenty-one, but as he lowered his head, pulling Josh into his throat again, watching his lithe body writhe on the comforter beneath him, he had to wonder who was seducing whom.

Josh certainly had enough agency for the both of them.

"Okay, then," Josh murmured, spreading his legs to give Liam better access. "So you want me to come first—then we'll see about the fitting in."

Liam had, in fact, been thinking he had to pull off, *had* to pull off so he could make it perfect, could master Josh's body and make him come all in the same thrust, like maybe somebody who hadn't done this before might dream about. But this… this carte blanche to Josh's body, the joyous acceptance of orgasm as inevitable, that made all the difference.

Much like the family's capers, things didn't have to be perfect to be right.

And he wanted to taste, to savor, to swallow, so badly.

He lowered his head again, stroking with his mouth, his fist, his tongue. With his other hand, he groped… erm… explored between the taut skin of Josh's cleft until….

"*Very* nice," Josh breathed, widening his legs more. "I like—ah!—the way you think!"

Liam let a little spit trickle down as he milked Josh's cock, and he wanted to stop and enjoy the details—the shape and size of the thing, the tremble of Josh's slender legs as he fought not to wrap them around Liam's head.

Oh God, Liam wanted him to wrap those legs around his head.

He wanted to be trapped here, pleasuring Joshua Felix Salinger, for maybe the rest of his life.

But time and sex move on, and Josh was young. With an arch of his back, he lost the fight with his thighs, and Liam felt them, stronger than they looked, wrap around his ears while Josh's heels dug into the muscles of Liam's back. His fingers knotted in Liam's curls, and Liam kept sucking, kept stretching with his fingers, until Josh cried out, the sound raw and joyous from a young man with such amazing poise. With an unhampered thrust into the back of Liam's throat, Josh spasmed and came.

Liam moaned, the taste of come sending him over in a dizzying shock. He moved his hands and wrapped his arms around Josh's waist, swallowing Josh's cock and his come and his raw joy while he convulsed and spurted, hot and vital, in his own briefs.

Josh fell back against the sheets with a soft, suppressed sound of pain, and Liam pulled away from him, not sure whether to be embarrassed or triumphant.

"Are you good?" he asked, wiping his mouth with the back of his hand.

Josh let out a sound between a gasp and a cackle. "My God, yes," he said, finally relaxing on the coverlet. "But I'm gonna need a minute—"

"Take all the minutes you want," Liam said, feeling stupid. "I, uh… I've got to go… uhm, clean myself up."

Josh lifted himself up on his good elbow. "Really?"

Liam squeezed his eyes shut. "I am so embarrassed."

Josh's hand had clenched in Liam's curls and then released, and now he clenched again, tugging upward. "Don't you dare clean a thing," he said softly. "Come kiss me and we can start again. Come *everywhere*. You have no idea how turned on I am."

Liam was going to take him up on it, but then he saw Josh's half-closed eyes, and he caught a half-hidden twitch of pain from the pressure they'd put on his shoulder.

"Nice try," he said, giving Josh a chaste kiss on the lips. "I'll be right back with a washcloth, some clean skivvies, and my dignity." And the tablet of painkiller Josh had neglected to take before he'd gotten into the shower.

In ten minutes, after a scowl from Josh at the painkiller and some shifting of clothing, they were back in bed, this time under the covers, about to press play on the movie again. Except this time, Liam stuck his arm out and invited Josh to lay his head on Liam's shoulder, because by God, they'd earned the intimacy by now.

Josh did, snuggling in against him in the bed, making unconscious little puppy grunting sounds that were incredibly at odds with his usual natural elegance.

"What?" he grumbled as Liam smiled gently down at him.

"Nothing," Liam murmured, kissing him on the top of the head. "Just… can we tell the world now? No skywriting, but can I be your stupid Interpol boyfriend—"

"How did you know what Grace called you?" Josh asked dryly.

"It's like I'm psychic," Liam returned in kind. "And you can be…." Six months he'd waited for Josh to invite him back into his life, and now that he'd shouldered his way in, disregarding all the many, many reasons he should have let the boy be, he only had one wish.

"Yours," Josh murmured. "I'm yours. Just… remember. The hard stuff is in front of us. I-I mean, I was keeping my distance because I wanted to get better, yes, but I haven't forgotten—and you shouldn't either—that my family just spent almost two months pissing off a very dangerous mobster. *On purpose.* You took *me* seriously about giving me space, and I'm taking *you* seriously about now being our sticking point. We've done the thing. We've got more hashing out to do, but we're stuck. So much to worry about, but you and I are sticking. It's a promise."

Liam whispered, "I promise," and used the remote to kill the lights. Before his eyes had adjusted to the dark, Josh's breathing was in that familiar pattern, the one Liam had learned on the yacht. He was sleeping, and it was Liam's job to guard him.

But first he watched the rest of the movie, because it really was charming, and Liam figured he was a bad guy now.

Bad Guys

JOSH WOKE up around 5:00 a.m., wondering at first if it was because he had to use the bathroom.

Then—like Danny had taught him when he'd been a child—he'd counted the people breathing in the room. Danny had spent some of his own childhood in less-than-optimal foster homes and much of his adolescence hustling sugar daddies on the Jersey Shore. Knowing who was breathing in the room you'd been asleep in was an important skill.

Liam, check. His own breath, check.

Breeze from a window that shouldn't have been able to be opened?

Check.

And there it was.

"Grace," he mumbled, eyes still closed, "if you are watching me sleep, that's creepy as fuck."

"Maybe I'm a voyeur," Grace said, absolutely unrepentant. "Maybe I was hoping to see hot sex and now I'm disappointed."

"You were surfing porn at fourteen," Josh said. "It was gross and disturbing then, and I don't even want to think about what you're watching now."

"Like I have time to watch porn," Grace muttered. "I have danced *two shows* since we started planning this gig. I am *busy*, and now I am worrying about your weenie ass again."

Josh yawned, sat up, and held his fingers to his lips, casting a glance at Liam, who was lying on his back, one hand on his middle, the other out against the white cotton sheets. He looked vulnerable there, and Josh was reluctant to leave his side, but Grace wouldn't let them sleep if Josh didn't give him some reassurance.

Josh was still wearing his briefs, which Liam had helped him into earlier, and as he walked into the front room/kitchen part of the apartment, he grabbed a black hoodie from on top of the dresser near the door and one-handedly slipped it over his head, then wiggled his good hand out, leaving the other sleeve and shoulder flapping over his immobilized shoulder.

"That's stylish," Grace poked, and Josh eyeballed his friend's black microfiber turtleneck and yoga pants.

"The undertaker called," Josh told him. "He wants that outfit back."

"You're just jealous because I make it sexy," Grace returned, and Josh smiled, partly because Grace was right and partly because they could go back and forth like this for hours, much to the despair of everybody who knew them.

"Want anything?" Josh asked. "Before you answer, I want orange juice."

"I brought doughnuts," Grace said, "because I love you."

And while somebody *not* in their family might have interpreted that as banter, Josh knew that from his friend, it was the purest and sweetest of truths.

"Thank you," he said sincerely. "If you ate all the cream-filled, our friendship is over."

"I ate all the jelly-filled," Grace said with a lascivious laugh. "'Cause—"

"Don't finish that sentence." Josh went to the fridge and one-handedly pulled out the OJ and the milk, wondering who'd stocked up. Maybe Liam had, since he'd obviously arrived earlier that day, but maybe Phyllis, the housekeeper at the mansion, had known he was coming and had ordered a delivery. It was funny how many tiny strings could be pulled to make his life easier. He tried not to ever take them for granted.

Together they sat on stools at the counter and tucked into the small box of pastries that Grace had brought from the shop around the corner. Hunter kept a penthouse apartment in a building about four blocks away, an older Gothic building with gargoyles and hardwood floors and stone cornices. Josh rather loved it. Hunter, of course, had converted the apartment into a giant open area, with a gym mat and exercise equipment in front of a dominating window, a bed on one end, a kitchen on the other, and a couch with a view out the window if there was not a sweaty man lifting weights to block the view. The doughnut shop—mom and pop owned—sat between the two buildings, and Josh and Grace had done the doughnut ritual more than once when Josh had stayed in the city, particularly after the more violent rounds of chemo.

"So…," Grace said leadingly, his voice laced with innuendo. He dipped his raspberry-filled, powder-sugar-coated piece of heaven into his glass of milk and then took a bite so big raspberry squirted out the end into the milk. He did this on purpose, Josh knew, because they'd both done this as kids. Josh's stomach hadn't done dairy since he'd gotten sick, but he still watched Grace happily because it meant *somebody* knew what doughnuts were for.

Josh didn't ask "So what?" because he and Grace had always confided in each other about sex, from Grace's first wet dream (fraught with wonder) to Grace's first blowjob (fraught with worry from Josh's end because Grace had been high and getting higher every day) to Grace's first buttsex (Grace's term, of course) to, finally, Grace's first times with Hunter, confessed quietly as though Grace had been afraid that being with somebody he cared about would get snatched away from him by the king of the trickster gods himself.

And for his part, Josh had talked about Greg, his sweet make-out buddy in high school, and Sean, the closeted policeman, and their few awkward, resentful encounters, but never about Nick, not even the one abortive kiss that Josh had regretted immediately and Nick had both feared and yearned to pursue.

And not one overnight—not even when Josh and Grace had shared an apartment in the city before Danny returned for good. Josh would wake up, give whatever Grace had brought home the night before breakfast, cab fare if needed, and on more than one occasion, a good frisking to make sure nothing like, say, cash or credit cards walked out the front door. Then he'd woken Grace up, made sure he'd taken his prophylactics that morning, and endured the horrific blow-by-blows of intimate physical details he really didn't want to know.

"So," Grace said now, "did his penis have a split at the end like a cloven hoof?"

"No, that was your date," Josh said with a shudder. He sighed. "I miss milk—no, don't give me yours. I'm sure Phyllis has oat milk at home."

Grace patted his shoulder in true commiseration. "Maybe it'll come back, the little bacteria thingies that let you drink the original moo-juice." He took a milk-sopped bite of his doughnut and squeezed out some more raspberry jelly to make the milk pinker.

"So…," Grace prompted again, and Josh knew he sort of owed Grace the salient points.

"He made me come—spectacularly, I might add, and I fell promptly asleep."

Grace sputtered doughnut into his hand and then grabbed a cloth napkin from the corner of the counter to clean up. "That? That's all you got after six months of stopping midsentence, staring out the window, and picturing his manly abs or whatever?"

"I didn't even get to see him naked," Josh muttered glumly. Then he cheered. "But the kisses were *amazing*."

"See, that's important," Grace said wisely, as though, on an emotional level, Hunter hadn't been his one and only lover. "The kissing… it's more than the buttsex, right?"

"Sure," Josh said evasively, but Grace wasn't fooled.

"Which you will have someday," he added loyally.

Josh smiled at his friend, loving him fiercely, and figured he owed Grace one of Liam's closest secrets for his faith in Josh's love life. "Want to hear an amazing fact?" he asked. And why not? Josh knew all about Hunter's dead lover, Paulie, and how Grace had agonized at first that he'd never be able to live up to a perfect dead guy. It was a good thing Hunter had the patience of a, well, *hunter*, because he'd managed to *patiently* explain *many times* that he cared about Grace, alive, more than he ever cared about perfect dead guy, dead.

"*Yes*," Grace said, pausing at the end of his doughnut. He often did that, Josh noted, because he'd probably been born understanding that life was fleeting, and happiness was too, and the end of the doughnut needed to be appreciated.

"The reason he got into Interpol so young was because the first agent he contacted—about Danny, because Liam's smart and had figured out that Lightfingers was behind some local art thefts—"

"Before they were friends," Grace clarified, but again Josh knew this wasn't because Grace had *needed* it cleared, but because sometimes Grace kept track of things better if he repeated stuff.

"Yes, it was during the becoming-friends phase," Josh told him. He'd spent the last year assembling timelines in his head revolving around Danny, and some of them were heartbreaking and some of them were exciting and some of them were… just Danny. In a way Josh had come to appreciate his father more, seeing him this way. Danny had missed his family—missed *Josh*—so much, but when he wasn't in Chicago celebrating milestones, giving drive-by hugs, or sometimes checking him and Grace out of school in the suburbs and taking them for pizza in the city, he was out and about, living a life, curating an underground art dealership or reading voraciously, he also… was Danny. Causing chaos because he could.

"So, the first agent he contacted *what*?" Grace said, obviously hanging on Josh's every word. Julia and Felix were Grace's parents in all the ways that counted—they'd been there through much of Grace's childhood and all the adolescence, the worrisome parts and the awesome parts—but Danny had been Grace's *idol*. Grace's parents hadn't bothered to come to his bedside when he'd almost died and they'd been in the same city. Danny had come to Josh's important stuff from half a world away, and had even, Josh knew, snuck into Grace's hospital room that one awful time to reassure Josh that he'd be okay.

"The first agent Liam contacted about thinking the person responsible for the weird art *relocations* in Liam's neighborhood slept with him, promoted him, and then went back to his wife."

Josh said that with a certain edge, not toward *Liam* but toward this nameless, faceless man. Unlike Felix and Danny, who had gone into their situation with eyes wide open and full agency, Liam had—Josh had no doubt about it—been seduced and deceived. It was an old story, but for somebody as self-sufficient as Liam had been, it had probably hurt.

Grace grunted. "Hunter still does wet work sometimes," he offered. "Remember that crew that helped us out in the desert in May?"

Josh nodded. They'd been busy, but Kadjic hadn't taken *all* their time.

"Anyway," Grace continued, "apparently he and Chuck went back and took care of some of those Gestapo assholes with some help from, you know, that other crew."

Josh cocked his head and thought of how to explain that was probably information Grace shouldn't just spill to anybody.

"I'm not telling anybody," Grace said patiently, as though he'd read Josh's mind. "I'm telling *you*, in case, you know, you wanted Hunter to do you a favor."

Josh chuckled, taking Grace's love for all that it was. "Kind," he said, "but not necessary. The reason I told *you* was that"—Josh's smile turned embarrassed—"I wanted you to like him," he admitted. "Because, you know, he's great, but he's human."

Grace's smile was luminous. "Like us," he said, then scowled. "Except you, Perfect Boy."

Josh groaned. "So Cancer Boy, Recovery Boy, now I'm Perfect Boy?"

Grace sniffed, pretending he wasn't jealous. "It was a *really* good op," he said.

Grace had this way of preening where he turned his face up to the gods and smiled, rocking his shoulders to music unheard.

Josh had this way of *parroting* that action when Grace let loose with one of his rare compliments, and he did that now.

Grace snickered. "We're so stupid," he said happily.

"Unbelievably," Josh agreed.

"But are we stupid enough to have *two* doughnuts?" Grace asked.

"No," Josh said. "But *you* are stupid enough to have the maple bacon bar and give me a bite."

Grace nodded sagely. "We *are*," he said. "We *are* that stupid."

And they were.

Josh sent Grace off around 6:00 a.m., after promising that he and Liam would be at the Glencoe mansion at five—no, four. No, wait, *three*, because he, Grace, Stirling, and Molly hadn't played videogames in *forever*.

"Fine," Josh sighed at the end of negotiations. "I'll be there at *two*, but *you* have to leave through the door this time. Because it's late and I worry and I didn't see any climbing gear."

"I've got secret pitons secreted all over this side of the building," Grace said with a sniff. "The sides *look* like slick marble, but it's a façade—so easy to make sure I've got footholds."

"I don't care," Josh said implacably. "And I'm going to text Hunter and tell him you left here so he's not worried."

Grace muttered, "Everybody's worried—so much easier when nobody cared," as he slid out the door like smoke.

"We always cared!" Josh hissed, sticking his head out the door to make sure Grace heard, and then he closed it tightly and locked it before going back into the bedroom and struggling with the tilt-and-turn window.

"Skinny fucker," he muttered, taking in the very narrow margin for Grace to wiggle through. "I swear if his head gets any bigger, he's going to get stuck."

A warmth at his back warned him, and Liam was draped over his shoulder, doing the catch on the window himself.

That done, he hugged Josh gently from behind and nuzzled his ear.

"Nice of him to visit," he said dryly, "but did you have to tell him my most embarrassing secret?"

Josh winced and turned in his arms, capturing his mouth for a taste of sweetness—sleep breath and all—before he answered.

"It was important," he said soberly. "Grace respects you, but you're, you know, law enforcement. He wouldn't really *trust* you—not with me—unless he knew you were one of us."

"Sleeping my way to the top doesn't make me a criminal," Liam said, sounding baffled.

"No, but it does make you… you know." Josh kissed him again, briefly. "Bent." Liam tugged at the hem of the awkward sweatshirt, and Josh ducked his head so it would clear. "And it means you understand what it's like to be human."

Liam's hands, broad and work roughened, felt so good smoothing along Josh's tender skin. Josh sighed and leaned into his chest, kissing the defined ridges of his pectorals reverently, wishing there was a light on somewhere so he could see if there were freckles here *too*. As he'd mentioned to Grace, he hadn't even seen Liam completely naked yet, and he felt *cheated*.

He felt cheated now as Liam framed his hips with those hands and rested his chin on the crown of Josh's head.

"Honest with me, Josh," he said. "Scale of one to ten, how tired are we?"

It was on the tip of his tongue to say "Four! Let's go!" but honesty… to someone who'd been raised as a thief and a grifter, it was the gold standard of currency right there.

"Seven," he sighed. He let out a breath. "And I'm going to have to be up in a couple hours to have some protein to counter those doughnuts."

Liam shifted and rubbed Josh's biceps under his T-shirt. "That's a… lad."

Josh snorted.

"I'm just saying, we can't do this unless you're honest. I won't coddle you if I know I can trust you. You do understand that?"

"I do," he promised. "Back in bed?"

"Sure, but will Grace be back? Does he have a key so we don't have to let him in?"

Josh snorted. "He never has a key. He set pitons in the side of the building so he could scale it for *fun*, and the doorman knows him by now. You couldn't keep him out of this place with a flamethrower."

Liam chuckled, and Josh added, "But my phone's on the charger—let me text Hunter."

"I'll get it," Liam promised, kissing his shoulder. "Just, you know, settle in so I can settle in next to you."

Josh did so, getting himself and his wretched shoulder comfortable while Liam texted Hunter. He grunted at the reply and continued to text and grunt as he climbed in after Josh.

"What?" Josh asked as Liam sat, bare-chested and dear, squinting at his phone in the ambient light from the windows.

"Hunter wants to know if you ate all the doughnuts," he said.

"No! There were, like, a dozen," Josh mumbled.

"He's asking if Grace can come back and get the box. Apparently he was supposed to be getting doughnuts for *them*."

"The place is still open," Josh said crossly. "Tell Grace to—"

At that moment they barely heard the door open, and then Grace's stage whisper, all the way from the front of the apartment.

"I'll leave some for you, Mr. Interpol Man. You can have sex now!" And then he was gone.

The gentle click of the door was barely detectable, and Liam set his phone in the charger with a huff. He turned toward Josh in the moonlight and said, "You're a matched set, right?"

Josh nodded soberly. "Salt and pepper shakers."

"Okay, then. Next time tell Mr. Pepper he gets one chance to break into a place I'm sleeping before I turn the alarms on."

"That won't deter him—"

"Okay, then tell him the truth," Liam said gruffly. "Tell him, unless he *really* wants to catch us having sex, he needs to respect some boundaries."

Josh sucked wind through his teeth. "He'd wait until we were done," he said.

Liam shook his head and then lay down, rolled to his side, and wrapped his arm around Josh's stomach. "Good to know," he said grimly. Then he chuckled. "Also good to know is that he won't be here tomorrow morning, after we eat and brush our teeth."

"Why?" Josh asked in all innocence, thinking about doing some research for the meeting being planned at his parents' house.

"Butt stuff," Liam said harshly, proving he really *had* been awake for most of Josh and Grace's conversation.

Josh choked on a laugh and then… oh… *thought* about what that meant. He must have made a sound because Liam cuddled closer and breathed in his ear. "You're thinking about it, aren't you?" he asked.

And Josh was—about the newness and the sensations and about the trust and about….

"Yeah," he whispered.

"Good," Liam said, nuzzling his ear. "I will protect Grace with my life, Josh Salinger, but remember that there's some stuff that's only meant for you and me."

"Understood," Josh said, pleased with the boundary. His eyes were closing while his body tingled, and he knew he'd have good, rousing dreams. "Love you, Liam," he murmured, not aware he'd jumped months of romantic interaction with one phrase.

"Love you too, Perfect Boy," Liam said, laughter evident in his tone.

He wanted to say, "I'm not perfect," but he was so much more than asleep before he could even get the words out.

Counting Stars

LIAM HAD planned his trip to Chicago weeks in advance. While he and Josh hadn't been writing anything personal to each other, he *had* been on the email chains that followed the strategy meetings for luring Kadjic to the area, and he'd known the night before would be important and possibly dangerous.

Still, waking up with the sun streaming through the blinds of Danny's pied á terre in Chicago instead of Liam's own dusty flat in London took some adjustment.

Feeling Josh's fingertips dancing across the skin of his shoulders was perhaps the most mind-blowing adjustment of them all.

Yes. Yes, we did that. We even said big important words. Come on, Liam my boy, it's time to make that shit stick.

He'd never wanted anybody like he'd wanted Josh Salinger. Not just the lithe body and the dancing brown eyes, but the entire package.

Listening to Josh disclose intimate details to Grace over doughnuts might have been a bad moment if Liam hadn't known it for an important one. If Grace knew, *everybody* knew (although hopefully not about Alec Lawson, because dear God!), and if everybody knew, that meant Josh was as committed as Liam was.

"I don't think you understand," Josh was saying fractiously, bored with resting in the berth but half asleep again already. "Yes, I want to get better because I want more goddamned life, right? But I... I'm the hope of my family, do you understand that?"

"I'm the oldest of six, Josh. I've been helping my mother pay rent since I was fourteen. Of course I get it."

But Josh shook his head. "No, you get pressure. And...." His scowl softened. "And you get pain. I'm so sorry. Because that sounds hard. But... but you told me your little sister, Tanda, the whole family was rooting for her to go to university, right?"

Liam nodded, thinking he hadn't reckoned on Josh's steel-trap brain remembering all of Liam's random conversation. "Yes," he said slowly. "She aced her O levels—she's going to go far, be a barrister, I think."

"So the whole family is looking at her, thinking, 'Life's been hard. It's hurt. And we've lost things nobody will ever know about, but if only she can make it, it will all be worth it.' Tell me I'm wrong."

Liam had swallowed then and vowed to go home and write Tanda and tell her how proud he was of her and how he'd understand if she chucked the whole barrister idea and became a roadie for her favorite band.

"You're not wrong," he said through a dry throat.

"Well, I don't have all your brothers and sisters. But I've got three parents who sacrificed ***everything*** *for me. I have an uncle who relocated his business, practically so he could be near me. My mother, yes, but Leon's a good guy, and he loved his brother, and he is sincerely trying to be my family. And… and I shanghaied Hunter and Chuck into my little circle of friends, and Carl joined up on his own, and they brought boyfriends and old friends, and Stirling, Molly, and Grace and I have been ride or die since grade school, and even Tienne, who didn't want anything to do with us for a while, fell in love with Stirling and… do you see? Me, breathing in and out, got all this together, and then I threatened to die on everybody."*

"And stop breathing in and out," Liam supplied, his own heart feeling sickly and stuttering thinking about it.

"And I can't do that," Josh said. Liam watched his amazing brown eyes grow shiny and red-rimmed. "I can't. Even when I want to sleep, I have to remember I can't sleep forever, because I. Am. My. Family's. Hope."

Liam nodded, understanding the pressure now. "And you don't want me to add to that," he said, the pain of needing to step back almost unbearable.

Josh had let out a little sob then. "Just hold my hand," he whispered. "I can do it if you help me."

And Liam had held his hand as he'd slept, still twitching because chemo did all sorts of damage as it healed.

Liam took a deep breath, that conversation fresh in his heart as he felt Josh's gentle touches.

"What are you thinking?" Josh asked from behind him.

"Well, first of all, what are you—"

"Counting freckles," Josh said promptly. "Every time I think I can stop, I lose my place." Liam felt the playful kiss at the base of his neck.

Liam smiled in spite of the grimness of the memory. So many reasons for him and Josh to step back six months ago, but none of that discussion had centered about what was happening *now*.

Liam, knowing Josh would be in danger, simply couldn't step back one minute longer.

"I'm sorry I couldn't wait," he said, rolling over when he felt Josh's fingertips stop their dancing.

"I'm not," Josh replied, searching his face for clues of regret. He swallowed and gave a little smile. "I wanted you there so bad," he whispered.

Liam cupped his cheek. "Why didn't you ask?"

"I… I wanted to prove I was okay. I could do it." He let out a little laugh that was the first time Liam had ever heard Josh sound scared. "I've never seen Danny so scared, Liam. We *really* need to find a way to get Kadjic—get him to the authorities, shoot him into outer space, strip him of his power. I don't care how, but Danny's offered to bolt twice a day for the last six months, because he wants us all safe. If I'm their hope, I'd better not let them down."

Liam let his own fingers dance along Josh's surprisingly strong jawline, down the tender curve of his neck. "Impossible," he said softly. "And none of them expect you to do it by yourself. And as for Lightfingers…." He let out a breath. "I was in that alley. I saw what Kadjic did. And Danny… he was at his lowest at that point, so he probably felt… hell. Helpless and sad and inadequate. But you know what I remember that I bet he doesn't?"

"What?" Josh asked before turning his head to kiss one of Liam's fingertips. He may not have a lot of experience as a lover, but his instincts were spot-on.

"Earlier that day," Liam told him, tilting his head back and shivering, arousal starting deep in his belly, "I ran across this group of street kids, drawing on the sides of buildings and on scraps of paper and anything they could get their hands on with packets of wax crayons. And I was thinking, 'Why crayons, why not food?' when I realized that most of their scraps of paper had held sandwiches and bread. And I asked one of the little girls where she got these luxuries, and you know what she told me?"

"Lightfingers?" Josh said with a smile.

"But she said it in French," Liam said. "Took me a minute. My French is not that good. Anyway, the point is, Danny at his lowest was still able to feed children, bring them joy, and save Tienne in that alleyway. I know he's scared—which means he's smart—but he's also not alone, and by God, he's not at his lowest. Not now, right?"

Josh nodded and relaxed in to Liam's touch, like the reassurance that his family could take care of itself was what he'd needed to become all Liam's in that moment.

Liam felt drawn to the kiss inexorably, and he was surprised and startled when Josh jerked away, holding his hand in front of his mouth.

"My breath," he proclaimed, voice muffled, "is *heinous*. If I have my way, you will *never* know how bad my morning breath is."

Liam took Josh's hand gently and moved it away. "*Nobody's* morning breath is great, Josh. I…." More confession here. "Every now and then I—" Oh Lord. He'd almost said "cop a fag," but that was a little *too* much London's East End for Josh. "—sneak a smoke," he finished. "Leftover from my flatfoot days. If I'm not careful, my breath is *hellacious*, and you have my permission to kick me out of bed then. This?" He swooped in for a quick kiss, which wasn't bad, really. "This is human. We can deal with this."

"You will *never* smoke in front of me," Josh said, eyes narrowed. "Ever. I will *beat* you. Do you understand?"

Liam grinned. "You bossing me around already?"

Josh scowled. "Cancer *sucks*," he said direly. "Don't tempt fate. Do you understand me?"

And suddenly Liam understood far more than Josh probably intended.

"I get it," he said softly, running his own fingertips along Josh's clavicle, which was more prominent than either of them would have liked. "It was a close call this year."

Josh rolled out of bed so fast Liam was afraid he was going to bolt out the door. "I," he said resolutely, "am going to go brush my teeth and use the facilities and rinse off my body. Then I'm going to eat. Then we're going to *return* to this moment, right here, and… uhm…."

Liam, who had been startled—and more than a little disappointed—saw a mottled flush travel from Josh's navel, up his chest, and along his naked shoulders, and hid his own expression with his hand.

"Butt stuff?" he asked, when he was sure he had his voice under control.

"Maybe," Josh said with dignity and swept off to the bathroom.

Chuckling to himself, Liam toddled off to the other bathroom to do the same. Perhaps, someday in the future, they could roll over and have relaxed morning sex, but right now, he got that Josh needed more control than that.

Well, the boy's life had been sort of a circus ride, no matter how much his three parents had tried to give him stability. Of course, given Josh's intelligence, curiosity, and damned confidence, Liam doubted he would have been boring in any circumstance, but the extra layers added on by a life of, well, skirting the law, even at a young age, probably made being in control as often as possible important.

I know, for example, why he tends to veer toward law enforcement—do you?

Liam spent half his shower cursing Felix under his breath and the other half wondering what he and Josh would do next.

PLAN, APPARENTLY—AT least for part of the morning.

He got out of the shower and dressed in sweats to find Josh, dressed in thieves' clothes, munching his way through a bowl of fruit, yogurt, and granola.

"I thought you said protein," Liam protested before throwing his underwear into the hamper in Josh's bathroom.

"Yogurt *has* protein," he mumbled absently, studying a tablet that he must have brought in his duffel on the way over. "And also some nice bacteria that helps my stomach recoup what it lost when chemo tried to kill me. So some things you should know about last night's fallout—grab some food and be ready."

Liam went through the small refrigerator and found, to his delight, bagels, cream cheese, and salami. He eyed that last speculatively, and then glanced at Josh and then back into the refrigerator.

"Eat the salami," Josh said dryly, although it did not appear he'd looked up. "If nothing else, I have breath mints."

"Try not to kill the romance," Liam grumbled, and when he glanced Josh's way, Josh was giving him a mischievous grin.

"You showed up when I needed you," Josh said happily. "Achievement unlocked. There's only one thing I need you to do after that."

Liam's expression softened. He knew the answer to this one. Any idiot would.

"Stay," he said.

Josh tilted his head. "We all have our damage. Stay."

"Understood. What are you looking at so fiercely?" He grabbed the bagels, schmear, and spicy lunchmeat and put them all on the counter before pulling out the toaster, all while listening to Josh reading the morning family report.

"Well, Carl told us that Kadjic managed to slip out before the FBI Art Theft Division got there—"

"Big surprise," Liam muttered.

"Yes, but also not a big surprise was that Celeste apparently didn't even know who the guy was—her words—and she had no idea why the painting seemed to anger him so much."

Liam snorted. "A lie?" he asked.

"Oh, definitely a lie. I heard her say his name twice a day for six weeks. She knew he was coming."

Liam frowned. "But she obviously knew that was bad news from a LEO perspective. I never did catch whether or not the girl invited him or just ran in his circles. How *did* he know whether to show up or not?"

"We baited the hook," Josh said. "Danny knew that Kadjic loved Dizzy Gillespie and the Chicago jazz movement. I think it had something to do with the hats."

Liam blinked. "Hats?"

"Fedoras?" Josh asked. "You know, all those movies with guys in fedoras and turtlenecks snapping their way through jazz clubs? Apparently Kadjic's a fan."

Liam gaped, nonplussed, until a bagel popped out of the toaster.

"Weird," he managed as he turned to his breakfast.

"No, not really," Josh murmured, making another note on his tablet. "What's *your* favorite music?"

"Punk," Liam said, not even having to think. "But that's sort of, you know, a London thing—even an East End thing."

"So," Josh said, "if, say, the lead singer of The Clash actually painted in the style of your favorite artist…." He gestured at Liam to fill that in.

"There's a street artist I like," Liam said. "Don't know his name, only his tag. Coyle." He said it with the Gaelic pronunciation, "Kelly," and was surprised when Josh spelled it out for him.

"Yes, that's it. How'd you know?"

Josh raised his eyebrows puckishly. "We ran into him when my family was wandering around Europe, when I was a little kid. Sweet guy. Loves fairy tales, proud Irishman, has a daughter about my age. I think Danny and Felix financed him—gave him enough money to live on until he made it big mainstream, and also kept him going so he could do his street art."

"I didn't know he was mainstream," Liam said, impressed.

"Under a different name," Josh said. "Anyway, they called it a grant, and he gives them a painting once a year to auction so they can keep giving out grants. Nice guy."

Liam chuckled. "Of course," he said. "But back to Joe Strummer coming back from the dead and painting street art."

"Well, what if he painted street art while he was *alive*," Josh said. "And you got a chance to, I don't know, own a piece of that wall for your giant loft—"

"Tiny dusty flat," Liam corrected dryly.

"With a fabulous art collection," Josh supplied. "Anyway, if *you* were a power-hungry oligarch, wouldn't *you* come buy that chunk of wall?"

Liam nodded. "Okay, so yeah. I get it. You baited the hook with a very public exhibition, and then fucked with it. Nice hint of cruelty. That's how you knew he'd show up, *and* how you knew he'd flip out."

"Exactly," Josh said. "And we knew Celeste ran in his circles, so that's why her loft. Besides, it was in Chicago, and we want to take him out on *our* home turf."

"Fair," Liam said. "So he managed to squirrel out of meeting the FBI—"

"Big surprise. BTW, if anybody asks, Carl's here right now debriefing us for the insurance company."

"I'll be sure to toast him a bagel," Liam said dryly.

"Well, he *was* going to come by," Josh said, his mouth quirking, "but apparently oversharing with my obnoxious codependent does have an upside."

Liam massaged his forehead with one knuckle. "So good to know."

"But there's more," Josh said, tapping an item on his tablet. "While we were making out—"

"Making love," Liam supplied without glancing up from prepping his bagel.

"Doing naked things," Josh clarified, eyes dancing, "two things were happening. Number one, somebody was taking a poke at my ID."

Liam almost dropped his bagel. "I'm sorry?"

"We knew it might be challenged," Josh said. "I'm not really a celebrity, but Felix and Julia are out a lot on the society pages. Danny has managed to keep a low profile after that appearance on TV last year, so Stirling backstopped 'J.D. Morgan' to the moon. The ID held—Stirling, Danny, and Tienne have built a system the military would envy—but Danny says somebody's been pretty insistent with it. There haven't been any breakthroughs, and nobody's thought about facial recognition software yet, which is good, but we can't expect that to last."

"What does that mean for us?" Liam asked, concerned.

"It means we need to get our shit together," Josh said with a shrug. He glanced up as Liam placed his bagel on a napkin and a glass of juice on the counter at Josh's side. "But that starts this afternoon."

"Yes, I heard." Liam walked around the counter and perched on the stool next to Josh's. "Two this afternoon. Why? Why did it have to be so early?"

Josh gave him a winsome smile. "Because I wanted to play video games with my friends. With you. Also my friend."

"More than friends," Liam grumbled playfully. But he was as weak as the next man; he needed to hear it.

"Yes," Josh said, and he leaned his head on Liam's shoulder with that pliancy and sweetness Liam remembered from the yacht. Not weakness, he thought, wrapping his arm around Josh's shoulders and leaning back. He sighed, some of his insecurity leaching out.

"What was the other thing?" Liam asked.

"Well, the other thing was that phone—remember the one I gave Danny?"

"I do," Liam said, mostly because *he'd* been the one to give it to Danny.

"In the time Kadjic was close to me, we managed to clone his phone."

"You what?" Liam practically jumped out of his chair.

"We weren't sure it would work," Josh said soberly. "People come up with encryption as fast as other people can come up with encryption blockers. It was a gamble, and it paid off. Not completely—we don't have a total phone list or all his passwords. But we *do* have a list of calls and locations he made within twelve hours after the clone."

"What happened then?" Because that had been while they'd been asleep, content after a hard evening's work.

"According to Stirling, all his passwords automatically changed, because he's got an algorithm on his keychain. But our computer guys—and between Danny, Stirling, Tienne, and Carl, we've got something of a squad—were all busy, busy bees until then. We don't know if he's been hacked or not, but we're pretty sure it's 'not.'"

Wow. *Wow*. This was more than Interpol—or any crime fighting organization really—had done in the twenty years since Kadjic had begun his rise from street thug to kingpin. Suddenly Liam realized the true delicacy of Josh's situation. He hadn't wanted to attract Kadjic's attention—not really. *None* of them wanted Kadjic to remember what they looked like. But he would have wanted to be close enough long enough for the cloning software to work. *That* was why the careful soft shoe of people running interference during the caper. Divert, divert, divert… steal all of Andres Kadjic's information in one fell swoop.

"Can you tell me what you all have planned?" he asked, suddenly worried for the caper, for the danger, for plans that might once again put a lever between them and pry them apart.

"No," Josh said, "because I don't know. I… I have the whisper of a plan, you understand. But you've seen us plan before, right?"

Liam nodded. What happened wasn't always… *linear*. It was instead a result of *gestalt*, the collective. Josh's "crew"—his family and friends—had at their disposal a truly boggling amount of talent, creativity, and intelligence. Josh may walk in with one sort of plan, but one person could throw a pebble in his path and he'd pivot in mid-stride, and the entire planet would pivot with him. They'd get to the same goal, but their journey could vary wildly—the night before was a prime example.

Right down to the hospital visit and Josh's return here, in Liam's care, instead of back in the mansion in Glencoe.

"You going to eat that?" Josh prodded, not moving his head from Liam's shoulder.

Liam shoved a bite of bagel in his mouth and chewed gamely.

"Good," Josh murmured. He sat up. "I'm almost done here, and you've got to keep up your strength."

LIAM FINISHED his breakfast and put both their dishes in the dishwasher. Then, conscious that in Josh's world, the clock was often ticking, he moved behind Josh, who was busy tapping away on his tablet, and slid his arms around Josh's slender waist, resting his chin on Josh's shoulder. This new familiarity thrilled him, but he wanted more.

"Almost…." Josh's fingers flew on the keyboard.

"Take your time," Liam murmured, then tickled Josh's ear with his lips.

"Augh!" There was some honest distress in Josh's tone. "I didn't mean to send that!"

Gently, Liam took Josh's earlobe between his teeth and gave a delicate nip.

"I, uhm…."

Still tormenting the ear (and he loved that Josh's seemed to be so sensitive), he slid his hands up under Josh's slim-fitting black shirt and palmed the soft skin of his stomach, the nearly smooth skin of his chest, noting the small but defined muscle groups. He was careful of the shoulder, although he'd noticed Josh had left the brace off when he'd dressed. Mindful of the bruised tendon, he stroked the skin.

"How's this doing?" he asked, making sure his breath tickled the whorls of Josh's ear.

"Tender," Josh admitted.

"Maybe you should—" Liam ran his lips down the cords of Josh's neck. "—take a break."

"I should resend… oh!" Liam had tweaked a nipple.

"Josh?" Liam murmured.

"What?"

"Later."

"Oh hell. God. Yes." Josh tilted his head back against Liam's shoulder, giving him complete access to his neck, his ear, anything he wanted.

Liam stepped back and whirled the stool seat around so Josh was facing him and took his mouth, because that was the *real* thing he wanted, Josh's engagement. And when Josh opened his mouth for the kiss, hands coming up under Liam's hooded sweatshirt to knead and explore, the gratification, the reward, was so damned sweet.

How long had they waited? A year? Six months? A lifetime? Like Josh's capers, time ceased to be linear between them, two magnets whose separation changed nothing about the strength of their connection, except maybe made it stronger.

Josh let out a sound—wanting, pleading, unbearably young—and Liam pulled back and reminded himself for the hundredth time that he needed to let Josh lead, but he was also the one most likely to keep his head.

"Come on," Liam gasped. "Bedroom."

Josh complied, and Liam was careful to take the hand attached to the uninjured shoulder, and to guide him gently.

"Grace has sex in all these weird positions," Josh said. "Are we going to do that?"

Liam grunted. "Can I express my absolute indifference for what Grace does in bed?" he asked.

"Okay," Josh said, sounding a little lost. "But I don't have a lot of other—"

Liam sat him on the bed and took the hem of his shirt. "Careful," he murmured. "Let me help you here."

Josh allowed himself to be undressed, and then Liam fell to his knees before him. "Josh?"

"Yes."

"What are you afraid of? We did this last night. It was good, right?"

Josh's shy smile would be the death of him. They'd be old and gray, and he'd see that hint of embarrassment, of self-effacement, and his heart would have had enough, and he'd be carried to glory a happy man.

"It was wonderful," Josh murmured. "But you waited for so long—"

"So did you," Liam told him, taking his good hand. "I know you're worth the wait. Am I?"

Josh leaned down and kissed his forehead. "Oh yes."

"I want to make love to you some more," Liam whispered. "God, if nothing else, I want you to *feel* like mine."

Josh cocked his head. "So do you want *me* to feel like yours, or do *you* want to feel like I'm yours?"

Liam blinked at him, trying hard to parse that, and Josh laughed.

"Both," Josh chortled. "Let's say both." And then he lowered his head a little more and captured Liam's mouth in a kiss.

Ah, God. So sweet. And more than sweet was Josh's laughter, his playfulness, his desire.

Oh…. Liam rose, cupping Josh's face in his wide-palmed peasant's hands. *Especially* his desire. He shed his hoodie and felt Josh tugging at his pants with one hand, grunting in frustration.

Liam took the task from him and said, "Can you, just this once, let me do some of this?"

"I want to see it," Josh grumbled, but he kept his injured arm in his lap, telling Liam that it hurt more than he'd ever admit.

Liam chuckled weakly, shoved his sweats and briefs to the floor, and stood there naked for Josh's perusal.

He worked out when he could—swam and ran when he couldn't—but thanks to that little trip to the Caribbean he'd seen pretty much all the men in Josh's crew in their swimming trunks and had conceded that he needed to give up ever being the prettiest or the most fit. But Josh didn't seem to be disappointed as he gazed at Liam's body in appreciation.

In fact, he appeared to be in awe.

"You do good things for my ego, boy," he said softly, cupping Josh's cheek again.

"You," Josh told him. And then, using his one good hand and his mouth and his tongue, he took Liam's cock in his palm and began to explore.

Liam's breath came out in a long hiss, and he closed his eyes, accepting Josh's ministrations with as much grace as he could manage.

His nipples were hard in the air-conditioning, and he felt blatantly exposed here in the bedroom, but mostly he was being devoured, kissed, explored by the man he felt like he'd wanted all his life, and he wanted to be *enough*.

Josh squeezed him, his touch firm and exploratory at once, and then lapped at his head eagerly.

Liam made a noise and threaded his fingers through that glossy black hair, not to pressure, but to touch.

"Good?" Josh paused to ask.

"Amazing," Liam breathed. "I won't last."

That low, self-possessed chuckle almost made Liam spend, and his fingers in Josh's hair trembled as he knotted them, tugged backward.

Josh gazed up at him like he was something, like he was important, and said, "I'm open to suggestions."

"Stand," Liam said gruffly. "Let me help you off with your clothes. Let me lay you back, put pillows down…." *Make love to you like you're precious. Keep you safe and never, ever hurt you.*

Impossible, he knew. Even lovers who had nothing to lose inflicted tiny darts. Alec Lawson had been a horrible snob. Without knowing it, he'd insulted Liam's family, his mother working two jobs, his siblings—some straight and narrow and some struggling to find their way—and his father, his poor drunken, devoted, bungling, stout-hearted father, at least three times a day. Liam had put up with it because he'd been younger, and Alec was his superior, and the relationship hadn't been equal in any sense of the word.

But it had given Liam a sense of what he wanted to do *now*, which was to keep his tiny darts to himself, to use words and actions to build and not break down.

To touch this fine body, laid out before him, with his soul in his fingertips, his heart in every brush of flesh.

But not with silence.

"Settled?" he asked, after he'd fidgeted with pillows and Josh was splayed out before him, pale and gazing up with dancing eyes.

"Like fine china," Josh replied. "Are you going to touch me soon, or is this an excuse for another nap?"

Liam gave him a flat look. "I would like this experience to be repeatable, thank you. If you're thinking 'Oh God, make him stop moving because I hurt,' then I have failed at my job."

Josh's burble of laughter was almost like a stroke upon his skin.

"I'll tell you before it gets that bad," he said. "Now kiss me and fuck me and let me enjoy my decisions."

"Aye, Captain," Liam murmured and took Josh's mouth again, and this time there was nothing to stop them.

Every kiss was fire, and the next soothed the burn but stoked up the heat. In a moment Liam was completely consumed, his finesse and good intentions gone as his breath ratcheted up. His urgency drove him against Josh's body, needing the headiness of skin on skin.

Josh arched his back, wrapped his legs around Liam's hips, and bucked, and Liam trembled with need. His hands suddenly shaking, he reached for the lubricant in the end table and fumbled for it, bringing it between their bodies so he could stroke Josh's entrance with it and stretch with a gentle finger.

Josh made a sound then from deep inside that spoke of hard want, and Liam thrust two fingers in, not so delicately, and Josh's next sound was pure need.

"Please," he whispered. "Please… I'm so ready."

More stretching, though, and then Liam was there, at the gates of heaven, and careful of Josh's expression, of his noises, of the urgency of his heels thrusting against Liam's ass and the vulnerable line of his throat as he gave Liam everything he'd ever needed, Liam thrust.

Gah! So tight! And Josh kept begging for more, for deeper, all the way, please—

"Ah!"

For a moment they were locked together, as close as humans could physically be, and a droplet of sweat plopped from Liam's forehead to Josh's shoulder as Liam trembled, his weight on his elbows as he gazed at Josh for permission.

"Go," Josh begged. "Please. Don't stop now."

He started slowly, and Josh's breathy moans drove him on, faster, faster, harder. Oh God, he should be mindful of the shoulder, of Josh's inexperience, but as he tried to slow down Josh cried out, his body trembling, agonizingly close to climax, and Liam had no choice.

He drove himself inside with all his force, his want, his need, and Josh's orgasm announced itself in a *roar* of completion that tipped Liam over. He buried his face into the hollow of Josh's neck and shoulder and groaned, the sound coming from deep within as he poured himself, body and soul, into the one man in the world he'd searched the world for.

His breathing was still coming in harsh gasps when Josh let a little pain sound out, and Liam pushed up off him.

"Do you want I should—"

"Move and I'll kill you," Josh mumbled, flushed and happy. "Now kiss me and tell me I'm pretty and tell me that was as wonderful for you as it was for me."

Liam chuckled, and from the dreamy expression that crossed over Josh's delicate features, he could tell Josh felt that right where they were joined.

"I hope you're ready to be saddled with me for life, boy-o," Liam murmured. "After that, I don't think I could leave your side again."

Josh's smile was still dreamy, and he threaded his fingers through Liam's hair, probably sending the ringlets into fabulous disarray. "Oh, like I'm letting you go now," he purred. "Now kiss me, like I asked, or I'll get pushy."

Liam's smile felt like it took his entire body to achieve, and he nipped playfully at Josh's kiss-swollen lips until Josh took his mouth and ravished him.

And still moving inside his lover, they began again.

Ladies and Gentlemen I Present You....

THEY FELL asleep eventually, Josh tucked inside Liam's embrace like he'd apparently always should have been, only to be awakened by the alarm from his phone on the floor.

"Crap," Liam mumbled, finding his own phone on the bedstand. "We should be *leaving* now."

Josh ran his lips over Liam's bicep, practically purring. "We can be a little late," he said, conscious that he was the one who'd said they should be at Glencoe at two. "We can get some lunch, take our time…."

"Wow," Liam said, chuckling. "If your parents had known this was what it took to get you to relax—"

"*Don't* finish that sentence," Josh said, laughing. Carefully, he swung his legs over the bed and took stock. Lower body? Completely debauched, ass a little achy, everything else floaty. Perfect. Upper body? Shoulder hurt like hell and, oh, hey, headache developing from who knew? Not eating enough? Eating too much? Endorphins? Anti-sex chemo residue? Whatever. Josh was tired of his fragile body's fragile body reactions. He wasn't giving up what he and Liam had done, *literally* to save his life.

But he must have made a sound, because Liam was out of bed and heading for Josh's shaving kit. He came back with a glass of water and a slightly stronger painkiller.

"Thank you," Josh said meekly. "Why does my head hurt?"

"Dehydration," Liam said with an evil chuckle, and Josh echoed it. Liam was still standing by him, hand out for the cup with the water, and Josh wanted to touch him. He handed Liam the cup and ran his hand over Liam's taut stomach, his smooth ass. Josh, who was surrounded by muscular man-gods, appreciated Liam's fitness without the showy muscles.

This was a man who could hug you and make you feel safe without cracking your skull on his biceps, and who could also hold his own in a fight.

It was a physical feature Josh found particularly appealing, especially now as he reasserted his familiarity with as much of Liam's body as he could reach.

"Mm… none of that now," Liam murmured, capturing his hand. "We really do have to get a move on."

Josh stood creakily and leaned into Liam's body. Liam set the water down and pulled him tight. "If I said 'I love you' right now, would it sound clingy?"

"Yes," Liam murmured, kissing him. "Say it."

"I love you."

"I love you too. No more pushing me away."

"No more," Josh promised, leaning his head on Liam's shoulder. He didn't want to admit it, but he wouldn't have the strength to do that—never again.

THE HOUSE was full, even at two o'clock, and the kitchen, as usual, was bustling. Phyllis was there, directing her minions, some of whom were prepping for dinner that night and a few who were making sure there were snacks available for anyone dropping by.

Phyllis had been a fixture in the mansion at Glencoe since Josh was very small. A midsize woman with spiral curls of brown and gray, she'd first taken the job because it allowed her to get her doctorate in philosophy while not requiring her to *do* anything with it—not teaching, not publishing, both of which she abhorred. She'd stayed because they'd become a family.

Now she greeted Josh with a smile, because she saw him nearly every day, but Liam? Liam she greeted with a squeal and a hug and a "I was so happy to hear you were back!"

"You know I only came back for you, my sweet English rose," Liam said, and Josh chuckled because he'd really played up the East End in his voice.

And Phyllis ate it up with a spoon. "Oh, my good lad you are. Come to steal away this'un now that 'es come to his senses?" She'd been born and raised in Chicago, but she gave that accent her all.

"Hey!" Josh laughed. "You're required to be on my side!"

"It was making you crabby," she said primly. "Now here." She shoved a plate of sliders into Liam's hands. "Take these downstairs to the others. They're excited to see Josh. Apparently they can't have a proper breakdown of a job without him."

"I thought that's what you were doing this morning on your tablet," Liam muttered, following Josh through the kitchen.

"No," Josh said, thinking about the bare minimum report he'd gotten from Danny. "They were taking it easy on me."

"I think if Interpol knew how much work criming was, they'd simply raise the minimum wage in most countries and watch the crime rate drop overnight."

Josh chuckled because it was true—at least for the things that he and his friends did. "Well, taking care of a population usually stops a lot of bad things," he said, not even wanting to think about how often the Salingers had stopped the rich and the corrupt from hurting people out of sheer entitlement.

"But that takes me back to my question," Liam said as they made their way through the bustling kitchen—where they'd take the entrance to the dining room and from there down the staircase to the basement den.

"What question?" Josh asked. "Hold up. Marco!" He smiled with genuine pleasure at Phyllis's head chef—and Josh's in-house caterer for the night before—who was currently cleaning the sides of a mixing bowl with a spatula. "Hey, I wanted to thank you for taking the gig last night. The feds give you any trouble?"

"Me?" the handsome young chef asked. "No, I'm just the caterer. We were hired by Celeste to do the job. Here, have a canape, they're delicious."

Josh chortled. "Good. Is Tor here tonight?"

Torrance Grayson, Marco's boyfriend, was also one of Felix's premier anchors on his news network. Torrance split his time between Marco's cottage on the property and, when he had to work late, his own apartment in the city. The night before he'd been taping a show, but he'd been their very compelling face man since they'd started this endeavor, making sure that whenever the crew's exploits hit the news, the first spin of the event was to shine the spotlight on the bad guys and away from the people who'd exposed them.

"He'll be here for dinner and the meeting afterward," Marco said. "I guess I'm invited downstairs too this time."

"Not for dinner?" Josh asked.

Marco rolled his eyes. "I'd rather cook," he said frankly. "Danny's list of items we can't talk about at the dinner table is up to two full pages on his phone." He shuddered. "Liver fluke people. *Liver fluke people*, Josh. I don't *care* if the *X-Files* did it first, I don't want them showing up during a dinner *I* cooked!"

Josh grimaced. "That wasn't Grace, was it?"

"No," Marco said grouchily. "*That* was Stirling. Apparently he and Tienne have been binge-watching old shows."

"Well," Josh said diplomatically, "we take some, uhm, digesting to get used to."

Marco glared at him. "Get out," he said.

"I'm sor—"

"It's my kitchen," Marco snapped, gesturing imperiously with the spatula in his hand. "Get out!"

"Wow," Liam muttered. "Is he always that touchy?"

Josh winced. "I think we were a little more tightly wound than usual before this job," he admitted. "Grace, Hunter, and Carl had been out of town, pretending to be Lightfingers while we set up the job and the ID, and they got back and, well, things got a little, uhm…."

"Out of hand," Liam said dryly.

"I was going to say up to our usual energy," Josh lied.

"Sure you were."

By this point they'd made it through the dining room and were heading toward the stairs. Josh held his hand out for the railing and drew air through his teeth. "Dammit," he muttered. "Fucking Kadjic."

Liam sighed and paused at the landing, his brush of fingers against Josh's shirt noting the absence of the sling. "Listen," he murmured. "I need you to not downplay this thing with your arm tonight."

Josh glared at him. "It's no big—"

"It's a very big deal," Liam said. "Because I need the lot of you to take him seriously. He's a *very* dangerous man."

"Oh, believe me," Josh said grimly. "We know. But they've got to trust me in there—"

"They'll trust you more if you tell them the truth," Liam said without bending.

Well, that was a part of him, Josh knew. A very *attractive* part of him. He could hold his own against Josh, against his family, against the things they took on. "I don't lie to my crew," he said. "But I'll try not to blow it off either."

Liam kissed his forehead. "Thank you. Now proceed before these sliders get cold. They smell delicious."

Well, Josh thought with a certain amount of satisfaction, he and Liam *had* been rather active that day. The sandwiches they'd downed as they hurried toward the garage to leave hadn't quite hit the spot.

The den was dark, lit only by the giant TV screen where characters from *World of Warcraft* were being pursued by bad guys and each other in search of treasure.

"Are you doing a raid?" Josh asked. "Without me?"

"No," Stirling said, still very focused on the screen. "We're all building up our characters so we can wipe the floor with you."

Josh snorted. "No. No. Not going to happen. Has never happened. Will never happen. Grace, watch out, Molly's orc is going to—"

They all grimaced as Grace's character—a lissome elf—separated into two pieces and toppled in a pile of animated blood and gore.

"Wow," Grace said. "We're on the same team."

"We're building our characters," Molly said primly. "All's fair in—*Tienne*! You little bugger!" But she said it with pride.

"You told me," Tienne said, his accented voice sounding extremely pleased. "You told me to practice being ruthless in video games, so I did. You weren't paying attention."

"No, I wasn't," Molly said. "And you're totally forgiven. We want you to live, that's all."

"Harsh," Liam said in Josh's ear.

"Well, he wanted to be in on going after Kadjic," Josh said. "I think Molly's been giving him ruthlessness lessons."

"I'm good at it," Molly said, tilting her head over her shoulder so she could beam at them from one of three couches, all facing the screen. Her hair—mounds of red spiral curls with separate curls dyed in a dark rainbow of streaks—was bundled up on her crown for video games, but Josh had no doubt she'd have it down after she dressed for dinner. Molly was a talented actress—and strong and aggressive enough to be muscle when Chuck, Hunter, and Carl were otherwise occupied—but she was also a beautiful young woman. While she complained copiously that all the men at the Glencoe mansion (besides Leon, of course) seemed to be gay, Josh was sort of glad she hadn't settled on anybody yet, because nobody seemed good enough for her.

But speaking of Chuck, Hunter, and Carl….

"Where's our muscle?" Josh asked. "And is Carl going to bring Michael?"

"Chuck and Hunter are running an errand," Grace said. "And by running an errand, I mean chasing down Celeste's drug dealer and getting him to spill about her finances."

"She spends ten percent of her trust payout on coke every month," Josh said, not sure whether to be disgusted with the woman or to feel bad for her. So much potential, so much waste. "We knew that when I got the gig."

"Yes," Grace said patiently, "but her dealer works for somebody, and they were hoping he'd have a line on where Kadjic disappeared to after he dodged the FBI."

"Ooh, good idea," Josh said. "What about Carl?"

"He's at the airport, picking Michael up." Carl's boyfriend, Michael Carmody, was also their mechanic, and he kept their assorted vehicles, including their planes, maintained and ready to roll at a moment's notice. Josh's little silver sportster was currently parked in the mansion garage, but he knew for certain that during the painfully uncertain fall and the long winter and spring, Michael had kept his car sheltered in the big airplane hangar they rented out and had kept it tuned up, cleaned, and ready to roll while Josh had been too weak to pick up a spoon, much less drive.

"Okay, so after dinner, then?" Josh asked, making sure.

"I'm sorry," Stirling said, his customary dry humor making a sly appearance. "Did cancer slow your ability to plot *and* play video games?"

Batting her eyelashes, Molly held out a controller and patted the open spot on the couch next to her. She was sitting on the good couch—Tienne and Stirling were on the bad couch that spilled all the occupants to the broken springs in the center, and Grace was sprawled on three beanbags on the floor.

Josh took the end of the good couch, and Liam, to his surprise, set the sliders down on the coffee table, grabbed one for himself, along with a napkin, and made himself comfortable on the carpet near Josh's feet.

"You want to play?" Josh asked, but he was already pulling up his character and outfitting it, taking his cues from the practice adventure everybody else had played.

"An elf?" Liam asked.

"He likes to be pretty," Grace said. "He's vain. You should know that about him."

Josh felt Liam's hand encircle his ankle.

"I'm aware," he said.

"Forget pretty," Josh told them. "What else am I missing about last night?"

What followed was something he and the crew had done many times, which was to debrief while splitting their attention elsewhere. It drove some people absolutely batshit—but for Josh and his friends, it became a training ground for paying attention to all the things at once. Incoming information, environmental dangers, strategy pivots, all of it swirled around them like their characters swirling around on the screen.

By the time the training adventure was over, Josh had heard every bit of gossip Molly and Hunter had picked up while working the catering floor, including who in the crowd had known Kadjic was coming and how they felt about that. Besides chasing down Kadjic's phone leads, Stirling had spent the morning doing thorough background checks on those folks and cross-referencing those names with people who used some of Celeste's other services—her drug dealer, her company's research and development team, their political analysts—to see where the power structures lay. Josh added to this knowledge with things he'd picked up working in Celeste's employ, and Stirling and Grace, when not moving their characters from place to place, picked up tablets lying next to them and added the information to a shared document.

Molly used her spare time to add faces to the bios.

Tienne added to the conversation by connecting his contacts in the art world—because that was important to Kadjic too—and Grace would consult the list whenever one of the people from Carl's report rang a bell.

By the time they were done playing videos—and it was getting time to go upstairs and change for dinner—they'd managed to organize and prioritize the information gathered from the caper the night before, and they had no doubt there would be more to add that night.

And Josh had managed to build up some life points and some strength points in his elf, Grace's character had gotten killed multiple times for no reason at all, and Tienne, in a fit of temper, had called Grace an annoying pooh-head and a scattered, cat-brained shitbird, both of which had sent the room into gales of laughter and made Grace preen like he'd earned high praise.

Well, Tienne, slender, blond, and as ephemeral as a summer wind, was notorious for his easygoing nature. Pissing him off that much in a video game really was something of an achievement.

"Okay, then," Josh said, yawning as he set down his controller. "I've got to go change—"

"Nap," Grace supplied.

"Dinner's at six!" Josh protested.

"Dinner's at seven," Liam said. "It popped up on everybody's phones while you were otherwise involved." He stood then and extended a hand, which Josh found himself needing. "Nap?" he asked solicitously.

"Only if you build up a character while I'm napping," Josh said on a yawn. "Next time, we need to be beating the snot out of you while we're doing this."

Liam grunted. "You think more of my intelligence than I do," he said. "I'd just as soon study your notes while you're all resting your brains. That was more impressive, but I don't think it's necessary."

Josh gazed at him, troubled. "These skills keep us safe, Liam," he said earnestly. "Please think about it."

"I will, boy-o—if you concede on the nap."

Josh yawned again and gave up—gave up on being frustrated too. "Fine," he said. "Grace, if I'm dressing up, you have to wear something besides thieves' clothes."

"I know, I know," Grace muttered. "I'll blow everybody's eyeballs out with my color."

"Dear God," Tienne retorted. "Is there no end to my indignity? If you must, could you at least let Molly dress you? She's very good with color, and she's even better with clothes."

Molly beamed at him. "You and my brother need to marry so you're officially in my family."

"First, we will find you a man," Tienne said magnanimously. "Because we want you to have one, not because you need one."

Molly had stood up, and now she kissed his cheek. "Are you taking notes, Stirling?"

"And we also want you to stop whining about it," Stirling said, giving her a "I'm a brother, so I can pick on her" smile.

"Apparently not," she said, flicking him on the back of the head as she passed.

They made their way up the stairs, and then passed through the dining room to the back staircase, where they made their way up one more flight for the bedrooms. Josh had a suite, and when he noticed Grace splitting off to come with him and Liam to the suite, he made a grunt of unhappiness.

"Really?"

"You sleep," Grace said. "I'll go over stuff on my tablet. I've got a thing in my brain. I want your stupid Interpol boyfriend to talk to while you're all recovering and shit."

Josh yawned again. "Fair," he said. "Stupid Interpol boyfriend, are you okay with that?" He opened the door to his suite and gestured everybody inside, grunting with the damned pain in his shoulder.

"Painkiller time," Liam said perceptively. "Kick off your shoes and get in bed."

Liam went for water while Josh did as ordered, the exhaustion taking over as soon as his head hit the pillow. After he'd washed down his meds, Liam bent over and kissed him. "Tell us if we're too loud," he murmured.

"Too much quiet bothers me," Josh said.

And then he was asleep.

GRACE WAS gone by the time Liam woke him, but Liam had freshened up and dressed nattily in an outfit Grace had apparently culled from, well, everybody.

"Marco's pants," Liam qualified, "although they're a little loose around the waist. Chuck's suit jacket—which fits me great, but I suspect it was tailored to fit him quite tightly. And Hunter's plain blue dress shirt, which is perhaps the best fit of all."

"Nice," Josh said. "I'm sorry. I should have had you bring a suit from the apartment."

"I didn't bring any suits to the apartment," Liam told him, searching through Josh's wardrobe for something dressy but not over the top. "Danny emailed me that Kadjic would positively be there, and I thought, 'I absolutely can't let him do this without me.' I took two trains and three connections from Paris to Chicago and got there just in time."

"Wow," Josh murmured, accepting a tie from him that he hadn't particularly liked until Liam put it in his hand. "You do know how to make a romantic entrance."

"It paid off," Liam said dryly, fetching a sleek black dress shirt that really *would* look good with that sapphire-blue tie.

"I'm glad you think so," Josh said, taking the shirt. "I *can* dress myself, you know."

"I know," Liam said. "This is part of me being proprietary and possessive. Give me a few months and I'll get this shit under control."

"You know that for certain?" Josh asked, taking the clothes to lay out on the bed.

"It's a guess," Liam admitted. "I've never been in love before."

"Oh." Suddenly all Josh could do was stare at the clothes on the bed, thinking that Liam could produce a lime-green-and-magenta paisley jacket and he'd put it on after a revelation like that.

"Don't let it panic you," he murmured directly in Josh's ear while holding out a slim-fitting pair of black slacks. "I got all my panic out on the yacht in January. You didn't see because you slept through most of it. All I could do was look at you and think, 'If anything happens to him, my heart will stop beating. That's terrifying.' So yes. I've come to grips with that. This is the next phase is all."

Josh shivered. "You think I don't have my own panic attacks about you?" he asked, thinking about how badly he'd wanted Liam to take their information/gaming drills seriously.

"I got that feeling when you tried to get me to play video games to strengthen my thief skills," Liam said, voice dry. He picked up the tie, which was suddenly dazzling. "Don't worry, boy—lad…."

Josh kissed him, enjoying the banter, the closeness, and the physical permissions they'd given each other during lovemaking the night before and that morning. They'd fallen in love ages ago, but consummation was so, so sweet.

"Josh," Liam finished fuzzily, looking pleased. "Why do you object so much to 'boy'?"

"Because I'm the baby," Josh said, smiling but not happy about it. It was a unique position of privilege and pressure. "I want you to think of me as grown."

Liam gave a low, filthy chuckle. "I think we've covered that," he said, and Josh bussed him on the chin and then ducked, because they could be arguing about this forever, and it was time to get dressed.

THE DINING room table had been somewhat reconfigured in the last six months. For as long as Josh could remember, it backed up to a long bench against a wall, and six to eight people could slide in on the booth-style seating on that side while the rest gathered in chairs on the other side of the banquet table or at the ends. Until Danny's reintegration into their lives, Felix and Julia rarely had a full table, so they'd mostly dropped the wings, kept the extra chairs in storage, and entertained four to six people at a time.

That didn't work so much for the family as it was, so they'd moved the table out to the middle of the room, kept it sturdy, and replaced the booth-style seating with individual chairs—also sturdy. They weren't entertaining guests in tuxedos sampling wine anymore—they were dining with family, with big, strong, solid men and women who disliked tiny, delicate furniture.

While Marco reported the staff found the new configuration easier to serve, the result for those sitting down was mostly the same, with the exception of being able to excuse one's self to the restroom with much more ease if you were sitting on what had once been the wall side of the table.

Josh liked the changes, almost unilaterally. He and Grace and sometimes Stirling and Molly had done a lot of homework at the old table, munching snacks Phyllis had provided with little more than a hair tousle and a "You're welcome—don't spoil dinner." Well, not homework, really. The four of them had finished that at school. This was more… side-quest work. But they'd been together, and they'd been working toward a goal, and their presence had helped erase some of the silence and loneliness left by Danny's absence.

Josh had a lot of fond memories of Felix and Julia being out on the town, doing something important for the company, and of coming to sit by Danny as he researched or plotted or simply educated himself on something he hadn't known before. All three parents had given him a thirst for knowledge, but Danny had given him a *delight* in it.

Josh loved that the table had changed to accommodate so many people who delighted in the same things he did.

It was only halfway full as he and Liam approached, but he noticed that Grace—instead of sitting to Hunter's right, which would have left two seats open—had chosen his left, which meant Josh had to sit between him and Carl.

"Nice," Josh told him, tugging on a straight lock of black-and-(this week)-pink hair.

"What?" Grace asked, batting his tawny eyes ingenuously.

"Ignore him," Carl said. "He's being a jealous prick, we've already told him so, and Michael has threatened him with not being able to babysit the next time his children come over."

"A blatant lie," Grace said primly. "Those kids love me, and he wouldn't deprive them of the pleasure."

"As long as you foot the bill for the repairs again," Michael said mildly, which was only fair.

"Hey, we fixed your plumbing problem," Grace said.

"And also fixed that whole 'lack of a sunroof' problem," Carl muttered, referring to the high-powered jet of water that had blown a hole from the upstairs toilet through the ceiling.

"The skylight looks so much better," Grace told him.

On the other side of Hunter, Josh heard Liam say, "Good God, what happened?"

Hunter made a little grunt and rubbed the spot in the middle of his forehead that was probably wound tightly enough to catapult a grape into space if he lay on his back and just let go of the tension caused by his significant other.

"Next time," Josh said, exerting whatever control he'd *ever* had over his best friend, "you ask Chuck and Hunter how to fix the plumbing. Or the electricity. Or the internet."

"I fixed the internet," Stirling said. "Carl could hack the Pentagon from his house, but he keeps refusing to race me for it."

Carl gave Stirling the soft look you'd give a favorite nephew. "But don't think I don't appreciate the gesture anyway," he said. He and Michael had bought the house (or rather, Leon had bought the house *for* them) in late November, after they'd helped solve the mystery of what happened to Leon's brother, Josh's father. The structure had been perfectly sound and had needed zero improvements when they'd moved in, but between Michael's three precocious children and their choice of Molly and Grace as their favorite babysitters, the same could probably not be said now.

It was a good thing Michael was so good-natured and Carl so unflappable, Josh figured, but he still wouldn't put Grace in charge of so much as microwaving pizza bites without explicit instructions and a list of ABSOLUTELY DO NOT DOs.

"Wait," Liam said at Grace's elbow. "Weren't you two going to get a dog—"

"Oh Jesus," Carl muttered.

"No," Molly said, shaking her head.

"Oh for fuck's sake," Hunter swore.

"For the love of God," Chuck said, sauntering in with his boyfriend, Lucius, on his arm, "don't even get us started on the fucking dogs."

Josh turned to Chuck, impressed by the natty blue-striped brown suit he was wearing, including a tie of such lustrous brown it looked almost like velvet. Lucius—a smaller dapper man with a slight widow's peak of brown hair and classically handsome features—wore his own understated suit, this one charcoal gray, but judging by the look of adoration on the quiet businessman's face, his absolute devotion to Josh's munitions-and-transpo guy hadn't lessened one iota in what amounted to a year of a long-distance relationship.

"Nice suit," Liam said. "Did you say *dogs*?"

"Nice accent, son," Chuck needled. "Good of you to show up at the last moment."

"And where were you?" Liam and Chuck got along quite well, actually, but Josh rather suspected Liam's dynamic with most of his team was the same dynamic he had with his large, rowdy family back in England.

"Me?" Chuck baited. "Me and Lucius here were at the party across the way from Miss Celeste's party. We caught all the overflow guests who fled after the po-lice came so they could gossip with other rich people. Picked up all sorts of tidbits."

"And Charles was on call for a distraction in case Josh needed one," Lucius said proudly. "Which he didn't."

"What did you pick up?" Carl asked curiously.

"That the insurance investigator was dreamy," Chuck replied, holding his battered hands to his impressively broad chest.

"Fuck off," Carl retorted. "I was just asking."

"No, really," Lucius said, taking his and Chuck's spot farther down the table. "Carl, you cut quite a swath among Celeste's guests."

"Oh hell," Danny muttered, entering the room. Danny was dressed in a close-fitting black suit with a black dress shirt, no tie—the formal version of thieves' clothes, Josh thought fondly—and unless he was being Benjamin Morgan, happy art docent of the Chicago Art Institute, who wore tweed and corduroy, it was the outfit that made him most comfortable.

"Why's that bad?" Michael asked, hand protectively on Carl's arm.

"Because I'm stuck being an insurance investigator for this gig," Carl said. "If too many people in Kadjic's circle remember me, it means our cast of bit parts has been stretched a little thin."

It was one of the reasons they'd put Chuck and Lucius in the party three floors down from Celeste's when Lucius had found the invitation in his mailbox. Chuck was a brilliant chemical engineer and a very talented getaway driver—but he was six feet three inches tall, with red hair, freckles, and a Texas drawl that could shake timber. Carl was just as tall, but his blond, green-eyed looks were a little less noticeable.

"Alas," Hunter said, "Molly and I have a run on the catering gig."

Molly grunted, shaking out her curls. “Speak for yourself. I heard two people last night try to link me to that thing we did in the winter before we nailed that sweatshop owner to the fucking wall. Apparently my hair is attracting notice, dammit.”

“Wigs?” Stirling asked, a sort of neediness in his voice that Josh understood.

She grimaced. “I’ve done wigs, little brother. They’re like wearing a furnace on your head, particularly if you’ve got a lot of hair underneath. I may straighten it and dye it blond.”

“That’d be a shame,” Liam said. “Maybe a cut? Or a simple plait might do.”

“A blond braid would be a change,” she admitted. “Or maybe dark brown… or auburn, like Chuck’s!”

“Green,” Grace said smugly. “I hear green goes great with vampire skin and freckles these days.”

“I don’t see it in *your* hair,” Molly muttered.

“Pink’s hot this summer,” Grace replied with a catlike smile.

“Green makes him look jaundiced,” Chuck said flatly. Well, Molly *was* his favorite.

Molly gave Chuck a kissy-face, and he laughed, the sound infectious.

“Dogs,” Liam said. “Sorry, Chuck, I know you like to make an entrance, but somebody mentioned *dogs*. Last I heard, the bet was that Michael would get either the most out-of-control giant puppy in the entire kennel or a dog that makes Methuselah look like a teenager. I still don’t know who won.”

“You had a bet on that?” Michael asked, his limpid brown eyes practically swallowing his narrow face.

“Yes, we did,” Carl said, gazing fondly at his mate. “Now tell the man who won.”

“Wait….” Michael frowned. “Was there another category? Old, destructive—”

“Ginormous,” Molly said. “I had money down on ginormous.”

“Tiny,” Grace said. “I had tiny and mean.”

Michael stared at all of them. “But which one of you won the bet?” he demanded. “Because I got one of each! I got old and ginormous and young and destructive and ginormous, and two old and blind and two tiny and mean!"

"Hunter," Josh said, shaking his head. "He had *his* money on *plethora*, and he cleaned us all out."

"I bought a damned fine gun with that money," Hunter said, with zero regrets.

"You should have bought me a dependable dog sitter with that money," Carl told him. "We turned our backyard into dog heaven, complete with a dog door into the laundry room, which will forever smell like wet dog, and so far we can't find a single person who's willing to stay at our house, use our air-conditioning, eat our food, and clean up dog poop for a living wage."

"Students," said Josh and all his student-aged friends.

"Carl, my man," Grace told him. "You should have asked us sooner. Perfect job for students. Don't worry about it. I'll have you two people willing to split the wage as long as they can eat your food and watch your TV."

"Thank you, Grace," Carl said, truly grateful. And then he brought their attention to the elephants *not* in the room. "Where's the grownups?" he asked, because by this time Danny, Felix, Julia, and Leon were usually there.

"I don't know," Josh murmured. He'd been thinking about his mother for much of the day. Not *all* day—those hours with Liam had been delicious and necessary, but Josh's mother usually would have been downstairs when they'd been playing video games, just to check on him. As much as a boy *didn't* want to have his mother poking into his romantic life, Josh also knew she'd fussed over him sending Liam away for the last months. She'd promised the night before that her fainting spell had been caused by too many nerves on an empty stomach, and he wasn't to worry, but, well, his mom. The whole world worshipped Julia Dormer-Salinger, but that was only because they hadn't been able to get the word out to aliens, where universal adoration would make her reign complete.

"We're right here," Julia said cheerfully, entering the room on Leon's arm with Felix gallantly on the other side. "Is Tor here yet?"

As Julia bent down to kiss his cheek, Josh searched her face for something—*anything*—that would tell him what the delay had been about, or any hint at all about the night before. All he could get from her—or any of them—was a sort of blinding happiness that was at odds with the soul-eating worry that had consumed the lot of them since they'd first seen Kadjic's message, written for Danny and submitted in code on Stirling's *not quite* hacked system that January.

"No, ma'am," Chuck said. "Tor's going to be a little late. Apparently there was a rather spectacular art theft last night, and Torrance is getting out the follow-up story before he comes in from Chicago."

Julia gave a gracious, interested smile as Leon pulled the chair out behind her and settled her in. "Oh really," she said. "Has there been any news as to who would perpetrate such a heinous crime?"

Grace snickered. "Sometime this morning," he said, "the *real* painting appeared in the house of one of Dizzy Gillespie's heirs, to whom the painting was actually willed. He'd had no idea it had been recovered, but he was ever so grateful to find it hung on his wall."

Josh cocked his head at Grace, impressed. "Was this before or after you brought me doughnuts?" he asked.

"Definitely before," Grace said, doing his little facing-sunshine dance.

"You didn't even tell me," Josh said, genuinely tickled. "I was going to do that this week."

Grace kept dancing. "I have hidden depths," he preened.

"You do indeed," said Danny, seeming pleasantly surprised as Felix held the chair for him as Leon had for Julia. "Thanks, Fox," he said fondly. "You didn't need to—"

Felix kissed his cheek, Danny blushed, and the whole table stopped to watch.

After a collective breath, Julia said, "So did Tor want us to hold the table or—"

"Tor wants you to start now," Torrance Grayson said, walking into the room with a large bowl in each hand. "And Tor's bossy boyfriend told him to bring the first course."

"Which is…?" Julia asked.

"Basic salad," Tor said, bemused. Marco was a top-rated chef—he usually went a little more adventurous. As Liam took the bowl from him to place at one end, he added, "Somebody will be out with a dressing selection in a minute."

Julia clapped her hands. "Perfect," she said happily. "I was really in the mood for basic ranch, lots of croutons. He really came through. Brisket for the main course?"

"Sure," Tor said. Torrance Grayson was a trim man with a pointed chin and large blue-gray eyes who looked both trustworthy and droolworthy on screen. The downside to his expressive features was that his confusion was easy to read. One of Julia's favorite things was good food, and she, Felix, and Danny (and Leon!) had offered Marco worlds to stay at the Salinger mansion to create food for them and their guests. When they weren't feeding their family, they were often feeding celebrities or businessmen—Marco was in high demand, and his cachet was growing by the gig.

Brisket and ranch salad wasn't usually his thing.

"I was in a mood," Julia told him mildly, and her delighted smile returned. "And now it's a good one!"

Once Tor had set the food down and taken the last remaining place, the other servers came in bearing "fixings"—bacon, cheeses, croutons, eggs, various vegetables and dressings in trenchers—and for a moment everybody's energy was taken serving themselves family style and digging in.

Josh glanced down the table to see Liam skeptically poking at a bowl of olives and another one with feta in it. "Green salad," Josh said. "Olives, feta, some oil-and-vinegar-based dressing—it's really very good."

Liam grimaced and grabbed the croutons instead, and Josh laughed. Liam had been very blunt about his "plain" tastes when they'd spent all that time on the yacht, and Josh was suddenly looking forward to teaching him a whole lot of fun things about food. His parents hadn't dragged him across Europe at seven for him to be dependent on chicken nuggets and potato chips *now*.

"But why's it called a salad bar?" Grace said next to him, as though they'd been in the middle of a conversation. "Is there alcohol in the dressing? Chopped brass in the lettuce? Where does that come from?"

"From restaurants where they used to set everything out on a counter so you could choose your ingredients," Josh said. "Buffets. How bad were *you* fishing for a topic?"

"See?" Grace asked. "Why don't they have fish bars? Where you walk up to a counter and choose fried flounder or swordfish or smoked salmon—"

"They do," Stirling said. "It's called a fish market, idiot."

"Have you been to a fish market?" Tienne asked dreamily. "All these muscular men—"

"And women," Molly said.

"Calling out to catch and then throwing hundred-pound fish at each other. It's amazing."

"Ooh—I want to throw fish," Grace said, shoving a bite of salad in his mouth that was mostly cheese and ranch dressing.

"Like that weird Muppet character who uses them as boomerangs?" Michael asked. "My kids love that guy!"

"Mm…," Grace said thoughtfully. "I don't know if that guy's my Muppet alter-ego. I think I'm more Animal."

Everybody stared at him.

"What?" he said, on another amazing bite of mayonnaise and cheese.

"Nothing," Josh murmured. "I just… I think we all agree. Perfect. You nailed it."

Grace preened some more, then turned to him. "And you're Kermit."

"I thought I was more Scooter," Josh said, although he was secretly pleased. "Danny's Kermit."

"Felix is Kermit," Molly said thoughtfully. "Danny is Scooter, and you're Robin, the little frog."

"Always size," Josh sighed dramatically.

"And I'm Miss Piggy?" Julia asked archly.

"Are you an ass-kicking beauty with impeccable taste and amazing shoes?" Chuck drawled, and Julia's genuine laughter was also her concession. Miss Piggy she was.

"Does that make me the Count?" Leon asked, obviously hoping to play.

"One, two, three giant yachts!" Danny teased in the Count von Count's Transylvanian accent, and Leon's brilliant smile tugged at Josh's heart. He'd worked so hard to become one of them. Josh was suddenly so very glad he hadn't driven the man away when he'd been sick and defensive and feeling small. He wondered if he should tell Leon that, though. They had never really cleared the air.

"So who's Gonzo?" Hunter asked, interrupting his thoughts and surprising them all.

"Do *you* want to be Gonzo?" Josh asked, because he'd sounded genuinely concerned.

"No," Hunter said. "I just… you know. Need to know there's a Gonzo in the universe."

"I'm Bunsen Honeydew," Stirling said proudly.

"And I am Beaker," Tienne said.

"Scientists." Stirling's quiet beam was almost as proud as Grace's *not* so quiet one.

"And already a couple in canon," Tienne said, bussing Stirling on the cheek. That quickly, they were in their own little test tube, and the conversation flowed around them.

"I'd say I'm Gonzo," Tor said, chewing thoughtfully, "But the thought of Marco being Camilla the chicken—"

"Camilla was a beard," Marco said, walking in from the kitchen with a tray on his shoulder and a tray rack under his arm. "We all know Gonzo's soulmate was Rizzo the Rat."

"Since you refused to sit down with us," Tor said acidly, "I'm not sure you get a say in the table talk."

"Don't be ornery, Gonzo," Marco retorted. "I just didn't want to hear Grace profane my food again with whatever the hell it was the last time I sat down."

"*Don't* repeat it," Julia barked, and they all turned to Grace, who shoved another bite of ranch-flavored mayonnaise in his mouth like he hadn't been about to refresh everybody's memory.

"What about Carl and Michael?" Marco asked, busing the finished salad bowls from most of the table. Josh watched as Grace worked to finish the rest of the ranch dressing.

"If you drink it straight from the trencher, I'm never eating with you again," Josh murmured under the voices of the rest of the table.

"There's a reason I'm not supposed to know it's in the house," Grace whispered back, sounding genuinely baffled. "It's like a weird sickness."

"Hunter, take his bowl," Josh said, and while Grace glared at him, Hunter took the bowl *and* the trencher and handed them to Marco.

"Nice lift," Liam said in admiration.

"You sit at a table with thieves," Hunter muttered.

Over their byplay, Michael said, "Carl's Rolph the dog and I'm Shrimp Louis! Get it? 'Cause I'm small, and Carl's trustworthy, kind, and funny"

And once again, the entire table was struck silent.

Lucius said, "That could be the most adorable thing I've heard said at this dinner table. This conversation is almost too wholesome for us."

That pronouncement was followed by raucous laughter and much throwing of dinner rolls, which normally Josh would have participated in.

But as he looked around for reactions, he noticed that Julia and Leon were holding hands and gazing into each other's eyes, nodding, before Julia reached out and took Felix's hand as well.

There was something very… intimate, about the four of them, Danny included on Felix's other side. It was like they had a secret that nobody else would understand.

"You saw that?" Liam asked around Grace's back.

"Yeah," Josh murmured. "I wonder what that's all about."

"They'll tell us," Liam guessed, as Josh's mother sent him a coded look from under her eyelashes. "Whatever it is, they can't keep it a secret for long."

Brass Tacks

"WE NEVER did figure out which Muppet you were," Josh said as they descended the staircase into the basement again. Phyllis and Marco's minions had already walked coffee and cookies down there, along with some portions of a pudding dessert that Liam was both fascinated with and afraid of. My God, he knew everybody worked hard for fitness, but they must burn some calories to eat like he'd eaten that night.

"Easy," Liam replied. "I'm the police bear."

Josh probably would have stopped dead on the stairs, but they were two of the first going down, so he just let his voice crack. "A what?"

"You know—whenever they need a policeman at the end of the show, I'm the copper who shows up and takes the villain to the nick. The police bear."

Josh squinted at him. "Grace," he called, because the boy was behind them, "was there a police bear in the Muppets?"

"His name was Bobo," Grace said happily. "He was really ugly."

"I don't like this solution," Josh said. "Find another character."

"I don't see how," Liam said. "It's not everybody who can pull off Shrimp Louis or Rolf the dog."

"Wasn't Fozzie a police bear at one time?" Josh asked.

"You remember that and you don't remember Bobo," Liam muttered. "No wonder I got sent to the bleachers for six months."

"I have never actually seen you in uniform," Josh told him, exasperated. "As far as I'm concerned, you live in a trench coat or a madras shirt."

"Or my suit jacket," Chuck added. "We'll have to work on that."

Liam suppressed a sigh. It occurred to him that overcoming his own embarrassment with Josh's money should have been something done during their separation, but he'd been so busy worrying, it hadn't occurred to him that he needed to adjust to having table service in

Josh's home, or a cast of characters so brilliant that of course they'd get their own Muppet and their own movie. Liam couldn't afford to be a supporting player in this relationship—he needed to step up and be a leading man.

"In London," he said, "I wear a cheap tan suit. It's riveting. I'd rather be seen in a madras shirt."

"Or without one," Josh replied puckishly, and Liam felt his cheeks warm.

"Or without one," he answered with dignity.

Josh winked and went to sit down behind the AV outlet so he could project his computer—or Danny's—on screen.

"Josh," Danny said, "let me and Felix sit there for tonight. You sent us everything you had, and we…." He gave a brief smile, and Liam caught the tiredness—happiness, but also tiredness—in his eyes for the first time that night. "Fox and I spent some time strategizing after Stirling got us some of the data from the cloned phone. I think we actually have a plan."

Liam expected Josh to bristle at this, but he didn't. Instead his face opened, and some of the tenseness, the drive that had only seemed to fade when they'd been making love, drained out of him.

"It worked?" he said breathlessly. "Last night worked?"

Danny's smile was as relieved as Josh's. "It worked," he said, and Liam recalled all of the fishing nets the crew had cast for information the night before. Not just the cloned phone, but Leon and Julia in the crowd at Celeste's and Chuck and Lucius downstairs. Hunter and Molly mingling with the staff—even Marco back in the kitchen and Carl doing double duty as an insurance investigator and con man. All of them had been fishing for information.

That's why they'd spent so long staging the theft, baiting the hook, setting the hook, and making Kadjic's manic thrashing the centerpiece of the night.

The real con hadn't been the theft, or even yanking Kadjic's chain. Josh, tapping on his keyboard that morning and consolidating information during video games—none of that had been frivolous.

Liam's discussion with Grace as Josh had been sleeping told him that. The young dancer's famously firefly-like attention had suddenly narrowed, and he'd spent that quiet hour walking Liam through a detailed people map of the party attendees the night before, including diagrams of who was more important than whom when it came to analyzing Kadjic's details.

Interpol would not have approved of the Salingers one bit, but they wouldn't have been able to match them in efficiency or accuracy of information either.

"So," Danny said as the rest of the crew filtered in and settled down, "Fox and I are running this one, because Fox insisted, but I've got Liam and Josh here front and center. Liam because he's had personal experience with Kadjic, and Josh because he's been running the show thus far and he's why we have what we've got. So has everybody visited the restroom?"

He glanced pointedly at Julia, who rolled her eyes and nodded, which made Liam curious, because as far as he knew, Julia Dormer-Salinger *never* used the restroom, nor did she snore, nor did she pick her nose. It was all unfathomable.

"Excellent," Danny said. "Does everybody have their dessert of choice? Take a few minutes and gather, because as soon as I'm hooked up here, we're on the clock."

There was a quiet mingling then, and Julia, Liam noticed, *did* make a quick dash to the washroom—there was one in Stirling and Tienne's bedroom suite, which was adjoined to the basement den with a door.

He caught his breath as something occurred to him, and then he glanced at Josh, who appeared to be oblivious.

He caught Danny's knowing smile, though, and the other man raised his finger to his lips and mouthed "Later" softly.

Liam's eyes widened, and he glanced at Josh again, thinking of the sober way he'd carried the burden of being the family's hope.

Would this event set him free, Liam wondered with a painful swallow, or would it rob him of things he knew were true?

And on the heels of that thought came another, more pressing thought.

They absolutely positively had to put Kadjic behind bars—but more. Like a snake, Kadjic's venom was potent enough that not even death would render him harmless. If Danny was to keep his promise to the family and not disappear, taking the risk of Kadjic's wrath and an all-out war with him, then they absolutely had to come up with a strategy to destroy him, and they had to do it on a timeline.

And suddenly Liam understood why Josh had been sidelined and Danny and Felix looked so tired.

Josh had been wounded, and he and Liam had shit to sort the night before, but everybody else, it appeared, had been all hands on deck, because if all hands *weren't* on deck, the coming storm would sink the bloody ship.

Three minutes later a bowl of pudding dessert was thrust into Liam's hand by, of all people, Carl.

"Hang tight," he murmured. "It's going to be a bumpy ride."

The big man disappeared, aligning himself with Chuck and Hunter near the bottom of the stairs so they could act as sentinels and guardians to the rest of the group, and Liam turned to find Josh glancing down at an absurdly large napkin full of cookies.

"Phyllis gave them to me," he said. "Which was weird, because she hasn't forced me to eat cookies since I was ten years old."

Liam opened his mouth and then realized he had absolutely nothing to say, and he was relieved when Felix, this time, called the group to order.

"Carl, hit the lights," he said, and in a moment the big projection screen at the far end of the room, which had hosted video games that afternoon, now held the image of a man they were all well familiar with.

"Andres Kadjic," Felix said. "Age fifty-five, started as a street thief in Russia and grew to gang leader, and then, being unusually clever and *very* ruthless, he had his street gang at the time—*Nozh*, meaning 'knife'—literally kidnap the head of the underground cigarette trade in Russia. The man was released and allowed to run his own company, but Kadjic is suddenly a twenty-percent partner, and boom. He has gone from street thug to businessman. He has grown in myriad ways, which we will discuss further, but never forget that he started off as a street fighter and he will continue to be one until the day he shuffles off this mortal coil, hopefully sooner than later."

"So a people person then," Hunter said, surprising Liam with a bit of snark.

"Oh definitely," Danny said dryly. "He loves people. He loves them hurt, trafficked, addicted, and bleeding—and he's got his fingers in all the pies to make sure that happens as often as possible."

There was an injured silence in the room.

"Too close to our hearts, beloved," Felix said softly, and Danny gave a brittle shrug.

"We know what he is, we know what he's done. And after last night we know exactly which pies he has his fingers in, and that's what we're here to talk about today."

Everyone in the room took a collective breath, and Liam remembered the fragile, broken thief he'd found bleeding in the alleyway ten years earlier. *I've been trying to drink myself to death for a year now, and I finally found a shortcut.*

Danny Mitchell, healthy, happy, and shored up by the love of his family, was worth every law Liam had violated, every blind eye he'd ever turned.

"Well, then," Felix said, his voice gruff, "let's continue. We've got a lot to cover."

"I think," Danny said, "that Liam will back me up on this. The hardest thing about bringing Kadjic down has been not just his lack of visibility—he's uncanny about staying hidden when his operations are going down—but also the sheer number of businesses he's working on. If we take out one business, for example, say *gun running*"—they all nodded, remembering when they'd put a considerable dent in his operations that January—"he can easily rely on his other businesses to fill that hole until the first one is up again. He's literally a hydra. Cut off one head and it grows back three-fold."

"That's, uhm, bleak," Carl muttered, and the rest of the room was with him. "You got any good news for us?"

Danny sent his friend a droll smirk. "If all I had was bad news, I would have left already to throw myself on his mercy," he said acerbically. "I'm only giving you background here. Kadjic isn't simply a villain with awkwardly shiny shoes—"

"And deeply in need of a skin-care regimen," Julia added.

"And some *manners*," Grace added.

"And a breath mint," Josh said with deep disgust.

Danny's smirk deepened. "Anyway, he's a business octopus, and we need to examine that before we bring him down." He turned toward the man he loved with all his heart. "Which is where Felix comes in. Fox?"

Felix Salinger had a sort of mythic grandeur about him, Liam thought. When Danny had been recovering in that hospital room in Morocco, Liam couldn't imagine who would be a match for Lightfingers, but once Liam had met the tall, broad-shouldered, leonine business magnate, Liam had seen it. He'd also seen how Danny had ended up with Kadjic when deep in his cups, because the two men were the dark and bright side of the business magnate's coin.

"The thing is," Felix said thoughtfully, "Kadjic's business is very much like my own." He sent a shadowed glance toward Danny, which told Liam he hadn't been the only one to reach the two-sides-of-the-same-coin conclusion. "I like to diversify, and I work with lieutenants and VPs to make each leg of the business as strong as possible. Lucius, your business is built on the same model."

"Yes," Lucius said, cocking his head. "But as you may recall, it's not exactly invincible." The Salingers had met Lucius when he'd been fighting both outside and inside enemies with an eye to not only destroying Lucius's electronics business but also his hidden shelters for abused women.

"No," Felix said. "But it *is* harder to attack strictly from the outside, particularly when an astute businessman is at the helm. But last night Danny and I were thinking—"

Danny let out the oddest sound then, a sort of schoolboy's snicker that caught Liam completely by surprise.

"Heh heh heh heh…."

"Danny, don't be rude," Julia said, but her own face was lit up with an almost eldritch amusement.

"What were you thinking?" Josh prodded.

"We're dying here!" Grace demanded.

And Danny turned to all of them, his expression a combination of Pan, Loki, Coyote, and Puck. "What I was thinking," he chortled, "was how utterly freaked out Kadjic must have been when he ran out of there. I mean, I know we were all worried about the op, and we had jobs to do, and Josh here had to visit the hospital one more goddamned time, but don't you see?"

"I saw him," Molly said, her own amusement showing. "He was literally *purple*, he was so angry."

"Oh God!" Hunter said, as though just remembering this. "He knocked over a tray when he hit the second floor. He was tracking a canape napkin all the way down the stairs!"

There were some more snickers, and then the room erupted into chuckles, a hearty, honest laugh from people who had been far too tense for the last six months when they'd realized that Kadjic knew Lightfingers was alive and the whole crew had gone on red alert.

When the laughter had faded, Grace said the one thing they all should have been thinking.

"Why didn't any of us laugh before now?"

"Because we've all been too afraid," Danny said bluntly. "But that's where we need to change, children. Because what Fox and I have planned for our finale in this case is going to take *everybody's* talents, and we're going to need to have fun."

"So," Chuck drawled from the back of the room, "I'm always in the mood for fun, Danny. What do you have in mind?"

What followed next, Liam had to admit, was as intense a briefing as he'd ever gotten at Interpol, followed by a slew of follow-up questions that would have put the international task force assigned to bringing down Kadjic to shame.

The five basic "heads" of Kadjic's operations were drug smuggling, gun smuggling (recuperating, of course, from January), human trafficking—primarily abducted girls from Slavic countries to serve as sex workers in the United States—illegal gambling, and art theft.

"That last," Danny said thoughtfully, "is more of his personal hobby than a pillar of his operations, but we need to keep it in mind because it *is* close to home, and as of yet we don't know where his home actually *is*."

"Where was it ten years ago?" Leon di Rossi asked, then hesitated. "I mean, we *are* allowed to bring that up, right?"

Danny gave him a mild look. "Yes, Leon. We're all in this mess because I slept with the wrong mobster. Of course we can bring up the past."

"That's not true," Julia said, and before Danny could protest, she held up her hand. "No, Danny. I know that's why he's after you, but think about it. We wrecked his plans any number of times before he caught you hacking one of his stooges. Gunrunning, drugs, information—hell, I'm sure some of his girls have passed through Lucius's doors. Am I right, Lucius?"

Lucius nodded soberly. "Many," he said. "And you all have been helping me scare up jobs, resources, and new IDs for them for the last year."

"Exactly," Julia said. "Danny, you're free to give us all the information you can, but I absolutely refuse to let you feel badly about it for one more minute, do you understand?"

Danny gave her a fond smile. "Of course, precious."

Julia preened and then got to business. "So about Leon's question—where *is* Kadjic's home?"

Danny shook his head. "It's a closely guarded secret," he said. "It was back then, and I can't imagine he's gotten less paranoid. But here's the thing. I know we said Kadjic's like a hydra, but we can also think of him like a big stinky onion. Thanks to all those frantic phone calls—and then some basic business calls—we've got a feel for where the different legs of his business are and a list of his lieutenants. If we go after the different pieces of his business, one at a time in quick succession, we can peel away at his security measures. Our hope is the more hot water his business gets into, the more he'll need to retreat to his home and his art, which means more to him than all the other."

"How do you know?" Liam asked curiously. *This* had been a vital chunk of Andres Kadjic's personality that his own sources had missed.

"Because I was *there*," Danny said. "The whole reason Kadjic picked up on me is because he saw me palm an authentic antique Berber necklace from a street vendor and then leave it in a museum drop box. The bugger stole the necklace from the drop box and presented it to me as a gift. I spent the rest of the night trying to explain to him why I didn't want the thing as a gift—I'd admired it for the craftsmanship but didn't covet it—and when I woke up, well, I was still drunk, and nobody here wants the details. But the *point* is, while he didn't know *Moroccan* art or jewelry, it was because he was so fixated on European art and jewelry, and he *really* had a thing for the nineteenth century British and French artists, which was unfortunate, because he was skipping his entire cultural history."

"Yes, Danny," Felix said dryly, "that was the unfortunate thing about Andres Kadjic. He liked Degas."

Danny snorted. "But moving on.... He talked about his home and how it was full of the most beautiful—and the most stolen, I'm sure—art, but he never gave me an address or even a country. All I know is there's a waterfall nearby and snow in the winter. So like a lot of our gigs, we'll have to improvise, but in the meantime, well, we have some ideas."

"Thanks to Josh's caper with the painting," Felix said, "we not only know what will draw him out, we also know what will get under his skin. He's absolutely sure Lightfingers was responsible for what happened last night, and he has vague suspicions about J.D. Morgan as well, although so far the ID has held."

"So we need to protect Josh?" Grace asked, and Danny and Felix both gave him sympathetic expressions, but it was Liam who got it first.

"No," Liam said, staring at them like they'd both gone mad.

"Now hear us out," Danny started.

"No," Liam repeated, feeling a little more panicked.

"Oh!" Josh said, because he wasn't stupid and he'd figured it out.

"No," Liam said, imploring him with his eyes.

"Yes!" Josh said. "It's perfect!"

"It's *dangerous*!" Liam's voice was rising, and even though Josh was narrowing his eyes and glaring at him, Liam couldn't help it.

"I bet they have more planned," Josh said, sounding excited. "Don't you see it?"

"I see it. I see you out alone, roaming the world, with Kadjic on your heels—"

"Oh, like any of us will let him go alone," Grace snapped. "If you can't keep calm, Mr. Interpol Man, we'll kick you outside for all the planning meetings."

"Seriously, Liam," Josh snorted. "You're planning to desert me now?"

"No!" Liam repeated, feeling the panic flutter in his chest. "No, but I am not enough."

"I think you should listen to the plan," Josh replied, infuriatingly calm. "I mean, seriously—"

"*You could get hurt*!" Liam yelled at the same time Julia said—not yelled, but *insisted*, "Honestly, Liam, do you think I'd approve of anything foolhardy? He is my first born, after all."

A silence rang through the basement as their voices faded, and Josh held up his hand.

"First," he said, cocking his head, "Liam, I love you. Yes, everybody, we're there, take a breath, get over it, it's love. Liam, I love you, but we could all get hurt. I want you by my side, not in my face, so take ten deep breaths and let me deal with the other thing going down here."

Liam swallowed and then followed Josh's deductive reasoning to the one place he'd been pretty sure it would go.

"Mom?" Josh said, cocking his head and grinning. "Is there something you'd like to tell us?"

Leon let out an absolutely besotted chuckle, and Julia gave him a sideways glance and blushed.

"I think you already know," she murmured. "I'm due in February."

The cheer that went up from the gathered family shook the floorboards of the great Glencoe mansion.

THERE WAS hugging—so much hugging—after that, and Tor's boyfriend came down to replenish the desserts and to stay, this time, for the rest of the briefing. Tor caught him up, and Marco could be heard saying, "Oh! Okay. I get it now. Brisket and ranch salad. I'll have to get used to that."

"The first time it was steak," Felix said happily, and Liam noticed that Danny and Felix were squeezing each other's hands with joy.

Danny, noticing the attention, gave him a wistful smile. "You don't understand," he said softly. "The first time she was pregnant, Felix was the first person she told, because she was desperate and afraid. I was the second, so we could come up with a plan. This time…." He smiled and peered across the room to where Molly and Julia were hugging and crying and hugging some more. "This time she has this entire room to celebrate with, including the father, who couldn't be happier." His eyes grew shiny as Josh stepped up to Julia for his turn to be hugged. "And her son, whom she couldn't love more. We'd planned to wait until the end of the briefing. This changed our plans somewhat, which was why Felix and I took over, but make no mistake, young Liam. This is a good thing."

Liam nodded, his hands still shaking. "But what you're planning to do," he said, keeping his voice down. "You're going to make our boy a *target*?"

Danny's eyes lit wickedly. "Oh, ye of little faith. I get it, you know. I've seen you work. You go out into the field with a couple of operatives, chase down leads, get intel back, chase down more leads. Come on, Liam, *think*. How are we different?"

Liam's mind flashed to the night before, when Josh had dislocated his shoulder by crashing into a wall. He hadn't landed on the balcony alone—he'd had people tending his clothes, helping with his injury, keeping an eye on his cover. And himself, making sure Josh knew he wasn't alone.

"I'll be with him." Liam wasn't sure if he was begging or if it was a vow. He knew what he'd prefer, but he'd just had it driven home that he wasn't in charge here.

"Did you hear the boy?" Felix asked, the lines at the corners of his eyes sexy and kind and oh so wise. "You two are in love. Far be it from us to get in the way of that."

"I'd say they're too young," Danny began, but Felix laughed and stopped him with a kiss to the temple.

"Hush," he murmured, and Danny winked at Liam and closed his eyes, obviously as content as he could possibly be.

And again Liam was yanked into the past, but this time it was Danny in the hospital, begging to be let out so he could wander the streets of Morocco and drink himself to death—or die of sepsis.

The man sitting across from him now, gazing fondly at the sister of his heart and her beau, was a man who had worked hard for this moment of peace and happiness.

Liam had to trust that he wouldn't sacrifice his son for it any more than he'd sacrifice his lover.

"A plan, you say," Liam prodded, but Felix shook his head.

"Hush," he said. "They'll calm down in a few more minutes. Look at her, Liam. She's shining."

They all were. Surreptitiously, Liam pulled out his phone and took a picture of Josh, smiling shyly at his uncle Leon while shaking his hand.

"Who you sending that to?" Danny asked.

"My mother," Liam said softly. "She's been begging me for a picture so she knows what he looks like. I think this one will do."

Eventually people *did* settle down, returning to their seats with napkins *full* of sweets—and, for most of them, extra napkins for happy tears.

And Felix picked up the dropped thread.

"Okay, then," he said. "So you all know part of the plan. Josh and Liam are going to be our distraction, and they are going to be a moving target. Again, thanks to last night's op, we know where his base of operations is for each of his major businesses. So what we propose is a two-pronged operation, one with plausible deniability baked right in."

"There are a lot of us," Danny said. "And we all have special skills and the ability to think on our feet, and several of us are quite adept at running the tech or masterminding an op. So we can quite probably have Josh and Liam—posing as Lightfingers or Lightfinger adjacent—running all over the globe to get Kadjic's attention—"

"Wait!" Grace crowed. "I get it! I get it! Josh and Liam go to a place, *be* Lightfingers, and Kadjic goes running to where he thinks Lightfingers is. And then, while *they* skedaddle, *we* sneak into his operation and make it go boom!"

"Big, bad-a-boom!" Danny confirmed, quoting an old movie. "Exactly, Grace. But wait—we've got some other wrinkles."

"Each team taking down a Kadjic operation," Danny said, "needs to be seen in Liam and Josh's company at the time of the operation. So if a big red-headed guy blows up a depot carrying illegal weapons in Kazakhstan…."

"I need to be seen chauffeuring Josh and Liam around at the same time," Chuck supplied. "How do you aim to do that?"

"A number of different ways," Felix said, "including airplanes, disguises, electronic signatures, and time delays. We need Kadjic to be closing in on Josh and Liam in London, get news of his gun depot in Barbados, run there, hear a description of Hunter and Chuck, say, and then have his surveillance on Josh and Liam pin Hunter and

Chuck back in London. And by the time he gets a handle on that one disaster, Josh and Liam need to be in Prague with the two people who are going to, perhaps, lead the authorities to his sex-trafficking hubs coming out of Russia, Ukraine, Poland, and Serbia, all while Kadjic is watching them wander through the city to see the sights, steal a few paintings, and wander on. And then, just when he thinks he's found Lightfingers again—"

"Somebody hits his next business," Tor said. "Boom!"

"Exactly." Danny and Felix glanced at each other and nodded, and Danny went on. "We need it planned, right down to the doubles, and we need to keep him hauling ass from one part of the globe to the other. We are going to make him absolutely insane, and while he's staring at the people he thinks are going to lead him to me—"

"We're dismantling his operations, one leg at a time," Liam said. "But he'll be kept so busy, he won't have time to rebuild."

"Exactly," Felix said. "And in the end, he'll run to the one place he thinks is safe."

"And by then," Danny added grimly, "we will hopefully have invaded that too."

"Interpol?" Liam asked, suddenly afraid for his friends, all of his friends, who had worked hard not to kill, and to work as bloodlessly as possible, unless somebody was aiming a weapon at *them*.

"Interpol," Danny agreed. "Yes, Liam—we'll skin him, dress him, roast him, and serve him. All your people have to do is—"

"Accept the silver platter," Liam agreed.

"But wait," Josh said, suddenly seeing the whole picture. "What will all of you be doing?"

Danny and Felix glanced at each other, and Felix spoke. "Besides directing resources, working comms and satellites and organizing that final con, we'll be—"

"Protecting me," Julia said softly. "Because I asked them to. And I begged—begged, mind you all—that Danny and Felix be here during my pregnancy." She was squeezing Leon's hand tightly as she spoke. "They'll be doing some traveling, but…." She swallowed. "I need them here." She sniffed and took an offered napkin to dab at her eyes. "Besides, this little episode is going to be costly, and we do need to keep the businesses running to fund it."

"And Kadjic will never suspect Danny if he never—as far as Kadjic knows—leaves Chicago." Felix looked grimly triumphant at that, and then he sobered. "And when we say Julia was begging, that was not an exaggeration. Danny and I do *not* like letting the lot of you go off into the world without us. That was never our intention. However, since Lucius and Leon have offered to supply us with transportation and extra pilots—"

"And myself," Leon said modestly, while giving Julia a beseeching look. "I, after all, do business in Greece and much of Europe, so I need to be positioned to be an asset—"

"No," Julia said mutinously.

"But darling—"

"You have children, Leon, and you made promises," she said, her face growing tight as she turned a glare to Danny and Felix, who both raised their hands.

"This was not our idea," Felix said. "Let Carl fly his plane, yes. Let him be on it while it's crashing, no."

"Hey!" Carl protested. "I've gotten much better!"

"He can land without hardly bouncing now," Michael supplied staunchly.

Carl gave his beloved one of those expressions that said he didn't know how to respond to that. "Thanks, sweetheart," he murmured.

"'Course."

"My own pilot can help," Leon said smoothly. "I, uhm… frankly, I would feel much braver if my own pilot was at the helm."

"*Hey*!" protested Carl, Chuck, *and* Hunter, their pilots.

"That wasn't fair," Julia snapped. "And remember the part about you having children—and one on the way?"

"You can't have it both ways," Leon said softly. "Either Danny and Felix here and me on the road, or me here and Danny and Felix on the road. I understand that you feel safer with them here—they have, after all, kept you safe for the last twenty-plus years, but you can't ask me to sit the whole thing out." His lower lip took on a hurt curve. "They always try to leave me out to protect you. It's finally my chance to play!"

Julia covered her eyes. "We will discuss this," she said after a moment. "All four of us." She removed her hand. "Suffice it to say, we need at least a month—"

"Two weeks," Danny said. "At the outside. Liam and Josh should be on a plane to England—"

"England?" Josh asked.

"Well, our first big boom is back in the Caribbean, where we know he's building up his gun supplies on another friendly island," Felix said. "We figured England for a week, the tiny island goes boom and…."

"And we're on our way to our next destination in the company of two people who look like the people who blew up the guns," Josh said. "I get it. Two different destinations, lots of—"

"Oh my God," Molly said, as though this had just occurred to her. "Are we going to put somebody in *boobs and a wig*? Please tell me yes. *Please* tell me that's part of the plan."

Danny snickered. "Well, it is now, precious. It can be." He sobered and made eye contact with everybody. "But we need to get to work. Felix is sending you info on every actual site that will be approached and assailed—we need *all* of the big brains in this room to be thinking of plans. Don't get all up in your feelings if we take somebody else's plan. You may be implementing it, because this is going to be big. Josh and Liam, you two are on sites of distraction—where can you be most efficiently *me*."

"Do you have a bucket list, Uncle Danny?" Josh asked eagerly, and Danny smiled at him beatifically.

"Oh, my boy, I'm sure I can get you some suggestions. How kind of you to ask."

"So four major ops and their distraction points," Felix summarized. "The fifth op depending on what we learn from the first four. Stirling, Tienne, and Danny will be our major computer power, although yes, I know the rest of you don't suck at it. But this way we can send Stirling and Tienne on the road with whomever is most in need, and they'll have hackers right there. I've leased us some extra time on the satellites—"

"You can *do* that?" Grace asked in wonderment.

Felix grimaced. "Well, technically, the network leases transponders all the time. Because this is breaking international, I obtained access to more along a broader spectrum so our commlinks will be unimpeded."

"And also to get the news out that the mainstream American news is neglecting," Julia said darkly, and the crew winced.

"Yeah," Liam agreed. "Sorry, you lot, but your networks are embarrassing right now."

"We know," Lucius said, sounding depressed. "Believe me, we know."

"So, yay Dad for the patriotic news coup," Josh said dryly. "And let's hear it for transponders in new places."

"And for work to do," Danny said. He glanced at Josh and Liam apologetically. "You're staying at the mansion tonight?"

"Yeah," Josh said, and Liam tried not to let his disappointment show because he'd harbored a deep hope for one more night in the apartment, alone. "We'll be at the family workout tomorrow."

"Excellent." Danny rubbed his hands together like a happy goblin. "We work best in gestalt, children, and I can't say I'm not counting on the lot of you to think us up a miracle."

At that point Julia let out *the* most *amazing* yawn, and the entire assembly stopped to stare at her as it seemed to devour all of her person, energy and all. When she was done, Leon cupped her elbow and said, "Ahem."

She gave him a beseeching look, but he shook his head. "We have an *agreement*," he enunciated. "Besides." His dark eyes—much like Josh's but older, more calculating, though still a handsome, depthless brown—swept the assembly. "I think we're ready to break up for the evening. It's time for everybody to get to their computers and analyze information, and time for you to rest."

"I am perfectly capable of—"

Leon kissed her, right there, and Liam watched as Josh's mother melted in his arms.

When he pulled back, he cocked his head, and Julia seemed to wilt against him. "That will not always work," she said crossly.

"No, it will not," he agreed. "So I'm taking advantage while I have it. Good night, everybody."

She gave him a droll glance but allowed him to shepherd her up the stairs with a good-night wave. As soon as they were gone, the happy gossip began.

"Did you know?" Molly asked Josh.

"No," Josh said. "But I feel stupid for not."

"You're going to have a *sibling*!" she practically squealed. "And Grace, you too!"

Grace wore a transported look. "More babies to sit on!" he said happily. "And we can take the new squashed baby to Michael's house, and *those kids* can sit on it. It will be *squashed baby soup*!"

"This baby will be more superbaby than Josh!" Stirling said, sounded excited. "We'll teach it electronics—"

"And languages and art!" Tienne added.

"And cars!" Michael said.

"And *theater*," Molly added.

"And safety," Carl muttered. "And Chuck, we know you're teaching all the kids to drive."

Chuck let out a maniacal l"You guys, did she mean it? I mean, I know Leon's a good dad, but… you guys." And for the first time Liam heard the forlorn note of the little boy Josh was trying so hard not to be. "You… you three were *my* parents. You're all… you know, still a team, right?"

Both of his fathers met his gaze. "Yes, son," Felix said softly. "She… I mean, she begged us to stay here with her, but I think as things get going, she'll probably cling to Leon and Danny, and I will join you all out in the world. But as for being parents together? Yes. I… what we've forged as a family—it's quite unique." He glanced around the room. "And that goes for all of you. Since March of last year, our family has grown *so* much. There's most assuredly room for one more. I…." He swallowed, obviously trying not to be emotional, and Danny took over.

"We'll stay family," he said firmly. "And I suspect we'll stay in the game. But right here, this place, will always be open to you. Your sanctuary. Your home. Whenever you all need it." His lips twitched in a faint smile. "Back before we met Julia and ever dreamed of a Josh, I dreamed of heists. I dreamed of revenge," he said with a modest tilt of his head. "I dreamed of riches and art and the ability to have a life full of books and knowledge and fun. I never, *ever* dreamed of the whole of us. I should have, but I didn't know I could have everything. I like it." His smile grew in both emotion and mischief. "I'm not letting it go now."

The meeting broke up after that, each of them to their own quarters. In the past, Liam had managed a guest room, often using one of the dedicated rooms of the folks who'd been staying in their city apartments. But tonight, he and Josh followed Grace and Hunter up the stairs, and instead of peeling off to their room, Grace grabbed Hunter's hand and led him to Josh's suite.

"Did you get all napped up?" Grace asked as they followed Josh into the room.

"Yes," Josh told him. "I take it you've got ideas?"

"*So* many ideas." Grace laughed manically. "I may need to fidget, though. And is anybody still hungry?"

"I'll go get snacks," Hunter muttered.

"Should we call Stirling and Molly?" Grace asked. "You and Stirling do the thing—"

Josh grunted and pulled out his phone. In a moment he said, "Stirling, yes. Tienne and Danny are plotting together. Molly and Chuck are working on something. Carl, Lucius, and Tor are grouped up, but Michael's going home because he's got to outfit the planes and start charting flight plans as we give them to him. And Marco's *bringing* snacks, so Hunter, choose your group."

Hunter gave Grace an unhappy frown. "Molly and Chuck are going to be doing munitions, transpo, and muscle," he said. "That's my area, but…."

Grace rolled his eyes. "But you need to be here to grab me by the scruff of the neck. Except you don't. I'm not going to do anything dangerous *tonight*," he said. And then he gave Josh a sneaky smile. "Except let our hamsters loose and watch them play."

Josh laughed and then glanced at Liam. "Where did *you* want to play?" he asked. "Everybody's going to need you in the next two weeks. Judging by what I've seen of Danny's list, we're going to have to become experts in international law overnight."

And for a moment Liam wanted to go see what the others were working on. But not tonight.

"Tomorrow," he said softly. "Tonight I want to be here."

A sort of luminosity broke through Josh's pure on-the-job expression. "Sure," he said. "Here is good."

So Liam grabbed his own laptop, pretty sure he was going to be doing a lot of "No, we can't do that stunt Tom Cruise did in that one Mission Impossible movie, because I don't want any of you dead" and settled in for the night.

Landing Gear

"JOSH—JOSH, LUV. Time to wake up. We're almost there."

Josh groaned and rolled into Liam's warmth, wondering where this delicious feeling of safety, of security, had been all his life. The heady smells of aftershave and wool had settled into his bones during the commercial flight, and since they were in first class on an overnight, their closeness had been guaranteed.

It was the first downtime they'd had in the two weeks since the big planning meeting, and with the exception of a few hours stolen deliciously in the downtown apartment, they had been intensely busy.

Josh's ability to plan all night, work out in the morning, and then run scenarios for the next twelve hours, was not what it had been the year before.

"No," he mumbled. "Wanna stay right here."

And oh! Liam's arm around his shoulders, like it *hadn't* been on the yacht when Josh had needed it so badly but had denied them, because needing wasn't loving, dammit. But now it was everything he'd wanted. But more because they *had* shared those delicious private hours, that sweet possession, those moments of bare skin, gazing into each other's eyes, and growing sober after laughter—those moments made them more, put into place all Josh had dreamed they could be.

"Come on, luv," Liam murmured. "You wake up now, we'll get through customs, and I'll get you to my flat. My brother's there. He's stocked the place up, aired it out. You'll be able to sleep off the jet lag, and you'll be ready for the day after tomorrow."

"Fuuuuuuuck…."

Because while the back end of the plan was subject to change, the first two phases were locked in and ready to go. But Josh and Liam needed to be in place. They'd draw attention to Lightfingers, Kadjic would be hopefully tracked to their location, and while they got the hell out of Dodge (or Paris, as the plan called for), something else—something big—would go down on the other side of the world.

But it was early morning now, which meant Josh got a day to rest, and, he had to admit, for him and Liam to be what they *hadn't* been able to be in the mansion: alone.

Still, Josh couldn't help but feel a sense of homecoming after they disembarked. Liam summoned a cab, and they were on their way to the once industrialized and impoverished East End.

"A lot of it was still slums when I was younger," Liam said, taking in the refurbished lines of pointed-roof brick buildings, and Josh nodded.

"I remember Danny and Felix were careful around Brick Lane and Whitechapel," Josh replied, those moments from his childhood when his family had been in Europe making for a happy memory. "But every year we returned they said the place was getting better and better. Banglatown is one of Danny's favorite places now—he used to write me about it, about the food and the color and the people." Josh had kept every postcard, every letter. When his mother and Felix had finally divorced, they'd had a sort of private family celebration that Felix could finally come quietly out of a closet he'd never meant to live in. Felix—who had probably been missing Danny at that moment more than he'd miss breathing—had gotten a wee bit drunk, one of the very few times Josh could remember that happening. Josh had run to his room and pulled out his shoeboxes full of letters, grabbing some of the more recent—including postcards from Banglatown.

Now, Josh wondered if Danny hadn't been to the East End to visit Liam, and the thought made him smile.

"Yeah," Liam said, but his own voice held hints of melancholy. "My dad had thought he was born to be a dock worker, and then when the neighborhood changed, when the jobs changed, he didn't know where he was anymore. It's one of the things, I think, that made it so hard to be himself."

"Mm…." Josh gave him a sidelong glance. If he was an open book when it came to falling for cops, he knew Liam was the same about wanting to *be* one. Funny, how such an old-fashioned symbol for stability, for peace, still held weight, even though history had born out that law enforcement was often the most lawless establishment of all. "I'm sorry about that," he said. "That's… hard."

Liam gave his own sideways look. "You would know, right?"

Josh shrugged. "Believe it or not, I didn't see Danny drunk that often. He was pretty good at hiding it, and—" He sighed. "—I think he saved the worst parts of it for Felix. Thinking back on it now, I can see he was so lonely. After we got back from Europe, he'd check me out of school sometimes and take me on field trips—museums, plays, ballets. It was like his entire life, when he was my age, he'd been poor and ignored, but once he had means, the only person he had to share those means with in public was his son. I-I see that cottage, the one Tor and Marco live in, and remember when Danny would get back from trips and they'd stay there. I wasn't allowed—and I don't think it was all because they were having sex. It was because Danny was… detoxing, I guess, from the loneliness of traveling without Felix. Fights, tears—whatever. I was never exposed to the worst parts of the situation. Which, you know, good parenting, but also…."

"Hard," Liam said. At that moment, the cab turned off into what had once been an industrial area, but just looking at the shiny scrubbed sidewalks and artful store fronts showed it had been recently gentrified.

The cab let them out in front of what had been an erstwhile warehouse but had now obviously been parsed into units, and the two of them grabbed their luggage and made their way through a makeshift lobby and down the hall to the elevator.

Liam took in Josh's expression in the elevator and laughed.

"The units are better from the inside, trust me."

Josh hadn't wanted to say anything, but the heavily scored concrete, low ceilings, and fluorescent lights had put him off a bit. He was very aware that not everybody could afford a mansion in Glencoe, but he and Grace had also made do with a modest allowance when they'd had their student apartment in the city, and they'd worked hard to make the place livable within their budget. He had to admit he was a little bit like Grace in that he was a hedonist and liked comfortable things.

"That's a relief," he said, and then Liam opened the door to his apartment, and he gasped.

The apartment itself *was* much nicer than he'd anticipated. Designed with a completely open floor plan, with the exception of what was probably a long narrow bathroom that literally took a slice off the big square space, almost the entirety of one wall was consumed with a bank of windows that Josh had seen wrapped around the building. The floor was still concrete, but Liam had buffed it to a shine and covered it with thickly padded, colorful wool rugs, both big and small, that marked spaces. A seafoam-green patterned rug sat under sturdy, plain, and comfortable-looking furniture in the center of the space that was obviously a living room. Another rug, this one turquoise blue and much more washable, sat under a small dining table of thick, bare wood, with matching chairs, each one featuring a cushion on the seat.

And in the back corner was a queen-sized bed with a fluffy white comforter and a few brightly colored cushions on top.

"Better?" Liam asked, before peeking in himself.

"Yes," Josh said, sincere but also laughing. "But I wasn't expecting it to be furnished with people as well as chairs."

Liam did a double take and rolled his eyes. "Robert," he said, sounding pleased to see his brother. "And Molly and Grace. You two got here quick."

Robert looked a lot like Liam—the dark freckles across the cheeks, dark brown hair without the curls, and a slightly crooked smile. But Liam's jaw was square and firm where Robert's was rounder and more boyish, and Liam—when he wasn't slouching in a corner, trying to be inconspicuous—had an upright posture and broad shoulders as well.

Robert's slighter frame wasn't unattractive—but it wasn't Liam, and Josh had grown quite fond of Liam's body of late.

"Sorry about that," Molly said cheerfully. True to her promise, she'd dyed her hair a wheat gold, keeping random streaks of mermaid pink. Then she'd straightened it and had practiced keeping it in a French braid down her back to her waist. The effect was actually quite lovely, Josh had thought, and while the streaks of color made her appear young and carefree, the straight wheat blond was almost plain compared to the spectacular sunset curls. "Chuck was flying with Lucius's pilot as his second. I didn't think Chuck could, you know, push the envelope in the air like he did on the ground, but I swear Lucius's guy was absolutely cloud white."

Grace's laugh was positively evil. "They're catching a sleep at Lucius's London condo and taking off tomorrow early, if Lucius's guy doesn't quit first."

"Poor Graham," Molly said, but she didn't sound sympathetic at all. "I really don't think he's got the stuff somebody like Lucius needs."

"Which is why they're not sleeping together," Josh said dryly. "I thought we were going to meet up tomorrow too."

Molly and Grace gave each other sly smiles. "See?" Molly said. "You see what I was saying?"

"He's trying to get rid of us?" Grace sulked, and Josh was tempted to massage his temples.

"No," he said slowly, "I just have dibs on the bed."

The two of them broke into raucous laughter, and Grace gave Josh a roughhouser's hug, shaking him while relieving him of his carry-on at the same time.

"You're so polite!" he laughed. "No, honestly, we just thought we'd check out Liam's family, torment them, freak them out about how scary we are, and then fade away to a hotel. We've got a room checked out in your name. It's all fine."

"My name?" Josh asked, absolutely positive they wouldn't be that stupid.

"J.D. Morgan," Molly corrected. "Don't worry, Josh, we've all done our homework." She gave Robert a cheerful grin. "But everything else is pretty much correct. We wanted to scope out Liam's family. Is this it? I thought we were promised siblings out the ass."

"I try hard to keep my siblings very much *out* of my ass, thank you," Robert said with a grin. "And no, I'm the second in line. Meg is next, Caleb is fourth, Patricia fifth, and Tanda is our youngest and our best."

Grace tilted his head. "Sorry, Liam, I guess your little sister is the pride and joy?"

"I don't know, Grace," Liam said, his accent growing thicker—probably with discomfort. "How excited would *your* family be if you became a copper?"

Grace snorted. "*My* family does not actually give a rat's ass if I live or die. Josh's family can vouch for that, which is why I live there now. But I do see what you mean. It would be a disappointment."

"And I followed in my big brother's footsteps," Robert said dryly, "so that makes us both disappointments."

Josh cocked his head, stifling a yawn. "You're law enforcement?" he asked.

"Oh aye—detective constable. Couldn't quite find the knack of rising the promotional ladder Liam did, but I do okay."

Liam snorted. "Not your fault the female superior officers were fewer and further between."

"Yeah, Liam was born with a lucky cock is all," Robert said, laughing. "But we do all right. Meg helps with her husband's business, Caleb's a *baker*, of all things, Patricia teaches little 'uns, but Tanda—she's going to uni and, well, yes. We're all proud."

Grace grunted, taking Josh's wheeled suitcase from his other hand and shooing him to sit on the couch across from Robert.

"Grace," Josh complained fractiously, but Grace scowled.

"We are leaving in a minute," he said, "and then you and Liam can crash. I'm on to you, Recovery Boy. Your mother laid into us all while you were napping yesterday before you left. It's our job to keep you healthy. No getting sick now when we're so close to the end."

Josh grunted and sank into the really comfortable cream-colored tweed. There was a vibrantly colored throw on the back, and he realized that he had to *fight* the compulsion to grab the throw, curl up on the cushions, and fall asleep, letting all of Liam's family wash over his head.

"Tell us more," he said to Robert on a yawn. "What's your mom like? Does Meg like her job? Are there nieces and nephews? Liam doesn't tell us anything."

Liam grunted. "We've been having planning meetings in your bedroom until twelve at night. Doesn't give us much chance for background."

Josh grunted. "We spent three weeks in a little berth in the Caribbean. You didn't tell me much then either."

Robert let out a little laugh. "Yes, Meg and Caleb are married—Caleb too early, Meg just right. Caleb has a little boy—the reason for the too early, but he and his wife seem to make it work. Meg has one of each. They're all right terrors. You can meet them tomorrow when they come over for breakfast."

Josh struggled to process this, but Liam, apparently, was right on top of it.

"When they *what*?"

Robert gave him a smug glance. "You tell us you're by for two days and bringing the love of your life with you, and you didn't expect this?"

Liam gave Josh a quick, embarrassed look. "I didn't say—"

"Oh the hell you did not!" Robert laughed. "We've heard of nothing *but* this boy for over a year!" Robert regarded Josh kindly. "We were all so very relieved to hear you're recovering from your illness, lad. Liam was in a state, trying to pretend he didn't care and most obviously caring. But we've been hearing stories of your 'Uncle Danny' for ten years now. I swear, wanting to catch a Lightfingers was one of the reasons I went after detective, now, wasn't it. So yes, you're coming by your flat today and leaving the day after tomorrow. From you, Liam, it's practically an entire Christmas visit. Of course Mum's coming by. In fact, she's texted me, insisting these two come sleep in her guest room at the house. Says she'll show 'em baby annuals and the whole kit and caboodle." He looked expectantly at Grace and Molly, his gaze seeming to linger over Molly's curves and wicked green eyes. "That all right with you two? We've got two twin beds, if that's all right."

Grace sniffed. "Girl cooties," he said with contempt. "We could sleep in the same bed and it would be like having a full-sized body pillow."

Molly stared at him, horrified. "It would not, you little pervert. I *shudder* to think of what you did with a body pillow before you met Hunter."

Grace let out a cackle. "Not even Hunter wants to know what I'd do with a body pillow before I met Hunter." He turned to Robert. "So yes, I'm gay, and yes, two twin beds are fine, and wait a minute…." Before Josh's eyes, he transformed into the charming young gentleman that Julia, Felix, and Danny had been trying to get him to be for the past ten years. "That would be very generous of you," he said. "Molly and I would love to accept. We need to Uber to our hotel to get our things first."

"I'll take you to fetch 'em," Robert said, smiling at him, obviously charmed. Then he turned to Molly. "And it would be a shame to be in bed with this one and mistake her for a body pillow, so I think two beds are best."

Molly—to Josh's immense enjoyment—blushed *hard* at this, the color sweeping from her neck to her forehead, washing over the freckles on her cheeks.

"That would be nice," she murmured. "The ride, I mean. Uhm, and thank you for not, uhm, arresting us when we broke in."

It was Robert's turn to cackle. "I could have sworn you had a key, you came in so smoothly. If you're as good as Lightfingers, I can see why he's such a prize for Interpol."

Liam groaned. "Shh, Robert—you're practically an information toxic leak."

Robert's smile remained undimmed, and Josh laughed to himself as he closed his eyes. Suddenly Liam was at his elbow, hissing, "Nope-nope-nope… come along, boy-o. To bed. I'll wake you up around noon to eat."

"No bed," Josh yawned. "Want to see your baby pictures."

Liam grunted, and Robert, still back in the living area, let out a quiet whoop. "No escaping it, brother—we'll show him all your secrets."

Josh mumbled something that might have been, "So nice to meet you," before he found himself sitting on the edge of the bed while Liam took off his shoes.

"I'm sorry I'm falling asleep," he mumbled. "I want to talk to your family."

"I suspect you will," Liam said. "In fact, given how much work we have to do tomorrow, I suspect I need to call them up and put some boundaries on how long breakfast is going to last."

Josh smiled and cupped Liam's cheek. "The job'll sort itself," he said. "I can't wait to meet your people."

Liam glanced up and captured his hand. "The job is dangerous," he corrected. "All things in moderation."

Josh shook his head a little giddily. "Tired of moderation," he said. "I want some *excess*."

"There will be time for that too," Liam promised. "Although I warn you, I don't think too much of you will ever be enough."

"Pretty," Josh hummed. "So pretty." He found himself laid sideways on the bed and the blankets pulled tight around his chin. "Tell Grace he can cuddle for a few before you come to bed. He'll get sad."

A rough hand on his brow and a sigh. "Of course. I need to talk to Robert for a bit anyway."

"Fucking cancer," Josh mumbled, because while his shoulder was mostly recovered, his stamina—ah, yes. Another year or so before he'd be able to take that transatlantic red-eye and run around for a day before falling asleep. Sacrifices.

He was almost asleep when Grace scooted into the bed in front of him, forcing him to wiggle back to accommodate him.

"Anyone else—"

"Would have let you sleep. I know. I'm needy. Shut up and tell me you're all right."

"Just tired," Josh said. Then he hugged his friend, truly able to relax because they were in this together like they'd always been. "Be nice to Liam while I'm sleeping."

"It's easy. He hasn't done anything embarrassing yet. Wait until we catch him with his mouth open, snoring. *Then* we'll do him dirty."

Josh was too tired to do more than smile while he drifted off.

WHEN HE awoke, Molly, Grace, and Liam's brother were gone, leaving him squinting in the grayish light coming through the tinted bank of windows. Blinking, he tried to remember if it had been raining or not as they'd arrived and decided that yes, it had been, and he closed his eyes and channeled Danny again, trying to count heartbeats.

Liam. There on the couch. Tapping furiously on his laptop, a bag of takeout on the coffee table in front of him.

Josh groaned and sat up, more to give him notice than anything else. Among other things, Danny had taught him how to creep out of bed so quietly nobody would know he'd woken up, a thing he'd done many times before Grace had come to live at his house, because he and Grace were frequently up to no good, and they didn't want to trouble the adults with pesky morality questions.

"You don't have to do that on my account," Liam told him, glancing up from his computer. "I've seen you get out of bed enough now to know you make church mice look like they're at a rave."

Josh smiled a little and put his hand out to balance on the wall. "Still tired," he admitted. "But starving. Please tell me your bathroom doesn't have a floor-to-ceiling window, because I need to stop there too."

"Your virtue is safe," Liam said, folding up the laptop. "Make yourself at home."

"My virtue's been pilfered," Josh corrected. "It's my dignity we're worried about." With that he toddled off to the bathroom, pleased to see Liam had pulled his own shaving kit out of his luggage and put it on the counter of the utilitarian bathroom. Liam had tried—there were thick bathmats and even a charming picture of a frog across from the commode—but the tile was stark white and the floor was still polished concrete.

Still, there *were* towels, and after accomplishing the necessaries, Josh decided to really start his day by washing off the travel.

He was enjoying the hot water when he felt a burst of cool air, and for a moment, he panicked, thinking, "Oh God, who's in my bathroom *now*?" Grace didn't care about his nudity, and Stirling didn't notice—and both of them had lived in the mansion with him for over a year.

But then the shower door opened, and in the confusion of the escaping steam, Josh could feel the heat of another body stepping in.

Breathing a sigh of relief, he leaned back into Liam's chest, pleased when he felt strong arms wrapping around his shoulders.

"I'm sorry I slept through your brother's visit," he murmured, tilting his head when Liam kissed the side of his neck.

"Don't be," Liam said, taking liberties with his earlobe that Josh didn't know he needed.

"But it's not fair," Josh breathed. Liam slid his hand along the tender concavity of his stomach, and Josh knew what it felt like to be aroused and comforted at once. "You know all my family, and I don't—oh!" Now there was a soapy washcloth being plied. Everywhere.

"My family's a madhouse," Liam said, his hands busy, intrusive… ah! So glorious on Josh's bare skin.

"So's mine," Josh moaned.

"So you'll get them," Liam said. "That's not the scary part."

Josh turned in his arms, needing to kiss him, to feel his soapy chest, to glut himself on Liam's skin as he hadn't managed to do yet.

"What's the scary part?" he asked, pulling Liam's head down so Josh could plunder that full mouth.

Liam struggled to lift his head long enough to answer. "You're the only one they've met," he whispered hoarsely. "You're the only one whose name they know. You're the only one—"

Josh kissed him again, a part of him thrilled beyond measure, too thrilled to be scared or anxious, and Liam took him in, magnified the kiss, ravished him with it, until Liam turned off the water and—still kissing—pulled Josh out of the shower, dried him tenderly and, kiss by kiss by step by step, took him to the bed.

Josh's shoulder didn't hurt anymore. He'd slept, he was clean, safe, and oh God, so needy!

"Hard and fast this time?" he almost begged.

Liam was reaching for something on the bedstand behind Josh's head. "Not going to last any other way," he said, voice thready.

In a moment he'd returned, a small bottle of lubricant in his hand, and with a short, savage kiss on the mouth, he adjusted his concentration to between Josh's thighs.

Josh bent his knees, splaying himself, still a little shy, but also—oh! "Oh yes," he mumbled. "I like that."

"Pay attention," Liam murmured against his neck, his fingers busy, spreading slick, stretching, arousing. "Someday you'll be doing this to me."

The image filled him, his own cock disappearing into Liam's body, Liam soft and begging beneath him. He moaned, and Liam ducked his head quickly, taking Josh's cock into his mouth and throat and pulling just as quickly off.

"You like that idea," Liam said and chuckled. He placed himself between Josh's thighs, and this time Josh closed his eyes, letting Liam's flesh fill him, push him, as he let himself float and merge, enjoying their clean, warm skin sliding softly as they moved.

"Oh…." He wanted to be clever. He wanted to say witty things in bed, telling Liam that this was *everything* he'd ever wanted from making love, that it was *more*. But only the soft sibilants of pleasure escaped.

And then the pleasure changed to urgency and the urgency to need. Soon he was bucking up against Liam in time, the sound of their sex smacking against the still air. Behind his eyes rushed white light, then blue, then red, as his climax exploded, and he groaned hard, bearing down as Liam rutted inside him, his own climax spilling, filling him, their spend hot and slick and absolutely a part of their lovemaking in a way Josh had never suspected.

They both cried out, spasms rocking them, and then they floated down, down, back into Liam's bed, soft and clean—or at least it was beneath the towel Josh sensed under his hips.

He laughed softly, opening his eyes, finding Liam's merry blue eyes searching his face.

"What?" Liam asked, sliding out of him as he rolled to his side, one hand on Josh's damp chest.

"The towel. Good planning."

Liam chuckled. "I… I keep thinking we should be having quickies in the closet, or I should be bending you over, taking you, and leaving you begging for more. Honeymoon sex, but I can't."

"Why not?" He rather liked the idea.

But Liam sobered and stroked the side of Josh's cheek. "Because I can't think of it being anything less than beautiful. Not right now. Maybe later, when I stop waking up and thinking, 'He's here in bed with me. He kissed me good night. It's all I ever wanted.' Maybe we'll have ravenous, carefree sex then. Now it's too important, you and me together."

Josh seized his fingers and kissed them, nibbling a little. "I wish I could argue with that," he said, remembering the months of wishing Liam was there, knowing the only reason he wasn't was that Josh's pride wouldn't let him be. "Maybe we'll know we can trust this when the sex doesn't have to be perfect."

"Are you complaining?" Liam asked.

Josh smiled at him and shook his head. Into the dreamy silence, his stomach spoke loudly, letting them both know that *somebody* hadn't eaten yet, and laughing, they both got up from bed and dressed, Josh in yoga pants and one of Liam's plain button-down work shirts.

Because Liam had placed it over his shoulders and kissed his neck and said, "Please. It's a fantasy of mine."

Josh grinned and slid it on, doing the buttons at the middle but not at his throat or around his waist. The shirt was big on him—he knew it would be—but he could see how having a smaller, more delicate lover could bring out the caveman in somebody.

He didn't mind. His own fantasy had been cemented by Liam's throaty chiding when they'd been in bed, and someday Josh would be the one topping, and Liam would be losing his mind.

In a few minutes, Liam was on one of the couches, presumably doing real Interpol paperwork on his laptop, while Josh rooted through their luggage for the carefully packed practice equipment.

"You sure?" Josh asked, pulling out the last battery pack.

"Yes, I'm sure," Liam said. "They won't be able to track us through the Chunnel. I bought our tickets with our other IDs—"

"Not your Interpol other ID?" Josh asked, because he *had* to, apparently.

"Yes, my Interpol other ID, because I'm as stupid as Grace accuses me of being," Liam retorted. "Or maybe I was there during the planning sessions, and I used the handy first ID that Tienne fixed up for me that's fully backstopped. Unlike yours, which should trigger Kadjic's paranoia in about a day."

"Sorry," Josh muttered, embarrassed. "I micromanage everybody else too."

"So I've been told," Liam replied dryly. "Now on. We take the train, do a one-day walkabout in Paris, including the Louvre, and *don't* steal the *Mona Lisa*."

Josh snorted. "Everybody wants to steal that fucking painting. Do you realize that it *was* stolen for two years in the early nineteen hundreds and—"

"Spent two years underneath some guy's stove while he had Italian nationals come peek at it and marvel that yes, they were a part of one of the greatest paintings on the planet. Yes, I know, because I was there when Danny told that story."

"I was *raised* on that story," Josh told him soberly. "Because the guy walked into the museum dressed like a schmo, then walked out of the museum through the back dock, and not a soul questioned him because he walked like he had the right to be there."

Liam took a deep breath, and Josh could see him processing.

"We walk like we've got the right to be there," he said softly.

"That's right," Josh said, setting the equipment down on the table. "We know how to disable the locks, the cameras, the security system, and when we leave, the attention's not going to be on the perpetrators."

Liam frowned, thinking about it, thinking about what they planned to do.

"No," he said in surprise. "It's not, is it?"

"Nope," Josh said, spreading out the lockpicks, the faux frames, the alarm buzzers, and the practice canvases on the mostly clean coffee table. "The trick is," he said, laying the equipment out in precise order, "to be so absolutely invisible that there's only one place for the attention to go. Care to join me?" He glanced up and held out a lockpick. Liam hit Save on his laptop, folded it, and set it down beside him, then took the proffered tool.

"Why yes," he said, "I'd love to play art thief Operation with you."

"Yes! Let's extract a kidney stone and replace a Rembrandt!" Josh told him happily, setting his phone up next to him. "Remember, we've got fifteen seconds to slip the canvas under the glass without activating the alarm. You ready?"

"Ready," Liam said, getting comfortable.

"Set, *go*!" Josh hit the timer on his phone, and they were off.

When Josh's family had been kiting around Europe when he was a child, they'd often stayed in second-tier hotels. Nice places, no bugs, no obvious drugs or prostitution, but the carpet wasn't new, and they were off the main drags with less visibility. The primary reason for this was to avoid any contemporaries of Julia's father—Hiram Dormer had his fingers in a lot of international pies, and the reason the family had escaped to Europe was to give them all a break from the constant implied violence of the mobster businessman. One of the unexpected benefits, though, was it turned out to be an excellent training and practicing ground for, say, a group of born grifters.

Josh remembered one time when a businessman had turned away from a woman at the base of the walkway leading into the hotel from the garage. The woman—while not a street-level prostitute was obviously a higher-class working girl—had been affronted.

"We had a deal," she said in shock. "You had your evening. You need to—"

He'd slapped her before she had a chance to go on and then turned on his heel, muttering, "Greedy fucking whore," as he marched away.

"Do we…?" Felix began, and then Julia had waved him off to track down the man's hotel room number while she went to console the woman and get her number.

The next day, Felix stayed back at the hotel to break into the man's room, get his information, and then put in a word with the man's company and his wife, while Danny, Julia, and Josh followed him on the street.

Julia had gone first, coming from the opposite direction, making sure to keep her stride loose and her expression haughty—she'd done her makeup and worn a wig to be much like the woman from the night before, figuring the man had a type.

And he did. His attention went directly to her, following her to his left as he passed.

Then Danny had come up behind the man on his right, bumped into him, and extracted his phone from his breast pocket.

And Josh had extracted his wallet from his back pocket without brushing his fingers against the fabric of the man's slacks.

They'd given the cash and credit cards to the woman—who had cried—and destroyed and disposed of the phone. When the man returned to his hotel, he found his reputation and finances in such thorough disrepair that he had to report to the American Embassy to avoid prosecution for trying to defraud an innkeeper.

And Danny had announced Josh had officially graduated from his course on lifting a wallet without the owner being the wiser.

Josh's fingers and fine motor skills were so inherently tuned—and so trained—by this point that he could run through the exercise of unscrewing the frame's backing while avoiding the contact points for the alarm unit several times over without breaking a sweat. But after a half hour, he glanced up and noticed that while Liam's fingers remained steady on their tasks, his forehead was a little damp.

"Food break?" he called kindly, and Liam grunted.

"You're taking it easy on me," Liam claimed, but he fell back against the couch and stretched his neck in relief.

"Well, you have other skills," Josh placated as they both rose and headed for the take-out containers on the counter.

"I am absolutely mortified by that phrase," Liam told him grimly. "Oh, Liam," he mocked, "it's okay if you can't get it up and you're a terrible lover—you have other skills."

Josh cackled. "Well, I think we just proved you *can* get it up and you're an *amazing* lover, so maybe don't take it like that."

Liam smiled in that self-deprecating way he had that turned Josh's key before wrapping his arms around Josh's waist and pulling him against his chest.

"I just… you know. I'm not a dyed-in-the-wool thief," he said.

Josh kissed his cheek. "I thought we both agreed my type is the man who catches thieves. You caught me. Be happy."

"I am." Liam gave him a squeeze before going for the plates in the cupboard. "Just, you know, don't let my family scare you off, okay? They, uhm, may have heard a lot about you as you were growing up."

"Now I find that *fascinating*," Josh said, sampling the green lamb curry and finding it mild enough for his poor abused stomach. He dished that up along with some rice, grabbed the fork Liam had left on the counter, and stepped to the side to let Liam make his own plate. Liam glanced at the small spot of food on Josh's and gave a crooked smile.

"Are you going to make me nag?" he asked gently.

"Let me see how this goes down," Josh told him. "It's getting better, and this is made with coconut milk, so that helps, but I never know."

"Nagging over," Liam said, much to Josh's relief. He appreciated people's concern—he did—but God, he was tired of feeling broken. "So now on to what's fascinating."

Josh grinned and made his way back to the couch, where he pulled up his legs cross-legged. To his surprise—and pleasure—Liam sat down next to him and leaned back so Josh could lean into him.

"It's fascinating that your family is so up on mine. Why is that? Why would you go home and say, 'Hey, I met this thief called Lightfingers—want to hear his story?'"

Liam smirked. "Not quite like that," he said, chewing thoughtfully. He closed his eyes, savoring the highly flavored Indian food, and swallowed. "I guess… see, I'd started out being a flatfoot—everybody got to hear those stories. I mean, I patrolled the neighborhood I grew up in. They knew half the people I collared, yeah?"

"Yeah," Josh said, nodding his head and getting it. A little bite of curry. He sighed, thinking he might be able to have seconds. It was good to eat again.

"But then… well, I didn't tell them about Alec Lawson."

"Because your sex life is your own," Josh filled in wryly, thinking about how the entire family had wanted in on *his* sex life, but he was surprised when Liam shook his head.

"I was ashamed," he said thoughtfully. "I… you know. I'd thought I'd discovered something really important—"

"You did," Josh said in surprise.

"And then I got… sidetracked, I guess. I was lied to and dumped, and I took a promotion for my silence. I was embarrassed, I guess."

Josh frowned, remembering Liam's dry wish for Josh to keep his secrets secret. "But you *owned* that shit," Josh said. "You took that promotion and you did a good job with it. You got closer to Kadjic than the rest of your organization combined. Didn't you singlehandedly clean up prison corruption somewhere too?"

Liam grimaced, and Josh realized he wasn't supposed to have heard that story either.

"Lightfingers helped me with that," he mumbled.

"Oh," Josh said, not liking the mortification on Liam's face at all. "So it's okay for us to go in as a group and do all the great stuff, but *you* don't get to accept help because you're a poor boy from East End and can do it all yourself."

Liam gave him a flat look. "No, that's not what I'm—"

"So our help isn't good enough?" Josh kept probing. "You're mad because the busts we've helped you with this last year weren't pure Liam Craig magic?"

"No!" Liam protested. "I love working with your family—that's not what I'm saying!"

"Then what are you saying?"

"I'm saying I was *used*," Liam burst out. "I let myself be *used*. I thought it was true love, but I was merely some strange on the side until—"

"Bullshit," Josh muttered, shaking his head and ignoring Liam's indignant gasp. "I checked him out, you know."

Liam's jaw dropped, and Josh scowled at him.

"Much like you asked around about Nick," he added, and now Liam flushed a little, the pink on his cheeks not quite drowning out his freckles.

"Nick is married with a baby," Liam said on automatic. "Just like you told me."

"Yes," Josh said patiently. "And so was Alec. Come on, Liam. You were so good at this with Danny. At looking at him and seeing him drunk and sad and thinking, 'He risked his life to save that boy,' and not pushing that you thought he was the infamous Lightfingers. I can read between the lines—it's practically the family industry. Why can't you look at Alec Lawson and see somebody trapped in the life they thought they wanted, who thought you were his ticket out? That's what *I* see. His wife wasn't the devil. He loves his children—every story I've read thus far bears that out."

"A lot, were there, in the last two weeks?" Liam asked dryly.

"I had them ready for work breaks," Josh told him, completely sincere. "But he gave you a raw deal—he couldn't propose marriage, so he fast-tracked you to the career you *could* have had if you'd been born rich with privilege, and you haven't let him down yet. Why would you be embarrassed about that?"

Liam gave a short bark of laughter and shook his head. For a moment, he concentrated on his food, and Josh did too, giving him time to digest.

Finally he stood and took Josh's plate, saying, "Want more?"

"Please," Josh said.

He returned with two full plates and sat again.

"Liam?"

"Your family," he said after a moment of chewing, "is important to me because Danny got clean. He took that chance in Morocco. I offered him a lifeline, and he took it. He poured himself into staying clean and being the best parent he could for you, even though he was thousands of miles away. You all—you all made mistakes. You all have your vices—yes, Josh, even you."

"I have no idea what you're talking about," Josh said mildly through a heavenly bite of curry and rice.

Liam chuckled sadly. "But you all forgive each other. I made the call, did you know that? Connecting Julia and Danny when he was asking for your parents to take Tienne in."

"No," Josh said, surprised.

"And all she wanted was for him to come home. He couldn't, of course. He said, 'How can I come home when I have to look up to see rock bottom.' But that whole moment there—my father was a drunk, and he drove his car off a fucking bridge, but we all still loved him. You would not believe the grief we got, coming up through school, me mum too—because we still loved him. So I guess I told my family about Lightfingers because I couldn't tell Interpol about him, and because I couldn't tell *them* about the things I did legally for Interpol. And because he was proof, you know? That our love wasn't misplaced, even when our father, God rest him, was a flawed, flawed man."

Liam's voice cracked, and Josh set his food down and moved closer to him, resting his hand on Liam's thigh.

"Why," he asked softly, "would you think that sort of forgiveness wouldn't extend to you?"

Liam sighed and leaned his head against Josh's. "All the people in my old neighborhood," he whispered, "worked their arses off to get by. Me? I slept with the right bloke."

"Yeah," Josh said, "but at the time, wouldn't you have wanted the happy ending instead?"

"Probably," Liam admitted. "But then there was Marrakech. And my idea of perfect… changed."

"Good," Josh said happily.

Liam turned his head and kissed Josh's crown. "You think that includes you?"

Josh leaned back so he could smile into those merry blue eyes. "I don't even imagine it wouldn't," he said archly, and Liam laughed and wrapped his arm around Josh's shoulders.

"How much do your siblings know about me?" he asked.

"Well, they don't know we're sleeping together yet," Liam said.

Josh stared at him. "Liam. We left them alone with Grace and Molly."

Liam groaned. "God. Yeah. Sorry."

"At this point they know I'm circumcised, and Grace can tell them how much you snore."

Liam scrubbed at his face with his hands. "What do you think Molly can add?"

Josh shook his head and rolled his eyes. "There's always the time the four of us broke into this one old bigot's store to put all his window mannequins in compromising positions," he hazarded.

Liam's chuckle sounded authentic. "All four of you?"

"Well, Stirling disabled the locks, Molly dressed them all in BDSM gear, and Grace slid in through the door and let the rest of us in."

"And you?"

Josh grinned. "My idea." He sobered. "Also, I kept Molly from beating the shit out of the guy when he was mean to Stirling. We worked as a team."

"Still do," Liam said softly. "Looking forward to seeing Stirling tomorrow."

"He's excited about running point," Josh said.

"And Grace and Molly?"

"Wherever needed," Josh said staunchly, and then, in the interest of truth telling, added, "Or, in Grace's case, wherever chaos will be most entertaining."

Liam shrugged, resigned. "Going to have to trust the boy sometime."

Josh smiled. "My whole life. Once—only once—has he really, really crossed a line, but he won't do that again."

"What happened?" Liam asked.

Josh shook his head. "I'm done with secrets. Let's run through the job a few more times and go to bed. We've got a lot to do tomorrow."

Liam nodded. "Fair. Will he tell me?"

"He would," Josh said, "for me. But it's like that alley in Morocco. There are some moments we would really just rather keep to ourselves. Life's complicated, Liam. You of all people should know that."

"God, you're older than your years," Liam muttered.

Josh had nothing to say to that, so this time *he* took the plates to the kitchen, and they went through the job three more times before bedtime.

JOSH WOKE up at seven that morning because Grace was watching him sleep.

"Are we doing this again?" he asked his pillow, not wanting to move from under Liam's protective arm over his backside. For such a sweet guy, Liam had a streak of protectiveness in him, and Josh wasn't going to argue with that one bit.

"Of course we are," Grace told him. "I thought that was part of our agreement. We would *always* do that. Remember when you showed up at Hunter's apartment, broke in, watched us sleeping, and then went back out and did us the courtesy of knocking?"

Josh scowled, not wanting to remember that night. He'd been so scared for his friend, so relieved when Hunter had been the one to find him, had grounded him, convinced him that nothing he'd done was so terrible that Hunter couldn't love him.

"If you'd *called*," he grumbled, "that wouldn't have had to happen."

"My bad," Grace said, meaning it. "But see? Turnabout's fair play."

"It'll be turnabout if Liam ever tries to sneak out of my flat with my wallet."

Grace grunted. "That was only a couple of guys."

"Yeah. And they were all stupid. What are you doing here again, besides creeping me out?"

"I wanted to warn you. Liam's mom's on the way with, like, breakfast in a cooler and grandkids and two sisters and Robert. By the way, Molly's got it bad for Robert. Please tell me he's as straight as he seems to be."

"Like an arrow," Liam mumbled from Josh's side.

"Really?" Josh said, this news surprising him more than the mother on her way. "That's *amazing*. I feel like we've finally broken the curse."

"Glad to sacrifice a sibling," Liam said, removing his arm (damn!) and sitting up, scrubbing at his face. "When did you say my entire family is coming?"

Grace squinted, and Josh wasn't surprised to see he already had an earpiece in. "Well, Molly asked to drive Robert's tiny car, so she misrouted the whole family by going the wrong way down some road I can't remember. I think you've got about ten minutes. Josh, your dragon breath could knock a murder bird out of the sky. Go groom."

"Our equipment's still on the coffee table," Josh grumbled. "If I'm gonna groom, you need to best man."

"Was there ever a doubt?" Grace asked. "I'll even steal the rings."

"That's my boo," Josh told him, grabbing some clothes from his suitcase.

"So, Liam," Grace said as Josh headed for the bathroom. "Did you ever break fifteen seconds?"

"No," Liam said, and Josh could hear the peevishness in his voice.

"What was Josh's record?"

"Nine point five," Liam said reluctantly.

"Mine's seven. Get dressed. Don't worry if I see you naked. I have a boyfriend—it's all academic appreciation at this point."

"Josh!" Liam complained, but Josh was ducking into the shower for a quick one at that point because Liam had to learn to fend for himself.

Fourteen hours later, in the Caribbean

"I CAN'T BELIEVE I'm the ringer for Molly," Lucius muttered, and Chuck's low laugh made him want to ruffle his feathers like a duck.

"Well," Chuck said, "next to Michael, you've got the slightest build, and Michael's walk is too…." He didn't want to say prison, but his old boyfriend—and the love of Carl's life—*had* spent two years incarcerated, trying to make himself as slouchy and small and unobtrusive as possible.

Chuck had the sad feeling it hadn't worked, but Carl seemed to make the man happy now, and that's all Chuck ever wanted.

Unfortunately, being happy for the two of them wasn't enough to keep Lucius out of drag.

The key, they'd decided, was to have one ringer for each pair of them. The crew was all so distinctive in their looks. A few simple cosmetic changes and some quick flights of fancy, and anybody trying to keep track of who was responsible for the Lightfingers' crimes *and* the Kadjic sabotage was bound to be thoroughly confused.

And—as the four Salingers had been *very* adamant about—the actual crew would never be recognized in Kadjic's circles. Ever.

Which meant Lucius now sported long blond locks, padding in his leggings, and a modest set of breasts, as well as some subtle makeup.

Chuck said he looked adorable and charming, but hopefully because Chuck knew what the special jock was tucking under, as that was Chuck's leaning in a mate.

"So," Lucius said, twiring the umbrella in his fancy drink, "we know which boats are going out to the island, right?"

"Yup," Chuck said, eyeballing the *very* unsavory batch of merchant sailors as they loaded up their cargo. His and Lucius's balcony perch overlooked the bay of Saint Kitts and Nevis, the small island with an even smaller island about ten miles off its eastern shore.

Lucius saw one of them, who would look very much like Hunter if Hunter had short blond hair—which he did now—make a quiet move with his hand against his thigh. Chuck sighed, running his fingers through his own newly brown hair.

Next to Hunter, Michael—who had rainbow sprinkles in his own dark hair, much like Grace—gave a little nod, and together they finished loading the guns on the doomed ship.

"Not that I don't love your company," Lucius murmured, "but don't you have something you should be doing?"

Chuck winked and stood graciously, like a swain called regretfully away from a date. He bent to kiss Lucius—an honest kiss between them, in spite of the subterfuge—and said, "Don't forget it's got to be the *roof* of the hotel room or your satellite won't connect. We need you to have eyes on us to send Carl to go pick us up."

"You mean I *shouldn't* let the four of you die in the middle of the Caribbean?" Lucius asked tartly.

"That would be preferable, yes," Chuck said, mimicking Lucius's precise tones. Before Lucius could pout, Chuck said, loud enough to be heard, "Don't worry about the check, darlin', I'll pay on my way out. I'll call you, 'kay?"

Lucius cocked his head and gave Chuck a "you asshole" glare from heavily mascaraed—and admittedly mysterious—hazel eyes, and Chuck winked and trotted out of the restaurant, making sure to pay in cash on his way.

Three hours later, Lucius was on the rooftop lounge of his and Chuck's carefully chosen hotel, his own earwig catching the chatter between Chuck, Hunter, and Michael as they, each on their own ship on the way to Kadjic's new gunrunning center, decided on the specific form of sabotage for each engine room.

The boats—hastily gathered by Kadjic's crew to make up for the debacle in early January that had put a decent-sized dent in his operation—were a mismatched fleet of junkers if Lucius had ever seen one. But they represented three cargo holds full of high-profile deadly weapons, and if *those* bad boys could sink, and the cargo on the island could be destroyed, Kadjic's gunrunning would be permanently underwater.

Lucius listened, resisting the urge to gnaw on his cuticles until they bled, until he heard Michael and Chuck say, in tandem, "Say the word and we can set a five-minute fuse."

Then Hunter said, "Fuck it. I'm using the C-4."

"Just like I told you," Chuck murmured.

"Shut up, Chuck," Hunter said. "Give me three more minutes."

In Lucius's head—and only in Lucius's head—Danny's voice said softly, "Operation Rembrandt complete, signature engaged. How're we doing?"

"Three to five min—" Lucius began, and then, on his screen, one of the three dots he was following disappeared. Far out on the horizon, a ball of flame could be seen erupting from somewhere on the wickedly blue ocean.

"Lucius?" Danny asked.

"Come on," Lucius muttered, and he heard a cacophony of voices. "*Hunter? Michael? Chuck? Who the fuck was that? Hunter! Are you there! Michael? Fuck-fuck-fuck. Chuck!*"

And then, cold as iced steel, came Carl's voice. "Hunter's fine. Michael, Chuck, blow your loads. Nobody laughs. Not a soul."

"Exiting now!" Chuck and Michael called, and the next two minutes were full of panting breaths and chaos as, presumably, Chuck and Michael hauled ass up to the deck of the two cargo freighters and lunged off their respective starboard sides.

"*Lucius*!" Danny demanded.

"I'm waiting!" Lucius gasped, suddenly aware that he'd been holding his breath. "One of the ships went early!"

Another moment of hoarded oxygen, and then Carl said, "Lucius, I've got them. Sorry—I got wind on another channel that Hunter had been made. I sort of blew a hole in his ship before they could converge on him while he was installing the C-4."

"Hunter?" Lucius said in surprise.

"I'm fine," Hunter grumbled. "Carl, it's official. We're brothers. Paperwork's in the mail."

Michael's breathless laughter could be heard. "You guys—always underestimating him, I swear."

And then Chuck's own coughing and sputtering. "Well, he is the best-looking blond of the lot of us."

"I'll carry that compliment to my grave," Carl said dryly. "Okay, now that I've used one of my RPGs, does anybody have an idea how to blow the guns on the island up?"

Chuck cackled, presumably rifling through the supplies Carl had been loading up on his small cabin cruiser as the others had been infiltrating the cargo ships.

"Don't worry, brother," he said happily. "We're in my wheelhouse now."

"Lucius?" Danny enquired delicately.

"Fine," Lucius said, feeling faint. "They're fine. They're on to stage two. It's fine. It's fine. It's all good."

"How are you doing?" Danny asked, his voice kind.

"I finally understand," Lucius said in wonder.

"What?"

"Why Molly's so dead set against boob sweat."

Danny's cackle sounded a little unhinged, but then, why wouldn't it.

"I'll tell them to engage," he said. "Let me know when stage two is complete."

"Sure," Lucius said. "Dear God. Next time, *I* want to be on the ship!"

Operation Rembrandt

"I SWEAR, I'M still full," Josh mumbled as he, Liam, Grace, and Molly all disembarked from the train in the middle of Paris.

"Well, yeah," Liam said, thinking fondly of his mother's "full Irish" breakfast. Ham, potatoes, eggs, sausage, toast, and—probably because Grace and Molly begged for it—fruit. And beans. Mustn't forget beans, because toast and beans were a staple no matter how much the yanks complained. "Another reason to only go home every few months. Mum can cook, but it's all starch. Potatoes, turkey pot pie, big gluey pots of pasta with sauces inspired by three cultures. She's great—but everything needs its own little dish of Tums."

Molly chuckled, and the four of them glanced around to get their bearings. "Palais Royale," she said. "This platform."

"Is Stirling in place?" Josh asked.

"Café St. Honoré," Molly said. "He's got a good view out the balcony, he says, and he just got there. He and Tienne have some time to linger."

"Good." Josh took a deep breath. "You guys give them a hug for me, okay? I… I really miss having everybody nearby."

"Any news?" Grace asked, and it was a sign of his absolute faith in Hunter that he didn't sound nervous at all.

Josh—who had been listening on his earbud to Danny's relayed information—nodded. "They're about to start stage one," he said. He grinned at Molly. "Lucius apparently has a whole new respect for you, in case you were wondering."

Molly grinned. "At *last*," she said, and then she gave Liam a sly glance. "Think maybe we could put your brother in the same room with him and Chuck? They could, you know, talk me up?"

Molly and Robert had bantered back and forth much like Molly bantered with *everybody*, but Liam had caught some speculative glances on both their parts, and he had to agree with Josh on this one: Molly was *due*.

"Of course," Liam said dryly. "But honestly, Molly-girl, all you've got to do is show up and be yourself. Robert won't know what hit him."

"Keep him," Molly said, pleased. And then their second train drew near and they all hopped on.

The minute they jumped on, they separated, with Josh and Liam going one way and Molly and Grace going the other. Liam could see Grace pulling his stocking cap over his sparkly hair as he went. They would enter the museum at five-minute intervals, each one of them dressed in black, with a black stocking cap, black baggy khakis, a long-sleeved microfiber shirt, and skillful makeup that evened out everybody's complexions, making Josh's pallor and Liam's ruddy cheeks match Grace's tawny complexion and Molly's vampire white. Molly was wearing a binder and shoulder pads, which made her look stocky and sexless but not feminine, which was the point, and the others had used similar prosthetics inside their clothes.

They were all close enough in height, Josh being the shortest, Liam being the tallest, for them to appear hauntingly similar.

The effect for the cameras would be the four of them, crisscrossing the museum, nobody in the same place long enough to do the *whole* job, everybody smoothly doing their part and hiding it while Stirling played merry-hob with the shockingly small number of monitoring devices kept by one of the world's biggest museums.

And of course with Tienne playing the shill—the innocent helpful bystander who was so very good at distracting attention.

They'd run through the con so often, their feet seemed to carry them without conscious thought.

They split up completely when the train let them off, circulating through the Palais Royale mall underneath the Louvre. While they were there, Josh bought—as planned—two cheap string backpacks in pale yellow, the kind people used to keep their water bottle and sunscreen, and Liam, at another vendor, bought two in the same pale yellow color. They both wore a similar pack—in black—on their backs, and their new purchases were quickly balled up and shoved in their pockets as soon as they left the shopping concourse.

And then, Josh first, they made their way into the Louvre. They had twenty minutes to get to their places, and it was both the longest and shortest time Liam had ever spent inside a museum. His heart leapt in his throat the minute he split off into the ancient world displays.

"Ooh.... Sparkly!" Grace said into their commlink as Liam eyed old Egyptian graffiti on a temple. With amusement he saw that the translation was along the lines of "My commander can suck dick."

"Remember our mission," Josh hummed.

"Remember my side quest," Grace hummed back, happy as a pig in slop at the Galerie d'Appollon. Liam didn't approve of the side quest. But then, he figured the Louvre could be short one giant pink diamond if it meant Kadjic's guns, drugs, and human trafficking operations could all be halted in their tracks.

He did have to suppress a smile, picturing Grace tooling through the opulent settings of some of the crown jewels of French royalty. Grace's side quest had been chosen with Grace in mind. First, it slaked Grace's urge to steal just to prove he could, and second, it provided a distraction when they needed one the most.

"Okay, losers," Molly whispered. "I'm in."

"Will it be Dolce and Gabbana?" Josh chided.

"Givenchy?" Grace asked.

"Bite me, morons," Molly said amiably. "I'm stealing the diamonds to put on my own creation. One day this Marie Antoinette thing will be wearing Thieves' Clothes, TM pending."

"Ooh, did you already buy the name?" Grace asked.

"Mmmaybe," Molly teased. "Liam, you there?"

"Do you people really talk to yourselves this much?" Liam asked irritably.

"It looks like we're on our phones," Josh said, which Liam knew, because he'd run ops before, but this... this was quite different. "Yay, Bluetooth. We don't even need to touch our earpieces and glance over our shoulders."

"You wankers are making my arse sweat," Liam told them baldly, feeling cranky. My God, they never shut up. It was like they knocked over museums for kicks.

"Well, stop sweating," Molly said. "I see Tienne coming. Josh, you almost at the target?"

"Just planted the goods," Josh said. "Grace, you at your mark?"

"Sparkly acquired," Grace purred. "Give me ten seconds to hit the alarm."

Liam turned and started ambling toward the stairs. They'd clocked three minutes to get from the ancient worlds section to Josh's spot by the old European masters—in particular, Rembrandt van Rijn.

Okay, then. So the guards would be coming from Liam's left toward the stairs—mark.

"I've got the guard entrance from the south," Molly murmured. "Mark."

"I've got the east entrance," Liam said. "Mark."

And then, from nowhere, Tienne joined their comm-party. "It is me! I'm here. I'm running. Like planned. The guards are after me! Josh, is the underwear in the bathroom?"

Liam must have made a choking sound, because Stirling's voice came next, sweet and indulgent.

"Don't worry," he said. "You're all encrypted. Tienne, say 'mark.'"

"Who's Mark?"

And while everybody—including Liam—tried to control their laughter, a shattering alarm exploded the peace of the Louvre.

"Shit," Josh muttered. "Grace!"

"I went early," Grace said, sounding so pleased with himself Liam had to swallow the obvious retort.

Stirling had known Grace far longer. "Do you brag about that to your boyfriend?" he snapped. "Goddammit—the guards are coming *now*!"

"Running faster!" Tienne hummed. "Mark's coming early too!"

"Lucky Mark," Liam muttered.

"Mark!" Tienne cried, and then Josh said "Oolf!" like he was supposed to, and then he whispered, "Dammit, Tienne, ouch—no, don't stop—keep going to the bathroom!"

"Oh! Sorry! So sorry!" Tienne called—and it sounded like he was talking loudly, as though running away from the person he'd accidentally shoved up against a wall. "On my way!"

Liam's guards had shown up by then, and he braced himself for impact in three-two-one—"Oolf!" He unobtrusively propelled himself underfoot at the same time Molly greeted her guards, the scuff of the guard's hard-soled shoe against his shin painful and then forgotten. For a moment, the comms were full of the Liam and Molly show: "Oh my God, so sorry—no, let me help you up! Oh shit—didn't mean to—oh no, I'm—oh wait—no! I'm just trying to help!"

The two of them, sacrificing their bodies and definitely their dignity, managed to trip up the guards rushing toward Grace's burst alarm, and by strategic placing, managed to keep them out of the hall where Josh was hurriedly replacing a reproduction of a lost painting with the painting itself.

In Liam's head he could hear Josh singing, "One-two-three-four-five-six-seven-eight-nine-ten-eleven-twe-el-elve!" with a familiar jingle in the numbers. Liam had to smile—it was the same counting jingle he'd hummed when they'd been working the night before. Liam had needed to learn the thieves' bits just in case, and he assumed Molly could have stolen the diamond or dismantled the clear plexiglass frame for the painting almost as quickly as Josh or Grace too.

"Twelve?" Grace asked, intruding on Liam's mental picture of unscrewing the tiny bolts, replacing the modestly sized sketch, and then fitting the bolts again.

"Twelve?" Molly whispered.

"Twelve?" Liam asked, backing away before the guards arrested him for their assortment of bruises.

"*Twelve*," Josh muttered, and Liam breathed a sigh of relief.

"Everybody's clothes are in the bathrooms," Josh said. "Ten minutes to change. Break."

Tonight, Liam thought, when he'd literally rinsed away the sweat in his armpits and asscrack and held Josh in his arms, he'd ask Josh where the expression "Break!" came from. The crew used it a lot, and he wondered if it was a sports term, since their basement meeting room was decorated with the colors and logos of every sports team in Chicago.

His mind was wandering, a stress response, he knew, and he pulled it into focus again as he spotted his bathroom. Every one of them had a different restroom to run into, and every restroom had a yellow backpack with a worn, nondescript T-shirt in it, and a pair of pants in anything but black.

Tienne was waiting in Josh's bathroom so he and Josh could exchange clothes. Tienne wore a white shirt and tan baggy shorts, and within minutes, he was escaping wearing all black with a yellow backpack that held a rolled-up reproduction of Rembrandt van Rijn's *An Angel with Titus' Features*, which had disappeared from circulation when the Nazis had stolen it in the late 1930s.

They didn't think the authorities would care that the reproduction was missing, since the real one was now hanging in its place, and Danny did like his trophies.

Twenty minutes later, Liam was back in the Palais Royale shopping center, his yellow backpack on his back, the black one wadded in his pants pocket, while the Louvre, he was sure, was swarming like a hornet's nest.

"How we doing, gang?" Josh asked, and Liam glanced up to see him walking briskly toward their exit platform.

"Grace and I are heading for the airport," Molly said. "Peace out. Good job, everybody."

"Liam, don't let Josh die," Grace said, and Liam grimaced, because of course he said it.

"Josh can take care of himself," he said, and was relieved by Josh's gentle snort.

"Tor and Marco are in place for our signature," Stirling said. "And I just got word that stage one is complete on the other side of the world."

Liam let out a breath. Stage one had been the most dangerous part.

"And I'll be sitting next to Josh in five," Liam said.

"Off to Germany to meet our next team."

"Good work, everybody," Josh said. "Comms off."

Liam watched as Josh hit the bud in his ear, and then, to Liam's horror, he staggered. It was almost imperceptible—if he hadn't been watching to see if Josh was okay, he would have missed it. In spite of their plan to meet when they sat, Liam picked up the pace, coming alongside Josh and slipping his arm around his waist.

"Almost missed you," he said, breathing with relief as Josh let him support some of that slight weight.

"I'm here," Josh said, his breath coming fast.

"Adrenaline?" Liam asked kindly.

"Didn't expect to crash so hard," Josh muttered. "God, I'm glad we're not flying to Germany."

"Not too much longer," Liam said, kissing his temple.

There were big screens along parts of the mall concourse, showcasing things to visit in the Louvre, and suddenly the one in front of them erupted with a breaking story.

The volume was turned down, but Josh and Liam got a good view of the famous glass pyramid above them, and the hologram bounced off one of the panes into the pathway to the museum itself.

It featured an outstretched hand, beams of rainbow light coming from the fingertips.

"Nice job, Stirling," Josh murmured as they rushed past.

"Did Tienne design that?" Liam asked. He'd only heard the caper finale described as "the signature."

"Oh yeah. Danny gave the specifics, though. He said Kadjic's smart but unimaginative. It's why he keeps stealing and hoarding art. He doesn't understand it himself—he just wants to keep it from other people."

"Nice," Liam said thoughtfully. "So Danny's rebranding. Instead of 'Lightfingers,' meaning 'thief,' he's becoming 'Lightfingers, the spreader of light.'"

"Exactly," Josh said, and they passed under the archway to the train platform. Josh's ankles wobbled on the raised bumps alerting pedestrians of directions and platforms, and Liam pulled him a little closer.

"So, should we—"

"Here's our platform," Josh interrupted, like he knew what Liam was going to say.

"I guess not," Liam muttered. God, this sucked. He'd never realized that taking on the care and feeding of a lover meant taking over from a perfectly competent group of parents who had already proven they'd go to hell and back for their son.

"Please," Josh said as they came to a halt, waiting for the train that would take them to a hotel in Bavaria where their luggage had already been sent.

Liam sighed. "We get some rest before the next one, right, boy-o?"

And Josh must have been tired because he let this slide.

"It'll take a week for the others to get into place," he said. "But we need to do some sightseeing in the meantime."

"Sightseeing I can handle," Liam told him. "But steady bedtimes and solid food will make me a very happy zookeeper in the meantime."

"Fair," Josh said. "Besides—Michael really hasn't seen anything outside the US besides the Caribbean so far. If we're going to be smuggling him around the world, we should show him and Carl a nice time this go-round."

Liam allowed himself to be distracted. "It's funny that he's the one with the big scary passport—of the lot of you, he's the *least* inclined to break the law."

Josh didn't have time to agree. The TGV/ICE came to a halt just then, and they jumped on, Liam shouldering his way through a dense crowd that was off-putting to a lot of Americans, before spotting two seats facing forward and dragging Josh into the one next to him.

Josh sank gratefully, leaning immediately against Liam as the rest of the car filled up.

"You doing okay, boy—"

"Fuck," Josh muttered, and Liam's tongue froze and then his heart and lungs and then his stomach and then his balls.

A small stream of crimson dripped from Josh's nose as he dug frantically through his pockets for a microfiber cloth to sop the flow.

BY THE time they pulled into the station in Bavaria, Liam was thoroughly wrung out, not from the gig but from worry. In spite of Josh's reassurance that he needed to take his iron pills and get some sleep, Liam couldn't help but remember the entire year previous, when the state of Josh's health had stood like a cinder block between them.

He reached for his phone a dozen times to tell Danny and Felix that it was time to pull out, to get another point operator for the scheme, because Josh wasn't ready yet.

He didn't, though, because Josh would probably accept and forgive a romantic betrayal a lot easier than a betrayal of a secret to his family. The one thing Liam had learned in the past year was that this family's currency wasn't in cash, gold, or diamonds—it was in trust.

Josh trusted him right now, but Liam had to figure out how to get him to trust that Liam would work with his family or not at all.

Liam summoned a rideshare in spite of the short, maybe four block distance to the hotel, and in no time at all the two of them were bathed, changed, and Josh, at least, was ensconced on the couch, a throw wrapped around his shoulders while he ate a hearty soup.

"Good?" Liam asked, coming out of the bathroom and toweling his hair.

"It's not hasenpfeffer," Josh said dryly.

Liam gave him a blank stare.

"You know, hasenpfeffer? Rabbit stew? Didn't you ever watch Bugs Bunny cartoons?"

Liam snorted. "No, and you shouldn't have either. Those didn't always age well."

"Politics, schmolitics," Josh chided. "If you don't think a rabbit in a dress is funny, we've got nothing in common."

"I'll give you that," Liam said, flopping down on the couch next to him. "When do our guests arrive?"

Josh took another bite of soup, giving Liam a sideways glance that said he wasn't feeling great, and if Liam hadn't been there pushing things, he would have shoved the bowl aside.

Liam gave him a stern glare, and he sighed.

"Tomorrow morning," he said. "And they should probably sleep for a day or two, and then we're off scoping out the next job."

"Good," Liam said. "So we'll do the same."

"Don't you want to do the tourist thing?" Josh asked in surprise. "I know you get to travel a lot, but…." He smiled winningly. "Bavaria. Andechs Abbey is close by, and there's several schlosses."

"Castles," Liam supplied dryly, because, dammit, he *lived* in Europe.

"Yes, but schloss sounds so much grander, you think?"

"It does," Liam agreed, cupping the back of his neck. A soft shudder seemed to encompass him then, and Josh melted a little farther into the very comfortable couch and took another bite of soup. "You all comfy, boy-o?" Liam asked.

"Yeah," Josh admitted, and Liam took the half-finished bowl of soup from him.

"So you need to listen to me, because I don't want this to be a fighting point. It needs to be an agreeing point."

"Go on," Josh said, swallowing.

"I won't keep a secret from your folks any more than I'd keep a secret from you, do you follow me?"

Josh, looking mildly embarrassed, nodded. "Yes, I follow."

"So here's what we're going to do. I am willing to hope that today's little incident was no more than pushing yourself too hard these last weeks, plus travel, which always whacks it out of you even if you've been doing it from the cradle, understood?"

Josh swallowed. "Yes."

"Good. So we'll take some days of rest—real rest. If we sightsee, we take a car, walk around for a bit, take the car back. No scaling walls, no hiking that dreadful hill to Andechs Abbey, which is a shame because their beer is first-rate."

Josh sighed. "I haven't even been able to taste it—everybody says that."

"Well, we'll have to come back," Liam told him gently. "But if you're up to full strength by the time Carl and Michael get here, I'll hold my peace, we'll do the gig, and you'll see your doctor when we get back to the States. Fair?"

Josh nodded like he was off the hook, but he wasn't.

"But if—" Liam had to clear his throat. "*If*, even *once*, you scare me again like you scared me on the train today, we will end up at Europe's famed social health care quicker than you can ask how much it will cost. Do you understand?"

"Don't rub it in," Josh mumbled. "Everybody in America knows you're more civilized than we are."

"Well, some idiots put the City of Batshit Crazy in charge," Liam said with compassion. Most folks in Europe felt sorry for their friends in the States these days. It was a terrible place to live right now—they could either fix it or flee. He was proud, really, of Josh's family for working so hard at fixing it. It was one of the reasons he was here.

"I'm really okay—" Josh began, but Liam shook his head and allowed some of his fear to show.

"Boy, I'll forgive you if you're not okay," Liam said, wrapping his arm around Josh's shoulders and pulling him close. "I'll forgive you for getting sick on me in the middle of this adventure and making me call your parents and tell them this happened on my watch. You know what I won't forgive you?"

"Dying?" Josh asked, and Liam's heart twisted, knowing that it had really come that close in November, and he and Josh hadn't even been allowed to *be* then.

"Pushing me away again," Liam whispered. "Not again. So you get used to that. You give me an honest evaluation. So right now, scale of one to ten?"

Josh grunted. "Five," he admitted. "I'm fucking exhausted."

Liam let out a slightly easier breath. "Fair. Stay honest. If you're not at a seven by the time Carl and Michael are up and about, you and I will go to the doctor, and if it's more serious than iron and sleep, we call your parents, understand?"

"Yes," Josh said, all the fight apparently beaten out of him by what had mostly been a pretty awesome day.

"Fair." Liam shuddered the last of his own stress into the couch, which he had to admit was extremely comfortable. "Now what are we watching?" He indicated Josh's computer, which was all set up with a movie, something mindless and entertaining and not in German, which Liam was fair at speaking, but his brain wasn't up to it today.

"*Reacher*," Josh told him, and Liam let out a delighted laugh.

"Trying to see how the other half lives?" he asked, indicating the title character's enormous size and muscular physique.

"It's so not fair," Josh grumbled. "Have you *seen* Chuck, Hunter, and Carl? Their bodies are *made* to stack muscles."

Liam kissed his temple. "Yeah, boy-o, but you've got a *really* wrinkly brain. Nature's got to balance these things out, yes?"

"The thought of you stroking my brain is absolutely terrifying," Josh said. "Let's watch the stupid show."

He was asleep before the end of the first episode, and Liam did what he hadn't done since they'd gotten back from the Caribbean in January.

Carried his boy to bed and tucked him in.

He was almost as insubstantial now as he had been then, and Liam thought he should maybe have a private chat with the one parent guaranteed to not lose his shit.

Because if he didn't, Liam might lose his own.

"TIRED WITH a nosebleed?" Danny asked as Liam crouched in the bathroom, feeling like he was texting his wife or something.

"Yes. He—I made him promise if he didn't feel better after some rest, we'd call you, but…."

"Nosebleeds are scary," Danny said soothingly. "I get it. But he's also right. The doctor said there could be lingering anemia, and his recovery period isn't anywhere near the three years they recommend. Of course, Josh was always an overachiever, but sometimes…."

"You can't rush healing," Liam murmured, and curiously enough he thought of his own father.

"I like your plan," Danny said. "Hold him to it. And call us if anything else happens. I'll put a line to his doctor now, and so if you *do* have to go in to the medicos, he'll be ready with Josh's records."

"Okay," Liam said, feeling better. "Good. I just…." How to say this.

"Needed a grown-up in the room," Danny supplied.

"Well, that's embarrassing."

"My boy, we are all high maintenance in this crowd. You may or may not have figured that out, but big personalities are often scar tissue over big damage. Second thoughts?"

"Absolutely not," Liam said fiercely.

"And witness," Danny said smugly.

Liam had to give him points for that, and then he rung off. Adrift a little, and not quite as tired as Josh but with the edge of his worry blunted, he finished off their dinner and then settled down to watch Josh's show.

It was entertaining, he thought with a yawn, finally exhausted. But he really did prefer his wrinkly brains to his giant biceps. It was a personal sort of attraction, and he'd stand by that choice any day.

Schloss

JOSH SLEPT for sixteen hours after they arrived in Munich, waking up around noon the day after arriving because—what else?—he had to pee. When he got back from the bathroom, he glanced around the suite and realized that Liam had eaten breakfast with, probably, Carl and Michael, and then taken off with them. He'd left a plate on the table, under a cover, with breakfast potatoes, fruit, and some sausage on it, and a text on Josh's phone.

Back by one. Carl and Michael are going to their room to rest. Love you.

Josh managed to devour everything on the plate, and was contemplating going back to bed when Liam arrived, breathless and buoyant, a small tourist bag in his hand.

"What?" Josh asked, smiling at him, thinking this would be what he looked like coming in from a morning run, or home from work after stopping for groceries.

Josh and his friends could be snarky and sarcastic, their brains constantly in motion, their edges honed by a vision of a world that was inherently unfair and needed constant tinkering. Liam, Josh thought, just liked helping people. He'd been proud of being able to help his mother with his younger siblings and proud of knowing his community when he'd been a flatfoot. And while Josh didn't think Liam realized it, what he'd done for Danny in that alleyway in Morocco had been extraordinary. It hadn't been the move of a law enforcement officer the way Josh's country understood law enforcement—but it *had* been the move of a compassionate person with the power to make things better.

It was that, perhaps, that had started the zing in Josh's blood. Not the story of Morocco, of course—Josh hadn't learned about that until long after their first meeting.

But Liam stepping up to help Josh and Stirling out of the van that night, and the way he'd simply caught Josh in his arms. All that compassion, all that surprising strength.

And whether Liam understood it or not, he was, by virtue of having a level head and a heart stouter than his brain was wrinkly, the grown-up in the room. There would always be tension, Josh thought, smiling besottedly and not caring. Josh knew how to be a crew leader—he'd watched Felix and Danny and Julia his entire life, and decided *that* was what he wanted to be. It was why he had never settled down on a major at school. The learning—*all* the learning—was the point. And then you used that knowledge to *fix* the things, make the world fair, level the playing field for people who needed the help.

Liam had simply learned to help. He didn't "lead a crew," he *cared* for a crew. That first kiss on the balcony in the dark had been the thing Josh needed with all his soul when he'd needed it most. From his first moment of contact, back in the alleyway in Morocco, Liam had been there—right down to trying so hard not to tell them all to shut up in the Louvre.

Now Liam held up the bag, somewhat triumphant. "Hair dye, tourist T-shirts, and, uhm…." His cheeks, usually a pale backdrop for those amazing freckles, turned ruddy. "And socks," he admitted. "I did not pack *nearly* enough socks."

Josh laughed, delighted. "Felix and Julia sent me to Europe on a school trip once, the summer after Danny left. I think they were trying to make me feel better, but I remember Julia talking to my father after one of the parent meetings." He straightened his posture and mildly cocked his head, assuming his best impersonation of his mother. "Felix, I don't think he'll fit in with the other boys."

And now he raised his chin and puffed out his chest, like his father when he was owning a boardroom. "Well, why not, dearest?"

"One of the other mothers asked how many socks we should pack, and the counselors replied we should purchase a brand-new package of twelve socks, be prepared to never see a single one of them again, and be grateful for that."

He gave his best Felix-trying-not-to-boggle impression. "I think maybe our Josh is a bit more mature than those other boys. Should we go ourselves and take Dylan Li with us?"

Liam had settled down next to him and was gasping with laughter at that point. "Oh my God," he choked. "That was amazing. So did you?"

Josh shrugged. "Of course. They were my parents." He smiled in reminiscence. "Grace and I were going on the London Eye for the second time. My folks were done with it, but Danny slid on, took a selfie with the two of us, and then slipped away when we disembarked. They didn't have a clue until they were looking through the family photos at the end of the trip." He sobered. "The expression on Felix's face…. God. I never want to feel loss like that."

Liam captured his hand. "Me neither," he said soberly.

Josh stared at their entwined fingers for a moment. "Maybe this was why I put us off for six months," he murmured. "This thing in me, what I feel for you, it was enormous after those weeks on the ship. But now, now that we've… *become*, I guess, we just keep *becoming*, more and more and more. I wasn't strong enough then. I was, quite frankly, too scared for myself to be a good lover for you. I… I mean, I'm tired, not gonna lie, but I feel like my heart's stronger, if that makes any sense. Strong enough to accept all that you are."

Liam kissed his knuckles. "Lots and lots of pretty words, pretty boy," he whispered, "for a very simple man."

"It's easier to be perfect when you're simple," Josh said, smiling at him. "And just because most of us have an IQ of buzzenteentwelve, that really doesn't make our lives any easier."

"Buzzenteentwelve?" Liam echoed, his mouth pulling in at the corners as he suppressed a smile. "Is that a Josh IQ, a Grace IQ, a Stirling IQ, or a Molly IQ?"

Josh couldn't help the giggles. "I think you have to combine the four of us to get above buzzenteen," he said. "The twelve is all Grace."

Liam snorted.

"What?" Josh asked. "What was that noise for?"

"I do email your parents about you," he said.

"That's sneaky." Josh had known that—he had—but as open as his family could be, he suddenly wondered what they said about him. "What's it mean?"

"It means," Liam said, grazing Josh's knuckles with his lips, "that they're pretty sure you fucked off on those tests you and Grace took so Grace would have the higher numbers."

Josh groaned and hid his face against his shoulder. "No," he said. "They told you that?"

Liam nodded soberly. "Danny said he'd never been prouder of you—it was one of the world's greatest grifts. Kept you in the same classes, made sure *you* didn't get transferred to a different school, and—" Liam regarded him with such profound admiration, Josh had to squirm. "—gave Grace something to cling to, something to make him feel better about himself when he needed it most."

"Oh God, stop," he muttered.

"No," Liam said. "You opened your heart to me in a big way, Joshua Salinger. I want you to know I understand *all* of what you are."

Josh gave him a shy smile and watched something complicated happen to Liam's expression.

"Josh, do you have a middle name?"

Josh shrugged. "Daniel," he said.

Liam let out a ragged laugh and pulled Josh against his chest. "Of course it is," he whispered.

Josh sat there, feeling safe, and for a moment his restless, overpowered brain didn't demand a damned thing from him, other than that he allow Liam to love him.

He would never understand people like Kadjic, he thought fuzzily, or any of the other people he and his family had waged quiet wars against. Why would you sell drugs or traffic humans or deal in weapons or anything else destructive and awful when you could sit and have a simple conversation with a good human, and he could make your world shine?

He allowed Liam to push him back to bed some more, and he woke up at six when Carl and Michael came over, amazing Bavarian takeout in bags hanging from their hands.

For an hour they ate schnitzel, wurst, potato dumplings, and apple strudel while Michael and Carl talked about Neuschwanstein Schloss, where they'd spent most of their day.

Josh held his tongue for most of the meal, letting Michael talk about the wood finish of the great canopy beds and the floors and moldings, as well as the tapestries and fine fabrics that decorated the rooms in King Ludwig's celebration of being rich and comfortable and liking nice things.

It was hard—he had to stop himself from asking about security, or the Rothschild jewels, or the painting stolen by the Nazis and saved by the Monuments Men, but Carl caught his eye and shook his head.

Josh remembered that shining faith Liam had in him, that he was more than a buzzenteentwelve IQ, and calmed down.

Josh had been coming to Europe since he was a child, but Michael had grown up hard in the Texas panhandle, and for most of his life, he'd assumed that his marriage to a wife he loved but didn't desire and their children would be the extent of his world. He was a criminal, so getting a passport would have been damned hard if they hadn't had Tienne forge one for him, and kiting around the world as a member of the crew and Carl's boyfriend was an adventure he hadn't once dreamed about, not even when he thought he was reaching for the stars.

Carmichael Carmody had earned the right to babble on and on about a castle, because he'd never believed such a thing existed in the world.

Josh relaxed into the dinner and allowed Michael's wonder to infect him, allowed himself to get happy about visiting a monument to love.

Finally Michael wound down and seemed to realize he'd talked through the entire meal.

"I'm sorry," he squeaked in the middle of waxing rhapsodic about the topiary garden and the labyrinth in the grounds. "I'm… I bet you guys see this stuff all the time."

"But never through your eyes," Josh said earnestly. "It's *so* much better listening to you talk about it than it was when I came here in high school with my class."

"Your class took you to Germany?" Michael said, breathless with surprise.

"Our suburb is *really* rich," Josh apologized. "I mean, the bad part of that is that we take things like Neuschwanstein for granted, and we shouldn't. You were there for a couple of hours and *look* at everything you loved. That's really the way to do it, Michael. Did you take lots of pictures for your kids?"

Michael's smile peeked out, revealing teeth that hadn't been fixed with braces when he'd been a kid but so much heart. "Oh, I did. I bought them all teddy bears and reproductions of the carvings and the sculptures and the paintings. Carl's going to post them tomorrow for me, since, you know." His smile turned mischievous. "Not supposed to be here and all."

"I've got a package I'll need you to send to my mom," Josh told him, thinking about the giant pink diamond Grace had stolen from the Louvre. "I'll need to get one of those stuffed bears first, though," he said.

Carl nodded placidly and took a lingering bite of schnitzel. Carl was forever watching his weight, but Josh noticed he'd slimmed down *a lot* in the last year and hoped he'd stop watching. Carl's placid demeanor and absolute calm turned out to be one of the crew's biggest cons—Carl was an outstanding boxer and tied for second for their best muscle, and he was nearly as smart as Josh, Grace, and Stirling, knew a number of languages and, best of all, how to navigate foreign legal policy and bureaucracy. A few extra pounds didn't detract from his effectiveness in the least.

Now he swallowed and settled back from the table with a replete sigh. "You're being very good," he said, "but would you like to know about the security now?"

Josh closed his eyes in gratitude. "You really do love me, don't you, Uncle Carl?"

"Never doubt it, kid," Carl said kindly. "Now for starters, the security system around the sparklies is *very* much the same as it was with the Louvre."

"Glass case, contact point alarm system—"

"Heat and touch activated," Carl finished. "We can freeze the server monitoring the pressure points and the temperature, but it's still going to take some real speed and sleight of hand to replace the fake with the real one. There's a security guard at the entrance and exit to the bedroom where the jewels are showcased, and we need a plan to get their attention. The problem is…." He sucked air through his teeth, and Michael filled in the missing word.

"Ambience," he said decisively, his twang sounding more pronounced than usual.

"Ambience?" Josh asked, blinking rapidly. It was a word he hadn't been expecting.

“That’s the word,” Carl agreed, and he reached into his pocket and pulled out fliers and maps of their target. “Listen, the Louvre was better guarded and more public. We all know that. And their security system was top notch—that’s why your team was bigger. But this place isn’t only *smaller*, it’s less crowded and less noisy. And there’s not just *fewer* people, there’s *much* fewer people. There were at least five minutes today when Michael and I were the only two people in a room, minus the security guards. Using Tienne as a shill and Grace as a simultaneous feint was brilliant, but that’s too noisy for this. There’s a hush around this place. It was built to be a refuge for King Ludwig, and also a *fantasy*, his own personal mental vacay, but dreamy. We can’t have art students doing parkour through the hallways. It’s disrespectful.”

Josh grinned at him. “I agree. But while I *didn’t* know about the extra guards, I *do* have an idea.” He smiled at Liam. “So, how game is Interpol?”

Liam squinted at him. “Game?”

“Well, we’re not technically taking anything—”

“A rather brilliant fake,” Carl said soberly, “of a casket of enamel painted on silver, surrounded by a king’s ransom—literally—of jewels.” He shuddered. “I can’t believe you put it in your luggage and brought it here.”

Josh grinned and glanced around conspiratorially. “Want to see it?”

Michael’s eyes almost bugged out.

Josh went to his luggage and found the special compartment holding the casket, which was about the length and width of a paperback book, with a depth of about four inches, in an elongated octagon. And it *was* exquisite, encrusted with the brightest of jewels: rubies, sapphires, emeralds. It had been commissioned in the Victorian age by one of the *many* Rothchild heirs for his daughter and later stolen by the Nazis when they’d plundered Paris.

After it had been returned by the famed Monuments Men, American soldiers whose job it was to save the treasures of the world from the predation of monsters, the Rothchild family had gifted it to Neuschwanstein so it could belong to the public. It was part of *many* treasures in the castle from the same bequest.

Except Danny had stolen it fifteen years ago as a present for Julia, who had been—by her own account—blue. Josh was old enough to start school (although they'd pull him out in a year or two), and while their household was warm and happy and full of laughter, it was also not what a young wife and mother dreamed of as a child.

And according to Danny, it had started to hit the three of them that they'd signed onto this grift for life.

Danny had apparently been in and out of the mansion at Glencoe at this time. Julia and Felix had been busy building Felix's empire out of the crumbs Julia's father threw her, and Phyllis was there for Josh if Danny warned them he was going to be gone. Josh remembered that—Danny sneaking into his nursery, giving him a hug, and promising to bring back a gift. He never went back on those promises, Josh remembered, until the time he'd left for good.

One night he'd gone into Josh's room, said he'd be back in two weeks, and had returned with a gift for Julia and a science kit for Josh.

Josh never knew what he'd brought back for Felix, but this had been the period when they'd always reunited happily, before Danny's drinking had begun to infect the family like a scotch-scented plague over the sun.

"It's beautiful," Michael said reverently, gazing at it as it sat on the table in a puddle of silk. "What made Julia decide to give it back?"

Josh shrugged, remembering the moment she and Danny had shared.

"She said it was never really hers in the first place. It's one of the few things Danny ever stole that he felt bad about. It had been saved from the Nazis and bequeathed to the public—but look at the pictures painted on it."

He held up his phone to use as a magnifying glass so they could get a good look at the etchings on the tiny silver panels and Carl and Michael gasped first, then Liam, who had done the same with his phone.

"Oh," he said, glancing at Josh.

The pictures, to a one, were of a lovely woman, dressed in full Victorian regalia, and her child. Whether walking hand in hand under almond blossoms or playing on a swing or eating dinner, the little boy wore bloomers, and the woman had the elaborate coif of the age, but they were obviously very happy in each other's company.

"For his daughter and grandson," Josh said. "Unfortunately, the daughter died in childbirth with her second child, so the casket has always been in public circulation, but Danny—well, he said that you grew less self-centered with age."

"Back then, what mattered was I saw a pretty thing for my loved one, and I wanted it," he said. "But this one haunted me. This treasure truly belonged to the world, and I stole it for my own. This isn't a rope of jewels shoved in the back of a museum that will never be shown again. This one is haunting. I found a replica—a good one—and replaced it, but I think the world should have the real thing again, don't you?"

"And this was a good time to replace the thing," Carl murmured. "How very Danny."

"Yes," Josh agreed with a little smile. He glanced at Liam and then at Carl. "So since we're going to advertise the return after I'm out of there—"

"Wait," Michael said. "So this isn't a switch?"

Josh grimaced. "Well, this one doesn't work unless they realize it happened. So we're going to have to simply put this one side by side with the other one, close the case, leave a marker that says 'Lightfingers was here,' and get away scot-free."

"Well, why don't we just set the casket down and run?" Michael asked, looking at everybody.

Carl snorted, the sound pure offense. "Because that's a terrible thing to do to Danny's reputation! No, this thing was stolen, and the replica has sat, pretty as a baby's first smile, on a green velvet cushion under a glass box for the last fifteen years. We need there to be both a subtlety and a flair here."

"Okay, then," Michael said slowly. "So we need to set the two boxes side by side and have somebody come in to… whatzit?"

"Authenticate it," Josh said, nodding. "Ideally, yes. So Carl's right. It can't be a smash and grab or art students doing parkour. It's got to be a 'now you don't see it, now you do,' sort of thing."

"So," Liam asked speculatively, "why did you ask me how game Interpol is?"

"Well," Josh said, giving him a kind glance, "how about we do this—and I know it's terrifying for all of us—but partly on the up-and-up. Liam and Carl distract the guards with some—"

"Not Liam," Carl said, making Josh blink. "I know you're trying to make him legitimate here, and it's a nice thing to do, but it's too suspicious. Liam shows up and the box shows up? Whether his job backs him or not, suddenly Liam's got a mark. He's been pretty pristine in all of our adventures so far—let's keep him that way."

"So what do you recommend?" Liam asked. "Because I saw that coming and I was on board."

"It's easy." Carl shrugged. "I saw five or six pieces my company ensures while we were there. Two of them were in the bedroom. I call the guards over, point out the weaknesses in the alarm system—and there were several—and while I'm doing that, Michael freezes the wires from the alarm to the wall, which gives you the five seconds to break the contacts and replace the box." He dusted his hands. "Easy peasy."

"Well, what do *I* do?" Liam asked, sounding miffed.

"Cover me on my way out," Josh said. "Also, you're in charge of the signature."

"What *is* the signature?" Michael asked, and Josh, feeling thick, stood up and went to search his luggage again.

"Actually, when we go out tomorrow—"

"When *you* go out tomorrow?" Liam said, catching his eyes.

Josh was going to shake him off; he was good at it. But he'd promised. He'd *promised.* "Six," he said.

"Not good enough," Liam said firmly, and when Josh felt the argument tripping on his tongue, Liam softened his voice. "You promised."

Josh sighed. "Can we at least go out to eat? Do some errands? Sightsee a little?" He tried his most winning smile, and Liam shrugged.

"Nap in the afternoon, early bedtime," he maintained, and Josh conceded.

Or, well, he yawned. Concession was sort of implied.

"Fine," he said, digging in the pocket of his luggage. It was more than a zipper—everything about the luggage was specially made, including the hidden pockets in the regular pockets. After a moment he produced a stack of fifty holographic stickers wrapped in plastic and pulled out another that he showed to everybody and then stuffed back in the bag.

"Once we pulled the job in France, we figured Kadjic'd be on the alert for things. He won't need the big gesture anymore—the small shit will catch his attention. So put these out tomorrow. Backs of traffic signs, park benches, that sort of thing. A couple in an area. Be subtle, don't get caught. We picked Munich because he's got enterprises nearby—nothing big enough for him to be visiting, not after all the shit that went down two days ago—but big enough for his people to start talking about the logo popping up. And, I shouldn't have to remind you…."

He paused with the stack of stickers extended to Carl.

"Don't get caught on camera," Carl said blandly. "Trust us, Josh, we're not stupid."

Josh handed the stickers over. "I know you're not," he admitted. "I'm just frustrated at not being able to go out and do it myself."

"Well, here." Carl pulled out a handful. "Trust me, I've helped Michael's kids with stickers. That will feel like buzzenteentwelve."

Josh grinned at him, because that number was sort of a family favorite, and Liam grunted.

"So," he said, "how much *is* a buzzenteen? Is it more or less than a googolplex? Is it smaller than infinity and bigger than a baker's dozen? I feel like I need buzzenteen maths now that I'm road-tripping to perdition."

"I figure," Michael said complacently, reaching for another slice of schnitzel, "that a buzzenteen is the amount of minutes left in the workday when you woke up really wishing you could stay home and watch TV in your pajamas."

"Times the percentage of your day you spent imagining you could squish your boss's head," Carl said, nodding sagely.

"Oh! I get it," Liam said. "So buzzenteen is the number of meetings I have to have before I dodge out of the next one and go solve the case myself."

"Or the number of heartbeats you have between when Grace goes early and you're actually supposed to be sprinting through the Louvre," Josh said with an exaggerated wipe of his brow.

"I get it now," Liam said, tugging on Josh's hand so he'd sit down. "Buzzenteen maths. I now have a new skill."

There was some laughter, and then they went back to fine-tuning the plan. Tomorrow might be a rest day, but in four days, they were going to have to pull off the job and take the train to Prague.

Four days later, in a warehouse in Colombia

MOLLY GOT *really* angry when people didn't know history.

"Did you know," she whispered, setting the explosive charge in the corner of the warehouse, "that when the farmers in this country were offered a chance to grow food instead of cocaine, they jumped on it? Did more to cut down drug trafficking than any amount of policing or violence?"

"Yeah, darlin'," Chuck said over comms from another warehouse, where he was doing, presumably, the same thing. "Do you know why they started growing coca in the first place?"

"Because the US paid them to in order to fund an unjust war in Nicaragua," she grunted.

"I know all this," Grace muttered from his own structure—there were three giant warehouses in Kadjic's compound, which Leon had needed to bribe, hack, and in his words, slither, in order to pinpoint. Lucius was in the pontoon plane, hidden in a cove of the nearby lake, which was almost dead from the pollution of processing Kadjic's cocaine, and he was, presumably, keeping an eye out for any more planes or transpo coming into the compound.

Hunter was… eliminating guards. Many of them were tied up and gagged—but not all. It was a bloody business.

"I'm just saying," Molly continued, leaping lightly to the ground on the other side of a massive stack of packed drugs, "that our country has a lot to answer for, and that was before the mad orange king."

"Darlin'," Chuck muttered, "can we not talk politics when we're trying to do some good along with the personal revenge?"

"Sure," she said, trying not to tug at her breathing mask. None of the guards wore them, but then, a lot of the guards had that twitchy appearance of addicts. The drugs themselves were triple-wrapped and packed—they'd already eliminated the guards around the processing buildings and set the unwilling workers free. Molly, Chuck, and

Hunter all spoke Spanish—and Chuck and Hunter spoke *Colombian* Spanish, because like most dialects, a regional difference was like a whole other language. They'd shooed the workers far, far away from the processing plant and gotten promises that they wouldn't return to their families or their villages until dawn.

Most of them had been dazed and tearful, many of them older women who weren't suited for sex work but were still trafficked in their own country.

It made Molly happy to think they'd be going home, but at the same time, she hoped they were *far* away from these warehouses before dawn.

If their crew did their job, they'd take out an entire branch of Kadjic's drug business. His cocaine operation would be completely defunct, and since he employed almost all local help, unless Kadjic was willing to move to Colombia, endure the heat and the humidity, and rebuild the machinery—from trafficked workers to hired muscle to actual infrastructure—he was going to have to kiss a third of his profits goodbye.

And thanks to Leon's shipping business, Hunter, Carl, and Chuck had plans for the shipment of opium from Afghanistan that was another third of Kadjic's drug empire.

And once those were up in flames, they had a list of suppliers to send Nick, Josh's friend in the police department, who could take advantage of Kadjic's distraction and take out his meth distribution system entirely.

And when Molly and Grace had been on their way to Colombia, they'd gotten word from Julia that Kadjic's last known location had been Paris.

It was going according to plan—they were sending doppelgängers of each other across the globe until Kadjic was sure Lightfingers had accomplices everywhere, but he couldn't find them *anywhere*.

Stirling, still in Europe and doing the research with Danny while the rest of them did the jobs, was currently ferreting out Kadjic's human trafficking operation in Czechia, while Danny put the finishing touches on the Lightfingers caper that would bring Kadjic to them in Prague just in time to see the destruction of the third branch of his empire.

It was a dangerous operation, but the ultimate goal was to lure Kadjic into the open in such a state of mind that he finally led them to his own den, where his most prized stolen art pieces resided.

And once he was there, nail him to the legal wall.

Daring? Yes.

Risky? Oh, definitely.

But Molly loved daring and risky—and she was having the time of her life.

Except for this whole cocaine everywhere thing.

While not as foolhardy as Grace, Molly had experimented with illicit drugs as a teenager. She'd been lucky. Her foster mother had called her on it almost immediately and had said all the right things: Molly was smart and beautiful and most importantly, loved, and adolescence may have hurt (because it *always* hurt), and Molly—abandoned as a toddler and in the foster system until she was eleven and Stirling was ten, had baggage that even her lovely foster parents couldn't lift—shouldn't risk throwing away the good things no matter how painful the bad.

Molly may still have gone Grace's way, which had almost killed him, except for Stirling, who had overheard Stella's conversation and stalked into her room after Stella had left.

Then he'd called her a selfish fuckheaded asswipe.

And then he'd cried.

And boom, Molly didn't have a drug problem anymore.

But she still remembered cocaine, because that had been the most fun. It had let her dance all night and get good grades and keep up with Josh and Grace and Stirling, who all seemed to have metabolisms of pure rocket fuel.

In the following months, she'd learned—mostly from Josh's subtle hints—that they got that way from *practice*, all the time *practice*, and that's when the ultracompetitive dance practices with Josh and Grace had started.

And she'd never been tempted, not once, to do drugs like she'd done as a teenager, but she still remembered cocaine.

She didn't want a grain of it up her nose. She didn't want it thundering through her bloodstream. She'd taken her adulthood and made it *hers*, and yes, there'd been a few romantic decisions she wished she hadn't made—nobody ever found true love on a club floor, or if they had, she'd never met that person—but drugs hadn't been part of any of it.

She wanted to keep it that way.

Unbidden, Robert Craig's earnest face passed behind her eyes. She'd had some time to talk to Liam's younger brother, and she'd been struck by the decency in him, the quiet strength of his family, gathering together, the support they gave Liam in spite of how far from his roots he'd gone.

The night Liam and Josh had arrived in England, she and Grace and Liam's siblings had stayed up talking, exchanging stories and such, and she realized how much of Liam's time with the Salingers had made it home to the East End.

She'd been asked everything, from how many bad guys she could beat up (from Liam's youngest brother) to whether she really did make her own clothes (from Liam's older sister) to a wistful request to see her and Grace dance (Liam's youngest sister). That last request they'd agreed to, putting on an impromptu exhibition to Grace's favorite classic rock song—"Come Out and Play" by Offspring.

Grace had gotten his own fair share of questions, and the whole time they'd answered, bantering back and forth like the siblings they'd become, Robert had sat there, eyes on her face, large and blue like Liam's, and a thoughtful expression, as though life had somehow surprised him.

That night Robert offered to show her to her room in his mother's big house, which was partially paid for by her children, who had moved her out of the tiny flat they'd grown up in. She now watched her grandchildren, and her youngest two grown children still lived at home, but they had "guest rooms enow," Robert said broadly and then smiled. Molly was pretty sure his accent wasn't that deep, and he'd been being playful.

When they'd gotten to the doorway, he'd done the most unexpected thing.

While Molly was looking for that often-elusive way to untangle from an awkward social situation, the kind where you get to know somebody too well over too short a time and you didn't want that magic to end, Robert had kissed her.

It was a simple kiss, gentle, a little bit of tongue, but her mouth had fallen open in surprise. He'd gone a little further then, and before he could get *too* forward (and oh, it had been so long, and she'd been so willing), he'd stepped back.

"We okay, then?" he asked.

She'd nodded, still speechless.

"Good," Robert said, kissing her forehead this time. "When you and my brother are all finished with this super-secret mission of yours, I sure would love to see you again."

She'd stared at him, suddenly seeing the appeal of Liam, whom she'd almost thought too plain for their Josh, and blurted, "You know my hair is really red. It's wild. I have no idea how long this pressed straight blond thing is going to last. My brother will kill me if I don't dye it back."

Robert grinned. "I can't wait to see it, Molly girl." And in spite of the fact that Chuck and Carl called her this all the time, this was the first time it had ever sent a thrill down her spine, and she'd almost wept with the awesomeness.

The next day during brunch, before they'd run off for the train station, he'd caught her hand and told her, "I meant it, last night. You come back. We'll see London right."

And even though, like Josh, she'd had a lot of chances to explore Europe, she couldn't imagine having seen London like she'd see it through this man's eyes.

So here she was—she and Stirling had avenged their foster parents, her little brother had found the quiet artist geek of his dreams—and she adored them both—and Grace and Josh, whom she loved almost as much, looked like they were going to live, and that hadn't been a given for either of them at different times over the last five years.

She had so many amazing uncles and a big sister in Julia and best friends, and now, after whining about it for two years, she had a prospect, a *really* lovely prospect, to date, and she was surrounded by the one truly stupid thing she'd ever done in her life.

Cocaine.

She felt like this was some sort of test. And it wasn't even like she was tempted, but just to have this shit all around her was terrifying.

Chuck spoke in her ear. "How we doing, Molly girl?"

Not Robert, but, well, Chuck was pretty solid as a big brother/uncle, so it did have some warmth in it. "Almost done," she whispered. "I've got one more charge to set—"

Lucius's panicked voice intruded. "We've got a swamp glider coming in. It's going to pass me right up, but someone must have sounded the alarm—"

"Shit!" Hunter swore. "We've got soldiers coming in this way. Chuck, grab a gun and get out front."

"Me and Grace will blow the warehouses," Molly said hurriedly, "and Chuck said something about getting the processing center too."

"I'll get it," Grace said. "Molly, ten minutes—go!"

"*Everyone off comms*!" Hunter ordered.

And the next eight minutes were a blur.

Molly knew it was eight minutes because she'd set her watch the minute Grace said ten. Her body was prime and muscular and fleet; she managed to scramble around her warehouse and then finish Chuck's while Grace finished his structure and went to the processing center too. The humid darkness around them was filled with gunshots and swearing and the occasional scream, and Molly, while surprisingly experienced in things like this for someone who didn't have a drop of military aspirations in her blood, worked hard to keep her thoughts focused and professional as she set Every. Fucking. Charge.

It felt like a hundred—in reality, it was only six.

But her watch said eight minutes, so since she couldn't use comms to check on Grace, she used the shadows to hide her sprint toward the long narrow building that had the tables in it where the product had been boiled, condensed, processed, cut, and bagged. Chuck had been going to do that one. He knew how to set the blasts so all the open powder on the tables didn't get aerosolized, becoming a mist of stuff nobody wanted to breathe.

But Molly was thinking *task*. She wasn't thinking *consequence*.

And there she was, thinking *task-task-task* and also *two minutes, a minute fifty-nine, a minute fifty-eight, task-task-task, a minute fifty-seven—*

When the processing building went kaboom, and Grace hollered, "Masks on, people!"

And Molly closed her eyes, pulled her hat down over her face and mask, and dropped to a crouch to avoid the rolling cloud of frosty death.

Most of her safeguards—her clothes, her posture—protected her from the bulk of it, but she still felt the tingling on the skin of her ears, the back of her neck, through the knees of her camouflage cargo pants.

She was alert enough that when Grace flew toward her, grabbed her arm, and practically dragged her through the forest until they had cover, she could stand and assist in her own defense.

"Goddammit, Grace," she gasped through the double layers of cloth over her mouth, "You went early."

"I am *so* fucking high right now," Grace gasped back. "The tarps weren't pulled tight on the other end. Gust of wind blew product in my face. Lucky *time didn't stop*. I'm buzzing so hard."

"Shit! Hold still!"

If somebody was overdosing on an opioid, they used Narcan to speed up their metabolism.

If they were overdosing on cocaine—which was *really* hard to do given how easily the drug was metabolized—their blood pressure was so high they risked stroking out.

So Molly—hell, all of them—were carrying small doses of lisinopril, which was designed to lower the blood pressure, just in case.

She had to grab Grace and force him to stand still to pop two tiny tabs in his mouth and make him dry swallow.

And then she watched him to make sure she hadn't overdosed him on blood pressure medication, which would cause his heart rate to drop.

They didn't have time to stare at each other long, because that's when the other three warehouses went up, a roar like a C-4 lion and a chemical eruption of hell throwing a fireball into the dappled black night of the jungle.

Molly was high enough to scream when they went off, her self-control gone, and Chuck's voice in her ear was panicked.

"Molly! Are you and Grace all right? Molly!"

"High as a fucking kite, Chuck, but breathing!"

"Grace?" Hunter said, his own voice strangled.

"Oh my God," Grace said. "If this had happened when I was seventeen, I would have gone back for another face full!"

"Oh God," Hunter muttered.

"Don't worry," Grace said. "It turns out, *drugs suck*!"

And then he bent over, ripped off his mask and his balaclava, and threw up in the bushes.

Molly held his head and pulled a bottle of water from her cargo pants, and together they went back to hiding in the bushes and listening while Chuck and Hunter did dangerous soldier things that they would ordinarily help with, but picking up a gun right now when their vision was swimming and the world had a fuzzy rainbow edge was a bad idea.

An hour later (or a year or a buzzenteen years later), Hunter's command of "Everybody back to the exfil. Lucius, start her up!" was met by Lucius's hearty, "Thank God!"

Molly and Grace untangled themselves from their huddle, as they'd come down from the dangerous high, both of them too fucked up to go grab a weapon and help. Self-awareness was a wonderful thing, and they weren't so cocky that they believed they were soldiers. They were thieves, and they could use weapons, but not like this.

"God," Grace muttered. "I'm fucking useless."

Molly started to laugh.

"What?" he asked.

"When I was seventeen, I would have snorted that off your dick and told myself you were straight."

It wasn't funny—it barely made sense—but Grace started to laugh, and then she laughed some more, and together they dragged their sorry asses back to the plane.

Chuck held her as Hunter took off, and Lucius, as though very conscious that Hunter wanted so badly to hold Grace himself, was treating Grace with the tenderness of an older brother to a younger sibling with the flu.

Once they were in the air, Grace said, "So did we do it? Can we move on to phase three now?"

Hunter's low, rather tortured groan was enough to tell Molly how badly they'd all been scared.

"A break," Chuck murmured. "We've got two weeks to rest and plan in Prague."

"I wonder if Robert would meet me in Prague," she slurred, thinking that if she hadn't been stoned she never would have said it.

"I'll ask him to come myself," Grace said. "After what we just did, we deserve all the things."

Molly laughed a little and wondered how she'd make this sound not so scary to Stirling, who still couldn't risk losing her.

And then she wondered how honest she'd be with Robert, who had told her he'd like to see her—red hair, curls, and all.

A man who could deal with her curls? Maybe that's what she'd needed all along.

Drops of Blood

THE GROUNDS of Neuschwanstein were stunning—wide and green, dotted with mazes and topiaries, and with the fairy tale castle in the background. Liam kept turning his face to the crystal blue sky, trying to raise his spirits to that level of beauty. But he couldn't. Josh kept saying he felt fine, but Liam's heart kept thudding weirdly in his stomach, so maybe Liam was the one who was sick.

But Liam had a clear picture of the night before, after a day touring Munich. Neuschwanstein wasn't the only castle in Bavaria, and the lovely greenery, even in late August, along with the reflective lakes, all displayed a certain… precision aesthetic, Liam guessed. A serenity and beauty that seemed to give every moment a fairy tale age. They'd eaten heartily, had some *amazing* light ale, and taken the S-Bahn across the city, getting off where they pleased.

The trip *had* been work to some extent. With suggestions from Carl and Michael, who had come the day before, they were mapping escape plans and alternative routes to the train and bus stations so they could split up if they needed to the next day and regroup in Prague. Their luggage would be shipped before they left the hotel, and they'd be doing the job, hopefully slipping away before a lot of chaos ensued, and then hopping on the train. If everything went well, they'd travel in pairs. If it didn't, well, they now knew the city, didn't they.

And Liam would be perfectly sanguine with all of that, except the night before….

They'd been so happy. Honeymooning, in their way, tumbling into the suite—and Liam had yet to get used to the posh rooms the Salingers rented—still laughing from watching a street magician outside the restaurant. The poor man had been either new or drunk or simply bad at his job, because they'd both spotted every move he'd made. At the end, Josh had dropped euros in his hat anyway, because, as he'd told Liam, at least he'd been *trying*, and Liam had loved him so hard right then—the heart of the boy, he'd thought helplessly. Who couldn't love the heart of him?

Their coming together had been laughing, with clothes being tossed everywhere, their hands lingering on each other's skin, their kisses playful. Liam could still feel the little thrill in his stomach when he realized that for all Josh's slightness, for his age, his chuckle was *deep* and throaty, male and adult.

The combination was as heady now as it had been in July at Celeste Buenaventura's terrible party, and Liam wasn't sated yet, wanted more and more. Josh's mouth, his taste, his laughter—Liam craved it *all*.

He'd had Josh his favorite way, underneath him, on his back, legs wrapped tightly around Liam's hips, little gasps of pleasure coming from his parted lips, when suddenly his body had gone slack.

He'd tilted his head to the side, and Liam had been horrified to see the drops of blood, black and oily in the dark, as they flooded his upper lip to the pillow.

While Liam had pulled out and run for a towel, Josh had rolled sluggishly to the side and mumbled, "Suddenly so dizzy… sorry… sorry…. God, so sorry."

Liam had come to his side, crouching naked next to the bed, heart thundering as he wiped the blood away and cleaned up the bed.

"No sorry, boy-o," he'd whispered. "Did you know it was coming?"

"I swear I didn't," Josh mumbled, obviously exhausted by the episode. "Fuck. Fuck." He took in gulping breaths through his mouth, and Liam had him sit up, running away to gather a bottle of water and a basin so he could rinse and spit.

A few minutes more and Liam pulled up the covers, as much to keep Josh warm as to avoid seeing him, pale and vulnerable and naked and sick, when they'd been in the throes of lovemaking not long before.

Liam found his own pajama bottoms and a T-shirt, and he turned on the bedstand lamp, sat, and smoothed Josh's hair back from his forehead.

"Did we overdo it today?" he asked softly.

"No," Josh muttered. "And not the day before either." He'd been so patient about rest days, and so excited about exploring the city—as well as scoping out the job. While Josh Salinger may not have paid a lot of attention to *schoolwork*, no matter what his grades said, he was obviously a big fan of *homework*, because Liam couldn't fault his professionalism when it came to a job.

"Then what—"

"Anemia," Josh muttered. "I swear it's anemia. I—" He swallowed and took a breath, like he was pulling on his grown-up pants, and Liam was glad one of them was.

"We have to do the job tomorrow," he said grimly. "Grace, Hunter, Chuck, Molly—they are putting their lives on the line tonight so we can go execute a cakewalk after a little bit of public defacement. It *must* get done, and while Carl's got the fingers for it, Michael doesn't—not at all." Michael's hands were scarred and callused, which was great for a mechanic, but not so awesome for a thief. "And you need to maintain plausible deniability. Carl was right. We can't drag your job into it—not now."

Liam didn't give a flying fuck about his job. He *thought* he had. In fact he'd been damned proud of himself. He'd thought he was a pretty solid officer. He'd made some busts he was quite excited about—some with Danny's help but some without. But now, watching the dedication of this bunch of thieves and grifters, Josh chief among them, who were willing to throw their own lives and safety on the line in order to simply balance the scales, Liam thought his job was the least of his concerns.

"Bollix the job," he said softly. "If I need to, I can do the drop—"

Josh shook his head. "No, you can't, Liam. You'll get pulled in for questioning if you get caught, and there goes the whole plan. No. Like it or not—and cakewalk or not—this whole thing hinges on me right now. I swear, I'll sleep in Prague. I'll even see a doctor in Prague. I'll fess up to the whole crew *in Prague*. But…." He gulped another lungful of air. "But tonight, I'm going to take my iron pills, have a midnight snack, and…." His mouth quirked upward, the first sign of true regret Liam had seen regarding what they'd been doing when this episode had begun. "And hopefully still be held by my boyfriend, who won't be scared off by a little blood."

Liam swallowed and nodded, stroking his cheek.

"Not scared *off*, luv," he said hoarsely. "Just scared. God, please don't tell me I can't be scared."

Josh closed his eyes then and captured Liam's hand on his cheek. "I'm scared too," he whispered. "Is that—can I say that? I-I'm so tired of being brave for everybody. I almost *died* last year. I remember fighting so hard for each breath, and Danny and Felix, they *prayed* for me, and I think they both told God to fuck off a long time ago. And I couldn't tell my mom—I couldn't—because I didn't want to let her down. And now I have you and…." He trailed off for a moment, and Liam wanted to soothe him, to calm him down, but God, he also really wanted to hear the end of that sentence.

"You have me and what?" he prodded, not proud of himself, but, well, Josh already knew him for his flaws.

"And I'm happy," Josh whispered. "My mom is finally happy. Danny and Felix are happy. I… I mean, I'll always worry about Grace, but he's finally happy and might not die tomorrow. And I have you. And you love me, and my heart is so… so full. And I don't want to lose that. I could live in a trailer in the middle of nowhere and never see a sky like today again as long as you loved me and my people were okay. But first…."

Liam saw the tear, saw the fear coming, and welcomed it. Oh God. His Josh, so snarky and full of life and determined not to ever let his illness or his hurt bring him low.

Liam rested his head next to Josh's on the clean pillow and kissed his forehead as his boy wept silently.

"It's okay, being scared," he whispered. "It's okay to let me see. How will you know I'll still be here if I never see you need me?"

"I'm sorry," Josh whispered, tiny sobs in his voice. "So sorry. I'm sorry. I'm sorry."

He'd fallen asleep that way, still weeping, and Liam had hovered over him until his breathing evened out. Then he'd cleaned up and brushed his teeth and crawled into bed on Josh's other side and held him tight.

And cried against his neck and hoped Josh slept through it.

It was okay if he didn't—Liam wasn't afraid of Josh knowing he was weak.

He had so many worse things to fear.

AND NOW, approaching the long drive to the castle via bus, Liam's fears were churning in his stomach with the bagel sandwich he'd split with Josh.

Protein, fruit, carbs. Solid food—not so much it weighed him down, but enough to nurture him.

Liam had even made him eat blueberries with his yogurt.

God, anything to feel like they weren't helpless against the sudden shifts of fate.

As the bus came to a halt, Josh and Liam disembarked casually, tourists excited to see King Ludwig's stone-and-marble monument to whimsy, and neither of them glanced over to see Carl and Michael getting out of a cab that they'd taken at the same time. Carl looked awkward in jeans, Josh had told them dryly. Carl needed to stay in slacks and a polo and do rideshare and not public transpo. He was a solid member of the team, yes, but a chameleon he was not.

Besides, Carl was going to talk shop with the security officers there, so he needed to appear somewhat professional.

Michael, on the other hand, had dressed casual, like Josh and Liam, in cargo shorts and T-shirts and ready to hop onto public transport on the way home.

Which was why they'd planned this down to the second. If their exfil was the tourist bus, they couldn't be the first—or the last—tourists on it.

"How you doin'?" Michael asked Liam as they loitered near a topiary. Josh was sitting nearby, taking pictures and apparently chatting with somebody cheerfully, and Liam was still a disinterested tourist. They hadn't sat near each other on the bus, but Josh had given him a subtle bump with a rub of his thumb on Liam's wrist as they'd disembarked, probably to still Liam's nerves.

It was kindly meant, but God, Liam was still shaken after the night before.

"He's not doing great," Liam confessed. He'd promised not to call Danny or Felix. Somehow this entire enterprise had boiled down to "Just let me get on the train to Prague!"

Michael *hmm*ed. "Yeah. He is a bit peaked."

It was such an old-fashioned word, delivered in Michael's unapologetic twang. Liam smiled at him, liking the smaller man more with every meeting.

"He just wants to make it onto the train for Prague," Liam said. "He's pretty sure it's a bout of anemia, but…." He didn't want to talk about the two nosebleeds or the exhaustion. Didn't want to talk about Josh's face going pale in the moonlight, and the way his eyes had unfocused and his body had fallen away from Liam's, limp and flaccid and unresponsive.

"We worry," Michael said, and Liam guessed he'd know. Earlier that year Carl had gotten injured by a lucky knife throw in the middle of an op, and a month after that had broken his wrist. Michael's boyfriend *seemed* like a safe bet in the worry department, but Michael apparently knew what it was like to worry about that guy who jumped in and did important things.

"Yeah," Liam agreed. He let out a little laugh. "I was thinking I'm the one with all the danger on the job, but it turns out this is what it's like to love somebody who misses jumping out of buildings."

Michael nodded. "You know, I've only known Josh since he got sick. You know the one thing that's always struck me about him?"

"What?" Because Liam had heard an earful from Josh, from the others, about who Josh *wanted* to be, who he'd been *before* he'd been ill, but this… this was how Liam had known him too.

"He's thoughtful," Michael said. "Like the other night, when he really wanted to talk about the job, but me, I was just…." He gave a self-conscious smile. "But he never interrupted me, never once said, 'Yeah, Michael, I know, I've been here before.' He asked me about my kids. Whole time he's been sick, he's been thinking about other people. Even you, I'd reckon. I think you've got the right of it, you know. You love the person you got, and if they're down, you hope for the times when they're not. But in the meantime, you… you know, love the person you got."

Liam smiled at him, that tingle of being in the presence of good family giving him some confidence for the next few hours.

"Capital advice, mate," he said, and Michael's grin was triumphant.

"I even got the accent and the fancy talk and all. You're good people."

Liam might have hugged him, but at that moment Josh stood and stretched and, without looking at either of them, ambled toward the castle.

It was time.

Josh was moving by himself, but Liam and Michael stayed close, partly so Liam could give Michael cover while he got into the corner of the room where the alarms were placed. When the contacts holding the glass case together were broken, a signal would be sent to the alarms to sound. It was an old system, but a good one, and Michael had a small aerosol can of liquid nitrogen that would freeze the wires and the signal box that enabled the alarm.

Liam's job was to cover for Michael as he got into place to freeze the wires, and then, while Carl engaged one guard talking about Serpentus, to go engage the other guard while Josh made the drop.

For a moment as Liam entered through the great doors, held open for the daytime tourists, he was distracted by the beauty of the castle itself. The woodwork—walls, floors, moldings, cornices—all of it hand-carved or lathed, lovingly oiled, and kept dust free, created a vast space of vaulted ceilings, rich tapestries, beveled-window crystals, and art, glorious art, on every wall, on stands and shelves, all of it well-lit and showcased for its full beauty.

Liam made a sound of want. He wanted time to linger here, to read the placards and the histories, to investigate the artists, the donors, the pure history of the place, but he couldn't. He was on a timeline and—

"We have forty-five minutes before the bus," Josh murmured, coming up behind him silently as he gawked at the entryway. "Find one thing, one glorious thing, and stare at it and study it until you get lost in it. Then it's yours when the job is done."

Liam glanced at him, took in his pixilated smile and the hectic color in his cheeks.

Was he well? No.

But he was having a damned good time.

"Suggestions?" Liam asked.

"Upstairs bedroom," Josh said promptly. "There's a stained-glass oriel in the bedroom. It depicts the swan knight, Lohen… something or other." He grimaced. "But there's swans and knights and the sun coming in, and it's a place you can sit and gaze out at the world—even though we can't actually sit there. Anyway, it's lovely."

"And you?"

Josh grinned. "In the shelves above the dining room there's a Fabergé egg *also* donated by the Rothschilds."

"You're not going to…," Liam inquired delicately.

"No, no," Josh said. "Besides, Grace already did, when we were in high school. We got almost to the airport before I saw it and made him take it back." He scowled. "Stupid Grace. *Almost* got us busted when we were here without our tour. Anyway, we never steal each other's targets. That's a bad way to maintain a friendship."

Liam raised his eyebrows. "Of course it is."

"I just want to visit it and tell Grace nobody's pinched it but him." Josh gave him a devil-may-care grin and waggled his eyebrows, and then Liam and Michael were on their way to see an oriel.

THEY WERE *almost* late to hit their mark, hurrying down the stairs on cat feet.

"Wow," Michael said for the umpteenth time.

"I'm at a loss," Liam said, trying to pull his brains back into his head. "So that's an oriel."

It was an odd, pretty word to describe what was basically a reading nook of grandiose, glorious proportions. The window—shaped by panels into a semicircle—protruded from the side of the castle, giving anybody sitting on the embroidered satin cushions a view of the topiary-strewn garden outside. The panels were decorated by an ornate frieze of stained glass, culminating in an obelisk at its peak, depicting Lofgran, the Swan Knight, the heraldic coat of arms for the castle itself. The effect *was* fairy-tale-esque, because apparently Ludwig II knew his enchantments, and Liam and Michael had spent a great deal of time doing what Josh had advised—taking it in.

"Glass and tape and solder and…." Michael blew out a breath. "*I* am full of wonder. I am so glad I didn't miss that this trip—we were all on the first floor last time."

Liam chuckled weakly and glanced at his wrist unit—and put on a little more speed.

He and Michael had time to slow down and calm their breathing as they entered the first-floor library and saw Carl talking to the security guard.

The security guard's back was toward them, and Carl, while not acknowledging Liam or Michael in any way, managed a faint flicker of his eyes to his right, and Michael peeled off toward the wall unit while Carl moved subtly to the left.

The security guard never even saw him.

Liam walked behind Josh, who was checking out a tiara with a series of truly resplendent teardrop-cut diamonds suspended along the bottom edge. As he passed, he nudged Josh's fingertips with his wrist and got a twitch in return.

He was the last in place as he pulled the security guard aside and asked him if there were any more stained-glass oriels in the place, nodding soberly as he got an answer not merely for Neuschwanstein but for several other of the Schlosses around Munich.

Josh turned, and, as Liam's watch buzzed, began his study of the jewel-encrusted casket, glowing in the sun.

Liam had never had an out-of-body experience before, but as he listened to the nice security guard speak with pride of this castle that he'd guarded for twenty years and expound on the importance of the Swan Knight heraldry to King Ludwig's family, Liam's soul seemed to rise up above Liam's thundering heart and count silently to itself.

Ten for the picking, one for the placing, one for the closing, one for the turning, ten seconds, nine, eight, seven—

Michael appeared from around the corner and sauntered by, indicating he'd frozen the wires for as long as possible and….

Josh was on his way out now, posture as relaxed as Michael's, and Liam was back with the nice security guard, who was only a little older than he was, and looking, well… oh.

Liam gave him a truly grateful smile and said, "I would love so much to stay and talk more, but my bus is leaving, and I will be flying out tonight."

The guard seemed satisfyingly crestfallen, and he slipped Liam his card, asking shyly for Liam to call him later.

Liam said he'd try, but he was already turning around and heading out the door, legitimately worried about the bus as he went.

He caught up with Josh right as Josh swore and pulled his T-shirt up to his face.

"Shit," he mumbled as Liam took his elbow. "Make sure I don't get any on the rugs—my God, they're priceless."

"I'm surprised you have any left," Liam said bitterly, and to his surprise, plan be damned, Michael took Josh's other side.

"Here we go, buddy," Michael said. "Let's get you outside." And quietly, he added, "I've got an extra shirt in my pack. You can wear it and use that one to sop the blood." Michael and Josh were of a size—two of the smallest in the group, sans Grace and Tienne.

Dad, Liam thought blindly. Michael was such a good solid father figure. It was hard to overestimate how much dad energy could calm a situation down. Liam had always been the dad energy in his house—it's what happened when you were the oldest. But he couldn't seem to summon that now, not when his lover, oh God, his *everything*, was bleeding and sick.

They made it outside in time to board the bus, where Josh hurriedly changed into a T-shirt with a Pokémon character on it, laughing a little as he held his own *Chicago the Musical* tee up to his nose.

The original plan was for the three of them to split up even on the bus ride, but Liam couldn't make himself do that. He took the seat next to Josh's and murmured, "Is it done?"

"You know," Josh panted, obviously fighting the sudden weakness that had beset him the night before, "you keep saying you love me, and then you insult me, cut me to the quick, by suggesting things like this. I'm starting to doubt your sincerity."

In spite of the worry and the adrenaline thundering through his bloodstream like timpani, in spite of the seriousness of what they'd done, Liam smiled.

"You'd better believe I'm sincere," he said, pulling out the card that poor Horst Tiesler had given him. "It's not like I don't have other offers, mate."

Josh tilted his head back and gave that wonderful, terrible jumping-off-buildings grin. "Lucky me, I'm a thief," he said. "Stole your heart already."

Liam gave a broken laugh and leaned back against the seat, squeezing Josh's thigh. "How you doing, thief of hearts?"

Josh seemed to melt under his touch. "My head is killing me," he confessed. "Could you pull some ibuprofen and water from my pack?"

"Protein bar?" Liam asked hopefully, but Josh shook his head.

"Real food," he said apologetically.

"Steak tartare and schnitzel?" Liam teased, because Czech food, which awaited them in Prague, was traditionally pretty rich.

"I'm missing London and gyro," Josh said dreamily. Well, the kiosk Liam had taken him to on the way to the train station had been one of the best, with seasoned lamb and cucumber-mint yogurt that Liam missed when halfway across the country.

It was also not nearly as rich as steak tartare.

"When this is over," Liam promised rashly, "you and me—we'll stay at my flat and sleep in and then go explore and…."

"And spend more than two hours with your family," Josh said. "You have good people, Liam."

Liam did—but right now, all his worry, all his heart, was invested in the thief of hearts at his side.

Liam's watch buzzed as the bus rattled down the road, and a text from Carl appeared.

Clear. Good job. Alarm never went off.

Liam glanced at Josh again, and his eyes were closed as he seemed to go deep inside himself. Liam had seen him do this on the boat, when his weakness and recovery had seemed overwhelming. He'd close his eyes and find the solid place inside that would keep him tethered to this earth.

He pulled out his phone. *Text Danny*, he tapped, knowing that Carl would be in the back of a rideshare and wouldn't have to argue with Josh about this. *Tell him Josh needs to visit a doctor in Prague.* Carefully, trying not to be obtrusive, he felt Josh's forehead, and found it hot and dry. *Tell him he's spiking a fever and has had two more nosebleeds.*

Fuck.

Yeah. See you in Prague.

Tell the kid he was amazing.

Will do.

And now Liam could see how Josh could boil his life down to "after the job." The job was done—they had a bus ride, a long train ride, to rest, to plan, to hope, to worry.

To wonder what their lives would be after this big job that would make them all safer in the world.

And suddenly Liam realized how very little his own job meant to him now. For much of the ten years after that first encounter in an alleyway, Danny had fed Liam tips to find the true bad guys Interpol investigated, and with a little steering from Liam, his department had managed to ignore one small-potatoes, mostly altruistic thief. The things Danny *had* stolen—he was especially fond of sparkly things from corrupt crime families, which he would steal on the heels of replacing priceless works of art—had usually been excesses of rampant greed on the part of the original owners. He'd once stolen some oligarch's second yacht—it had been recovered after being pawned for cash, which, Liam knew because he'd asked Lightfingers himself, had been given to a local homeless shelter, because Danny had been in a mood.

The things Liam had been chasing had been much like the things the rest of the team was chasing now. Guns. Drugs. Human trafficking. That had been good work, he'd thought then.

Now he was on the wrong side of the law but the right side of history, and his team was doing more good in three months than he'd done with government resources in the last five years.

He'd do this for the rest of his life, he thought wretchedly, hand convulsively squeezing Josh's thigh again as he watched the beauties of Munich pass by before his blind eyes. As long as he could have his thief of hearts beside him.

Prague

MAYBE IT was because he'd had three parents, but Josh had never wanted one more than the other there for comfort. His mother, warm, maternal, or Felix, strong and masculine, were both great at feeding that place in a child that needed to be reassured and cared for. And Danny, kind, funny, intuitive, had been completely wonderful. Although admittedly during the years he'd been missing from the household, Josh had rather hoped for Danny more than the other two because it meant they could see each other.

This last year, as awful as the cancer had been, had filled up Josh's reserves of Uncle Danny a little, repaired some of the damage done by missing him.

And the stories—from Liam, from Carl, from Tienne, even obliquely from Danny himself—had given Josh some insight into why Danny had needed to stay away. Josh's generation was good at telling people they needed to take care of themselves before they could care for others. Danny had been doing that—fixing things in himself that had been damaged even before Julia and then Josh had come along—so when he returned for his family, he could be this *force*, this amazing, kind, avuncular figure of fun and reason and fair play.

And Josh's Uncle Danny, who in spite of hurting—of screaming inside, Josh could see now—had been there through so much of Josh's adolescence, even though it meant being in proximity to the one person who had hurt him the most.

So when he opened his eyes in the hospital in Prague, he was not surprised to see Uncle Danny there, the window behind him dark with night. But he was so terribly grateful.

His eyes burned as he let down the guards he'd held in place, the fears he'd held back. Because Liam had been trying so hard to be strong, Josh hadn't wanted to freak him out more.

"There you are," Danny said with a smile, his eyes tired. "I've been texting your mother. She seems to think you were sleeping late simply to annoy her."

Josh found he was too tired to smile back. "That's a lie. She's been trying to get me to sleep more since I was seven."

"Yes, but now that you're grown, she expects more," Danny rejoined, but the levity was forced, even Josh could see it. Apparently Danny felt it, because his demeanor softened, became less brittlely cheerful. "Or maybe I should say she hopes for more," he said quietly. "How are you, my boy? And not the 'I'm fine' you fed to Liam. He saw through that, by the way—it's why he stopped asking."

Josh nodded, barely remembering the ambulance ride from the train to the hospital. Liam had told him they'd arranged for the ambulance to meet them in Prague about midway through the train ride, when "resting" became more like "loss of consciousness."

The ambulance had been the compromise between taking a cab or Liam demanding they stop the train and administer aid *immediately*.

Josh groaned and looked at the now-familiar lines of fluid—a saline drip and the more ominous red blood transfusion—being administered into ports in the back of his hand.

"This again?" he whispered, grateful his head had stopped pounding. Anemia did that, but so did leukemia.

"We don't know," Danny said softly. "You could have been right the first time—anemia from overdoing it. You should have seen a doctor in Munich, but Liam said you were being stubborn."

Josh's lips finally twitched. "He was hurting himself not taking me without my consent."

"Why didn't you go?" Danny asked.

"Superstition," Josh said baldly, because that's what it boiled down to. "I kept telling myself if I could just get the job done, then I could sleep and—"

"*Bollix the job*!" Danny cried, and Josh blinked.

"Danny…?" Josh said, genuinely surprised.

Danny shook his head and put a hand against Josh's temple with as much reverence and absolution as a priest. "It was never about the job," Danny whispered. "It was about doing something together. Don't you get it, Joshua Daniel? *Together* means you have to be there too."

"That's not entirely true anymore," Josh told him, suddenly feeling like the parent. "Grace, Molly, Chuck, Hunter, Lucius—they risked their *lives* the other night."

"That was our choice," said a familiar voice, and Josh rolled his eyes and hey, there was his headache. And his best friend. Together at last. "We love you, Recovery Boy, but I'm not getting a face full of cocaine for you. I was *down* for that clusterfuck. You talk about fixing the world? That shit was *prime* for being blown out of existence, I shit you not."

Danny's glance toward Grace, who was apparently curled up by Josh's feet—he could see him now—was affectionate. "Eloquent, Dylan Li," he said. "And you shall have to elaborate on the face full of cocaine. Sounds… invigorating."

Grace shuddered, sitting up and rubbing his eyes. For the first time ever, Josh could see the beginnings of a beard on his friend's usually smooth face. He would have to tease him later.

"Blew chunks like a *boss*," he admitted. "Molly force-fed me the liso, and *blech*. In case I ever wanted to do drugs again, now I don't. Hooray!"

"But how did it happen?" Josh asked, curiosity overriding the headache and weakness and the awful feeling of being near tears.

"A gust of wind through a plastic entrance tarp while I was setting the charges," Grace said, shaking his head. "Oh my God—*right* in the kisser. Had a cloth mask, but fuck me, next time I'm going full WWI gas mask because that shit was *heinous*. Blew the charge early, I was so hyped. It was a goatfuck." He grinned tiredly. "And then we get here and you're in the hospital again. I could cheerfully kill you."

Josh felt those tears again. "But you won't because you still love me, right?"

"Yeah," Grace said, dismounting the foot of the bed and coming up to hug him, in spite of the driplines and monitors and such. Carefully, because he'd had practice, he climbed in next to Josh and snuggled. "Still love you. Liam loves you too, by the way. We had to pry him from your side—he wasn't smelling too great. You neither. Get a shower, hippy."

Finally situated, Grace's body went limp, and Josh was pretty sure he'd fallen immediately asleep, like he did.

"Well," Danny said, wiping his face, "that was a timely break to save you from getting chewed out. Are you ready now?"

"They were counting on me," Josh whispered. "I didn't want to let them down."

"We could have done something else," Danny told him, smoothing Josh's hair back from his forehead with a cool hand. "God, Josh. What have we done—your mother, your father, me—what have we done to make our love feel conditional?"

Josh closed his eyes and swallowed. "Nothing," he said. "I just… you all gave up so much for me. How could I fail?"

"You can't," Danny told him, and Josh heard the sob in his voice, and maybe that little sound allowed him to finally get it. "You are such a good—*truly* good—person, Josh Salinger. Not simply smart. Not simply clever and fun. *Good.* Your heart is so pure. You can't let us down. Not if you get sick again. Not if you quit the game—"

"I love the game," Josh told him, closing his eyes. "No quitting the game."

"Okay, then. So maybe don't play it until it kills you, okay?"

Josh nodded. "I *would* enjoy some more time with Liam," he confessed.

"Well he… he's been in love with you probably before you met," Danny told him. "I'd say it was a fairy tale—"

"We just came from a fairy tale," Josh said, remembering the oriel and the egg. "Remind me to tell Grace it's still there."

"My egg?" Grace asked groggily.

"Yeah," Josh mumbled. "I checked—still real."

"Good night."

"Fairy tales aren't as hard," Danny said, ignoring their byplay as he often did. "Relationships take work, and you know that work, my boy. You've forged some first-class relationships, and they've forged their own. But you need to take Liam as seriously."

Josh swallowed. "I do, Uncle Danny," he said, his heart on his sleeve. "I… feel like he's everything I'd ever hoped for. It really is like magic. Like you couldn't be there for me, so you created my perfect mate by telling a witch all about me, and she made me a Liam to patch any holes you might have left."

"You," Danny said with a smile, "are getting a wee bit daffy. I'll be sure to tell him about it when he gets back."

"Where is he?"

"Felix took him to the hotel to wash up. Grace wasn't wrong about him getting a bit ripe."

Josh frowned. "How long have I been here—wait, Felix? Who's with Mom?" He tried to push himself up on his elbow and fell back against the bed, partly because Grace was holding on to him and grumbling, but mostly because his arm—oh fuck, his arm. What in the hell had happened to his shoulder?

"No-no-no—no getting up," Grace growled. "Stop talking and listen. My God, let me sleep."

Josh scowled but did as commanded.

"The train pulled into Prague the morning before yesterday—"

"I lost two days?" Josh gasped. They'd only had two weeks to plan!

"And your mother is here. She adores Prague, and she made me promise to take her around to show her the sights. She says she owes me for seeing it without her so many times. Also, she has plans to decorate my apartment—says it's 'bland.' But she'll have to wait until all our fellow miscreants clear out. Right now half our party is there, and half of them are at the Mozart, courtesy your rich Uncle Leon, who apparently owns a great deal of stock in that one."

Josh blew out a breath. "We know a lot of rich people, Danny."

"And a lot of people not so rich," Danny agreed. "I don't know what to tell you. But what's to do?"

"So what's everybody doing?" he asked, the exhaustion suddenly hitting him hard.

"What you're about to do," Danny said softly. "Sleep. Don't worry. We'll plot next week."

What was he not saying?

"What's next week?"

Danny sighed. "They took a biopsy of your bone marrow this morning, which is why your arm hurts. Tomorrow we'll know if your cancer's back. If it is, by next week we'll know how we're going to treat it."

"No…," Josh mumbled. "No… plan without me. Please." His eyes were closing. "Liam… tell Liam…."

Liam could take care of the family while Josh was sick. But Josh had fallen asleep as quickly as Grace. Goddammit. He had so much left undone.

HE WOKE up to bright morning sun, and a… a different presence at his back. A little bulkier, snoring softly, and something about the scent—clean, yes, but a little darker, more cedar….

"Liam?" he mumbled, and his mother, ethereally lovely as always, moved to close the blind so the sun was deflected to the ceiling and not in Josh's eyes.

"He's sleeping, darling," she said, turning toward him now that her task was done. Impeccable. Julia Dormer-Salinger always looked impeccable, he thought proudly. She was wearing a pale blue pantsuit, with a cream-colored blouse and a rope of pearls at her throat. Her hair was done up in a twist, and her makeup—always subtle—had masked some of the ravages of sleeplessness and worry.

But not all.

"Sorry to drag you out here," he mumbled.

"Not at all," she said sweetly, taking a seat next to his bed and picking up a paper cup of tea. "It's nearly September, and Prague is just breathtaking. It's a treat to come out this time of year." Her expression dimmed. "Unless, of course, I'm worried about my child. Not so much of a treat then, is it."

"Sorry," he said again.

"The person you should apologize to is lying right behind you," she said gravely. "You promised the world to him, Josh—do you understand that?"

"I don't want to let anybody down," he said.

"Oh, bollix the rest of us," she said sharply. "*He's* the one who's been waiting for you. We've had you. Do you want to break his heart?"

"Uncle Danny yelled less!" he complained, somewhat unfairly, and she gave a ladylike and delicate snort.

"Uncle Danny never had to convince you to do your algebra," she told him crossly, and he could see the marks of crying on her features and felt even worse. But instead of yelling more, she reached out and feathered that lovely healing mom-touch across his forehead.

"Don't mind me," she said softly. "Apparently it's a good thing I didn't have a whole day care center full of children, because I'm not great at balancing worry and pregnancy. And I'm not only worrying about you—although you do your share, let me tell you. The men try to keep the details from me, because my 'delicate condition' scares the raisins out of them—all of them. It's hilarious and terrifying. But I've caught some of the transmissions and…." She shook her head. "My God, the risks you all are taking. I can't believe I thought I could nap and retire during some of the planning stages and you all would carry on without me. Did Grace tell you about the cocaine plantation job?"

Josh's lips twitched. "Something about him and Molly getting a face full of cocaine and how drugs are bad."

She eyed him sourly. "That's exactly what I got, and given that's the sanitized version, I think we should both be having a retroactive panic attack."

His shoulder still hurt, and his body felt like it was under a giant dollop of molasses. "Sure, Mom. I'll get right on it."

She let out a sigh and slumped back into her chair. "I'm sorry," she said after a moment. "I… it's strange. I've never in my life had so much good fortune, but for the first time in my life I'm—"

"Afraid of losing it all," Josh filled in for her, understanding exactly.

She stroked his brow again. "Yes," she murmured. "That. Okay. I promise not to overreact, but you—you have to promise me something too."

Oh no. He knew where this was going. "Stay back with Stirling for this one?"

"You're very bright," she whispered. "No matter what the biopsy results are, yes. Please. For me?"

"Whatever," he grumbled with little grace. "It's not like I can move much now anyway."

"How very adult," Liam said into his hair.

"Wait until I exact promises from *you*," Josh said, starting to fall asleep again.

“Yes, I’ll keep your family safe,” Liam said softly.

“How did you know?” But he was asleep before Liam could answer.

LIAM KNEW because Josh had been saying it in his sleep for the last ten hours.

He’d gotten back to the hospital early in the morning, after catching a few hours of sleep at Danny’s apartment and updating everybody there on his condition. (The team seemed to have split itself up into older and younger regarding the apartment/hotel sitch. Hunter, Grace, Molly, Tienne, and Stirling had taken over Danny’s apartment, while Chuck, Lucius, Carl, Michael, Tor, and Marco were staying with the “adults” in the hotel. Weird.)

When he’d returned to the hospital, he’d found Danny, pale and hollow-eyed, trying to console Grace.

“We can take care of ourselves. Why won’t he fucking sleep!”

“Hush, pet,” Danny had murmured, his arms around the young man like any parent’s would be. “It’s okay. He’s going to be worried with all our near misses.”

And Josh had muttered, eyes not opening, “Liam? Liam, take care of them. Keep them safe.”

And helplessly, like being swept away in a wave, Liam was back on the goddamned yacht, when the family had been about to leave to take care of the business that had drawn them to the Caribbean in the first place and Josh had been sentenced to staying behind.

Take care of my family.

And Liam understood about families, about knowing they were strong and fragile, and knowing that the loss of one member, only one, could shatter the peace of the many until the unit repaired itself with duct tape and superglue and sad, bleeding shards of their hearts. They both knew what he’d been asking, and Liam had jumped into the boat for Gunrunner’s Island without a qualm.

His only regret then had been that he and Josh hadn’t yet kissed.

Well, they’d kissed now. They’d made love, and it had been everything Liam had dreamed. And here he was, being given that same choice again. Stay with his… his *person*. More than a lover, more than a friend, the one human that fate seemed to have gifted him with, and he was in *need*.

But more than that, Josh needed Liam to help keep his heart whole.

He'd barely looked at Danny and Grace after that. He'd crawled into bed behind Josh, the spot still warm, he suspected, from when Grace had slept, and he'd pulled his heart close.

"I'm here, boy-o. I'll take care of them. Don't you worry."

"Liam," Josh mumbled. And then he'd relaxed and, thank heaven, slept.

Liam sensed a shifting around the room then, and since he hadn't slept well or long the night before, he dozed for a bit. When he woke up, Danny and Grace were gone, and Felix was there.

Because of course he was.

"How are we doing?" the big man asked, and he was wearing a sport coat, polo shirt, and slacks, his lion-mane of blond hair tamed by an expensive haircut, like any other buzzenteenillionaire out on a holiday. (Liam rather enjoyed buzzenteen maths now that he'd gotten the hang of it. Saved him a lot of work on adjectives like "polished" and "urbane" and "posh.")

"I'm sorry," Liam said, before he knew it would come out of his mouth. He started to move, thinking to get out of bed and meet Josh's father eye to eye, but Felix shook his head and held out his hand.

"You would not believe how many conversations we've had with one person or another in this very position," he said, mouth tilting upwards slightly. His mouth stayed the same, but his eyes grew shiny as he added, "Even Stirling, who promised Grace that he'd make sure Josh wasn't lonely when that lot went to Greenland. Had to keep myself from bawling like a baby when I saw that. Those kids…."

"I hear they had a rough go of it with the drug job," Liam said, remembering Molly and Chuck's raucous retelling of the adventure in Colombia. Hunter hadn't laughed as they'd been telling that, though—apparently that wound of worrying about Grace was slower to heal these days.

"Some of them," Felix admitted. "Stirling, Tienne, and Tor and Marco have actually been having the time of their lives, from what I understand. They got to Munich right as your little stickers and such had been noticed, and somebody asked about the two caskets."

"Somebody?" Liam queried, catching the extra inflection on the word.

"Tienne," Felix said. "He's very good at doing his job and then just fading away, like the Homer Simpson meme."

Liam chuckled. Everyone knew that one.

"So Tor was there to cover it," Liam said with some satisfaction. That had been the plan. Stirling and Tienne had also, on a smaller scale, been responsible for other light shows like the one in Paris, and apparently Tienne had been training up—he'd managed to tap the pocket of one of the biggest right-wing politicians in the States, who'd been visiting Paris as they'd been leaving, and then Stirling had spread the man's passcodes around on the dark web, doing *amazing* damage to the man's reputation and finances. While not exactly planned or sanctioned by the group, it was in fact quite a coup. Stirling had flashed the Lightfingers symbol above the man's hotel that night from a projector on a timer, while he and Tienne were well and away from the site. So yes, if Kadjic was paying any attention *at all* to the news, he'd be chasing his tail, trying to track down Danny while at the same time wondering who was responsible for all the chaos of his businesses.

It would make even a very careful man *very* careless indeed.

"It *is* working," Felix said softly. "We just—we've become *very* cognizant, I guess, of all the ways this could go wrong in the past month. And then, while we were grappling with that…." He nodded his chin at Josh. "You exhausted yet?"

Liam gave him a level look. "I can sleep, sir," he said evenly, as his arms tightened ever so slightly around Josh's chest.

"Good." Felix bent to kiss Josh's forehead and then, unexpectedly, to ruffle Liam's hair, sending his curls into what was probably a stunning disarray. "You're good children, both of you."

Liam opened his mouth to say, at best, Felix was an older brother, but he found he couldn't. At his feet opened the terrible yawning pit of heartache where his father used to be, and that twin vine wrapped around his heart. *What a good, sweet man* vied with *what a terrible selfish git*, and for a heart-stopping, breathless moment, he couldn't figure out which should win.

Felix must have taken in his expression because he reached up to ruffle Liam's hair again, and this time, his hand stayed, tenderly, like family's.

"Good and bad," he said softly. "We love people for their good and their bad. It's a *stunning* realization that a human can hold our hearts so thoroughly, isn't it?" His mouth—full, expressive, with none of the tight wrinkles that accompanied a smoker's mouth or the flat lips of someone who never smiled—turned down at the corners again, and he sat back in his seat, although Liam could still *feel* those soft fingers in his hair.

"The day after Danny left, I… I sat and cried. Went into our little cottage and realized he'd packed up everything that mattered and left everything that didn't." Felix swallowed hard. "And I realized—our final fight. He'd goaded me. Pushed me into telling him to get out. Because the situation was killing him." He shook his head. "I cannot live through a moment like that again." A deep breath. "And some people may wonder why all of us are so willing to go through this for a man who cheerfully admits his worst, deepest flaws at the drop of a hat and doesn't spare himself when he does it."

Liam thought of his father, boozy and a little tearful, telling Liam that he was sorry they were poor, but Liam was a good little man who would help his mum when Liam's father couldn't.

Liam missed him so badly, booze and all. His father had known that Liam was gay—known, and loved him with no change except to teach him to punch. Liam had been able to walk into the schoolroom or the world with confidence then. No reason to punch when you walked like nobody's meat. But he remembered those moments, some of them unclouded by drink, when his father told his children, told *Liam*, that he loved them.

Those moments were everything.

With aching clarity, he saw how this family would rise in defense of their strongest—and weakest—member. Like peering through a window into his own heart, he saw how much it meant to him to be part of this quest, this thing he'd started by being a substandard Interpol agent but a decent human being.

"I don't wonder," he said gruffly, leaning his cheek against Josh's hair. Soft and thick, it needed a trim, because it was starting to curl against his collar and Josh liked it short.

Here, holding the man he seemed to be destined to love, Liam knew exactly why Josh couldn't sleep without knowing Liam would protect his family. Liam had spent much of his young-adult life protecting his own family. He knew exactly how Josh felt.

THE NEXT morning, Josh's room was… well, crowded.

Josh was sitting up in bed, bathed and dressed and tired and pale—and satisfyingly grumpy. He glanced from parent to parent… to parent to parent and shook his head in irritation. But he didn't let go of Liam's hand, and he endured Grace's semipermanent cuddle practically in his lap.

And was fully aware of the fifty-dozen people (slightly less than a buzzenteen, he'd told Liam, holding on to his humor by his fingertips) standing out in the hallway.

"But Mom," he'd protested, "what if… what if…." His voice dropped. "What if it's bad news?"

"Then we'll tell them all so they can cry together," she said softly. "Besides. What *if* it's bad news? What should we do then?"

He'd leaned against Liam a little harder. "Same thing we're doing now," he said softly. "We're all in Europe. I-I mean, I didn't stop doing this when I was sick last year. I kept on until I couldn't, and then I kept on when I could."

She nodded, her eyes shiny. "And that's what we'll do this time," she whispered. "But this time…."

And her eyes had flitted none-too-subtly toward Liam.

Josh had glanced at him, seeing his tightened jaw, his expectation to be hurt again, and couldn't do it.

"This time Liam's in for the haul," he said, not breaking contact with those dark blue eyes. God, he couldn't send him away again. Should *never* have sent him away, no matter how hard the emotions were.

But certainly wouldn't do it now that he knew what happiness looked like in Liam Craig's arms.

"Damned right I am, boy-o," Liam said, some of the fear in his eyes fading. Josh got it then, that Liam understood about circumstances. Cancer, death, even human weakness were sometimes beyond our control. But being there for another human being—particularly one you loved—was one of the few things a truly human being really had mastery over. "As long as we both shall live" was a heart-beating promise, and Liam had made it.

And now so had Josh.

So when the doctor made her white-coated presence known at the door, seven heads swiveled toward her, a handsome woman with tawny skin and crisp movements, her dark hair pulled back into a tight bun.

When she spoke, her English rang distinctly with a Slavic accent.

"There is quite a crowd outside," she said bemusedly. "These people are here with your consent?" She peered at Josh.

"Extended family," he said sheepishly. "Moral support."

"Well, they must have supported you quite well," she told him, "because while your iron is low, and your iron *and* glucose levels were dangerously low when you came in, your aggressive leukemia does not appear to have returned."

"I'm clear?" Josh asked, almost afraid he'd heard her wrong.

"For now, yes," she said, giving a severe glare around the room. "*However*," she added, "your iron and vitamin deficiencies are cause for concern. Did your doctors not give you guidelines about recovery, one of them being to not push yourself beyond your limits?"

Josh felt the flat gaze of all the people he loved most in the world piercing him with the scare he'd given them.

"I didn't know it was beyond my limits at the time," he said with his most charming grin. And yes—he'd learned to charm and to disarm with that smile, practically from the cradle. Danny had once warned him not to use his charm like a weapon, because odds were it would end up hurting the innocent, so Josh had tried not to abuse that smile—but he knew he had it.

This doctor, it seemed, was impervious.

"Mr. Salinger," she said severely, "what are you doing here?"

"My boyfriend put me on an ambulance, and this is where we ended up?" he asked, feeling like he was missing something.

There was a stunned silence. Liam thunked his forehead against Josh's shoulder, and the parents—all four of them—covered their eyes.

Grace shot up in bed next to him and said, "Oh my God you're stupid."

"I am not!" Josh retorted, stung.

"So stupid," Grace muttered. "Liam—it's your job now. Tell him why he's stupid."

Liam glared at Grace, who glared back, but it was Danny who intervened.

"Doctor, is there anything else?"

She nodded. "Yes—he can leave the hospital this afternoon, but he needs to be here every morning for the next week to have his levels checked and to get plasma and electrolyte infusions—along with antibiotics, because he is just primed for infection right now." And now she was glaring at Josh. "And this means that whatever you were doing kiting around Europe, you can very well put a kibosh on until you've recovered for at least a year. After you get the all clear to go back to the States, I don't want you *near* a plane for another six months at the very least. For God's sake, *rest*, young Mr. Salinger. Your records indicate you came very close to death less than a year ago. Give your body time to recover."

Josh nodded, feeling the tightness in his chest that indicated his iron was so low he *still* wasn't getting enough oxygen, and conceded.

"Honeymooning," he said faintly, leaning into Liam's arms. "We were honeymooning."

She gave him a slightly less exasperated glance. "Well, do it from home. I understand you have some accommodations in the city?"

"Yes," Danny said smoothly. "He's well set up for places to stay. Felix, Julia, do you want to make the appointments? Leon, Grace, could you tell everybody they can breathe again?" He glanced at Liam. "Liam my boy, you can stay if Josh wants you to, but Josh, since you're not checking out until…." He glanced at the doctor.

"Noon," she said adamantly. "After his first infusion."

"Yes," Danny said, forestalling any argument Josh would have made. "Then you and I have something to talk about."

Josh felt Liam standing up as well, and he turned to him in confusion.

"Oh no, boy-o," Liam said softly. "This, I think, is a conversation you have to have on your own."

Josh realized he was pouting and shifted it to a scowl instead. "Coward," he muttered.

"Lover," Liam said simply. "You need this convo, boy-o, or I haven't been paying attention."

Everybody shifted then, with the line of parents hugging Josh, because in spite of the scolding it *had* been good news, and then Grace—who was the last to go—glared at him and swatted the back of his head.

"Dumbass."

And suddenly Josh found himself saying Grace's line. "But you love me, right?"

And then Grace—who cuddled or swatted or broke into Josh's room or flat at fuck-all in the morning for a conversation—was hugging him.

And Grace didn't hug.

"You made promises," Grace said. "You and me, going out as old men, bungee jumping off an airplane. Don't break my heart."

"I won't," Josh said, his eyes burning.

"Going to go eat schnitzel," Grace muttered. "Fried meat—it's delicious." And then he drifted away like angry smoke.

Liam leaned forward, the last in the room, and kissed Josh's forehead. "This won't hurt much," he murmured. "But I think it's a long time coming."

And then the room had cleared out, and it was just Josh and Danny.

Danny wasn't particularly tall—a thing that Josh had always loved about him because *Josh* wasn't particularly tall. Sure, Liam could pass for tall at five ten or so, but after being surrounded by Carl and Chuck—both in the six four/six five range—for the past year and a half or so and being visually dominated by Felix all his life, Josh appreciated Danny's slender five seven.

Danny was *Josh's*. Josh had never needed to share Danny with a job or a spotlight. When Josh was a child, Danny had been more like a nanny than Josh's actual nannies. And right when Josh had grown out of needing a caretaker twenty-four seven, Danny had still been the fun parent.

Until Danny hadn't been there anymore.

Josh sucked in a breath to kill that thought, like he'd killed it for the last eleven years, and Danny blew out a breath and sank down next to him on the bed.

"Josh," he said softly, "you know how much I love you, right?"

Josh swallowed and nodded. "Of course I do." That terrible rift so Danny could clean up, get sober. Those postcards and letters and gifts. The surreptitious visits, the trips to Chicago where everything hurt so Danny could be there for Josh, who was the one person who *didn't* hurt.

Josh knew.

"Then you need to trust me," Danny said, leaning against him. Josh leaned back, his eyes burning. Fucking anemia.

Sure.

"I do," Josh reassured. He'd poured out his heart in his letters, telling Danny things he hadn't trusted with Felix or his mother. Of the three parents, Danny had been the first to know Josh was gay. He'd been the first to know Grace had been using drugs, the first to get Josh's panicked, anguished letter when Grace almost let that dangerous preoccupation kill him.

Danny had known about Josh's high school boyfriend, his doomed affair with Sean the closeted policeman, and his stupid, helpless attraction to Nick, who'd been married.

Danny had even suspected the thing—the tremendous, amazing, heart-changing thing—with Liam, probably long before Liam had.

Certainly long before Josh allowed it to happen.

"Good," Danny said, looping his arm around Josh's shoulders. "So if you trust me, you need to tell me the truth, okay?"

"I always do," Josh said, and now the tears started to slip from between his squeezed-shut eyelids, and he wished for Liam, who would tell him not to cry.

"Good," Danny said again. "So, my boy, my son, the child of my heart, the precious human who kept me sane, who made me want to clean the fuck up and get sober and keep being a parent and who dragged me back to a life I love beyond measure, you need to tell me, on a scale of one to one hundred, how viciously angry at me are you?"

Josh gasped, feeling as though he'd been struck. "I'm not—"

Danny shook his head and kissed Josh's temple. "Sure you are. I left. I know what it's like to have damage, son. My father was killed when I was four years old during a shooting at a convenience store, and my real mother died of cancer when I was nine. I was *furious* with them for a lot of years, and they were not nearly as culpable as I was for leaving you."

"You had to…." Josh whispered, shocked by Danny's revelations, things Josh had not known.

"I did," Danny agreed. "I had to leave. But you are not obligated to forgive me for it."

And that stung. "Of course I do."

"Oh bullshit," Danny said sadly. "Goddammit, Josh, this drive you have to be the king shit of grifters, to be the mastermind, to make this crew yours and damn your own health for doing it—"

"Kadjic is *threatening* our *family*—"

"*Then let me die fighting him*!" Danny shouted, surprising Josh enough to pull out from under his arm.

In his entire life he'd never heard Danny yell.

"Danny," he whispered, more surprised than frightened.

But Danny was wiping his own tears with hands that shook. Josh thought that for once Danny looked like a man in his early forties, instead of ageless like Peter Pan. Josh could see the gray hairs that threaded through the rich brown and the fine lines around his eyes and the corners of his mouth. Not a lot. But enough. Josh's Uncle Danny hadn't lived an easy life, no matter how light he made of the things that had hurt him.

A lifetime of telling people you'd been a helpless falling-down drunk for a number of years didn't lessen by one iota the strain of living through those years in real time, although they could make the present easier in the telling.

"Your drive," Danny said bitterly. "Your amazing, prodigious drive. Josh, I get it. I left, and you felt like whatever parenting I'd given you, you had to take it over yourself. And all I'd had to give you back then had been the game. You could pick a pocket at four. You could run a con at seven. You once brought us the diamond collar of a spoiled schnauzer when you were eight years old. You'd even assessed the karats. And we were so proud of you, son—but we would have been as proud of you if you'd been playing chess. Dancing." He emitted a broken laugh. "God, are we proud of the way you dance. Acting. How *very* smart you are. And… and I think the thing I'm proudest of is how you've gathered these people together—these separate, different people—and you haven't merely secured their loyalty and love to *you*, but your loyalty and love to *each other*."

"But Danny," Josh whispered, "*you* did that."

Danny laughed bitterly. "No, son. I arrived to help your father, remember? And you took me to pizza. And pizza led me to Stirling, Molly, Chuck, and Hunter. And that led us to a dozen people in that hallway who will cry tears of joy right now, because you are okay."

"Both of us," Josh said, feeling like he had to be clear. "That was both of us." Danny had brought Carl, Tienne, and Liam. Chuck had brought Lucius as a lover and Michael as a friend. Felix had brought Tor, who brought Marco.

Danny gave a faint smile. "You're trying to do math with a family the size of a hurricane, son. Don't bother. What matters is we are all swept away together. And they all love you. And for that I am proud. But you can't let my pride get in the way of what you feel."

Josh let out a sigh and tried to fight it, but now that Danny had said the words, it was all so very clear.

His eyes hadn't stopped leaking, but now his voice broke, and he shook from his hands to his heart. "How could you?" he mewled, falling apart at all the seams, destroyed from the inside out by the thing that *had* driven him, from his earliest memories to his adulthood. The thing he couldn't admit, because he knew it wasn't fair.

But fairness didn't matter now.

"I loved you so much," he rasped. "All I wanted was to be you. And you *left me*!" That last came out as a howl, one buried in his chest since he was ten years old, and he wanted to rage about the room and throw things. He wanted to—oh God, he wanted to *hit* this man who had only done his best by Josh, and Josh had never suffered.

But he had. The hurt… the hurt….

"*You left me*!"

All he had the strength for was to sob, and like he had for Josh's entire life, whether by his bedside or three thousand miles away, Danny held him. Took his pain and anger and turned it into love so Josh could sob and rage and sob some more.

HE WOKE up on a soft bed in a small, quaint bedroom with Moroccan tapestries on the walls and floor and satin drapes in blue and gold across the windows, with white silk flowing underneath.

There were shelves and shelves of books surrounding the room, making it smaller but, Josh thought sadly, also making it like the Tardis. A magic place that was bigger inside than it was out.

Danny's apartment. It must have been.

Liam was seated in an armchair by the side of the bed, doing something serious on his phone. He'd done that periodically as they'd traveled. He'd told Josh he was faking his job, but Josh knew he was also supposedly deep undercover and feeding Interpol tips on the Kadjic operations that the family had sabotaged so far. The sabotage—blamed on rival operations—had given Liam some cachet, because he'd been the first to report on not only the end of the operation, but also the roots—where Kadjic had gotten his guns, for instance, or which distributors would now be missing cocaine.

So he was not, in fact, "faking" his job; he was using Salinger intel to *do* his job, and giving the money from his promotions and such to his family to pay for his mother's big house, his sister's university experience, and to subsidize his other sister's business.

A good man, Josh thought achingly. Not necessarily an honest one—at least by the standards of his employer—but such a good man. A man who wanted to do good things in the world.

And who thought he and Josh were cut from the same cloth.

"I don't even remember getting here," Josh muttered.

"Really?" Liam said, after making one last tap on his phone and setting it down on the end table. "There was practically a fist fight for who got to carry you out of the hospital."

Josh was too tired to smile. "Who won?"

"Hunter," Liam said grimly. "Because Grace won. He told the grownups they were all too stupid to be trusted, and Carl, Chuck, and me that we were too tired from doing real work, and that Hunter was the only one he had faith in." He shrugged. "I am not exactly sure how that young man does it, but he does seem to drive the team when we're too big to steer."

"I hate emotional meltdowns," Josh said, his throat too raspy for I-told-you-sos. "How's Danny?"

"Looks like he swam through seven layers of hell to be your whipping boy," Liam told him. "What did you two say to each other?"

Josh tried to chuckle. Couldn't. "He said I was mad at him and I had a right to be."

"Mm." Liam took his hand as it lay on the bed, and threaded their fingers together. "And what did you say?"

"Mostly I reverted to a ten-year-old and screamed, 'You left me,'" Josh told him, the embarrassment trying to swamp him, but no. Still that curious, quiet emptiness. That anger had been driving him for so long. What would drive him now?

Liam kissed Josh's knuckles, and Josh felt the slippery heat of his tears. "What you said to him," he whispered. "Did it give you peace?"

Josh closed his eyes. "Yeah," he admitted, after searching himself for a moment. Liam's hand, hard and grounding, and the softness of his lips on Josh's skin. The last six weeks came flooding back. Honeymooning, Josh had said. And God, they'd had fun doing it. He opened his eyes again. "But I still want in on the game." At Liam's pained expression, he added hastily, "In a slightly less intense capacity. As long as…." He swallowed, suddenly nervous.

"What?" Liam asked, and his fingers had grown tighter, as though he was afraid.

"As long as you're with me. Us. But mostly me. I'm not in the game to prove anything anymore. Not to Danny, not to Felix or Julia. But I still love it. And I love you. Can we… can we still do this, be in this together?"

Liam's crooked smile, with the slight gap of the front two teeth, the charming freckles, the calm acceptance, the willingness to play the game with them, the drive to use all his knowledge for good—it was all, Josh thought achingly, he'd ever wanted. All he'd ever needed in his life.

"God yes," Liam answered, and then he lowered his face to Josh's, and Josh *felt*, for real, for the first time since he'd awakened.

And what he really felt was he wanted to kiss Liam Craig until the planets turned to dust.

THE CREW didn't seem to want to disperse as they left the hospital, which was frustrating because Tor wanted to talk to Marco alone.

And Marco was being stubborn.

"Tell them," he said as they hit the street.

"Marco," Tor muttered, "can we just, you know, have a minute to talk about this?"

"No," Marco said. "It's a perfect opportunity. Tell them."

"Tell us what?" Carl asked, and Tor glared at him, trying hard not to remember that Carl's level-headed advice had helped him actually *win* Marco that winter, when Tor had been dragging his heels.

"It's an idea," Tor told him, fighting the urge to check his cuffs or the lay of his suit jacket or for lint on his turtleneck. They were situated near the river, and it was the first day of September. Turtlenecks were perfectly fine in Prague.

"It's making him squidgy," Stirling said, a stealth observation from their quietest member.

They were walking down the street, practically en masse, the adults taking a car to Danny's apartment with Josh. Tor was wondering how all five of them fit in the car when Danny, seemingly coming from nowhere, said, "Squidgy's a good word for it, my boy. Torrance, why are you squidgy?"

Tor startled so badly he would have turned an ankle and gone down, humiliatingly enough, on the walk, if Marco hadn't caught his elbow and said, "Steady there, cowboy."

Tor shot him an irritated glance and tried to regain his cool.

"Can we not talk about it here?" he asked. "Jesus, Danny, I thought you were on your way to—"

"The hotel," Felix said. "And we will be. But first they're dropping Josh and Liam off at Danny's flat."

"Oh shit," Grace said. "I should be there. I made Hunter go to carry Josh, and—"

"And Hunter will join us at the Mozart for lunch," Felix said. "We're having a buffet sent to the suite in half an hour, and then Torrance and Marco can tell us whatever has been brewing between them since they arrived at the hospital this morning."

Tor shot Marco a dark glance, but Marco, curly hair blowing in the breeze from the river and dark eyes sparkling with "I told you so," gave him a sunny smile in return.

They hadn't eaten at the Mozart that morning, although the food was *very* good. But Marco was a classically trained chef, with accolades and apprenticeships up the wazoo. He could probably be the head chef at the restaurant of his choosing, but he liked his family, and he liked having a life outside of work, so he enjoyed cooking for the Salingers, where he often got to share his gifts with the higher profile names Felix and Julia's business brought into the mansion.

But when they'd jumped on board with the crew to help this op run, Tor had suggested that since they'd be in Europe, they check out as many places to sample as possible, and Marco had leapt at the chance. France had been delightful, as had Bavaria, and while Bavarian and Czech cuisine had much in common, Marco was still excited at tasting the differences, which was how they'd ended up having breakfast at the Michaelangelo Grand Hotel that morning.

The dining room had been clean and airy—much of Prague's architecture was modern—and Tor had enjoyed the impression of great windows overlooking the white linens as they gazed at the river outside.

But it wasn't the architecture that Tor and Marco needed to talk about.

They'd been waiting for their meal, which was, they'd been told, going to be a bit delayed. The morning sous chef was expecting his first child, and a replacement had yet to be found. While they were reassuring their server that all was well and the wait was acceptable, the table behind them was not being nearly so patient.

"I do not care if he's giving birth to the brat himself or popping it in the pot," came a thickly accented voice—a brutal voice. And one that Tor remembered from being on comms the night they'd switched the painting in Chicago. "If I do not get my food quickly, I shall take my money and my investment from this rathole and rip it like a torn limb until this cesspool starts hemorrhaging money. You tell your boss that, yes? You tell him that Kadjic gets his goddamned eggs benedict—"

"Right now," came the cheerful voice of another server. He'd added something in Czech that was probably the equivalent of "Here we go, Mr. Kadjic, there's no reason to overreact."

Kadjic had glared at the man—and thank God it wasn't a woman, Tor had thought, because the first server, the one he'd been eviscerating, had been female, and that note of condescension in his voice was galling—but the second server, obviously knowing the way his bread was buttered, had given a chipper wink.

Kadjic had relaxed a little and given the man's ass a pat as he finished settling the plates and left to fetch some extra sauce.

Tor and Marco had witnessed this—but not watched it. In fact they'd pretended to make polite conversation with their own server, who was looking so uncomfortable Tor thought she was going to be sick, while the scene had gone on beyond them.

Marco had then asked the server if he could speak to their chef before Tor could stop him, and he was left alone at the table to nibble on breadsticks and try hard to listen to Kadjic's muttered conversation with his two guards, who never left his side.

What he'd learned was *interesting*.

And then Marco had returned, face flushed with triumph and, after sitting down *next* to Tor, not across from him, leaned over and whispered in his ear, "I'll be working here for the next week. We must tell Felix and Julia—we've got an in."

Tor, who had hung out of helicopters to deliver stories and had, just that January, faced down a sitting US Congressmen as he revealed the man's investiture in his daughter's trafficking ring, found himself cold to the pit of his balls.

"No," he'd whispered, but at that moment, Kadjic barked something at his server, something cruel, and Tor had given Marco a thin smile that indicated "We'll talk about this later."

Marco—thank God—seemed as cognizant of the danger as Tor now was, and he'd smiled gently, kissed Tor on the cheek, and said, "Don't worry so much! The chef seemed to think my credentials were completely in line, particularly since it was only breakfast service."

Tor's mouth watered, purely a Pavlovian response. "Are you going to make your chocolate cream cheese muffins?"

Marco grinned devilishly. "Oh no—I have a brand-new recipe to try out—you'd better be here to eat!" And then his eyes had made a completely unconscious dart toward a target neither of them could see, somewhere over Tor's left ear, and all thoughts of Marco's rather sublime pastry chef abilities vanished, and so did Tor's appetite.

"No," he mouthed, but he swallowed the syllable.

"It will be delicious," Marco assured gently, and Tor wanted to tell him that it would be *dangerous*, not delicious, but he couldn't. They had to wait until they were far away before they even broached the subject.

At that moment, their food arrived, brought by a grateful server, who comped most of their meal to thank Marco for his service the next day.

As they ate—they'd gotten crepes, one savory and the other sweet—and Marco had waxed rhapsodic over the lightness, the texture, the sublime seasoning, both of his strawberry suzette and Tor's savory Florentine, Tor's busy brain was at war with itself.

The lover in him—a newly awakened human, but one he found he liked better than the cold-eyed journalistic opportunist he could be—wanted so badly to guard Marco's safety, to keep this ugliness, which he'd embraced enthusiastically, wanting to be the truthteller and the revealer of the forces the Salinger family fought, far away from this warm, sensual, amazing human being he loved.

But the cold-eyed journalist wasn't oblivious to the opportunity.

Kadjic had swept out of the dining room without leaving a tip by the time Tor and Marco were finished, and Tor was just about to launch into a well-reasoned lecture as to why this was a *very bad idea* when they got the text that Josh's results were in.

Gratitude swept Tor in no small measure. The torch he may have held for Josh Salinger had long since cooled to warm friendship, but it *was* friendship, a good one, and he loved Felix like a brother. His friend was going to be okay, and he knew the world was uncertain enough that health was no small thing.

So to have Felix guiding them to the Mozart—which was lovely in a Classical era, old-world way—to plan for the job had Tor doubting the wisdom of what Marco was obviously hoping to do.

At the same time he was raring to go full speed ahead.

His whole life had been about the truth changing the world for the better. But he'd seen enough wrong in his time, enough evil, to know that the truth alone couldn't do it. The opportunity to bring down somebody like Kadjic, who had done so much wrong in the world, was irresistible. Even if the whole thing went wrong and Tor ended up disappearing from the world young and unknown, *he'd* know that he'd worked to right a lot of wrongs.

And that was all very noble and self-sacrificing, but it didn't apply to Marco, whose only ambition his entire life had been to cook for people and make them happy.

Except Marco loved the Salingers too.

Tor's brain was whirling with it still as Felix guided them through the lobby—and God, in his entire life Tor hadn't dreamed of a place that made him yearn for *The Magic Flute* to serenade him to sleep on tapestried furniture beneath fantastical chandeliers.

"My God," Marco murmured. "This place…."

As they turned toward the elevators, they caught a glimpse of the great window overlooking the river, and both of them sighed softly.

"Come on," Marco said, smiling. "If we're going to die dramatic deaths, can you think of better scenery?"

"Shut. Up." Tor shook his head, the elevator dinged, and most of them shoved themselves inside.

Those who had too much nervous energy—Carl, Chuck, Tienne, and Grace—took the stairs.

ONCE IN the suite, after the buffet arrived, the lot of them made themselves comfortable on couches, stuffed chairs, dining room chairs, and the floor.

Molly, Grace, Stirling, and Tienne, their prodigies, were the ones on the floor, sitting cross-legged and sharing their plates of food. While he hadn't been a part of the group since middle school like the others, Tienne still managed to fit in, and Tor watched them enviously.

He remembered being in college, thinking he was invincible and everything was easy. But these "children" had seen real consequences, and he reflected that perhaps their insouciance in this moment was part of their strength. All four of them had proved they were capable of tough decisions, specialized skill sets, and impressive deeds.

Still, he was reassured by Marco's solid body sitting on the dining room chair next to his so he could eat the capers and lox with delicate nibbles and a fork.

"Good?" Tor asked, like he always did when dealing with his lover's specialty.

"Very much so," Marco told him, closing his eyes. "The salmon is particularly fresh. It's delicious."

While they were eating, Julia, Leon, and Hunter walked in, and for once, instead of standing sentinel near the front door, as Chuck and Carl were doing instinctively while cradling their plates in their hands, Hunter went to sit next to Grace.

Tor watched as Grace rubbed up against Hunter like a love-starved kitten and then offered the muscle-bound enforcer his plate.

Hunter took it, but not before rubbing back against Grace, a solid animal show of reassurance that somehow touched Tor deeply.

Grace had always been an enigma to Tor, but he understood love now, and that was what he'd just seen.

As Julia and Leon settled down *at* the table, their plates before them, Felix, with a nod from Julia, stood.

"Okay, everybody. Hit the head and get seconds now. In fifteen minutes we've got to be at our best. Before we start this planning session, is there anything we should know?"

And before Tor could think of how to phrase it, Marco blurted, "Kadjic's at the Michaelangelo, and I've got a job there as morning sous chef for the next week. Any suggestions?"

Felix gave a long, slow blink, and then another, and Danny burst out laughing.

"Holy shit, Fox, you should see your face."

Tor glanced around the room and saw that everybody was as flabbergasted as Felix, and he felt mildly better about being so up in his head about the matter.

From the table, Leon, who apparently had become a full-fledged member of the family, muttered, "What are the fucking *odds*!"

"My thoughts exactly," Felix muttered, as though released from a spell so he could talk. "Danny, are there any more of those pastries left? I feel like I'm due."

A Little Night Music

BECAUSE STIRLING loved Josh but also worked well in quiet (Liam assumed), Stirling was the one who brought Josh his laptop and the results of the briefing the day before.

Liam sat next to Josh as he got his infusion of plasma and saline, working on his own laptop and occasionally glancing up to stare at Stirling in surprise.

He'd loathed meetings and briefings his entire professional life. This sounded like, of all the goddamned briefings he'd daydreamed his way through, this was the one he'd wanted to attend.

"Really?" Josh asked, pausing in whatever search he was about to initialize. "Marco's working at Kadjic's hotel?"

"Yes," Stirling said, *not* pausing, which was what made Stirling a prodigy while Josh was simply brilliant. "It really was fortuitous."

"Good word," Josh murmured, his fingers resuming their tapping. "So what's the plan after that?"

Stirling grunted. "Well, first you and I perform magic and figure out exactly where the girls are being trafficked."

"Not magic," Josh said with a smile. "Logic."

"I don't see the difference," Liam interjected, because he wanted to be part of their rhythm.

"We swapped out ma for lo. But it's the same ic," Stirling replied, straight faced.

Liam chuckled, and Josh shot him a grin.

"And after the magic?" Liam asked.

"The fun part," Stirling said. "We organize the op to set the trafficking victims free, and it's going to be a big one." He glanced up. "Expect Felix and Danny to call upon your mighty law enforcement powers for that."

Liam nodded soberly. "So noted."

"Mostly for help placing the victims," Josh said, thinking. "I mean, we can set them free, I hope, but free isn't 'rescued' when you're in a foreign country without knowledge of the language or a passport. That's seriously going to be something involving the Czech government and Interpol."

Liam frowned. "They might have passports," he said. "Many sex workers are trafficked by scam artists. They get their passports expecting to be taken to another country to work legitimately, and then their passports are taken from them, and they're forced to go along. Maybe I should go on the op—I can search for the passports while everybody else is subduing the guards and freeing the victims."

Josh glanced up, suddenly stricken. "Without me?" he said, and it was one of the few times Liam had ever actually *heard* him sound like the boy Liam teased him for being. Just that quickly, Josh shook his head. "Ignore that," he said, giving a bright smile. "Momentary lapse. Of course. I'll tell Felix right now."

But before he could pull up the text function to do that, Liam settled a hand on the inside of his arm, careful not to dislodge the IV needle taped there, giving him lifeblood and strength.

"This," he said softly, "is how we get angry. I get we're working now, but you be sure to rage at me a little when we're alone."

Josh shot him a relieved, tired smile. "I can do that," he said, winking. Then he went back to work.

"So," Liam resumed, after Josh and Stirling had used the moment to communicate the new wrinkle, "what's the Lightfingers job? If the big half is freeing trafficked prisoners, what's the arts-and-crafts plan to tweak Kadjic?"

Stirling grinned, a startling expression on such a stolid young man's face. "They already have Kadjic's room number," he whispered. "Grace has broken into his room twice to move stuff around. Last night, while Kadjic was at the theater and hiring a rent boy, Grace stole *all* his silk pocket squares, the ones that match his ties. Molly's busy sewing them together into a miniskirt."

Liam and Josh both snickered, and then Josh glanced up. "She's not going to *wear* it, is she? When he can see her?"

Stirling frowned. "Not willy-nilly," he said. "We've had a blond at every op—I think she's going to touch up her roots when it's appropriate and shake her booty in public when it makes him froth at the mouth."

Liam heard Josh's sigh of relief.

"Afraid they'll bollix it up without you, boy-o?"

"Or worried for my friend's safety!" he protested. Then, to Stirling, "So is our endgame the same?"

"Well, first we're going to break through his protections at the Czech Port Authority," Stirling murmured, and then he and Josh both let out twin breaths of appreciation.

"Okay, then," Josh said. "We've got it."

"Got what?" Liam asked.

"Our route," Stirling said frankly. "See, we knew Kadjic had a hard-on for Prague, which, you know…."

"Nice city," Liam said, because there was no denying that the jewel of Czechia was very pretty—the old-style architecture, the bridge and the lights spanning the river. Almost every window held a view of old-world charm mixed with modern amenities.

"Really pretty," Josh said, nodding. "I hadn't been to Prague before. What I've seen so far? I can see why Danny loves it."

Liam listened carefully for any bitterness or any anger when Josh mentioned Danny's name. It wasn't like he'd heard any before—apparently Josh had been masking his real feelings of hurt even from himself—but now there was an appreciation of the man and what he'd done with his time while he'd been gone from his family.

"I want to come back," Stirling confided. "Tienne is in love with it here. He's been parkouring all over the place, and then he's found a studio where he can rent time, and he paints by the hour. It's really fun to watch."

Liam grinned at him. "Good plans to make," he said, and it occurred to him that the crew—all the crew—seemed to have a handle on things. This was a big project, but it was not the only project or their last project. There would be *after* the project, and since all of the crew seemed to have found their match, that *after* would come with happy romantic adventures.

The thought cheered him. The infusion room was an atrium, full of natural light, with a view overlooking the Charles Bridge. While not a port, the graceful stone arch was a landmark, and underneath it swanned the riverboat cruises that seemed to showcase so much of the charm of eastern Europe. Watching the riverboats come and go was a particularly stately pastime, so it wasn't like the place was dreary. But the sun sparkling off the water and the promise of a crisp nearly autumn day seemed beyond Josh's fingertips today, and Liam knew that had to be bringing him down.

"So we all agree, Prague is wonderful, and between Danny's apartment and the Mozart, we're being spoiled rotten," Josh said primly. "So do you want to hear about Hamburg?"

"Sure," Liam said. "You can wow me about Germany anytime."

"Well, to start with," Josh said, "we thought we'd be searching one of the major ports—Praha Smichov or Praha Radotin. But those ports are *so* big, they all have their own police units, and while human trafficking takes place through the big ports, there's a lot of big busts. And Kadjic doesn't traffic droves of people. He tends to traffic…." He swallowed, looking uncomfortable.

"High-value sex workers," Stirling filled in for him without inflection. "Boys and girls—and yes, I mean *boys* and *girls*. The average age of the workers under Kadjic's men in America is fifteen, which means…."

"Oh God," Liam muttered, feeling sick. "Yes. We've known this, but also that they are… well, pretty." Kadjic's people recruited for classic Eastern European beauty—and apparently for youth.

"Until they get hooked on drugs or get murdered or jump into a river on purpose," Josh said grimly. Well, his friend Nick wouldn't have spared Josh the details as they'd been rooting through Kadjic's activities in the States.

Liam wouldn't have either, but that didn't make him hate Nick any less.

"So we're *not* looking at the major ports?" Liam asked, going back to their main points.

"Děčin," Josh said decisively.

"Děčin?" Liam was surprised. The port of Děčin was a resort of sorts, attracting close to a million tourists of the yacht and sport boat variety a year. When one thought of human trafficking, they thought of miserable filthy conditions in packing containers with the inhabitants freezing or suffocating or otherwise dying of exposure. One did *not* think of Děčin, where the rich and beautiful kited about on yachts, thousand-dollar sunglasses in place and silk scarves streaming behind them in the wind.

"Think about it," Josh murmured. "Leon's yacht in the Caribbean. It's large—it accommodated twenty passengers, twelve crew easily—but it was small compared to some of the yachts in Děčin. Take one yacht that size and super-stuff it with… well, human beings. That's easily eighty passengers, and they would only need the boat crew and maybe ten or twelve overseers with weapons. And…." He looked sick. "I understand the training is… uhm…."

"Yeah," Liam said. He'd worked a case involving large-scale trafficking six or so years ago. The victims were repeatedly assaulted in the name of making them numb to whatever a client would do. "It's fucking brutal. So you think the training is accomplished on the yachts between Děčin and Hamburg?" Because that wasn't very far.

"No," Stirling said. "They're funneled through Děčin and Rotterdam and a couple of other ports, and they consolidate in Hamburg, and then they're on for a twenty-five-day ocean voyage to New York or New Jersey or Florida."

"You tracked all this?" Liam asked, and he shouldn't have been surprised.

Stirling gave him a beleaguered glare. "What do you think Danny and I have been doing as you two have been throwing Lightfingers shade all over Europe?"

"Paris and Munich," Josh said. "Not all over. Anything beyond that was Tor and Marco and you and Tienne."

Stirling chuckled. "Yeah, well, we did PR. You two did the actual theft/replacement things."

"It's Grace who's been the real hero," Josh said. "That pocket square thing was genius. And now with Kadjic's pocket squares becoming one of Molly's fashion creations—"

"And the original copy of Gustav Klimt's *The Maiden*," Stirling added, like that was no big thing.

"Oh my God," Josh muttered. "That was supposed to be *my* job!"

"It'll be like the Art Institute in Chicago," Stirling said soothingly. "You'll sit in the truck while Grace, Carl, Tienne, and Danny pull the job."

"That's nothing like the Art Institute," Josh said grumpily. "And remember how you and I almost got blown up?"

"What are you and I doing?" Liam asked, suddenly aware not only that Stirling hadn't said *he'd* be in on the art job but that this plan had been arranged without his input as well.

"You'll be with the rest of us, liberating the—"

"The *Spelyy Persik*," Josh cried triumphantly.

Stirling wrinkled his nose, and Liam tapped his marginal cache of Russian phrases. "Ripe peach?"

They all grimaced.

"Fucking charming," Josh muttered. "But yes. I traced the LLCs that owned the shell companies under Kadjic's umbrella until I found one that specialized in—and I quote—'maritime investments.' If you look at it, it pays for berths in ports, various vessels, gas, employees, which I assume means muscle and not the sex workers, and miscellaneous. It has a *huge* budget, so I'm thinking bribes. Look under 'Vessels' and 'Děčin' and here you have it. In Děčin, the *Spelyy Persik*." He let out a harsh breath. "The ripe fucking peach."

"Wait," Liam said again. "Stirling, are we doing both jobs at the same time?"

Stirling gave him a placid look. "Did I forget to mention that? See, Danny said it was one thing when Kadjic had to go across the world to get to us, but this time, he's splitting his attention damned close to the same city." Děčin was about an hour away from Prague. It would be close enough to put insane amounts of pressure on him, and for the crew to work the jobs in tandem. "It has to be done both at the same time, and then we have to *poof* while we wait to see if he'll go to ground so we can track him to his home next and, well, get Liam's people in on that."

"Why Gustav Klimt?" Josh asked.

"Why anything?" Stirling replied disgustedly. "I mean, *I* love the painting, although I've pretty much hated everything else Kadjic has liked, but I guess Kadjic has spent the last eight months trying to negotiate buying it from the museum. They refuse, because, well, *it's a fucking classic*. It's one of Prague's top ten featured pieces of art in a lot of lists. So if it suddenly disappears, Kadjic—"

"Will see it as a finger in his face. I get it," Josh said.

"*Both at the same time*?" Liam demanded, because *fuck* Gustav Klimt! It had finally really hit him that Josh was going to be on one side of the city while Liam was on the other, and as he stared at Josh in fury, he saw the absolutely calm expression of a man who had figured this out about three beats ahead.

"It'll be fine," Josh said softly. "I'm going to be in the truck running ops. I mean, it's not as good as the van we've got at home—"

Stirling snorted. "The hell it's not," he said. "Your Uncle Leon must *really* love you, because he came through in a big way. These are, like, secret police vans, retrofitted with modern equipment."

"How do you know it's not for my mother?" Josh asked, but he had a troubled expression on his face as he said it.

"Maybe it's for the whole family," Liam suggested, and Josh shot him a grateful smile.

But still, Liam could see the trouble remained, and he thought he saw the source of it.

"You want we should have supper with your mother and Leon tonight?" he asked softly, and Josh nodded.

"Apparently it's Josh's week to get healthy, both emotionally and physically," he said lightly, and Liam noted the use of the third person. It was something Josh and Grace did when they were talking about personal growth.

"It's a magic thing," Stirling said, completely serious. "Once you start having sex, it's like you *have* to."

Liam cocked his head. "Is it, though? Is it really?"

Josh winked at him. "Maybe it's a Salinger thing," he said, but Liam shook his head.

"Maybe it's that you and your friends are all really young," he said, the age difference hitting him again.

Josh shrugged. "Could be," he said. "Does that mean you're going to say no the next time I try to seduce you?"

Liam felt the flush flooding from his chest, along his extremities, and up to his ears.

"No," he mumbled, glaring at Josh as Josh resumed his relentless tapping. "So, Stirling, tell me again about the job? If we're splitting up, I think we need a *whole* lot more information."

"IT'S SO weird," Josh said as he and Liam caught a rideshare to the hotel. Stirling was meeting up with Tienne at the museum so they could scope out the place with Danny, but Josh was under strict orders to rest. Logistics—and the noisiness of the group as a whole—dictated they get a room at the hotel because Danny's apartment had become, in Danny's words, "A bohemian commune," and Leon had provided them with a private room on the same floor as the suite.

"What's weird?" Liam asked, feeling like his head was on a swivel. The idea that Kadjic was practically in *the same city* after his interaction with Josh—hell, with the entire family—was making him paranoid. He couldn't get over the absolute horror of being seen on the street, in a shop, at a restaurant by the mobster, who undoubtedly had access to a whole lot more muscle here than he did in the States.

"I *feel* fantastic. The plasma infusions are like a magic potion, but the time I spend getting them feels like the ultimate in being an invalid. I can't even explain it."

"Right, boy-o, that's weird."

Josh regarded him mildly. "And the bug up your nose is named…?"

"I'd rather not say his name," Liam muttered as they got in the back of the small vehicle. "Not in public."

"Freaking you out?" Josh asked, grinning.

"Too right," Liam muttered. "But tell me more about you feeling better." He offered a less-distracted smile. "I can't get enough of that."

Josh sighed and leaned his head against Liam's shoulder. "I'm hungry," he declared. "Can we get something amazing to eat on the way to the hotel?"

"Apple strudel?" Liam asked, eager to hear it. To his memory, Josh hadn't voluntarily eaten since he'd asked for real food on the train. They'd managed to get a pretzel down his throat before he'd really gotten scary.

"Schnitzel," Josh said. "I understand there's a fusion place that does garlic tomato breading on their schnitzel—Grace hasn't shut up about it. Want to stop there? It's about a block before we turn off into the hotel."

From the front of the Uber, a young woman with her hair done in several braids and tipped in purple, as well as sporting a nose ring, said, "I know the place. I'll stop there while you run in for takeout if you like." Her voice was lightly accented English, and while Josh engaged her in conversation—and arranged for Liam to stop for takeout, it seemed, Liam sat back and allowed himself to relax a little, as he hadn't done since Munich.

"So where are you from originally?" Josh asked. "Mm… eastern Canada? Maybe Toronto?"

"Good ear!" she said delightedly. "I've been here for ten years. My original job was as a nanny, but the kids grew up, moved out, and I'd fallen in love. I did not want to leave."

"Well, it is a beautiful city," Josh said.

"Not with the city!" the girl chortled. "With my girlfriend! I mean, Prague is beautiful and all, but as soon as she gets her passport and visa, we're going to Toronto immediately. I'm dying to get married, and my parents can afford to throw us the works, but not if they have to fly the whole family to Prague!"

Josh chuckled. "Absolutely fair. Well, I appreciate the rec for the food. The Mozart is amazing, but I miss eating on the streets of a city, you know?"

"You've traveled a lot," she said knowingly. "Always hoping to find that wonderful little hole in the wall that is magic for your visit to a new city."

"Exactly!" Josh crowed. "You understand. My best friend is here too. I'm glad he can do the exploring since I can't right now."

She was paused for traffic at the moment, but she took him in as he leaned against Liam.

"At the hospital—it was bad?" she asked delicately, and Liam knew without looking that his cheeks were hectic with his newfound vigor but that his face was pale with the almost chronic lack of oxygen.

"Not so bad," Josh said. "Bad would be cancer again. This is just getting too worn down before I was fully up to a hundred percent."

"That's still a shame, particularly when you are on a romantic vacation."

Liam felt more than saw Josh's eyes on his face, and some of the panic that had seized him on the train from Munich bled out of his body. He met Josh's eyes happily—but with a certain resignation. This would be life together. Whether Josh's body was 100 percent and he was pushing it to 120 percent, or whether he was trying to rest after pushing himself too hard, the anger at Danny wasn't the only thing that drove Josh Salinger.

Josh Salinger drove Josh Salinger. He wanted to see, do, be, explore, enjoy, manage *all the things*. And he was so bright, so competent at everything he tried, he could fool the world into thinking it was no big deal.

Liam understood what a big deal it *was*. It was Liam's job to catch him when he got knocked down.

"It hasn't been bad," Liam said softly. "I understand our balcony overlooks the river."

Josh smiled delightedly. "Some blankets—"

"—a heater," Liam added sternly.

"And some takeout. I mean, it's the *Mozart*. How could it not be romantic?"

"*That's* the spirit," their happy guide said. "But first let's stop for the takeout, and then let's get you back on vacation."

THEY MANAGED to make it into their room with nobody the wiser, but when Liam set the food on the table, he turned to find Josh standing suggestively close, staring at him with knowing eyes.

"Really?" Liam asked, but gah! The tender skin of Josh's throat tempted him, and Josh's long fingers in his hair tugged him down, down, down into a kiss… just a kiss… just Liam's hands, rucking under Josh's shirt.

Just Josh reaching behind Liam to knead his backside under Liam's slacks… just Liam's fractured "Ahhh…." into Josh's neck as his body flushed Defcon 1 in one quick grope.

"Naked?" Josh practically begged.

"Do you mind your strudel cold?" Liam gasped, but Josh's hands were already at his belt, and Liam was lifting Josh's shirt over his head. The bandage on Josh's arm didn't faze him, not this time. Liam had seen the needle in his arm, knew there would be bruising.

Josh could take the bruising, but he couldn't seem to live without Liam's hands on his skin.

Liam needed reassurance that his lover would be there, warm and vital, when they were joined, and wouldn't fade away a little at a time, like a picture, pixel by pixel.

But he wasn't going for the whole nine yards either.

"Lube?" Josh whispered as they shed their clothes on the way to the bed.

"Blowjobs," Liam managed, possibly his last coherent thought as he kicked off his slacks and Josh's hands found the bare skin of his thighs.

No arguments. Thank God, no arguments. Just their hushed breath, the taste of Josh's skin, the glide of shaking hands across his own. They ended up bare, sliding over each other, touching *everything*, Josh's hand across his chest a revelation, the stroke of his own hand on Josh's cock all the power the universe had ever known.

They kissed until they came, spending in each other's fists, Liam's body shaking so hard with need, with desire and emotion, that his cry into the dim room was involuntary and tortured, swallowed by Josh's kiss until their shaking stopped and they could breathe again.

Josh wiped them off with tissues by the bed and then tugged a throw over them to ward against the September chill. Liam turned and pulled him close as Josh lay on his back and leaned into Liam's kisses on his temple and cheek, and for a moment all was still.

"Okay?" Josh asked, his voice surprisingly hesitant.

"I needed it," Liam said rawly.

"I could tell." Liam didn't have to see his face to know the uncertainty that would pass across his features. "Why?"

And Liam hadn't been going to say it, had been going to take the fear of this in his chest, hauling along that moment like luggage, but he couldn't.

Apparently that's not how love worked.

"You almost passed out on me," he murmured. "I was inside you, and your eyes went glassy, and you started bleeding, and… and I was so scared. I just needed—"

"To see me okay." Josh breathed out. "I get it. I'm sorry."

And Liam was going to say it was fine, but taking a lesson from Josh's meltdown with Danny, he realized he shouldn't. "You should be," he said, with enough petulance to make Josh smile, but enough realness to let him know this was truth. "I… I trusted you to tell me if you were doing okay, Josh. I was so scared." It was the second time he'd said it. "I don't know how we happened. We shouldn't have. We were a moment. Then we were companions on the yacht. And then… one kiss and you were my *everything*. And you were right. We've been *honeymooning*, and we may have been working in between, but it's been the best part of my life here with you. Don't… don't take that away." He sounded like a child, so he knew how Josh felt. "I know there are things you can't help. But… but please, value your life as more than a mastermind or the glue that holds us together. God, if nothing else, value your life because I need you."

Josh turned to him, his eyes shiny in the darkness. "I think," he said softly, "that's all I've needed in my whole life. To be needed. All these wonderful people, trying to be the thing I needed. I needed to know I was important enough to need."

Liam smiled, but something small broke in him. "You need me too, right?" Oh God—how pathetic. In that one moment, he felt himself become younger and smaller than he'd been since his father had died, leaving him head of the house at fourteen.

"So much," Josh said, and then his beautiful boy—his stunning man—was kissing him, and Liam felt it, the force of him, deep in his soul.

He's going to be okay. We're going to be okay. We're going to make it through this okay.

We've got to. I can't see any other way.

A WEEK LATER, Liam was still holding on to that thought as they each scoped out the different sites for the job they were doing in three days.

Liam had spent the day before out at the dock as well, driving in a rented speedboat with Hunter by his side, his normally brown hair dyed blond and still short. When Liam's eyebrows went up, he grunted, "I've been growing it all summer for this gig. I swear I'm gonna keep cutting it short after this until the blond grows out."

"Has it been working?" Liam asked. "This switching of the hair?"

"I don't know. You'll have to ask Carl. He's getting his hair dyed red today so he can be Chuck at the museum. I gotta admit, this is probably a good idea since odds are better Kadjic's going to be there and he'll be less recognizable that way."

Today Liam was used to the blond hair—and Carl's red hair, and Chuck's blond hair, and Liam and Hunter were strolling up and down the docks, both of them dressed in pricey cashmere turtlenecks and jackets in response to the weather. Liam had seen Chicago's cold in the winter, but this crispness so early in the fall was still a surprise.

They both had watch caps on, in deference to the wind, but Liam found he was enjoying the trip. Děčin was a place for the rich. The women were all dressed *very* well, most of the boats were chic testaments to wealth, and the men who owned them were in a constant state of preening. The *sailors*, on the other hand, were intense, flush with their love of their crafts, of their vocations—there really was something about life on the water.

And the atmosphere was one of a last-ditch party. Because it got so cold so quickly, Děčin harbor tended to empty out near the end of August. Those who remained were making plans to fly to their intended destinations, perhaps lingering a week for shopping or other pursuits. They were far enough north that boating—even in a luxury yacht—was dangerous. Boats could be iced in as early as October, and any destination from Prague was at risk for bad weather.

This meant that the *Spelyy Persik* wasn't as difficult to spot as it might have been.

A mid-sized yacht, it was still a grand duchess in a thinning crowd of royalty, and maybe it was because Liam knew who was trapped inside, but it seemed darker, somehow, than the gaiety and ostentation of the pleasure boats in the area.

"Nobody on the decks," Hunter said softly, although his eyes seemed to be scanning every boat on this particular strand.

"Heavy exhaust from the rear," Liam said. This meant the ship wasn't well maintained, which it wouldn't be.

As they watched, a dockworker pushed a dolly full of boxes up the ramp, and a giant of a man, complete with watch cap, stubble, and a windbreaker unzipped to accommodate a belly, came out to sign for it. He pushed it in through one of the lower deck openings, and Liam engaged his tactical brain—but it was tough.

"The thing about boats," he muttered, "is the limited number of entrances and exits."

Hunter grunted. "And every one of them is through a guy who looks like *that*."

"And the engine rooms are full of sailors who are either working out of fear or are pirates themselves. Either way, assume they're enemies, and remember we're civilians and we don't kill enemies."

"Grace would say it's a shame we couldn't suck them up through the middle, like a straw." Hunter chuckled a little, and Liam could see it, that flash of what made a man like Hunter so over the moon for a tornado like Grace.

Well, after the last year or so of getting to know the young man and his bond with Josh, Liam could see Hunter's weakness was also his strength.

Sucking girls up through a straw in the center of the boat would be ridiculous, though the soldiers and sailors would see them and shoot them and that would be out. Now if they had a way through the *bottom* of the boat....

Liam sucked in a breath.

Well, he needed to sneak onto the yacht and find the girls' passports anyway. The situation had to be stealthy at some point. It wasn't like they could paint the walls with the blood of their enemies and then just stroll off the ship with a bunch of trafficked humans.

But still... a straw.

Behind the strand with the yachts and the cabin cruisers was a giant icebreaking ship, getting ready for its winter gig plowing through the dangerous waters of the North to make way for ships bearing supplies to ports living through snow nine months of the year. Ships that big were a maze of staircases and corridors inside, and to work on them, scaffolds and those portable nylon maintenance tubes were used to transport up or down in a timelier manner, hauling more equipment when needed or letting men slide down the tube when they needed to be on the dock quickly.

"A straw," Liam muttered, cocking his head.

"A straw?" Hunter replied, following Liam's gaze. "Really?"

"We'd need generators to pressurize the tube under the water," Liam said slowly. "So we'd have to borrow—"

"Steal," Hunter supplied frankly.

"Borrow," Liam corrected, "a whole lot of heavy-duty nylon fabric, like what you find on the bottom of a raft, some epoxy, a shit-ton of pumps, and some of that clear fiberglass piping that's stacked over by the ice cutter on the industrial dock, and—"

"A cofferdam," Hunter said shortly. "You really think we could build a cofferdam? Like an airlock? And then what? Have the victims escape down a hatch we cut into the bottom of the ship?"

"Do we have anybody who can do that?" Liam asked, and Hunter snorted.

"Chuck *and* Michael can both weld underwater. Michael took a course this spring, and Chuck took the refresher with him. Do you know how much those two assholes could make on that skill alone?"

"More than me, mate," Liam said, not even batting an eyelash. He'd *seen* the requirements for that sort of work, and he lacked the self-control and the hand strength and the willingness to stay underwater for longer than five minutes if he wasn't scuba diving in the Caribbean.

"We'd have to ask them," Liam said.

"Hey, we could ask them," Hunter mimicked. "It's a big job—we'd need most of the crew here for three days, while maybe a skeleton crew preps for the museum job."

Liam glanced at the boat again and thought about a hole opening up above the airlock a cofferdam would provide. Somebody would need to guide the victims to the hole and reassure them they weren't jumping to their deaths—and somebody would need to comb the cabins for their passports, somebody licensed to defend him or herself with force.

"We'd need to slip Molly in through the front," he murmured. "And she'd need to let me in through the service portal at the waterline."

"I'm sure Molly will be thrilled to ditch the museum job to wander a yacht full of minions and help people jump through a hole in the bottom of a boat," Hunter said, and Liam scowled at him.

"What?" Hunter asked.

"With you people, I can't tell if you mean that or not," Liam told him frankly.

"Oh no, seriously—she'll be thrilled," Hunter told him. "The worst part is Grace will wish he was part of it. He'll be mad that he can't do both jobs." After a pause, Hunter added, "As long as they say they can do it."

Liam nodded. "We should look for alternatives today before we meet. It's… you know… just an idea…."

"A WONDERFUL, AWFUL idea," Chuck said, his face lighting up with excitement as they indulged in Prague's version of Thai food in the big suite. "Do you know what that would take?"

"We'd need to borrow equipment to make the tunnel," Michael said, "and we'd need to work the pump for at least twenty-four hours before we could seal the cofferdam to the hull—"

"And we'd need to figure out a way to sneak Molly *into* the boat—" Hunter began.

"And then for her to let me in through the bottom port—" Liam said, but Molly glared at both of them and shook her head.

"I sneak in through the port the morning before the heist," she said. "I hide with the victims and spread the word. Liam, you don't need to come in. I can find their passports."

"I don't want you there without backup," Danny said unequivocally, and there was universal assent.

"But Danny," she said patiently, "we're going to be stretched thin. Who've we got on the museum job anyway?"

"Grace, Josh, Tor, Carl, and Tienne," Danny said. "Since the port job just commandeered the rest of our muscle and Leon."

"I can be muscle," Leon said, miffed.

"You *have* muscle," Danny said, "but you're like Fox—nobody's going to believe you're pit crew, Leon. We need you there with a handy rental yacht to take those girls to Hamburg with their passports and get them home."

"No machine guns for Leon," Felix intoned.

Leon humphed. "You know, my father made both me and Matteo work on the docks for years when we were younger."

"You were probably the belles of the ball," Danny retorted dryly. "When I met Fox, he was pickpocketing tourists in Rome, but every street kid for miles knew he was a rich man's son, which is why he's going to be bidding for the Renoir at the museum."

"I am not," Felix said. "I'll be at the docks with you. Tor can buy the bloody Renoir."

"He'll probably get a better deal on it," Danny snapped, which meant Felix would be at the docks.

"And there goes any cachet as a thief I've ever had," Felix said, scowling.

Danny snorted. "Because all that praise for your 'business acumen' isn't enough cachet for you?"

Felix's chuckle rolled richly. "Those six units of junior college weren't for naught," he said, referring to the forged credentials he and Danny had established so Felix could run the network he and Julia had inherited/stolen from her father. "And not that I don't look forward to being muscle," he said, grinning wolfishly at Leon in one-upsmanship, "but does that mean I'm *not* buying a Renoir that evening?"

"No," Danny said, sighing in concession and obviously changing plans with Felix's teasing. "Kadjic and company didn't spot Tor, and you're right—he's perfectly capable of playing the thwarted bidder."

"Thank you," Tor said smugly.

"Also," Danny told him with a sharp look, "since Marco will be working with the catering crew for the museum gala, he's going to need you to help him keep his cover."

Marco shrugged. "I make the canapes, I serve the canapes…."

Danny shook his head. "Don't be complacent," he said. "If somebody looks at you and says, 'Hey, haven't I seen you before? Chicago?' you say—"

"I say yes, my boyfriend and I have been taking a tasting tour of Europe so I can bring the flavors of Poland and Prague to my hometown," Marco replied smugly. Then he sobered. "You all have proven it many times," he said. "Nobody notices the help."

"Wait," Felix said. "Why isn't Lucius at the museum?"

"Because Lucius is helping to load trafficking victims into Leon's yacht to just get them out of the port to safety," Lucius replied testily. "It's all hands on deck, Felix—quite literally. Tor is less likely to be connected to Chuck. Like it or not, we've been busy beavers, and we're trying not to be seen too much. Tor's cover as the traveling journalist means it's *fine* if he's recognized."

"Way to go, face man," Grace said to Tor, who gave a smug smile.

"I'd say I'm more than a pretty face," he said, "but it's my pretty face that's getting me into the museum."

"I still say I could go in as J.D. Morgan," Josh said. "I was a legit art dealer in Chicago—I have credentials under that name and the whole nine yards. Why can't I be the negotiator for Tor for one of the lesser-known paintings on sale while Grace and Tienne lift the Klimt?"

"Because it took three weeks for that man's fingerprints to fade from your shoulder," Liam snapped. "No."

"Liam's right," Danny said, the pencil making more scratching movements on the legal pad. "That man had a really unhealthy fixation on you, Josh. And I know I'm probably the least reliable person on this subject, but…." Danny shook his head. "I *swear* I didn't mention a word of you to him while we were together. Not Fox, not your mother, and certainly not you. I was thrilled about throwing my own life down the toilet, but I didn't want even the breath of you touching him, not then, not ever. But from the moment he sat up and said hi to us when we were online, I've been living in *terror* that he'd figure out a connection, or that I had a family in the Chicago area. Whether he was trying to hit on you because you're his type—and you are—or whether he's got a suspicion because he's closer than we ever wanted you to be, I just don't want him to even know we're in the same hemisphere, much less the same latitude and longitude. Do we understand?"

"I get it, Uncle Danny," Josh said, and to his credit, Liam didn't hear a breath of resentment there.

"In fact," Danny muttered, "maybe *I* should do the museum job—"

"No," Felix said, putting a hand on Danny's shoulder that Liam could tell was designed to keep Danny from simply lifting up fueled by nervous energy alone and helicoptering around the room. "We need someone to distract the muscle from our end of the docks. That's you and me. I've got the businessman's cachet and the broad shoulders for working the equipment, and you've got the thief chops to slip in and doctor the docking records and manifests. We haven't had a chance to prep for this job, Danny. We need someone who can crack their computer *or* doctor their paperwork as well as charm them silly. Leon's needed to help with the victims, and there's going to be an awful lot of us armed with foil blankets and wearing hip-waders helping those poor kids across the river floor while they try not to freeze to death. All hands means all hands."

"Fucking gala," Danny muttered, tilting his head back. "I mean, it was hard enough we were planning to do this on the same night, but…." He glanced around the full room, where the crew had broken into small groups, everybody planning what they'd have to be doing the next day. Between Marco's information and Hunter and Liam's casing of Děčin, they'd realized that the *Spelyy Presik* was leaving the day after the Prague National Museum gala, which Kadjic was planning to attend. It made sense. Kadjic would conclude his business with the Gustav Klimt painting and then follow his own boatload of trafficked humans to make sure it arrived safely before the ports in Prague were blocked by snow. Marco had picked up on enough gossip to know that rumors of the "Kadjic Curse" were beginning to circulate.

"You would be amazed at what we're being blamed for," Marco had told them the day before, after arriving at the suite with two giant pastry boxes of heaven. "Apparently police have cracked down on Kadjic's distributors in the States—"

"Oh, that's us," Josh said. "Did you miss that meeting? We gave all our info to Nick so after the thing in Colombia he could really put on the pressure."

"Oh," Marco had replied, setting the boxes down and allowing the group to attack and scavenge, which was something that apparently gave him great pleasure when he'd been baking. "Well, he also blames us for a ship leaving the Middle East full of opium that apparently blew up—"

"My bad," Leon said. "Do you have a marzipan croissant?" he asked rather wistfully.

"Your bad?" Marco said, offering him that very thing. "How is it that's your bad?"

Leon had taken the croissant from him and shrugged. "Well, Chuck and Hunter were planning something, but they were spread quite thin. I, as you know, have left the more brutal parts of the import/export business behind me. However, a certain… acquaintance, who also wanted to go straight, asked me how I might trust him, and I said to not do any dealings with Kadjic." Leon shrugged and took a bite of the pastry, his savagely handsome features melting like a child's with pure bliss. "I had no idea he'd blow Kadjic's ship out of the water."

"Oh dear God," Julia said, as they'd all stared at Leon, appalled. "I hope he didn't get… or do I hope he did get…? I am both aghast and strangely heartened by this news, Leon. I have no idea what to hope for."

Leon grinned at her, flakes of butter croissant still in his beard. "Hope my colleague can stay straight and doesn't get caught," he said. "I certainly hadn't anticipated the move, and the colleague had been trying to make a name for himself, so I don't even owe him a favor."

Julia blew out a breath and moved forward to help brush the crumbs from her lover's beard, and Marco continued on with the list of things that had happened to Kadjic since the Salingers had begun their campaign, starting with the painting in Chicago. While the Salingers were really only culpable for about three-quarters of the list, what had come from the bit of gossip was the knowledge that Kadjic was definitely feeling the pressure. It was why he would negotiate the painting and then follow the shipment of girls out in what would ordinarily be a routine operation he'd have nothing at all to do with.

"Excellent," Danny muttered. "If Marco's right, this will do it. His empire is dissolving, his passion will have just betrayed him, and he won't be able to pin the fallout on a single person. This is when he'll go to his den to pout."

"How do you know for sure?" Molly asked, and for a moment Liam held his breath, thinking that this was the height of cheek, interfering with someone as cyclonic as Danny Lightfingers and the man who'd almost broken him.

But Danny proved, once again, why he had a room full of talented geniuses following him around the world to get rid of a monster—one Danny refused to take personally anymore.

"Because his empire is his ego," Danny said. Tienne and Stirling were in a quiet corner, each working on a different project, but within touching distance so their knees and shoulders bumped. "The thing that drove him to order Tienne killed was embarrassment. Tienne's father had made a fool of him when all the poor man had wanted to do was keep his son away from Kadjic's nasty fingers. Think about it. We have embarrassed him on a global stage many, many times. And while he still has more money than God, we have seriously disabled his ability to make *more*. When I met him he was just coming into his own, just becoming the boogeyman he is today. I remember asking him when it was going to be enough, and do you know what he said?"

Molly shook her head.

"He said when his footsteps make the world burn. Well, now they're making *his* world laugh. He's going to need to lick his wounds from that. And when he does, Liam's crew will have him."

"We could have him," Grace said, seemingly out of nowhere. The truth was, Liam had realized, Grace did his share of the planning, but in surprising places. While Josh was always solidly planted with his laptop, Grace was often dancing around other people's conversations. Liam had just finished hearing him do physics problems in his head to help Chuck and Michael figure out how much power the pumps would need to clear out the water for a pathway for their fleeing victims. While the water was cold, their risk of being discovered or of something going wrong with the equipment doubled for every yard of pathway they carved below the river's surface. It was imperative that they balance how much water they had to pump with the well-being of victims that they had to assume were underfed and weakened by captivity, so Grace's quick—and deadly accurate—calculations probably saved lives.

Now here he was, smiling waifishly at Danny and offering to… what?

"What would we do with him if we had him, precious?" Danny asked carefully.

The smile went from waifish to wolfish. "We're not angels, Uncle Danny. And Kadjic is a *very* bad man."

Danny nodded, taking Grace seriously as so many of the crew had learned to do. "It's a legitimate proposal," he said, and Liam was aware that the room had gone still around him. "And, in the heat of the moment, a number of us have dirtied our hands in such a matter." Liam had a memory of Gunrunner's Island and a small but significant body count, including a man who had assaulted Tienne. "But…." Danny swallowed and cupped Grace's cheek in a gesture that was pure affection. "No, my darling boy," he said softly. "I would never, in a million years, want you to put a thing like that on your soul."

Grace swallowed in turn, and the whole room could see his eyes grow shiny. In a move like a darting fish, he gave Danny a short, fierce hug before coming to sit next to Josh.

Josh stopped his relentless tapping to wrap an arm around Grace's shoulder and whisper in his hair, and Hunter left his stand as sentinel of the room to Carl and came to sit down on the floor by Grace's feet.

And Liam felt a contentment, an easiness, because these people he'd come to love weren't going to change in this endeavor—Grace *could* be a first-rate, terrifying assassin.

But he wasn't going to be, because the people who loved him wanted him to remain Grace.

And Josh—his Josh—had always been focused, always been super competent, always been their mastermind. And he'd always done his best for those he loved.

Liam thought that maybe they would be okay.

"So, Josh," Danny said, and Josh glanced up from the one-handed work he'd been doing on his computer. "How's the gala job going?"

"Well," Josh said, "lucky for us, Kadjic has a hard-on for somebody really well-known this time. That last artist was a little obscure, so we had to go into her house and break into her loft to search for lost canvases. This is Gustav fucking Klimt, and it's one of his most famous paintings, so it's in the middle of the Trade Fair Palace. And the reason this is good, Carl?"

Liam grinned because he'd originally been in on the gala job and had gotten to scope out the entire National Gallery of Prague.

"Because the Trade Fair Palace is in the dead center of town," Carl said. "And the gala is for another Klimt masterpiece, *Prince William Nii Nortey Dowuona*—"

"No," Molly said, turning her attention from the yacht schematics that Stirling had brought up for her. "Is that really the name of the painting?"

"It's a very handsome painting of Prince William, who was a prince of Ghana in the 1890s," Carl said. "It was stolen by Nazis and disappeared—

many feared it was destroyed. The painting was marvelous, but the subject was Black, and we know the Nazis were fuckheads about that."

"Still are," Stirling muttered. "Only now they're paid by the US government."

"One crisis at a time," Danny said. "Kadjic today, the mobsters in the White House tomorrow."

"Deal," everybody breathed, and Carl continued.

"So the gala is for the Prince William painting, which Kadjic doesn't want—"

"Because in spite of his fascination with Dizzy Gillespie," Danny added, "he is very much a Nazi fuckhead."

"Exactly," Carl said. "And this gives us some drawbacks and some bennies. One of the drawbacks, of course, is that the Klimt part of the museum is going to be rather full."

"And the bennies?" Danny prodded.

"The attention is going to be on the Prince William painting," Carl said.

"Also," Josh said, "that *The Maiden* is going to be in a slightly darkened corner of the museum because the Prince William is everybody's darling—as it should be. Now I've been directed to stay in the van, but Grace, Carl, and Tienne have been in and out of the museum, pretty much scouring the Klimt exhibit in its entirety, while I've been looking at schematics. Part of our problem is that *The Maiden* isn't a small painting—it's slightly larger than six by six feet, and hefting it out of there is going to be a challenge. But I think we've got an in—unfortunately it's tomorrow night and not the night after."

"What's our in?" Felix asked.

"A special cleaning crew," Julia said. While Carl had been asking questions as himself, she and Tor had simply been wandering around the museum like tourists, albeit Julia wore a disguise. Between them they'd managed a thorough casing of the place without exposing Grace, Tienne, Josh, and Molly, who had been getting a lot of exposure as of late. "They will be escorted by a docent with key privileges to get the nooks and crannies. It's my understanding that some of the, uhm, finer points of the alarm systems will be shut off so they can clean the frames of the paintings in that section of the museum."

"What's our gambit?" Danny asked.

"I made a painting!" Tienne said excitedly, breaking up the rhythm, but given the fond looks aimed his way, nobody seemed to care.

"Of course you did," Danny said, offering him a radiant smile. "And in record time too, precious—how did you do that?"

"Two weeks, Uncle Danny," Tienne said. "But it is fine. As soon as I heard Kadjic had been bidding on the painting, I started to research and plan. Stirling got me a studio—it's very pretty. I would like to paint there next summer. May I?"

"Of course," Danny said. "But for now, the painting…."

"Oh." Tienne gave a shy smile. "It is not my best, but," he gave a truly Gallic shrug, "it shall suffice."

"I'm sure it shall," Danny agreed with a nod. "Now, is it perfect, or…."

Tienne shook his head negative, quite pleased with himself. "A teeny tiny flaw," he said, almost purring like a kitten. "In one corner, where Kadjic's letters were before, I placed the Lightfingers logo. It's almost invisible, but I think…."

"Oh yes," Danny said. "They'll be looking for it." He sighed. "So here's our big question. Do we do the boat job on the same night we're doing the Klimt job, in spite of the fact that Kadjic won't be in either place, or do we wait for him to appear at the gala and do the boat job that night, risking that he'll be tipped off to the Klimt job?"

Chuck grunted. "I hate to put a number to this, Danny, but it's literally going to take us every second of the next three days to build a cofferdam, pump all the water out, and cut a hole in the bottom of the yacht. Besides, if we're smuggling two people *in*, they are going to need some time to figure that shit out too."

"Decision made," Danny said lightly. "We should still have people at the gala to keep track of what Kadjic is doing. If he's as paranoid as he was ten years ago, he'll get so much as a whisper of Lightfingers on the Klimt and take off for his bigger business venture, and we may need you all to run interference for us while we finish up. There's at least an hour between the two—it's long enough for an emergency escape."

"Besides," Marco said practically, "he's being driven by his own people around town, in his own vehicle. If you want an in to where his hideaway is—or even where his transportation hubs are—it would be a good time to plant a bug."

"Or a fish and some broccoli," Grace said, sounding insanely happy about this. Well, Liam understood that at home, stinking up the cars of rich douchebags was one of Grace's favorite hobbies.

"I'd rather you not this time, precious," Danny said mildly. "You're not merely facing exposure with this one. Kadjic will kill you. A tracker or a destination are both more than enough reason to park the van and do surveillance, yes?"

Grace sighed. "Yes, Uncle Danny," he said, melting against Josh again.

"That's my boy," Danny murmured and then sat back in his chair, rubbing the back of his neck. Felix moved behind him and started massaging his shoulders, and Liam watched as the two of them simply relaxed in each other's presence.

He glanced around, clocking the other members of the crew, and spotted a hole in their midst. "Where's Julia?" he asked.

"Resting," Leon said grimly, emerging from their suite bedroom. "She's been doing much of the surveillance on the museum, and she's quite fatigued."

Josh glanced up from his tapping and said, "She's doing okay, right?"

"Yes, son," Leon said softly, approaching them while the room lapsed into murmurs of fierce concentration. "I'll tell her you asked."

Josh gave him a thin little smile—not defensive but tired. "Thanks, Uncle Leon." He paused. "It's nice, you know, that you take such good care of her. Danny and Felix do too, but she deserves somebody special. And kind."

Liam had no other word for the look on Josh's uncle's face. He melted.

"You think so?" Leon asked.

"Well, yes," Josh said. He put more energy into his smile, although the night was moving on, and Liam could tell it cost him. "I mean, you showed up for me, and you sort of jumped right into the family, and that's great. I'm glad you did—I might not have said that before. But my mom… I mean, you know. My *mom* is sort of too good for *anybody*. But you understand that about her, and you work to overcome being a simple human next to a goddess, and I appreciate that." He swallowed. "I am *really* excited about the baby. She's got so much love to give. She was an *amazing* mom for me—and I didn't know how scared she was, although I understand that now. I think that with a partner, and my dads, and the whole family—I think she'll get to be a parent again in a whole new way. Thank you for giving that to her. Sincerely."

Leon's eyes had gotten shiny, and he palmed them like the macho Mediterranean badass he undoubtedly was. With his other hand, he reached down and squeezed Josh's shoulder, gently, and then bent over the couch and kissed his temple, like Liam had seen Felix or Danny do countless times.

"You are welcome," Leon whispered. "Thank you. Thank you so much for letting me join your family. I miss my brother—thank you so much for letting me know you and getting a little of him back."

And with that he turned away, going back to the bedroom, Liam presumed, to get his composure.

When Liam glanced up around the room, the only two people watching them were Danny and Felix.

"Good job, son," Felix said softly.

Danny simply held his hand to his heart and nodded.

Josh shrugged in embarrassment and then concentrated fiercely on his work.

Liam checked to see if Grace had caught any of that, but Grace was fast asleep on Josh's shoulder. It was only then that Liam caught sight of the clock and realized how late it was, how hard everybody had been working, and remembered that Josh had another treatment in the morning.

"Bed," he said softly.

"Just this one more," Josh whined.

Liam closed the laptop with gentle intent. "You can finish tomorrow. While you're at the hospital. Come on, Josh. This is a group effort, and we've got three days. You don't get to play if you get a nosebleed and pass out—that's the rules."

Josh gave him an anguished glare and then, to Liam's intense relief, nodded.

"Hunter?" Liam murmured, and Hunter moved from where *he* was doing calculations that needed a compass and triangle to stand and scoop Grace into his arms.

"Our room," Liam murmured, because the suite was busy and it only had so many attached rooms, and it wasn't like Liam and Josh were going to go have a quick shag right now.

Hunter nodded gratefully and followed them into the hallway, and soon Grace was deposited on one side of the big bed and Josh on the other.

"I'll be back to get him in an hour or so," Hunter said. "If you don't mind, can we crash on your hide-a-bed?"

"No worries," Liam told him, and then Hunter left, and it was just Josh and Liam while Liam pulled off Josh's boots. Like Grace and Danny, he was wearing thieves' clothes—which were great for sleeping, running, and stealing.

Tonight it would be sleeping.

"You did good tonight," Liam said softly. "I think your Uncle Leon needed to hear that."

"And now I feel bad for not saying it sooner. Guilt is a terrible thing." Josh said that last part on a yawn. "Liam?"

"Yeah?"

"Grace and I are going to take over Grace's dance school when this thing with Kadjic is done."

Liam smiled and sat on the bed. The two of them had so much potential—so many ideas. "Good idea, boy-o."

"You'll visit, right?"

"Aye. And you'll visit me. And this isn't our last adventure by any means."

Josh smiled a little, his eyes closed. "We were thinking about recruiting… maybe not perfect kids. Like, juvenile hall kids. Kids who need a break and have a certain set of skills."

"And morals," Liam said. "Don't take your good hearts for granted."

Josh *hmm*ed, eyes still closed. "I want to be with you as much as possible. Maybe I can come on your adventures when you're not coming on mine."

"Sounds like a lot to do, Joshua Daniel. Maybe you should rest up so we can get this done first."

"I love you. I love you so much. Nobody else could get me to go to bed early, you know."

Liam chuckled. "I am aware."

He lowered his head then and tried to put his soul in the kiss. And then he was back out and down the hall, in the thick of things, working with the family. *His* family now. Funny how that worked.

Easy as Klimt

STIRLING HAD been right; the van Leon had purchased for them was glorious. Small—the roads of Eastern Europe weren't as wide as those in America, and the small squarish vehicle with the name of a local cleaning service stenciled neatly on the doors was not nearly as hefty and decadent as their surveillance van in Chicago—but well equipped. Josh had even spotted a coffee maker tucked back in one of the cupboards.

The Klimt job had gone off *flawlessly* the night before. Tienne and Grace had slipped in, dressed in the purloined uniform of the specialized cleaners, and they'd managed to move the Klimt into a janitor's closet. There, they stripped the original canvas from the frame and replaced it with the forgery, and then they'd wrapped the real thing lovingly in an acid-resistant linen sheath and rolled it carefully into a waterproof, silicone-lined canister.

Which they left in the back of the janitor's closet with a giant label, in Czech, that said, *The Maiden* by Gustav Klimt.

They were not actually *trying* to steal the painting—much to Grace's eternal disgust. They were *trying* to let Kadjic know that they knew he *wanted* the painting. The hope was that, since the Klimt wing would be closed until the gala—the better to reveal the *Prince William*—the forgery and the original painting would not be noticed until there was a crowd of people to appreciate the… misplacement.

Tonight, Grace, who'd had his hair dyed white blond and streaked with strands of gold and violet sparkles that morning after the job, and Tienne, who was the only person in the crew who hadn't changed his hair because with his slender build and long blond ponytail, he could *also* be their blond woman, both wrapped colorful scarves around their necks and slouched about the gallery with tiny drinks in their hands, scooping hors d'oeuvres and lifting wallets in a desultory fashion while Carl made polite conversation with the chief docent.

All of them had their attention focused on Kadjic and his entourage, who kept stomping like theater thugs around the Klimt wing, first sneering at the Prince William and then eyeballing Carl with deep suspicion.

"Kadjic knows him," Grace murmured in Josh's ear, "but he can't place him. It's almost delicious. And Carl's not even trying to hide. He's using the same ID he used for the party. Who knew being an insurance guy made you bulletproof."

"How's Tor and my mother doing?" Josh asked. They'd been stretched so thin that while Marco was engaged in the museum's food facilities, Lucius had been forced to do basic manual labor on the dock to get the cofferdam into place and help the girls escape. Julia *had* been going to go on Carl's arm, but that would have been *too* much of a coincidence. Instead, she and Molly had planned her outfit carefully—complete with a red wig, temporary freckles, and green contacts. Pregnancy had added weight to her figure, and instead of bemoaning it, they'd capitalized on it, dressing her in a full green skirt and gold sweater.

She still looked stunning—as all the men in her life dutifully and enthusiastically told her—but she also appeared a little older and a lot more brazen and less reserved. To Josh's delight, she was fully playing into her role as Tor's literary agent and "a friend of his mother's," and Tor was a charming young friend enjoying her company.

"We're fine, darling," Julia murmured through what sounded like a full mouth. "And Marco's canapes are to die for. We'll need to kidnap that boy to get him back to Chicago, mark my words."

"No kidnapping necessary," Tor replied. "He can't wait to get home and try new recipes. I'm sorry, can I help you?"

From the van, Josh's hackles went up. He did *not* like the edge to Tor's voice, and in a moment, through Tor's and his mother's transceivers, he knew why.

"You look familiar," came the oily voice of the man they'd been torturing for nearly two months. "Why is that?"

Tor replied, "My boyfriend works as a temporary chef at your hotel, Mr. Kadjic. I've seen you there many times."

There was a stunned silence, as if the truth had been the last thing Kadjic had expected. "His eggs benedict is… unusual," he said, with the same inflection someone else might have used when saying "full of cockroaches."

"He uses his own recipe," Tor said. "If you let me know what you dislike, I'm sure he'll change it when it's your order."

"It is too late," Kadjic replied, as though Tor and Marco should have been anticipating his every need. "I shall be leaving Prague in the morning and dining on the road."

"Well, that's a shame," Tor told him. "I'll certainly neglect to pass on your lack of regard."

Josh had to cover his mouth to avoid barking laughter into his microphone before he caught the gist of what Kadjic had been saying. They'd known they might have to plant bugs on Kadjic's vehicle, but this new information only made that more urgent.

With the press of a button, he was talking to Grace and Tienne.

"Kadjic's with my mother and Tor—you guys need to get out to the parking lot, stat, and bug his vehicle before somebody spots the painting and goes apeshit."

"Hear you, Anemia Boy," Grace murmured. "Let me just slip out the side door—"

"No!" Josh cried. "Not the west entrance, you moron—it's alarmed!"

There was a sudden shrill electronic wail, and Grace's muttered, "Fuck." Then, louder, "Oh no! I thought this was how I got to the U-Bahnhof!"

Grace could do *many* things with amazing skill. Speak German was not one of them. But as Josh peered through the hacked CCTV feed and saw all the people gathering around him, trying to make him feel better as he—utilizing years of theater experience and getting away with everything sans murder—played the innocent fuckup, he thought perhaps with a face as beautiful as Grace's, nobody cared how dumb he made himself look.

Unfortunately that left only one of them to bug the car, which was half the reason they were there anyway.

"Tienne?" Josh asked. "Can you surrender your pass and go out the front?"

"Oui, oui," Tienne murmured. "Yes, I wish to leave a bit early. Too many cocktails—I am not so good with wine."

Josh fought the temptation to bang his head against his keyboard.

"I mean coffee," Tienne supplied apologetically. "Yes. I have been drinking Viennese coffee. It is not sitting well in my stomach. Apologies."

Josh checked out the feed and saw that no, nobody suspected Tienne, but he too was stuck in a social situation that he was unable to escape quickly. Well, hell—it was bound to happen. Too many jobs, too short a time—improvisation was the name of the game.

"Mom," Josh murmured, securing his earbud and grabbing the last two tracers from the drawer of tracking equipment. "Can you make nice with Kadjic for another five minutes?"

"Sure," his mother murmured. "Cobras aren't dangerous as long as you keep making eye contact."

Oh God.

"Five minutes," he repeated. "Then get the fuck out of there."

With that, he slid out of the back of the van and made a slow spin of the valet parking area. Carl had actually driven the van and given the keys to the valet while the rest of the party had arrived via public transport or on foot, but they *all* had a set of these keys, including Josh.

Okay, then. He spotted Kadjic's giant gas-guzzling American import in the corner and then scoped out the valets, who were running to and fro, and plotted a course that would get him to the town car while keeping him in the shadows.

It was slow going, and he was frustrated to find himself winded halfway through. God*dammit*, he was tired of this shit.

It wasn't until he got about three-quarters of the way there that he saw a valet heading directly for the back quarter and heard *everybody* shouting in his ear.

"Josh, he's leaving!" his mother said, while Grace said, "His goon just gave his ticket to the valet stand," and then, most concerning, was Tor.

"Shit, Josh—he spotted the forgery. He's yelling something at Carl's art docent now, and I think he's made Carl too."

"Almost there," Josh panted, sprinting for the town car. "Fuck me. It's going to be close."

All the times he'd jumped off buildings or danced for hours. All the times he'd pushed his body to its max, strong, fleet, graceful, and it turned out the most important race of his life was being run in a back parking lot as he tried to beat a valet who was attempting to finish his cigarette quickly before they both got to the same town car.

At that moment, something complicated went on in his ear—and, as usual, it had to do with Grace.

"Hey—ouch! The fuck!"

And then, that voice. "I *know* you." And, almost bewildered. "I *know* you. I've seen you on surveillance—you've… you've been *everywhere*!"

"Mister," Grace said, "I've never seen you before in my life."

Oh God—Grace. Who could rob a nun blind but couldn't *fucking lie*.

"Grab him," Kadjic muttered, and there was something jumpy in his voice. Josh pictured the jowly mobster with his eyes flickering in all directions. Had he seen Carl? Was he rethinking Julia? Did Tienne appear suspect? To Kadjic—so paranoid they didn't know where he actually lived—every interaction, every frustration of the last two months, must have been scrolling through his mind.

Josh hoped it was epic. He hoped Kadjic saw shadows that reminded him of old enemies and the faces of the dead he'd left behind in every stranger's eyes.

"Grab me?" Grace protested. "Grab me? Help! Help! I'm being—*oolf*!"

Oh God. Oh God. They had Grace!

"Josh," Carl said, his voice edging on panic. "They left. They're heading for the valet lot themselves. Somebody sounded the alarm for the Klimt, and he knows the game is on. You need to duck out of sight ASAP."

Josh didn't have enough breath to answer. The valet had stopped to shout instructions to two of Kadjic's thugs as they neared the entryway to the valet lot, and Josh was mere feet from the back of the town car. From this angle, Josh could see Grace, sagging in the grip of one of the thugs.

Grace.

Shit. Kadjic was approaching—Josh was going to get busted if he didn't find someplace to hide, and find it *now*.

He felt the trickle of blood from his nose as he fell against the back of the town car, fortunately in the shadows. He was hidden from Kadjic's party, but could still watch them advance, and he thought helplessly that most of the vehicles out in this area were low-slung growly sportscars that would probably give Chuck a hard-on but that he could hardly roll under without getting squashed.

The trunk latch rattled underneath his weight, and his panic and his breathlessness faded as his formidable brain took over.

He reached into his pocket and pulled out his lock picks, trying to remember if the valet had already clicked the alarm system as he'd approached.

He must have, Josh thought as he opened the trunk and slipped in, then closed it from the safety handle inside.

Nobody even saw him hide.

LIAM WONDERED how old he was now. He'd been about to turn thirty-one and feeling mighty old next to his young lover, whom he refused to relinquish, before Molly had opened the bottom hatch, the one level with the dock, so he could slip into the yacht, but that felt like it was a thousand years ago.

His path had been littered with moaning henchmen with zip-ties around their wrists—but only three of them.

"How many?" he asked softly as he followed her through the labyrinthine corridors.

"There's at least twenty," she said. "Right now most of them are up in the common room, whining about the rations." There was a touch of smugness in her voice. She'd been "delivered" that morning in a big pallet of boxes that had been transported to the cargo hold. The markings on the side had indicated steaks and pies, and discovering those boxes had been emptied had probably pissed a lot of the lower ranks off.

They'd be assuming the captains had all dined well that night. The captains would all be assuming they worked with thieves. That hadn't been the plan, but it was a windfall to sow dissension in the ranks before you robbed them of their cargo.

"Have you made contact with the victims yet?"

Molly gave him a fierce look. "Some of them are in a bad way," she said unhappily. "They'll need medical. I already contacted Felix and Danny, but they're going to need help swimming under the dock to the other ship."

Liam grunted and wished for maybe the more bloodthirsty mindset of a TV law enforcer. "Due process," he whispered to himself. "Due process. Due process."

One of the men at his feet moaned and spat, and Liam kicked him in the ribs.

That process was due, he thought sourly.

"How close are we to moving them out?" he asked her.

"Chuck popped the hull about ten minutes ago," she said. "I've got a quiet evacuation going, but I need to get back. You were right—we need you to get their passports, because they need some guidance on this end. You know where to go?"

He bent to the feet of the guy he'd just kicked and took in his clothes. Liam was wearing thieves' clothes—black sweats, black turtleneck, black balaclava. The guy at his feet had a green balaclava but pale, freckled features. Liam tucked his own hat in his pocket and grabbed the green hat, relieved when it seemed clean and not greasy.

"Think I'll pass?" he asked Molly, tucking the hat on his head.

"Definitely," she said. "These guys don't know each other's names. I hung out in the galley for a bit and listened in—those Russian lessons are really paying off, by the way."

Liam laughed softly to himself and wondered how many languages the Salingers knew between all of them. Maybe their next caper should involve the Middle and Far East so they could pick up different traditions and different tongues.

"Good," he said. "I speak a few words. And I definitely know 'The captain needs something from his quarters.' You keep the victims heading down the airlock. I'll get their passports. You ready?"

She paused, sober. "Any news from the other end?"

Liam gave her a warm smile. "Just heard from Josh—apparently his mother looked straight at Kadjic and he didn't recognize her. He said it was epic," he told her, using Josh's word. "So far so good, although they're hoping the painting switch will be discovered before the end of the night."

"Epic," she said, offering a fist bump. He gave her one in return, and she slipped off toward the engine room, where, he presumed, the three henchmen with head injuries had come from.

It was his turn now.

He'd been in on a few raids of human trafficking boats, although none as big as this one.

Still, the MO of keeping the captives' passports in the captain's safe was not new. Those were gold. Those were the things the captors would use to get the women what appeared to be legitimate employment when they reached their destination, and the things that would be held in reserve so the women would never try to escape. While the US was known for its draconian and inhumane measures toward illegal immigrants, they weren't the only ones, and human chattel had a value all its own. Being caught without a passport could be absolutely deadly.

Liam made his way up out of the steerage compartment, past the common area, and up another steep series of steps toward the captain's quarters. He passed one or two crew members, but not closely. They'd all been heading toward the chow line, and he was grateful. While he did speak his own limited amount of Russian, lying was harder in another language, and incapacitating an opponent took time.

It's one of the reasons he loved Danny and Josh's crew. It was worth it to him to plan an elaborate operation that would save lives and trauma.

"Liam, you there?" Stirling said into his ear.

"Da," Liam murmured, spotting the captain's quarters near the front of the main deck. He pulled out his own lockpicks and—thanks to Danny's tutelage during those long-ago visits to the rehab center—made quick work of the lock.

He paused to glance around, grateful the room was empty.

"Just entered. The safe is back behind the bar. Getting there. How's things on your end?"

"We have… uhm, disturbing news from the gala," Stirling told him. "And we have reason to believe Kadjic might be on his way with Grace in the car with him."

Liam almost dropped his lockpicking kit. "I beg your pardon?"

"And, well, they don't know it, but Carl said Josh was in the trunk."

Liam's vision went black. That fast. He felt himself going down, probably about to nail his head on the small, sharp-angled counters to be found even in the captain's quarters of this stingy, utilitarian yacht, and he caught himself, barely, with a hand on the back of a chair.

"Josh is what?" he asked, trying to breathe.

"Carl said it went bad fast," Stirling told him. "They're all in the van now, heading this way. Josh was about to tag the town car with trackers, so those, at least, are working, but Kadjic suspects, and we've got to get a move on."

"Fuck. Does Molly know?"

"She's got the girls coming out as fast as she can," Stirling said. "When you're done there, if you could… you know?"

"I've got her back," Liam said. The siblings would never look alike, but they'd never be apart, Liam knew. He wondered if his brother, Robert, knew what he was in for, harboring a crush on Molly Christopher. She was nobody to be trifled with—but she also deserved every bit of happiness her brother had found with the quiet, surprising Tienne.

That thought, of all things, grounded him. God, he wanted to go swooping into the night to rescue Josh, who had—what? Smuggled himself aboard the vehicle that Grace was about to get thrown into? But Josh had people swooping to his rescue. It was Liam's job to protect the people on this yacht, to help the captives, to have Molly Christopher's back.

Josh—whether physically weak or jumping out of buildings—was pretty adept at taking care of himself.

With a deep breath and a sense of purpose, Liam crouched between the small wet bar and the wall, pulled out the electronic gadget that would hack directly into the chip in the safe that held the code, and started his first robbery.

Passports first. Molly and the rest of the captives next.

Exfil after that.

Saving Josh's ass if he hadn't done it himself before Liam got there? He'd get there. It would happen.

Liam had to have faith.

"REMEMBER," JOSH murmured, "Don't talk."

"I am not stupid!" Grace proclaimed loudly, and Josh, jouncing in the trunk of the car and trying hard not to vomit, wanted to smack him.

From the front of the car—and in the commlink—Josh heard the confusion of the guard and the driver and of the very dangerous man in the back of the car with Grace.

"I know you're not stupid," Kadjic was saying. "You are an astounding thief."

"Prove it," Grace said, so much adolescent hostility in his voice that Josh winced.

"Did you or did you not switch the paintings in Chicago?"

"Which ones?" Grace asked—legitimately, but Kadjic could hardly know that.

"The Abercrombie!" Kadjic exclaimed, and Josh halfway expected him to choke on his own tongue with rage. "You know damned well that—"

"I didn't steal that painting," Grace said.

"I *saw* you there catering the event!"

"But I didn't steal the painting," Grace said virtuously. "Celeste's twenty-karat diamond—*that* I stole, but she hasn't noticed it yet."

Josh snorted. "I knew it," he murmured.

"I was very smooth," Grace said to both of them. "What else do you think I've done? Come on—I want to hear!"

"The Lightfingers forgery in the Louvre," Kadjic accused, his voice high and ringing with triumph.

"What are you talking about, stupid mobster man? I don't paint!"

"But I *know* you were there—I saw footage. There were six of you with black clothes and… and hats and masks and…."

"If there were hats and masks, how would you know me from a hat and a mask? Geeze, Mister, if you're going to kill me, kill me for that diamond. It's worth a *fortune*."

"*I don't want the bloody diamond! I want Lightfingers and the bloody Klimt you stole*!"

"That's *nasty*!" Grace retorted, sounding as wounded as a startled racoon. "I didn't finger anybody's bloody Kl—"

"I will beat you!" Kadjic screamed, and for a moment, Josh's heart stopped, he was so afraid for his friend.

"If you beat me," Grace said, "you'll never find the Rothschild Egg I slipped into a maintenance closet tonight. I mean, it's not fingering a bloody Kli—"

"You stole a *Rothschild Egg*?" Kadjic gasped, sounding as though slapped. "How did I not know about that?"

"Because you're all excited about lady parts? I don't know, you tell me!"

"Did you really?" Josh asked, forgetting that he wasn't supposed to be talking to his friend *right now*.

"I don't believe you," Kadjic said at the same time.

"Why do people *always* underestimate me?" Grace retorted. "Why doesn't somebody go online and check for it?"

And Josh realized he *had* underestimated his friend.

"Stirling!" he whispered, clicking his earpiece three times to change receivers.

"Josh?" Stirling asked, sounding frantic. "You okay?"

"Cramped," Josh admitted. "And would love some fresh air. But Grace just told Kadjic to look online for a stolen Rothschild Egg at the museum."

"Did he really?" Stirling squawked.

"*Does it matter*? Trace that request to Kadjic's phone, and then you can track him should he ditch this vehicle!"

"Oh my God. Oh my God—that's brilliant. I don't know if *I'm* that brilliant—"

"Please-please-please-please…," Josh whispered.

"I'm working!" Stirling practically sang.

Josh kept his begging to himself after that and tuned in to what Grace was saying.

"Well, did you find it?" Grace asked, presumably speaking to one of the flunkies.

There was a flurry of Russian, too fast for Josh to follow, and then Stirling said, "Woohoo! I found it!"

"I'll leave a tracer here," Josh whispered. "And one wherever he—"

"Josh, he's heading here."

"He's what?" Josh squeaked.

"What was that?" Kadjic asked.

Josh held his breath, and Stirling told him, "He's heading straight for Děčin. It worked—we spooked him. But he's heading for us, and we're not done yet."

"Shit," Josh muttered. He was thinking, *Reveal myself now or wait to see… reveal myself now or wait to see….* But at that moment Grace spoke up again.

"You found it," Grace said smugly. "I can tell. See? Left that egg right there. Why, did you want it?"

"I *wanted* the Klimt!" Kadjic snarled. "And now I get neither Klimt nor egg. What do you say to that, you rank guttersnipe?"

Grace started to cackle. "Mister, my father can buy and sell you for spare parts. You don't have to be born in the gutter to know how to snipe, you hear me?"

Josh winced, and in his ear, Stirling—who must have tuned in to Grace's frequency too, said, "He must be really scared."

"I should get their attention," Josh murmured.

"No!" Stirling yelped.

"No!" Grace yelped too.

"Stay there until you can really help him," Stirling urged.

"Fine," Josh grumbled, and he didn't state the thing he knew and they didn't. Even if the hatch popped, he would need help getting out. His body, the thing he'd valued for his independence, was giving out on him when he needed it most. Careful in the confines of the trunk, he rolled to his side, making sure not to crush his earwig. There was an emergency foil blanket back there, and he pulled it over his body, not sure if he was overheated from the engine or freezing from the fifty-degree coolness permeating the trunk, but knowing a shock blanket was never a bad idea. With a deep breath against the panic of claustrophobia and of knowing Grace was in the hands of their most mortal enemy, he closed his eyes and put his biggest asset to use.

Think-think-think-think-think....

Oh shit.

"Stirling," he asked, barely above the hum of the engine, "how's the op going?"

"Funny you should ask that," Stirling began, and Josh had to work not to pop the trunk and leap out of the vehicle as it ran.

LIAM'S SENSE of direction was best described as fair-to-middling, which was one of the reasons he always hovered over his laptop before an op. He supposed it had something to do with his mild dyslexia—remembering his left from his right was difficult and painstaking, but it wasn't something he made a big deal out of because people tended not to trust somebody when they had that problem.

It took a concentrated effort to zoom through the ship's corridors, climbing up to one deck and down to another in order to bypass the galley, and feeling the giant plastic-covered package of passports thudding against his hip from the black canvas satchel he'd brought in with him. Danny's idea, of course, or Liam would have been forced to shove them down the front of his pants.

In his ear, scenes from his nightmares played out while he tried to do his bloody job.

"Molly, luv," he sang, "I don't suppose you know how many girls you have?"

"Sixty-three," she said promptly. "How many passports do you have?"

"Sixty-five," he replied, his voice grim. "Any idea where to search for the missing girls?"

"Hold on," she said. "Some of the girls know English."

He let her do that while he tagged overwatch. "Stirling, how are they doing?"

"Grace has almost gotten himself killed at least three times in one conversation," Stirling said brutally. "And Josh keeps threatening to expose his position to shut Grace up."

"No," Liam said, his heart thundering in his ears.

"Oh *hell* no," said Felix.

"And fuck no," Danny said. Liam knew they'd both been escorting girls from the cold water of the river, where they'd had to swim the last twenty feet from where the inflatable path to the cofferdam gave out, under the dock that held Leon's yacht, and up the offered narrow steps into the bottom portal itself.

A volunteer Julia had secured from heaven knew where was there to give the victims hot soup and clean warm clothes and promise them their passports and a return to their homes, which Interpol would secure just as soon as Liam (Ha! Like he could do this alone!) broke them out.

And Chuck and Hunter were down below the ship, working whatever industrial magic they'd produced to keep the water pumped from the hole they'd carved in the hull.

Thin, he thought in frustration. *So many of us, and we are spread too thin.*

Well, they *were* attempting, in one fell swoop, what many government agencies had tried to do over the last fifteen years.

And they were so close to succeeding—but dear God, what the cost?

"Ideas?" Liam panted. In the silence after his last breath, he heard a sound—one he'd heard on the streets often, and one he was there to stop. With a frustrated grunt, he threw open the door to the cabin he was passing and took in the scene with one glance.

Sex slaves were often trained, and it was as brutal and as awful as it sounded. One girl was on her back, sobbing, and another girl was chained to a fixture in the corner of the room, and Liam didn't have time to be a good guy.

He didn't carry guns—but he did carry a telescoping baton and a short dagger on his belt. He pulled off the baton in one practiced gesture and telescoped it out in mid-swing. It hit the crewman assaulting the girl at the base of the skull and spine, killing him before he had a chance to turn his head. With a grunt, Liam pulled him off the girl, saying, "Found the other two girls—taking them to escape now."

Turning to the one on the bed, he asked, "All right?" in his threadbare Russian. She nodded numbly and stood, pulling the rags of her shirt around her, crossing her bare legs in what was obviously pain.

"Wash," he said, trying for gentleness. "Get dressed. We have little time to leave."

She swallowed, tears running down her face, and then swallowed again. And then showed far more courage than Liam would have been able to and set about the cabin, going far enough to pull the sweater off her rapist's back to cover her thin adolescent body.

It hung down to her knees, which was cover enough for Liam. He was busy picking the locks on the other girl's chains. The two girls embraced, sobbing, mumbling to each other in Russian, and Liam gestured them firmly out the door and down the stairs to the next deck,

He knew the word for *hurry*, and that was enough. As they ran, he with his telescoping rod held at his side, he tried his comms again.

"I ask again, ideas?"

"We've been discussing that while you were busy," Danny said, coming back online. "How much do you know about munitions?"

Liam grimaced. "Not as much as Chuck and Hunter," he said. "And they happen to be right under the ship."

"Good point," Danny said. "But they're going to need your help."

"Fair enough," Liam muttered, hopping to steady one of the victims as she stumbled. "Anything else I need to know?"

"You, uhm, do know how to swim, my boy, don't you?"

Liam almost stumbled himself. "Why? Why do I need to know how to swim? Danny?"

"Just answer the question," Danny soothed. "And then we know how to plan."

Liam said, "Yes. Yes, I know how to swim. Why do you ask?"

And then he wished he hadn't.

"NO," FELIX said as together he and Danny abandoned their post of escorting the girls and left it in the volunteer's capable hands.

"Fox, I need you to keep your wits about you—"

"I said no, you will not do this!" Felix cried, and Danny stopped as they were running and turned to cup Felix's cheek.

God, he was still so beautiful, Danny thought as he examined his only love's worried expression in the light from the electric lamps lining the dock. The high brow and Roman nose hadn't changed from their first meeting, practically as teenagers. But Felix had grown into his features, looking leonine and regal and masterful. Twenty really was overrated to forty, Danny thought irrelevantly, and he'd always hoped to find out how forty was overrated to sixty and beyond.

He still hoped for that.

"I promised not to leave you," Danny said softly. "I won't willingly, you know that."

"But he's a monster," Felix said, his voice sounding wobbly and young, when he'd always seemed the leader of the two of them.

"He is."

"And you barely escaped last time," Felix told him, as though the scars, heavy keloid, painful reminders along his rib cage, hadn't been there for the last ten years to remind him.

"And he has our son," Danny said. "And we promised none of our children were allowed to get hurt—but especially not that one."

Felix caught his breath and nodded. "Do you even have a plan?" he asked.

Danny managed to pull himself from the fear of the moment and shake his head. "You, Julia, Leon—when, oh when, will you people stop underestimating me."

Felix scowled, grabbed his hand, and kissed his palm. "Are you going to share?" he asked in irritation.

"Certainly," Danny said.

In his ear, Stirling said, "Danny, they're eight minutes out."

"Good," Danny said. "Now I need both of you to listen to me carefully. We can't risk too much communication—we have no idea when he's going to figure out we're all mic'd."

"Go, Uncle Danny," Stirling said.

"Go, Danny," Felix told him.

And while he and Felix strode to the upper parking lot of the dock itself, Danny spilled the plan while the enemy drew near.

"YOU UNDERSTAND what to do?" Chuck asked Molly. Liam had brought the last two girls down just as the others were disappearing through the emergency porthole Chuck had carved. After helping them through the hole and into the metal semi-sphere that they'd sealed to the curved bottom of the ship and then pumped dry, Chuck had squeezed through the hole, followed by Hunter, both of them trying not to grimace as their rather bulging biceps were scraped along the freshly melted edges.

Then Molly had slipped into the semi-sphere with far less trouble.

"Once the last of the girls is past the tunnel, I get the fuck out and turn off the pumps as I pass," she said. "And yes, I can swim to the surface after that."

"Hurry out of the water," Chuck said. "After this thing catches fire, there's no telling what will be in it, chemical wise, and we don't need your hair to turn green."

Molly grimaced. "Or my skin or my internal organs."

"Now you're getting the picture," Chuck said seriously. "I'm going to give us ten minutes here, ten minutes to find a way to scuttle the ship and then jump off the back when it blows. Danny said it had to be spectacular, so—"

"GTFO," Molly said. "I hear you, Chuck."

Chuck smiled at her fondly. “That’s my Molly girl,” he said. In a gesture of tenderness, he tapped her cheek with his knuckle. “Keep your skin on your body, precious—it’s where it belongs.”

And with that, he gave a fierce chin nod to Liam and Hunter, and Molly ducked her head out.

“Can you really rig this thing to blow in ten minutes?” Liam asked, following Hunter, who thankfully seemed to have a better memory than Liam when it came to directions.

“I can scuttle this ship in five minutes,” Chuck said grimly. “The trick is going to be rigging it to scuttle and then getting to the top deck to leap before it goes.”

At that moment they heard shouting, and Hunter said, “Showtime,” before pulling his knife out of a sheath at his belt.

Nobody wanted to fire a gun on the inside of a ship, when bullets could bounce or hit things that would make steam pipes explode.

But that didn’t mean they had to be nice to the people currently racing toward them with their hands full of things like mallets and giant pipe wrenches either.

Liam pulled at the dagger in his belt, positioned his baton, and crouching a little behind Chuck, got ready to pull cleanup duty.

They had nine minutes to go.

JOSH AND Hunter were really going to start checking Grace’s luggage before they left any place they stayed for longer than a minute. If Grace had stolen *half* the things he’d babbled about to Kadjic over the last twenty minutes, he was not only going to have an Interpol Red Notice posted in his name, he was going to be wanted by a number of private art patrons who were almost as powerful and far more ruthless than countries.

And the truly frightening thing was, Josh *knew* Grace wasn’t lying, because Grace *sucked* at lying, and he also knew the only reason Grace was babbling about all the—oh my God. *When* had he had a chance to get at the Queen’s jewel closet in London? Holy fucking shitballs! Josh was going to have to talk to Molly about that one, because *foreign policy* was established by what Camilla decided to unearth from the jewel trove, and Grace had stolen a tiara once rocked by Princess Anne.

And the only reason Grace was telling Kadjic about Princess Anne's asymmetrical tiara, once worn in the only magazine spread to actually make her both pretty and desirable, and how Grace had wanted it for himself, because he *loved* looking pretty and desirable and how his boyfriend was going to go secretly nuts about that when Grace wore it to bed (oh dear *God*!) was because Grace was *avoiding* telling Kadjic about the job at the Louvre and Colombia, which were the two things he'd had a personal stake in, and also not dropping a dime on the rest of the family.

Grace wouldn't rat them out if he could at all help it, but at this point, Josh was fully aware Grace might not be able to help it.

"Calm down," Josh murmured through comms. "Grace, my man, if you end up telling these people about what you do in bed, you will never get your dignity back."

"I have no dignity," Grace said, and it would have been a non sequitur, but at this point, he'd told them about the decision to turn his hair white, what his favorite ballet was, and how many lead dancers he'd blown before he settled down with his totally monogamous boyfriend. They were way beyond non sequiturs at this point.

"I have noticed," Kadjic said, sounding irritated and baffled. "Has it occurred to you that things might go easier on you if you simply stayed silent?"

"Mister, *you* kidnapped *me*. If you hadn't wanted to know about the time I rescued all the frogs from biology class you should have kidnapped somebody else."

"That is a lie," Kadjic said. "That is from American television. Nobody truly does that."

"Sadly not," Josh murmured, more to calm Grace down than to answer Kadjic.

"I didn't know they were already dead," Grace said glumly. "I opened the boxes and shouted, 'Hop away, little buddies!' and they just sort of slithered out, looking pathetic with their little hands in the air. And then they started to melt, because they were all frozen, and they just… you know." Josh could picture Grace, tongue sticking out the side of his mouth as he did his best impression of a dead frog.

Not one of their finer moments, no. Josh had felt stupid for not looking up how frogs were shipped to the biology teacher. He'd been fully okay with the assignment, but Grace… he just never knew when Grace's enormous heart had been going to engage. Apparently frogs had done it.

"Why are you telling me this?" Kadjic asked, clearly as bewildered as the rest of the world when faced with a tornado.

From elsewhere in the car, Josh heard an odd sound. It was like a bear… burping?

"Oh my God," Grace said in wonder. "Mister, is your hired muscle *laughing*?"

"Vlad!" Kadjic barked. "What—"

And the sound got bigger and louder as the guard—who probably didn't speak English well—processed the story. "Hop away, little buddies!" he hooted. "Hop away!"

Josh half expected Kadjic to rant, to rave, to grab Grace by the throat and threaten his life somehow, but he underestimated the man.

With an amount of composure Josh found chilling, Kadjic said, "Who *are* you? Were you sent to infiltrate my operation?"

The baffled silence from Grace's comm was actually reassuring. It meant Grace had some measure of control over what he said next.

"I'm a narcissistic kleptomaniac," Grace said, as though schooling someone. "With diagnosed ADHD and undiagnosed borderline personality disorder. Have you not been paying attention? I couldn't infiltrate a box full of dead frogs!"

"Oh, Grace," Josh murmured, not sure if his friend would hear him or not. "You are my brother and my best friend and a hurricane with a good heart. I let you down, is all. I should have researched the frogs."

"I should have known," Stirling said in his ear. "And Molly blames herself, because she was crushing on some guy and wasn't paying attention to us that night. We were all a team."

Before Josh could pass that on, Kadjic snapped—ostensibly to his driver—"Wait, are we at the Děčin parking lot?"

"Da." What followed was a flurry of Russian too quick for Josh's ears, but Stirling had apparently tuned into Josh's comms because he murmured, "He's asking which slip the yacht is in, and how far away they are from it."

"Where are we?" Josh asked. Tentatively he stretched his body, hoping he could move past the weakness that had gotten him in here and the stiffness that had set in while he'd been curled up in this confined space. Josh had always been much like Grace—unafflicted with either fear of heights or small spaces, but he thought this particular small space might give him nightmares after this. There was no padding in a trunk, and while there was light from the rear lights, it was tinted nightmare red and yellow. The carpet was rough under his cheek, and the surface was hard and unyielding—he could feel bruises forming on his hip from his position.

"You're in the upper parking lot of Děčin," Stirling said, sounding stressed. "Tell Grace to be ready to help you out. There's an exchange going on."

"A *what*?" Josh asked, but at that moment the car stopped and shit got real.

"A WHAT?" LEON demanded as he helped the last terrified, abused child—they *were* children, most under sixteen, fuck the monsters who did this to them—into the yacht he'd rented for the occasion. Leon paid very well, and the captain of the ship had instructions to pilot to Hamburg the minute the gangplank was withdrawn. At home, Julia was in charge of fundraising for a number of overseas aid groups, one for missing and exploited children in particular. It had enabled her to recruit volunteers, and the yacht—which was going to be a bit crowded, although not nearly as badly as the one they'd just come from—was full of people armed with blankets, food, clothing, and most importantly, the language skills and diplomatic ties to get these children home.

"An exchange, sir," Michael said, with such earnestness that Leon felt compelled to keep from laying into the younger man with all of the frustration in his soul.

The cofferdam and the long vinyl hallway attached to it required constant monitoring and pumping—pumping the air in and the water out so the young women could emerge under the slip and, thus covered, make the short swim to the ladder that took them to the rescue yacht's gangplank. Securing the equipment, installing it, and maintaining it had all fallen under Michael's wheelhouse, and given that he'd had about six hours to gather everything so he, Chuck, and Hunter could start the work under the yacht, he'd proven invaluable.

Leon could not—*would not*—dishonor that work by screaming at him like a drunken sailor.

"What, pray tell, are they exchanging?" Normally, they were all mic'd—but normally, on a job this size, there would be two people on comms. Leon had opted out. He'd be speaking in multiple languages to multiple people, and who needed somebody in your ear at a time like that? So hearing that Danny was going out to meet the *one goddamned person* that they had all worked so hard to keep him away from was not only a surprise, it was a gut punch to all of their hard work.

And Leon had *promised* Julia he'd keep her family safe.

He was new to this game—but he loved it. He loved the dedication to righting wrongs, the acceptance that humans were flawed, and the fact that the family looked eagerly for redemption at every chance.

But more than that, he loved the people. His brother's child, Josh, was as brilliant and as principled as Matteo had been—a shining celestial being. But hopefully Josh would have more time to shine than Matteo'd had. Leon would give his life—his soul—to see that happened.

And Julia.... Dear God, she was transcendent. Not merely beautiful—although her beauty left him blind to all else in the world—but as brilliant as her son. As principled. She'd admitted to him once that, unlike Felix, her pedigree was real. She'd graduated from Vassar at nineteen, and when he'd professed admiration, she'd waved it off. "I had nothing to do but study, Leon—it was part of grooming me to be a trophy wife."

Any man who listened to her speak, saw the wickedness of her wit or the deft competence of her compassion, and thought of her as a "trophy wife" didn't deserve a wife, much less a trophy.

And that afternoon, as she'd readied for her part to play, she'd called him up and reminded him once again of his one promise to her.

To take care of the family that had cared so beautifully for her and her son.

He had one goddamned job to do, and Danny was proposing a *what*?

Literally, as the kids would say, *what* in the *fucking hell*?

Michael stared at him as he tried to put all this into words and then backtracked. In two minutes, Michael had spilled it all. Grace's abduction,

Josh hiding in the back of Kadjic's town car, Danny's plan for scuttling the ship, which came with the corollary of getting their own ship the *fuck* out of the slip before that happened, and, oh, hey, Danny exchanging himself for Grace and Josh before—or was it during or after?—the explosion.

"An excha—" Michael started, but Leon didn't stay to listen. With a few terse words to the volunteer next to him, he warned her to pull the gangplank as soon as he left, since the last two girls had confirmed that Molly was behind them. With that, he abandoned his post at the hatch, hauling ass down the dock with Michael trotting after him.

In a few terse sentences he told the captain to pull out and head for Hamburg *immediately*, because the ship in the dock next to his was about to be scuttled.

Then he hung up and—feeling a twinge of sympathy for a sopping wet Molly, who had just cleared the cofferdam tunnel herself and was climbing onto the dock instead of the ship as she'd expected to—barked, "Come on!" to the two of them. Then Leon shoved his phone away and grabbed the keys to the SUV some of them had taken to the dock that night. Lucius, who had been serving as a lookout near the front of the yacht, joined them as they ran.

"Where are we going?" Michael panted.

"I'm going to the exchange," Leon told him. "You said the upper parking lot?"

"Yessir," Michael said.

"Exchange?" Molly and Lucius asked, and Leon waved them off.

"More running, less talking," he gasped. "Molly, Michael, you go get the SUV and wait on my order."

"Where am I going?" Lucius asked, and to his credit, he sounded like a runner in his natural stride.

"We're going to the upper parking lot to try to keep Danny and Felix from getting killed," he said, and because he was more a fan of free weights than running, he had to save his breath for the sprint.

LIAM HATED the smell of blood, he really did, and the smell of blood mixed with dank metal was right there with rotting garbage fermenting in piss as his least favorite odors.

He was sweating and breathless, and the hand and wrist holding his baton ached as though he'd broken his own bones, and his dagger hand and the blade itself were dripping with blood.

"Chuck, are you through yet?" Hunter asked, and he sounded breathless himself, both of them staring through the white-painted pipes and mystery fixtures of the engine room, now dripping red, to see if there were any more men with weapons running down to stop them from scuttling the ship.

"Almost there," Chuck sang, and the man at Liam's feet groaned.

Liam kicked him in the ribs, and he coughed and sputtered and fell silent. Liam scanned the surrounding hatches—there were several, one from their level, one from each of the upper levels—looking to see if there were any more henchmen.

"Think they know the cargo is cleared yet?" Hunter asked.

"I don't know," Liam said. He'd told them about Kadjic abducting Grace—and Josh climbing in the trunk—as they'd run. "I think Kadjic has his hands full." He gave Hunter an apologetic smile. "I gather Grace was being… uhm…."

"Grace," Hunter said, one side of his mouth pulling up. This man had no illusions about the man he'd fallen in love with.

At that moment there was a voice in his ear. "Liam?"

"Gotcha, Stirling."

"How long?"

"Got it!" Chuck called. "We're out of here!"

"Two minutes," Liam said, hauling ass after Chuck as he led them, as agreed upon, up the stairs to the hatch that led to the main upper deck.

"Exfil?"

"Off the boat, aft."

"You'll hit the water. It's deep enough. If you flatten out, you should be fine, but be careful of the boat's props. You'll get your earwig wet, so don't expect it to work. When you surface, the van will be in the lower parking lot. Lucius has the keys. I've got the equipment set up to track us. You can follow, and if Chuck drives, you'll catch up. I gotta go!"

"Go?" Liam muttered. "Go where?"

At that moment, Chuck swore. "You guys ready for another bout? I'll block, you kick 'em out of play!"

And with that, he swung his massive fist into the jaw of the first bad guy with a gun coming down the stairs. The guy fell sideways, and Hunter threw him over the rail while Liam got ready to handle the next one.

"How long?" Hunter called, sounding worried as three more men appeared in the hatch.

"*Two minutes*!" Chuck screamed at them. "*She's gonna blow in two minutes*!"

Liam knew barely enough Russian to translate, and suddenly they didn't have to hit any bad guys anymore.

But they did have to yell at them to run faster.

"DANNY, NO," Felix hissed, his heart as cold as it had ever been. Of course they had to get Grace and Josh back—there was no question about that. But dear God. Had he ever thought he'd have to make a choice between his lover and their son?

You did. You both did. Over two decades ago when you decided to give him and his mother a good home, the one none of you had grown up in. You both made a choice to choose them first. It's why he left, you moron. Because it was better for all four of you.

And he came back because we're better together, Felix reminded himself fiercely.

"Please, no," Felix answered in response to Danny's stony silence.

Danny gave him an expression of annoyance, putting his hand up to cup his ear as he listened to Stirling. When he was done, he nodded and glanced up to the hillside, searching, presumably, for the lights from Kadjic's vehicle.

Then he focused on Felix. "Fox, this isn't a death sentence. Stirling's got a fix on Josh and Grace—and me. But even if we're stripped of our earwigs, he's got a fix on *Kadjic*. Grace gave him some information to look up, Stirling tagged his phone, and now, even if they send a signal jammer to burn out *our* comms, Stirling's got a track on *Kadjic's*. So follow me. Let him take me and follow me. If we get Grace and Josh back, it's all worth it."

Felix nodded, his brain seeing the sense of it, but his heart….

He kissed Danny hard, desperately, needing him so much in that moment, his common sense checked completely out of the picture.

Couldn't this man see that Felix was nothing without him? He'd spent ten years as nothing, a shell, Josh and Julia his only ties to the land of the living. They'd kept him there, sure, and he'd never be sorry he'd kept the promises he and Danny had made—of safety, of shelter, of caring—but none of that had been for *Felix* until Danny had come back into his arms.

Danny pulled away, giving a shy grin that yanked Felix immediately back to twenty years ago, when they were practically children, and Felix had first let Danny kiss him in his tiny, airless garret room.

And then Felix had kissed him back.

"This isn't the last of me," Danny said. "I promise, Fox. I won't leave you. I meant it. Never again."

"You had better fucking not," Felix said thickly and then held him close, so close, against his chest, wondering if he'd ever learn to breathe again after this night.

At that moment, Danny cocked his head and parted from him, then whispered, "Go lay on the hill, there, in the grass. They can't see you, Felix. I need you to come get me!"

Felix nodded dumbly and hurried to do as Danny said, sliding into the weeds on the hillside, which were, as the fall rains threatened, high enough to cover his shoulders as he flattened himself to the ground. At that moment the car—an enormous luxury vehicle, black, of course—slithered down the last curve of the hill to the upper lot. The headlights picked up Danny, slouching insouciantly, looking for all the world like he wasn't waiting for his ex-lover and greatest mistake, the man who had tried to murder him in a back alley and left a twisting of scars on his ribs and worse ones on his heart.

In his ears there was a crackle, and Stirling said, "Josh is in the trunk—they don't know about him. Grace is in the back with Kadjic, and they're making the trade for him. Josh says there's a quick-release handle in the trunk. He should be able to open it, but he says he might need an assist out."

"An assist?" Felix asked, shocked out of his fear. "Josh?"

And Stirling, who while running comms on an op always sounded at least fifty years old instead of Josh's age, suddenly sounded much, much younger. "Felix, he hasn't said anything, but he's not sounding… great. I didn't want to tell Danny that, but I think the reason he ended up in the trunk was he was too weak to run anywhere else to hide."

Oh. "Oh no," Felix whispered, his heart aching. Of all the bloody times. Josh had been so conscientious since Felix had arrived from Munich. But the last two weeks had been a lot to ask from anybody.

Good God, the way that boy drove himself. Felix had seen it as a child—even before Danny left, he'd wanted to be the best at everything he tried. (Except test scores. Felix was aware that Josh had fixed his test scores to be slightly behind Grace's, but even that spoke to Josh's kindness and his intense loyalty.) And since embarking on this enterprise, this… this *adventure* to go out into the world and not simply tilt at windmills but slay the real giants, Josh's drive had amped higher.

Felix had been so relieved he'd allowed Liam back into his life. But Liam—for all that he seemed to be a very *good* boyfriend—was not a miracle worker, and Josh's body needed a year of peace in which to heal.

Felix would not object to that. That month at home, him and Danny working their actual jobs, Julia consumed with the joy of a pregnancy not only wanted but *celebrated*—and Leon, their new brother, who had come to him and Danny for counsel and for companionship every day—that had been golden.

And Felix wanted more of that peace. Jobs, yes, he thought yearningly, but he wanted jobs they could do from home. He wanted time with his family not fraught with danger.

But first they all had to survive this night.

Felix watched anxiously through the tall grasses as the car drew to a halt, Danny still illuminated by the LED lights, looking for all the world as though he were waiting for a bus.

DANNY TRIED to block the headlight glow, dying for a glance at Grace. He wished he'd known Josh was still in the trunk—he would have placed Felix closer to the main road so he could run, open the trunk, and get Josh out, all while Danny was occupying Kadjic.

And the thought that that's what he was doing—occupying the man and not fencing for his life—helped keep him calm.

Anything he and Andrejevic Kadjic said to each other would be inconsequential to getting Josh and Grace out of the man's clutches.

An enormous man emerged from the rear of the town car as it idled, and Danny dismissed him. Muscle. Yes, he could probably snap Danny's neck like a twig and probably had several weapons on his person—but Kadjic was the real killer, the commander of the troops.

"Andres?" Danny asked politely, and the man with no neck scowled and shook his head. So Danny raised his voice. "Andrejevic, get out here and face me yourself, you coward, and bring the boy with you."

The muscle backed up, and Grace emerged from the town car, moving jerkily as though pushed.

Kadjic himself emerged behind him, glaring through the mist now lightly peppering the space between the headlights and Danny.

"What are you doing here?" Kadjic asked, sounding shocked, and it occurred to Danny that while his empire had been collapsing, Kadjic hadn't thought to connect the flamboyant art thefts with the massive inroads he and his people had made at dismantling the branches of Kadjic's life work.

But Danny knew a little of Stirling's plan, and if Kadjic didn't know now, he'd figure it out in… how long? One minute? Two?

"Think, Andrejevic—I know it's hard for you. Too much cocaine, too many rent boys—but think. What could I possibly be doing here, on the night your favorite painting in the National Museum of Prague disappears, replaced by a stunning forgery?"

It was wonderful, in its way, watching the parade of emotions cross Kadjic's face, as he made the final connection, realized that he *wasn't* losing his mind, that Lightfingers *had* been behind the dissolution of his businesses *and* his personal ambitions. And that tonight, at a place where one of his biggest business assets had been housed, was where he found Lightfingers himself.

He paled and swallowed. "What… what did you do?"

And suddenly, Danny wanted to tell him.

"LET THE boy go," Danny said, allowing a small, unpleasant smile to cross his features. In profile, Felix could see it—all the evil Danny *could* have been. His childhood had been horrific, although he laughed it off when asked. He had literally whored his way to Europe just to get away from the Jersey shore, and then he'd stolen his way out of a rich man's bed so he could live free and do whatever he'd pleased.

He'd pleased to feed children half of what he stole to survive. He pleased to give Felix a hand out of a tight situation. He pleased to scam Hiram Dormer out of his trinkets to pay for the children Dormer had fathered by assaulting any woman who worked for him.

And when they realized that Julia had been Dormer's victim more than she'd been his daughter, Danny had pleased to sacrifice himself and Felix to help her.

The Danny Mitchell that Felix had fallen in love with *could* have been this vindictive demon he showed to Kadjic now, but Felix knew, would know until he died, that the real Danny was the laughing boy he'd taken to bed all those years ago, and the warm, kind, sensual man Felix would not relinquish in a million years.

"Why should I?" Kadjic asked, shaking Grace by the scruff of the neck.

"Well, for one thing," Danny said, "because his boyfriend is a trained killer who makes this one look like a kitten in a sandbox." He indicated the man with no neck who had cleared the car first. "I am not kidding, Andres—if you wish to survive the night, you will not give him a reason to come after you."

Grace—who had been unnervingly quiet, Felix had to admit—gave Kadjic a sunny smile. "He loves me," he said with absolute sincerity. "That nice man whom I have never seen before is absolutely right. My boyfriend will skin you with a shiv and use your meatsuit as a sack if you hurt one precious hair on my head."

Felix winced. Oh God. Grace. Every fiber of his being was telling him to stand up, to make himself a bigger target than Danny, a bigger target than Grace, to spar verbally with a monster, to engage him until they could get Liam there, get Hunter or Chuck to fire a lethal shot, get an entire Interpol army to take him down!

But the same reasons they couldn't do that from day one stood. If Kadjic died before his empire died, the harm would still continue. The entire justification for the past two months was to take Kadjic's empire down as well as to demoralize the man, to make him ripe for the plucking for law enforcement. To bring him to justice for crimes much bigger, much more destructive than what he could inflict on their small family.

Felix had lost Danny because he'd been thinking about his company—not the money, but that they'd trusted him, the employees, the people who'd invested with him. They'd given him their faith, and he could not let them down.

He'd been looking beyond himself, beyond what he'd wanted, what he'd *ever* wanted, and here he was, about to do it again, lose the man he loved because he was focused on the big picture and not the slight, unassuming, beautiful, amazing god of chaos who loved him.

"No," he said, not sure he'd said it out loud until there was a rustle in the grass next to him.

"Stay put," Leon whispered, breathing hard. On his other side, Lucius slid quietly and murmured, "Not yet."

Felix glanced from side to side, wild-eyed, and Leon caught his expression and chuckled soundlessly.

"I understand this is a family. We can't get into trouble alone—that's not right."

Felix grinned at him, charmed, as Julia must have been.

"The others are heading for the SUV," Lucius said. "I think Stirling had to take a moment to pack up his personal laptop."

"Why are we staying put?" Felix whispered, eyes back on Danny and his deadly verbal waltz with Kadjic.

"Wait for it…," Lucius whispered.

"*You wear my name*!" Kadjic screamed, shoving Grace aside to lunge for Danny, and Lucius and Leon had to actively restrain him as his muscles shrieked to put him between Danny and the man who'd harmed him.

"Your name?" Danny chuckled. "Hardly. I've got some ugly scars, you know, but you didn't finish it. You ran away for a coward before you could finish the last two letters. However, I've got the name of the love of my life tattooed on my ass, and that shit, as the kids say, is going nowhere."

"Really, Danny?" Felix whispered to himself, both amused and appalled. The tattoos had been *their* secret. But then, if there was ever a time to tell a secret….

"I'll rip him from your body as I rip him from your heart," Kadjic snarled, shaking him. Kadjic was taller than Danny, and outweighed him by a good fifty pounds, but Danny's mouth was curled up into that evil smile, and Felix would've put his money on Danny any day.

"You can try," Danny said, and Felix realized that this was the long game again. Find Kadjic's lair. Find the art he'd stolen, squirreled away, blackmailed from the world.

Fuck the long game, Danny. Let us get you out of there ***now!***

And then Kadjic started glancing wildly around, screaming at his muscle man in Russian as he, too, searched the immediate surrounds.

Oh hell.

Where the fuck was Grace?

Danny's smile widened, and as Kadjic shook him harder and Felix strained against Leon and Lucius's restraining hands....

Wait for it.

BOOM!

Forgetting stealth, the three people in the grass rolled over so they could scope the river below them, and stare in horror as the *Spelyy Presik* burst into flames, a handful of people throwing themselves off the aft deck and into the black water twenty feet below.

As Felix caught his breath, worried for his friends, he heard faintly—so faintly—Josh's cry of "*Liam*!" but before he could run to the back of the town car and pull Josh out of the trunk, Kadjic gave a howl of rage and threw Danny in the car, lunging in after him and screaming for the driver to pull away.

Their no-neck friend barely claimed his foot from the pavement before the car squealed up the hill and into the night, and as it disappeared from the circle of ambient light, orange from the burning ship, Felix saw the back hatch of the vehicle slam shut, obviously yanked from the inside.

"Oh *hell*!" Felix cried.

And Grace was nowhere to be found.

Reichenbach Falls

AT LEAST Grace was warm, because the outside temperature was dropping with every mile, and even beyond the exhaust and the smell of the tire and engine grease—and his own blood—Josh could catch the tang of snow.

"You're so stupid," he mumbled, about an hour into the drive. "You could have been free!"

"I'm stupid?" Grace mumbled back, cuddling into Josh closer. "You're too weak to walk! How could I know you were too weak to walk!"

"I'm sorry," Josh told him, trying not to shiver. "I'm so sorry."

Grace had tunneled under the foil blanket too—they wouldn't freeze to death here in the trunk, but comfort was at least a hundred kilometers behind and below them. "I was trying to plant the trackers. I didn't expect…." Josh tried to keep his voice from breaking. "I didn't expect…." He didn't expect his body to give out, not now, when they all needed it most.

Grace pulled him closer. "Why?" he asked softly. "Why now?"

"What?" Josh was trying not to cry.

"You were strong and fucking silent for a year—why does this hurt you so much now?"

Josh almost laughed. Who said Grace hadn't grown emotionally since he and Hunter had gotten together?

Which was the answer, wasn't it? Having someone in your life to lay your burdens on made you stronger, but it also made you realize how weak you were alone.

"You're so brave," he whispered. "Loving Hunter. It's so scary knowing they could leave, even if they don't want to."

"Liam won't leave you," Grace said. "I mean, you know, he might leave *Chicago*, but you don't have to stay there all the time either."

"I'm so muddled," Josh admitted, "as to how that will work. I've kept you out of school enough. You were going to get your degree and teach kids to dance, and you have shows to be in and—"

"And you'll be following your Interpol boyfriend around the world, helping him break into shit," Grace said with satisfaction. "And then you'll come home for months at a time, and you and I will raise hell. Don't worry, Recovery Boy—you can't ditch me." Josh *heard* his scowl. "Not that you didn't try. What was that shit?"

Josh had listened in horror as Danny threatened to trade himself for Grace, but at the same time, he got the plan. Danny trades himself for Grace, Grace swings around and picks the lock and lets Josh out, and then, when they were clear, the cavalry would rush in and the yacht would explode and hey, they'd track the car to Kadjic's lair, Liam would call Interpol, and Kadjic would be busted, his empire in shambles, his secret art collection discovered and released to the world—hooray!

Except Grace got to the trunk and found it open, but Josh was unable to do more than that. By the time Grace arrived, Josh was so weak he could barely lift himself up on his elbow to tell Grace to run.

And while Grace had been trying to wrestle him out of the trunk—all in silence because, of course, Danny was scaring the shit out of everybody as he sparred with Kadjic—the yacht had blown up.

Josh had watched his friends, and, hey, the man he loved beyond reason, leap off the aft deck and—hopefully—not get singed on their way down.

He wasn't proud of crying out then, and he was really not proud of the fact that, as soon as the car slid into first gear, Grace had leapt on top of him and yanked the trunk shut on top of them.

And Josh was back in the dark once more, with Stirling in his ear and a furious Grace on top of him.

And neither of them were able to speak above a whisper, because oh fuck, Kadjic *had Danny*, and if Kadjic had them as well, it was like having a scalpel to Danny's balls. They were leverage, and they both knew enough about the game to know that leverage over somebody was all you needed to bring them to their knees.

In the town car, the battle raged on, with Kadjic throwing swords and Danny dodging them and parrying with stilettos.

"You are looking older, Daniel," Kadjic purred smoothly after what had been a weighted silence. "Too old to be a—what was your word? Boy toy?"

"You only need to fear age when you have nothing to show for it, Andres. I'm not anybody's toy—haven't been since you tried to gut me in Morocco. How have *you* grown emotionally in the last eleven years?"

"My empire has grown by leaps and bounds," Kadjic defended, but there was an anger in his voice, a clumsiness that belied his belief in himself. Danny *had* grown—and Kadjic had no idea how much. But Kadjic was still the same street bully Danny had defied way back then.

"Has it?" Danny asked smoothly. "Has it? This wasn't your first shipment lost in the last two months, I hear. How's things coming out of the Middle East? Still up to your eyeballs in opium? What about South America? How's the cocaine flowing these days, Andrejevic? That used to be your favorite product—still the same?"

"You could not possibly…," Kadjic said, dismissing him but at the same time, Josh could tell, believing him.

Danny chuckled. "You'll never know, will you. I could get all of that information from creditable news sources, like I heard about the Rembrandt in the Louvre—"

"That was *you*!" Kadjic charged.

Danny chuckled again. "You think? I've got witnesses that say I was somewhere else completely that day."

"Where?" Kadjic demanded.

"Oh, wouldn't you like to know," Danny said. "But it doesn't matter. Because I wasn't at the Louvre. Nor in the Middle East or Colombia—"

"Munich?" Kadjic demanded suspiciously. "That tiara in England?"

"No," Danny said. "But it's been so gracious of you to allow me free rent in your head. Have you really been chasing me around Europe, hoping to find me with my hand in the till?"

"Are you telling me you've been out of the game for the last eleven years?" Kadjic sneered. "You dried out and gave up thieving?"

"Good God, no," Danny snorted. He paused. "I'm just telling you that you're imagining things, Andrejevic. Your empire is crumbling around you, and you are blaming an old boyfriend who hasn't thought about you in years."

"*You lie*!"

Josh and Grace both gasped softly, because they could feel the shifting in the car and knew something violent had happened.

When Danny spoke next, his voice was muffled—much as Josh's was—so probably through blood. "Of course you're right," Danny admitted. "I thought about you just the other day. I made an appointment with a plastic surgeon to get my scars removed."

The next sound was definitely a blow, and Grace whimpered softly in Josh's ear.

At the same time, Stirling—who had been so silent, Josh had wondered if Kadjic's men had run a jammer on the car—spoke up.

"You guys still there?"

"Yes," they both said, and then Grace bumped Josh with his nose, indicating Josh should be the one who spoke.

"Good," Stirling said. "We're still tracking you. I keep expecting somebody to jam our signal, but apparently Kadjic's busy freaking out, so, well done."

"Danny's keeping him busy," Josh whispered.

"Kadjic hasn't checked for an earwig, but I think it got turned off." The first time Kadjic had hit him, probably. Danny would leave it off then, and reactivate it when he had reason.

"Where even are we?" Josh asked, because that had been bothering him as the air got colder.

"You're about half an hour from a little village called Český Krumlov—it's supposed to be charming, but I don't think Kadjic is heading there."

"Why not?"

"Because his driver has been looking up stops for petrol in the village you don't usually do that when you're home. I think he's got a cabin tucked into the South Bohemian mountains somewhere, but if so, it's off the main mountain road, which is pretty curvy." There was a pause. "I hope you're not queasy, Josh."

Josh grunted. No, thank God, that had *not* been one of his problems. But he felt like he had to be honest. "Weakness, Stirling. Just… exhaustion. I may have to sleep soon. And I don't know if I can walk when it's time to get out."

"Fair. I'll tell the others."

Oh God. Josh was a minute away from passing out, but he had to know. "Liam…?" he whispered. "Chuck and Hunter and—"

"They're fine," Stirling said. "In fact the timing was like we'd planned it!"

Josh chuckled rustily. "You'll have to tell me sometime," he mumbled. "Talk to Grace now."

And then he fell asleep or passed out or whatever it was that took over his body these days.

But Liam was safe, and that was all he needed to know.

"*Fuck!*" Liam swore as he surfaced from the oily water, lungs aching and a suspicious burning in his side. "Fucking *balls*, that's cold!"

Hunter surfaced about ten feet from him with a sharp gasp. "Bracing," he wheezed, while Chuck popped up next to him.

"Somebody call search and rescue," he gasped. "My balls are in my throat!"

There was lots of swearing then, as they made their way to the slip where Leon's yacht had been. None of them talked about it, but they'd had a hell of a time not getting sucked into the rotor wash as the great bloody machine had passed by them, because they were alive now, and that's all that fucking mattered.

Finally they were wet, chafing, *freezing*, and piling into the comms van where Michael was waiting with clothes and—shockingly enough—coffee.

"Would you believe there's a coffee maker and an outlet?" he asked, pointing to the thing on the small counter under a cupboard. "I found it when I was tossing the place for clothes."

"Needed," Chuck said, gulping his coffee. He'd shucked his wet things and was huddling naked under a blanket while Hunter and Liam did the same. "Where are we going?"

"Let me get kitted," Liam said, and then, "Wait a minute—which one of us is bleeding?"

He'd seen the traces of blood on the floor of the comms van, as well as some of the clothes.

"You," Chuck said, at the same time Hunter said, "Chuck," and Michael said, "Hunter."

"Wait, me? Where?" And that was all three of them.

"Oh Jesus," Michael muttered. "It's *all* of you. Carl is not gonna be okay with all three of you bleeding!"

"Head," Chuck admitted, the blood smearing on his hand now that it had stopped mixing with the water sopping from his hair. "Fuck. Ouch. That makes sense. I keep seeing two of everybody."

"Bicep," Hunter grunted, lifting his own blanket to check. "Nasty. Anybody have gauze?"

Liam grunted, and now that they were out of the cold and nobody was trying to kill them, he let his endorphins flow back a little and took stock.

"Ribs," he said, suddenly worried. "Oh dear."

"Fuck," Hunter said. "Liam, stand up. Michael, do we have gauze, or am I ripping T-shirts? This is bad. You can actually *see* his rib!"

Liam hadn't been the only thug with a knife, but thanks to growing up poof in a rough neighborhood, he was the *toughest* thug with a knife in every fight he'd been in.

But that didn't mean someone else hadn't gotten one in.

As though someone had touched a live match on latent gasoline, pain swept up his side, obliterating the ache he'd been suppressing, and his vision dimmed. "Oh, hey," he muttered. "There we go." For a moment he fought nausea and thought dimly that this must be what Josh felt like after chemo or before a wave of weakness took him out at the knees.

The thought of Josh shored him up. They could not afford to give in to their injuries now.

"Where is everybody?" he asked. "Are we the only ones back at the dock?"

"I'll explain," Michael said, "but we've got to get going. Stirling said he'd leave a map for you. Liam, you can manage comms, right?"

Liam grunted. He was proficient, but thanks to the dyslexia that had plagued him since childhood, nowhere near Josh or Stirling's speed.

Josh isn't the only one who hates having his weakness paraded about, he thought, hating himself for only getting it now.

"I'll need Hunter's help," he admitted. "I'm slow on the read, mate. If somebody's typing, you need to read it out loud. Everything on the keyboard I can do by touch."

"Sure," Hunter said. "I'll get your ribs while you boot up. Chuck, get behind the wheel and aim for the road between the two that you see, and Michael, I would *love* to know where my boyfriend is, but then, I'm pretty sure we're all in the same exploding yacht there."

"Well," Michael said, "for starters, Josh and Grace are *both* in the back of the town car now, and Danny's in the front with Kadjic… wait, wait, wait… let me back up."

They all groaned as Chuck slid on the dry clothes closest to his size (too small!) and then got behind the wheel.

And then he started putting events together in a way that seemed to make less sense the more he spoke.

"So let me get this straight," Hunter said, after Michael had wrapped things up to a stunned and puzzled silence. As he spoke, Chuck was racing through a curvy mountain road, and Liam had to keep *willfully* forgetting that the man had admitted to not being able to see straight.

Aim for the road in the middle, indeed.

"Josh was in the back of the town car. Kadjic grabbed Grace at the museum, and Josh jumped in the back to follow him. Right?"

"Yes," Michael said. "Josh was going to put trackers on the vehicle, but the thing with Grace happened instead."

"Got it," Hunter said. "So Kadjic pulls up to the upper lot, and Danny's waiting for him because Stirling tracked the car."

"Yes," Michael said.

"Danny buys time and tries to exchange himself for Grace—it's working, and Grace tries to sneak Josh out of the back of the town car when the ship goes boom and all hell breaks loose."

"You're doin' fine," Michael said soberly. "Woohee, Chuck, you ain't getting' any slower."

"That middle road thing seems to be working," Chuck confessed. "Is it just me, or is there a hideous drop off on the right of the other two roads?"

"Ain't small," Michael said, taking a deep breath, and Hunter ignored them and continued. Liam, following the directions Stirling had left on the laptop for him, logged in and started pulling up various screens. *Julia*, *Carl*, and *Kadjic* all specified a different dot that seemed to be on the same curving path that they were on, moving through the same mountain range. Liam wanted to ask Hunter if he saw the words *Greater Bohemian Mountain Range* anywhere on the screen, because between the movement of the van—not inconsiderable—and his own jumpy vision, he could not fucking get a bead on anything longer than those names.

But Hunter was still getting the story. "Okay, so that's the town car. Tell me about Carl's van here?" he continued, still looking over Liam's shoulder.

"Okay, then," Michael said. "Leon had grabbed me, Lucius, and Molly by this time, and we were hauling ass for the upper parking lot. As we passed the comms van, he told Molly and Stirling to meet him by the SUV in the lower lot. Stirling stayed a minute to fix up the laptop for Liam, I stayed to tell you all what was going on, and Lucius followed Leon, and together they got up to the hill by the upper lot in time to keep Felix from going ballistic. At least that's what was happening on comms—Stirling relayed it to me as we were running. We were *still* running, 'cause there's, like, an extra quarter-fucking-mile coming from our side of the dock when Carl, Julia, and Tienne show up in the comms van from the museum. Carl throws open the door, shouts, 'Get in losers, we're gonna fight,' and Felix, Lucius, and Leon jump in and take off."

"He did not say that," Hunter said, and if Liam hadn't been so busy tracking the three dots and trying to figure out how to call up people's earbuds on comms, he might have joined him in his disbelief.

"Swear to fuckin' God," Michael said. "We heard him as we got near the lot."

"Good line," Chuck conceded, and Liam let out a pained chuckle, then a yelp.

"Fuck! Hunter!"

"You are *bleeding* all over the goddamned van," Hunter snapped. "Soldier up and let me dress this. Are we heading in the right direction?"

"Yes," Liam grudgingly admitted.

"Then stop staring at the screen. You can't magic him here with your brain power, so fucking chill. We're *all* worried. Have faith."

Liam was about to snap at him that he couldn't possibly know how worried Liam was, but then Liam remembered whom it was Hunter was worried about.

Hunter had resigned himself to feeling like this every minute of every damned day.

The least Liam could do was not give himself a massive migraine and let the man bandage his ribs.

"Fine," Liam said. "So, 'Get in losers, we're going shopping—'"

"Gonna fight!" Michael corrected. "Anyway, yes. They must be squished like sardines because there's seven of them in that comms van and we're a tight squeeze in this one."

"Given their proximity," Liam murmured, "I'm thinking Carl stopped to switch a few people into the SUV." Probably thinking, like Hunter had, that they knew where the vehicle was and which way it was heading, and they needed to collect themselves before they kept going.

"Yup," Michael said. His voice fell. "None of us are with our person. I mean, it don't matter, but…."

Liam gave a small smile. "It matters," he said. "But we'll all fight for each other anyway."

"Speaking of which," Hunter murmured, and Liam had to close his eyes and breathe through Hunter's ministrations. He was an able medic, but playing with the flap of skin just made everything hurt in living color. "You, sir, are a street fighter if I ever saw one. I mean, Chuck's a freight train, Carl's a brawler, but you're a fucking menace. That was impressive."

"Seconded," Chuck said from the front. "Man, you're a fucking danger. I feel like if we had Carl with us, we could take over small countries."

Michael chuckled. "Carl would do fine—but he wouldn't be around art, and that's his favorite."

"Better on the street than on comms," Liam said grimly. He took a breath and then another, and Hunter put another strip of plaster across his ribs. "Will I live?"

"I wouldn't get hit there if you can help it," Hunter said. "Now there's a beeping on the screen—it says Stirling. Put on the headset and mouse click the light. I think we can connect to the others now."

"Bloody fantastic," Liam said. "Could you get me a jumper or a tee or something? I'm freezing here, mate."

"Can do."

Liam worked the screen and put on the headset, and he was good to go.

"Liam?" Stirling said. "How you doing? Everybody okay?"

"We'll live," Liam told him. "Our earbuds are blown out, so good call on leaving Michael here and a headset. We're apparently following everybody through the…." He glanced at Hunter.

"Greater Bohemian Mountain Range," Hunter said.

"Greater Bohemian Mountain Range," Liam echoed. "Do we have any idea how far we're going?"

"Well, we figure past Český Krumlov," Stirling said. "That's a little town at the base of the mountains—it's where Kadjic's going to stop for petrol, probably. We need to hold back. We're all gassed to go, everything was filled this morning. We figure Kadjic's heading for his hideout, so this is our chance. You guys down with that?"

Liam wanted to say he goddamned was not, but as he glanced from Chuck, who was nodding, to Michael, who was doing the same, and Hunter, who gave him a grim nod, he realized that everybody here—*everybody*—had the same reasons to scream, "Stop this now!" But they weren't letting go of the main objective.

"Everybody here is a go," he said. "What's the plan?"

"Well, first," Stirling said, "we need to wait until Kadjic stops, and then Felix apparently has an idea. Something about the one thing Kadjic ever let drop about the place that Danny passed on to him. But we've got to see it first."

"So, driving blindly through the mountains?" Liam asked.

"Julia's at our wheel," Stirling said, confirming Liam's suspicions about people shifting in the vehicles. "Apparently she's been taking lessons from Chuck."

"God help you," Liam said. "Ping us if anything springs up."

"Will do. But hey, since you're closer to town, could you do me a favor? Could you look up Tor's comm and see how he's doing? Everybody wants to know how the painting caper's going, and he's the last piece of the puzzle."

"Will do. Let me ping him. Will get back to you."

"Fair. Out."

TOR WAS *not* happy with being left behind. But he *was* okay, and as he told Liam, the caper had gone like a dream.

"I recorded the bit," Tor said. "Marco came out of the kitchen to hold the camera—he's very proud. They discovered the switch, and Marco made a fuss about the closet being opened. It was brilliant." Tor dropped his voice. "I did spot a jeweled egg in there. I pocketed it in case there was a reason we took it. Do you know anything about that?"

Hunter, who had been listening with Liam, scowled. "I know my kleptomaniac boyfriend had a moment of nerves," he said into the shared mic, and Tor made a wheezing sound in his throat.

"You mean… you mean I helped with an *actual art theft*?"

Tor had always been their front man—reporting the good they'd done and leaving their methods to them.

"You okay there, boy?" Liam asked kindly. Well, he'd learned long ago that sometimes a thief's measure was greater than the sum of a man's conscience.

"No," Tor said. "I mean… *yes*! I'm a thief too!"

Liam and Hunter both chuckled, and for a moment, Liam felt a burst of hope, but it was Hunter who came up with the big idea.

"Hey, since you're, you know, resting on your laurels and all," Hunter said, "we're currently heading up into the Greater Bohemian Mountains. We think Kadjic's place is there, now that we know a general direction. Do you think you could…."

"Make computer magic," Liam said. "Stirling seemed to think I'd do what he did on comms, but with him and Josh out of action, we need a real hacker."

"It is a perk of the job," Tor conceded smoothly. Then in complete seriousness, "I'll try to have you plans and a deed of some sort in the next half hour."

Liam grunted. "You *are* a miracle worker," he said frankly, and then, in case Chuck drove them off a cliff between now and then, "I'm sending you my lieutenant's email—and my clearance code. Once you have the details, please send them to him. Tell them I told you he'd want the information." He paused. "Is that okay with everybody?"

"God yes," Chuck said from the front.

"Wasn't that our endgame?" Michael asked.

Hunter sighed. "If you insist."

"I don't," Liam told him sincerely. "You lot have done a lot of good in the last two months. There's no shame in wanting to finish this."

"Well, how soon will your goons, I mean guys, get there?" Hunter asked. "Because, you know, if things come up…."

"The nearest office is in Prague," Liam said frankly. "But they've got helicopters."

"Maybe give us a margin, Tor?" Hunter said. "We want to get our boys out of there without entanglements, right?"

"I hear you," Tor said seriously. "Let me get your destination, and I'll tip them off after you get there."

That decided, they signed off, and after a question to see if Chuck was okay—and some fumbling of ibuprofen so he would be—they settled into watching the mountain road unwind.

"JOSH," GRACE whispered. "Man, you've got to wake up. We're here."

Josh groaned and shivered and then stretched, part of him registering that he was much warmer than he had been, and another part gratefully acknowledging that the movement had stopped.

"Where are they?" he mumbled.

"Kadjic hauled Danny into the house. The driver just closed down the garage. We're clear."

"Good," Josh said. "You're going to need to haul me out of here and let me get my legs under me."

His blood had started to move sluggishly through his veins again, and while still exhausted, he could feel his adrenaline, finally, propelling him forward. Kadjic had Danny. They needed to find him. It was really that simple.

It took some doing—and they weren't as quiet as they should have been—but Grace finally had him out of the trunk, his limbs stinging enough to steal his breath.

"What now?" Grace asked, shivering. The garage was warmer than outside, but not by much.

"Stirling?" Josh muttered, tapping his comm. "Stirling, did we lose you?"

Stirling's reply was broken but still reassuring. "Ten min… here… out… getting… wait for us…."

"Finding Danny," Josh replied tersely, not sure Stirling could hear him any better than he'd heard Stirling. "Find us."

And then he tapped the comm again and signed off so the static didn't kill him.

Determinedly he took a few steps forward, relieved when he didn't stumble. In a moment Grace's hand was under his elbow, steadying him as they neared the steps from the garage to what was probably the first floor.

As they walked up the steps—lushly carpeted—Josh tried to put a finger on where they were.

"Cold," he said. "*Damp*. And what is that sound?"

"Rain?" Grace asked, puzzled.

"Too high up for rain," Josh said. "But it's water."

"Fountain?" Grace said, and Josh considered one of those indoor water sculptures and just as quickly rejected it.

"He's not here that often," he said. "Those mold and rust. And if he's got art here, it would damage the art."

As they moved up the stairs, one painstaking step at a time, Josh said, "And it's getting drier. He's got humidity control up here, but still—what do you think?"

"Waterfall," Grace said promptly. "Like Batman. It's the Batcave, but this is the bad guy."

Josh grunted. "I want to tell you that's stupid," he muttered, "but we're up here in the hills of Bohemia—"

"That is a made-up word," Grace told him indignantly. "Like buzzenteen."

"Swear to Gru it's not," Josh told him. "It was a place. It got conquered and then disappeared, but there's still the Greater Bohemian Mountains. And I think we're there."

"How can you know more passed out than I can know awake?" Grace asked grumpily. "And you're the one who's stupid, Mr. Can't Walk in Bohemia."

"I haven't been able to steal anything," Josh told him. "I've had to study maps. It's really frickin' boring unless you're grabbing weird shit from museums, so I hope I get better soon."

"You're just saying that to make me feel better," Grace whispered, his whisper indicating that they'd reached the landing and had to watch for people now.

The water sound was louder here—and in the distance, closer to the water, farther from the stairs from the garage—they could hear voices raised in anger, one of them Danny's.

"Follow that argument," Josh mouthed, and Grace nodded.

The floor under their delicate rubber-soled jazz slippers was a rich, burnished hardwood, with silk-and-wool runners that were probably worth as much as the carpet Josh had almost bled on in Munich. Reds, blacks, purples, the walls were painted in the same sumptuous, baroque colors, but that wasn't what caught Josh's attention.

"Oh my God," he whispered, rounding a corner and coming face-to-face with half a wall holding Rembrandt's missing painting *Christ in the Storm on the Sea of Galilee*.

"Isn't that…?" Grace asked, sounding stunned.

Famous? Yes. Stolen from the Gardner Museum in Boston in one of the most famous art heists in history? *Hell* yes. Thought to be missing forever? *Oh my fucking God!*

"Holy shit," Josh whispered.

And there was a series of Monets that had thought to have been lost during the bombing at Giverny.

And there, in a glass case, was….

"Is that from that big jewel heist at the Louvre?" Grace asked, staring at the circlet of emeralds framed in diamonds, with a tiara to match.

"And that is the third *David*," Josh said blankly, gazing at the case next to it, where a twelve-inch bronze casting of Michelangelo's *David* stood. There were two accounted for, and the third one was thought to be a myth.

"It exists," Grace said, sounding equally as blank. "Holy fuckballs. This place is the holy grail of thieves."

They kept going, keeping silent now, their footfalls almost inaudible under the sound of the waterfall that must surely be outside, or overhead, or sliding them down the goddamned mountain.

Then they rounded a corner and, like sunrise over a valley at their feet, the house—which had seemed to be close and labyrinthine thanks to the baroque walls, mahogany flooring, and jewel-toned rugs—blossomed into a spectacle of lights.

The sitting room, because that's what it must have been, was spacious, and it opened out into a view unparalleled by any Josh had ever seen. Lit by spotlights, a giant window that must have been made of pressurized glass overlooked a veil of water, the falls that had permeated the house with sound. They weren't crashing on the house, but rather, the house was recessed in the rocks underneath. The garage entry was behind the mountain, and then the house itself burrowed through, coming out here.

It was glorious, but Josh, who had never experienced a moment of vertigo in his life, wanted to cling to something with fear that the whole thing would hammer down on his head and they'd go sliding down the mountain at any time.

There were five people in the room: the chauffeur, the muscle, and a man who must have been the butler. Those three were obviously trying to make themselves invisible. They stood in various positions, subservient and expressionless, ranged around the other two people, who were obviously the stars of the show.

Danny was leaning insouciantly against that spectacular bay window overlooking the waterfall. The window was up on a rise of about six inches, surrounded by a platform, the better to give the people sitting on the chairs and couches ranged around the room a chance to appreciate the view.

Kadjic was pacing this platform, swearing at Danny, raging at him, trying to wipe that all-knowing, unpleasant smirk off his face.

He'd obviously done so with his fists more than once, and Josh's chest ached as he saw the bruises, the bloody nose, and the careful, injured way Danny was cradling his ribs with one arm while using the other arm behind him to brace against the window.

Oh God, Danny. So many people who loved him enough to keep this from happening, and still, he'd loved them too much to let them try.

"Look at it, Daniel!" Kadjic was frothing. "Look at this! All of it! It could have been *yours*. The art alone, do you not crave it?"

"It's lovely," Danny said, his words muffled from a rapidly swelling nose and probably some loose teeth. "You should give your decorator a raise."

"I *loved* you! Why would you forfeit all of this for that *child*!" Kadjic demanded. "Answer me! *Answer me*!"

He advanced forward, and Danny simply stood there, and as his eyes landed on Josh and Grace and then flickered away before Kadjic could be tipped off, his smirk changed into an expression of true serenity.

"Because," he said, his shoulders twitching in a shrug, "he reminded me of somebody I love."

Kadjic's blow never landed. His hand fell limply to his side.

"You have a child?" he asked, sounding as though this thought—the thought that Danny had anybody else in his life besides Kadjic himself—had never occurred to him.

"I do," Danny said. His mouth twitched. "More than one, in fact, although not related by blood. But they're mine. That boy in the alley? He's one now."

"The other one? The thief?"

"Yes," Danny said. "Oh, that one—he's more myself than I ever was."

Next to him, Josh heard Grace gasp, and he wanted to hug his friend, who had needed so badly to know this.

"Others?" Kadjic asked.

"You would not believe if I told you," Danny said softly, "how many. How very much I love them. How very much these riches do *not* mean, when you have that sort of love in your life."

As Danny spoke, Josh sensed movement around him, but he knew without looking whose footfalls those were. All of them—all of them—

had spilled through the house, probably coming from other entrances, clearing out the few occupants taking care of the house as they did so.

Hunter emerged next to Grace, wrapped an arm around him, and held him tight as Grace steadied Josh, and Josh looked wildly around.

Liam? Felix?

His mother came to stand next to him, her wig of earlier that evening pulled off, her face wiped clean of makeup. She offered her arm and whispered, "We're the misdirection, darling. Are you ready to play your part?"

Plan, Josh thought somewhat desperately. There was a plan.

In front of him, Chuck and Carl both quietly disarmed and restrained the chauffeur, enforcer, and butler—with some help from Michael and Lucius, who started a pile of the various knives, guns, brass knuckles, and saps that Chuck and Carl kept producing as they patted them down.

Julia spoke up. "He has a sister, for one," she said, "who would be very disappointed to see him further harmed."

"And a son," Josh said. "One who has loved him since birth and would be very, very unhappy if he's not returned safely."

Their voices made Kadjic whip around, and they could all hear his gasp as he took in the situation. "You…," he whispered wildly, eyes on Josh. "From the very beginning—*you*?"

"Me," Josh said, nodding in acknowledgment. "And my mother."

"I have people here who will *gut* you—" Kadjic began, but Molly strode in, her blond plait swinging behind her.

"And they are no longer mobile," she said with satisfaction. "Right, little brother?"

"Infrared indicates we got them all," Stirling said, striding in through the hallway Josh and Grace had come through. Apparently, while Josh and Grace had pussyfooted through the house, overwhelmed by the beauty, the rest of their party had been absolutely fed up with all that had come before.

"You…," Kadjic muttered, staring at Molly. "You—you've been… *you're* the one we've been looking for. *You're* everywhere! A blond woman—"

"Or man!" Tienne said cheerfully, at Stirling's side.

"And *you*!" Kadjic returned his ire—and his obsession—to Josh. "*You* were at the party. Who *are* all of you?"

"We're the orphans you created," Molly said.

"I'm the boy you tried to kill," Tienne added.

"We're the soldiers who fought against people like you," Chuck said with a nod at Hunter.

"I'm the insurance guy who had to clean up your messes," Carl said, his voice light even as he kneed the muscle in the throat for trying to take him down.

"And I'm the son of the man you tried to kill in an alleyway in Morocco," Josh said. "And I'm the man who's been planning the heists that have plagued your hopes all summer. Did you think nobody loved him, Kadjic? Did you think you could wreak the kind of destruction you have, all over the globe, and not earn yourself some enemies?"

Kadjic was focused on all of them, but Josh was concentrating behind him on Danny, who had locked eyes with Julia, and on the shadows, passing between the waterfall and the glass.

"Now?" she murmured, and Josh realized that she, Danny, and whoever was casting those shadows beyond the window must have been mic'd.

"Now," Danny said with conviction. "Give it up, Andrejevic. You have nowhere to go. Interpol is on its way, and according to our accounting, you have flat run out of the collateral to pay off your network to get you out of it. You're done. You don't even have enough to start over."

"I'll destroy *all* of you—"

"With *what*?" And for the first time, Danny's voice rose. "We've taken you, Andres. We've ruined your businesses, stripped you of your reputation. You have enough money to live well, perhaps, so perhaps you should flee into the hills to lick your wounds." He shook his head. "But you'll never be great again. Nobody will want you. I at least thought you were a good time when I was drunk and heartbroken and looking for death. But how much fun are you now? We took your crime, and can you see what's left? An obscene, sagging, lonely little man, and nobody, *nobody*, will even miss you when you're go—"

With a roar, and movements too quick to be halted, Andres Kadjic charged into Danny, and the two of them crashed through the window and out into the three-hundred-foot drop to the mountainous rocks below.

The glass cutter Danny had been wielding behind his back clattered to the floor as he disappeared.

Catch You, Catch You, Catch You if You Fall.

"READY?" FELIX called, and Liam wanted to scream, "No!" But he couldn't. His ribs blazing, it was all he could do to hold on to the guywire that kept him from pitching off the side of the house.

The water was falling fast, but there was not as much of it as it seemed. The house was obscured from the front but not hidden, and while working in the cold and the wet was difficult and slippery, Leon had produced some gloves and boots from Carl's van that made traction easier.

"I figured we would be working underwater," Leon said cheerfully. "We weren't sure which van would be where. I put them in both."

In passing, Liam thought the man was an amazing father.

Given a direction and a general vicinity, Tor had produced miracles. An hour after he'd signed off with Liam, the information had started pouring through the computer—specs, security systems, entrances and exits. Liam had passed it on, and in the remaining hour of the trip—all of them holding a ten-minute distance from Kadjic's town car lest the caravan of headlights alert him on what was essentially a deserted mountain road—they had determined the best points of egress.

There weren't many. A main door and the garage itself.

And the only window was the giant bay window overlooking the canyon.

And then, as they'd approached the edifice, a light had come on, making the house glow like a jewel behind the veil of water.

Two figures could be seen arguing, and Stirling, who had muted Danny's comms during the ride so they could talk and not distract Danny as he verbally fenced with an alligator, spoke into Danny's ear.

"We're coming. We're infiltrating the house in two minutes."

"Silently," he said subvocally. "I need an out through the window."

And throughout the three vehicles, pandemonium ensued.

Leon had taken control, forcing Tienne to give him a commlink as he'd told them, as though they all should have known, that there was water-rappelling equipment in the front van. All he needed was volunteers.

Besides himself, of course.

Before Stirling disabled the alarms and the crew had streamed silently through the great vaulted garage, searching for the various guards and household personnel, Liam, Felix, and Leon had begun their ascent to the roof of the house, recessed behind the waterfall.

It was then that Stirling told them Josh and Grace had apparently emerged from the car they'd all passed without a thought and were wandering through the house while the rest of them tried to be as silent as possible.

"It's fine," the young man said. "They're finding their way to the main room. We'll be able to herd them your way."

Herd them your way.

Herd them *out the fucking window*.

Liam was a little fuzzy on why this was such a good plan, but since Danny couldn't be argued with right now—he was currently getting the crap beat out of him in a whole other argument—Danny was the one calling the shots.

And Liam guessed he wanted the big finish.

Well, he did have one coming.

Still, as Liam and Felix were carefully negotiating the wet rock face—and he gave thanks for a plethora of Interpol training classes that made this possible—he couldn't help gasping, "Why are we doing this again?"

Felix paused for a moment, and Liam had a glimpse behind the urbane businessman to the hard face of the criminal he might have been without a Danny Mitchell to temper him.

"Because if Kadjic lives, we want him to think Lightfingers is dead," Felix said shortly.

"If?" Liam asked, panting and—gloved fingers gripping the slick surface like death—surveying the valley beyond the waterfall Kadjic had built behind.

In the moonlight it was lovely, rolling fields stretching out beyond the snow-tinted peaks, with the occasional farm or homestead cozied between gentle rises.

He wondered at Kadjic's determination to carve this house into the cliffside. How much had he disrupted, destroyed, ruined, to have this monument to his own greed nobody would ever see?

"If," Felix said grimly. "If."

And then they were at the window, positioning themselves to be able to swing in from the sides. Above them Leon was poised with two electric winches, one from each comms van—those suggested by Hunter and seconded by Michael, because apparently Leon wasn't the only king of preparation in the group. (At this point, Liam thought they could pull a genie and a magistrate from the engine compartment of the bloody comms vans and Leon wouldn't bat an eyelash.)

Liam still didn't have a comm link, so while he had a decent view of what was happening inside, he didn't have audio.

He wasn't sure he needed it, though. He could see the crew emerging a few at a time, could see the threats in the room neutralized, could see Kadjic frothing at the mouth. They hadn't just dismantled his businesses, they'd dismantled his *person*. Men like Kadjic didn't like being shown up, didn't like feeling weak or outmaneuvered or outthought.

Or outclassed.

And the expressions, the body language, the constant threats to Danny—all of it indicated somebody decompensating in real time.

"Pay attention," Felix hissed over the sound of the waterfall, and Liam stopped paying attention to what the others were doing (was it his imagination or did Josh look like pale death in black microfiber?) and started paying attention to what Danny was doing behind his back. The glass cutter wasn't subtle, the strokes weren't even, but every silent *scritch* was meant to weaken the structure currently keeping Danny from pitching through the air and onto the jagged rocks at the base of the falls.

"Oh God," he muttered. This was really happening.

His heartbeat slowed, and his stomach knotted as he realized, suddenly, exactly what he'd been tasked with. *Protect my family.* Josh would never forgive him if he bollixed this up.

So much faith in him, Liam thought almost desperately. So much hope that Liam could keep Josh's family safe.

"*Now*!" Felix shouted, and as Kadjic lunged against Danny, the glass behind him crashed outward, and the two bodies hurtled through the air.

Felix and Liam shoved off their sides of the house frame, both of them aiming for Lightfingers, who had kicked against Kadjic with his feet and held his arms above his head as he fell.

Liam got him first, seizing Danny's hand in midair, his ribs howling as he slowed Danny's descent. Felix closed in, their flesh smacking solidly while he wrapped one arm around Danny, keeping his hand on the guidewire.

Liam kept hold of Danny's other hand, and the three of them were winched up, one foot at a time, until they reached the recessed roof of the house, where they literally pushed Danny into Leon's arms so they could scramble into the alcove themselves.

Liam could feel blood drenching his ribs as he pulled himself to safety.

For a moment they stood, breathless, double-checking each other for new injuries, when their silence was broken by Felix.

He'd engulfed Danny in an embrace so tender Liam had to look away. It was so very apparent Felix was sobbing against Danny's neck.

"So," Leon said, coming up alongside Liam. "I think we should see how Josh is doing, don't you?"

New Day

IT TOOK two hours for Interpol to get there, and by the time they did, Tor had arrived in a rental, a flustered Marco by his side to play cameraman, and the rest of the crew had cleared out.

Felix and Leon had needed to restrain Liam to keep him from going with them. Josh was a mess, blood caking the front of his shirt, circles under his sunken eyes, his pulse thready and his temperature spiking.

"You need to stay," Josh told him, "and get your medical treatment here. Hamlet had it right, Liam—there needs to be reporting here. You need to spin it, otherwise they'll run fingerprints and we're all cooked."

"But God, baby—"

Josh's smile had been the shy one, the one Liam treasured. "You'll find me. Don't worry. It's not goodbye—it's just one more goddamned trip to the hospital." He scowled playfully. "Maybe from now on they'll start packing plasma in the comms van."

He'd kissed Liam then, hard, and Liam had responded with all his soul. But inside he knew. This wasn't over by a long shot.

Two hours after the kiss, Interpol arrived, and somebody *not* Hunter stitched up his ribs.

Two days later the trailer his supervisor had commissioned to house the Interpol agents and provide offices so they could categorize and report on all the artifacts in the house arrived. Coincidentally, that was the same day the forensics people recovered Kadjic's broken, bloodied body at the foot of the falls.

Not much of it was left, Liam was happy to report, but his fingerprints and dental records were still *quite* recognizable.

Two weeks after Kadjic's body was recovered, Liam was *still* at the Fortress of Vanity (as Josh called it in text now), helping to catalogue and source all the stolen artwork. His supervisor had said, rather happily, that the job would take years and had hinted to Liam that he might be in charge of the operation before it was over.

Liam didn't tell him that if *he* was left in charge, he might be found guilty of shipping some of the more memorable art pieces to a family in Chicago, for no other reason than he thought they might enjoy them when their original owners didn't seem to care.

He obviously was not the most reliable of agents at this moment.

Two weeks after that terrible temptation to steal art for the Salingers just because Liam missed them, Josh was given the okay to go back to the States, but Liam was still stuck in the fucking trailer, longing for one of the decadent hot showers at *any* of the hotels he'd stayed at during his journey and wanting to see Josh so badly he almost couldn't breathe.

He didn't even have their fingerprints to hide. Liam resolved to send Michael's kids a *case* full of toys since Michael had been the one to remember housecleaning, which he and the others had done before they left.

Liam got Josh's text when he touched down in Chicago, and sat in that awful sterile trailer, staring at his phone, his heart, his *soul*, feeling empty.

His supervisor was now Carter, who had taken his turn in rehab all those years ago and run with it. He was now an able administrator who trusted Liam since their days in the field together. Liam—knowing that Carter valued humanity and justice more than bureaucracy—had taken that first violation of the rules in shipping Tienne to the hands of the Salingers as his invitation to skirt the rules.

Carter, who had seen that Liam was a decent human being, had allowed for any elisions Liam made with his reports.

It had been a good working relationship, and Liam had no complaints.

Until now.

"Craig?" Carter said, coming up behind him as he sat in the trailer staring soullessly at his phone. "Anything wrong?"

Liam glanced at Carter—terminally single, sagging a little around the middle, hair thinning, living for the job—and his emptiness felt eternal.

"Oh," Carter said softly. "Time, is it?"

"Time?" Liam asked hollowly.

"You were always meant for greater things than just this unit," Carter said. "Husband, children, a life…."

Liam's mouth twitched "You knew I was gay?"

Carter snorted. "I *am* a member of Interpol, after all. I do have certain skills."

Liam swallowed. "I love working here," he said honestly. "I-I don't want to leave forever. I…."

"Consultant status," Carter said crisply, as though he'd been planning this all along. "Visit the UK office once or twice a year, give workshops. That way—" He shrugged. "—you can keep giving me juicy tips from time to time, but you and your young man can go your own way. And best of all…." He waggled his eyebrows and gestured to the trailer, the sole purpose of which was to allow for bureaucracy to chug along at speed.

"No paperwork," Liam said softly.

"Right," Carter said. "You're never goddamned good at it anyway. Give me a week. Can you wait that long? Then I'll book you a flight."

He didn't need to. A week later, Hunter, Chuck, and Carl landed in a private Prague airport, all of them rested, happy, and ready for trouble.

"Get in, loser," Hunter said. "We're gonna go fight."

Stepping aboard the jet was his first step on the path home.

FINALLY, *FINALLY*, Josh had the all clear from the hospital for limited activity. He was tired, weak, bored and….

Content.

Healing sucked. It was gonna suck, and he needed to get used to the fact that he'd set himself back a good long year with the entire Kadjic enterprise. But whatever he'd needed to prove about carrying on the family business, about being good enough of a son for them to have sacrificed so much, he'd proven it.

Best of all, he'd learned he'd never needed to prove it at all.

The anger he'd borne so long no longer plagued his heart, and he found that his stress over what to do next was no longer a driving, constant presence.

He was going to be bored—he could finally read all those books his professors had recommended for extra reading. His friends weren't going anywhere. Molly had spent a week in England with Liam's brother—he promised to do the same in Chicago—but she wasn't leaving. (Although she had chopped off her straight blond locks, and what was left was short ringlets that her brother still loved to touch when she was sitting at his feet. She looked adorable and claimed she'd lost twenty pounds of hair alone.)

Grace continued to share his time between the mansion in Glencoe and the dance studio and Hunter's flat in Chicago.

And Stirling and Tienne might live in the basement of the Glencoe mansion forever.

Carl and Michael still ate dinner with them once a week, as did Chuck and Lucius. And Tor and Marco weren't leaving the mother-in-law cottage anytime soon.

And the dads were… well, there had been arguing at first, during their first week back, but Josh was beginning to see the difference between an argument and a fight. Felix had been *terrified.* Danny had been ready to die to protect them all but very glad that hadn't been necessary. They'd needed to hammer their shit out first, and then they could be the family patriarchs that everybody else needed.

It had come. Like everything else with two such brilliant, headstrong, different people, it had been difficult—and difficult to watch—but it had been worth it in the end.

And Josh's mother continued to be smart, stylish, and *very* busy, and now? Radiant and madly in love with her child's father, who while spending the last month in Europe, making sure his businesses were in good order after their summer adventures, would be back in the beginning of November.

She seemed especially glowy today, as she and Josh sat on the newly installed marble bench in her mediation garden, both of them wrapped up against the pending snow of a Chicago October, but wanting to see the leaves on a glorious sunny day just the same.

Josh had one thing on his mind.

"Mom, you know you can't keep them."

His mother raised her fingertips to the lovely green necklet at her throat, a circle of emeralds, princess cut, each one surrounded by an oval of tiny perfect diamonds. It was stunning, it looked *glorious* on her even though blonds weren't supposed to wear green, and it was *so damned stolen.*

"I don't see why not," she said, sounding petulant and seventeen. "It's not like anybody knows we have them. Nobody even knew *Kadjic* had them. And honey, since he's given them to me, he hasn't stolen a single pair of my earrings—not once."

She'd said that when Grace had given her the giant pink diamond from the Louvre, as well. Every time Julia seemed sad or tired or overwhelmed with pregnancy at forty-one, Grace went to his luggage and produced another hot piece of jewelry. Hunter told Josh that he had no idea where the Princess Anne tiara was, but he thought Grace might be saving it for Christmas.

Right now, Josh dragged his fingers through his hair, which was getting shaggy. "But *Mom*, we're trying to instill certain habits here. And not taking valuables from foreign countries is one of them."

"But honey, we don't even know for certain they're from the Louvre heist."

"Mom, he didn't steal the provenance. It's going to occur to them eventually that those jewels went somewhere."

"No, it's not" came a beloved East-End–infused voice as its bearer traveled from the rear of the house through the garden.

"*Liam*!" Josh stood—slowly. He was still prone to dizzy spells, and he was learning. But once he was on his feet he ran straight into Liam Craig's arms, which were as strong and warm and wonderful as he'd remembered.

"Hello, boy-o," Liam said into his ear. "Surprised to see me?"

"*Yes*," said Josh. Liam had texted that he was trying for a flight over the next few days, but he hadn't said a word about finding one. "You got a flight?"

Liam snorted. "Right. Or maybe three assholes in a private jet gave me an hour to pack and told me to get my ass to the tarmac so they could turn around and bring me home."

"Chuck, Hunter, and Carl?" Josh asked excitedly. Of course they'd need three of them for a flight with that quick a turnaround. "I hadn't realized they'd even borrowed the plane. I had no idea…."

Liam gave a tired smile. God, he looked good, but like Josh, he'd lost weight in the last month and a half, and there was exhaustion in the circles under his eyes. *This is how he feels when he looks at me*, Josh thought, wanting to hold his face and kiss him and kiss him and kiss him.

But Liam set him down with an *oolf*, and Josh clung to him with more than affection.

They were still a little bruised and a little battered. Like Felix and Danny, they would need a reckoning, some jiggling in the puzzle boxes of their own hearts until the pieces learned to fit.

But for once, Josh was content.

It would come.

"They seemed to think you were pining for me," Liam teased, except Josh, thinking about his friends' concern over the last month, didn't think it was all in jest.

"And they missed their new playmate," he said, hoping to make Liam smile.

But he swallowed, and Josh realized that he'd just left the job that had driven him his whole life.

He needed reassurance.

"And I *was* pining for you," he said honestly, leaning his head on Liam's shoulder. "So much."

"Me too," Liam said softly, holding him close some more. "Apparently it doesn't matter if you send me away or I go on my own—away from you doesn't suit me anymore."

"Same," Josh murmured. But still… Liam's whole life had been spent trying to do a job he loved. "But you left. Are you sure?"

Liam's tired smile still did *amazing* things to Josh's stomach, crooked teeth and all. "I haven't technically *left*," he said. "I'm a *consultant* with detective inspector rank. They may still call me in on cases, but I have the right to refuse. But, you know, I thought since we've gone international now, you lot might like a chance to venture outside of Chicago once in a while."

Josh grinned. "My lot might," he said, and then he sobered. "But not right now. Not this year."

Liam cupped Josh's too-narrow waist with his big hands. "Joshua Daniel Salinger, I'll take a year off. Or three. Or five. Somehow, I don't think we'll ever get bored."

Josh had to wipe his eyes with his palms. "I don't plan to," he said, his voice a little broken. But he didn't *want* to break right now. He wanted to *celebrate*. Later they'd have time for Josh to fall apart in Liam's arms. *Later* they'd make love, slowly, carefully, immersed only in the glory of intimacy, not racing for a peak he couldn't afford to leap off. Not today. Not now.

But they'd get there.

"What *are* your plans?" Liam asked, but he'd turned, one arm still around Josh, the other including Julia, who had been somewhat trapped in her tiny corner of the garden and had been smirking as she pretended not to see their reunion.

"Well, right now," Josh said, taking his cue and dialing back his emotions, "I'm trying to convince my mother of two things."

"One is to give up the necklace, which I shall not do," Julia said archly.

"Nor should you have to," Liam said dryly. "As I was saying when I came outside, I happen to have the provenance on me—I saw it on Kadjic's inventory list, and, well, I guessed where it had gone."

"You have the provenance?" she asked, batting her eyelashes coyly. God, Josh's mother—she'd be beautiful and brilliant forever.

"In my luggage, milady," Liam said. "I'll get it later, and we'll consider it an early Christmas present, shall we?"

"Ooh, Josh, I like this in a son-in-law. Tell him he's scored big points with me here."

"Because catching Danny as he fell out of a window wasn't enough," Josh scoffed, and his mother pouted.

"Some would call that reminder in bad taste," she said.

"What was the other thing you're trying to convince her of?" Liam asked.

"To find out if I'm having a brother or sister," Josh said. "It's driving me and the dads insane. It's driving Uncle Leon insane. It's driving *Grace* insane, and he, in turn, is driving us *all* insane. Why won't she even *try* to find out?"

Liam's hand around his waist tightened. "It's like any good caper, lad. The surprises are half the fun."

Josh scowled at his mother but returned the squeeze. "You're pregnant at forty-one, Mom. Isn't that enough of a surprise?"

"Hush," she said and then lowered her voice. "But between you and me, I *did* have the test done. I want to find out how long it takes for Danny to break into the medical system and find out. I think he's already asked Stirling for help."

Josh chuckled and pulled Liam down on the bench next to her for the last few streaks of sunlight through the gold leaves and what might be their final glimpses of the heartbreak-blue sky of late October before the snows came.

No family was perfect—not even families that looked perfect on the outside. But *his* family, as sprawling and unusual as it was, had more than proven itself strong enough for whatever was to come.

And the man by his side had been part of that. Like Felix and Danny, they would have their storms, their disagreements, their rough patches.

But Josh hadn't only learned thievery and graft from his parents. He'd learned loyalty, kindness, and play, and now he knew Liam had those things in his bones.

The Salingers were a long way from being finished with the world, but for this moment, in his mother's garden, he and the man he loved had peace, and his family had joy, and as he and Liam had both learned the hard way, peace, love, and joy were the rarest, most vital riches any human could be gifted with, and they couldn't be hoarded.

They could only be given freely.

Josh Salinger and his family would be giving of their riches for as long as hard work, luck, and a little theft could provide.

Jitters, Jumps and Thieves: A Long Con Short

"So, Josh," Hunter said at dinner that night. "How you feeling?"

Josh regarded him with mild surprise—and deep exhaustion. Deep undercover in order to lure Kadjic out of hiding, he'd been doing an *actual* job while running the op from the mansion, and Hunter could tell he was exhausted.

But so was Hunter. Hunter thought maybe they could, well, solve each other's problems.

Josh must have seen something of that on Hunter's face, because he blinked away the sleep—and the headaches that still plagued him after chemo had robbed his body of a lot of his red blood cells—and obviously tried to think.

"That depends," he said muzzily. "How close are you to an actual murder rap?"

Hunter grimaced. "He doesn't have a show right now," he said apologetically.

"I know," Josh said.

"Chuck and I went out on a run yesterday. We were trying to corner Kadjic's main drug distributor in Springfield."

Josh grimaced. Obviously he'd heard about this. "I know."

"He hid in the trunk, Josh. Chuck and I are buzzing down the road at a buzzillion miles because, well—"

"Chuck is driving," Josh filled in.

"Yes, and suddenly the back seat of your little roadster pops open and Grace crawls into the car from the trunk and asks for a milkshake."

Josh's lips twitched, and Hunter relented. "Yes, it was sort of funny," he admitted. "But then we track the guy down, and Grace is like… doing grands jetés behind him, and Chuck is trying to lean on the guy and—" Hunter shook his head. "It's hard to lean on somebody like that when your boyfriend is looking like Peter Fucking Pan. It feels dirty. And I *know* Grace is an amoral little asshole who would sneak a lockpick between this guy's C1 and C2 vertebrae and render him unable to breathe, but… but he's smiling at me and drinking a milkshake and holding his foot over his head and—"

"I get the picture," Josh said, his lips still twitching. He'd put on enough weight that Hunter could see the dimple on his cheek popping in and out, and Hunter gave a sigh.

"Look, man, he needs you. I… I love him. I'd die for him. He may think we're just boyfriends, but I will put a ring on it one day when he's not looking, only…." Hunter couldn't help it. He was used to keeping his body language contained and his emotions even more so, but he found himself waving his hands around like he could produce the words to explain his frustration by magic.

"But we need a day out," Josh said happily. "I hear you. And actually, it's time to let him help plan the op."

Hunter sagged at the table. "Oh my God, thank you."

Josh nodded his head sagely, like he was doing a favor, but Hunter caught his lips twitching and felt infinitely better.

Josh and Grace ride again—the dynamic duo was being restored.

All was as it should be in the world.

"SO," GRACE said, his voice impossibly low, "what are we doing this for again?"

"We're practicing," Josh said, looking down from the balcony of the building two blocks away from the building he was supposed to be working at. They'd chosen this one because it had similar dimensions and composition to their target building, but the room they had access to for "practice" (as he'd told his parents) faced an alleyway and not a main street, the better to not attract attention.

"We've done this lots," Grace said, leaning over the balcony railing until he could lift his legs over his head while outside the railing's safety area. "Why are we doing it now?"

"Quit that, you idiot," Josh hissed. "People are *less likely* to see what we do here, but that doesn't mean you're invisible."

Grace—who had apparently learned *some* self-control over the past year, dutifully righted himself and stared at Josh, waiting for an answer.

Josh grimaced and looked away.

"Oh my God," Grace said, a shaft of pain so raw crossing his lovely features that Josh felt his own eyes water. "You… you can't."

"I can," Josh defended. "I just…." He sighed. "I've got to be able to do this, Grace. You know that, right? I'm the only one with access to steal the painting and time to replace it with the forgery. I'm the only one with an excuse to be there if I'm busted. I… everything we've put into this job, and it's gotta be me, but…." He sighed and tried to still the shaking in his hands.

"It's been a while," Grace said, his voice neutral. "Since we rappelled down buildings."

Josh let out a breath, glad that Grace, as ever, got him.

"It's been a while," he admitted, still holding on tightly to the other thing he didn't want to say.

But Grace—as ever—*got* him.

"You miss Liam," Grace said wisely.

"So bad," Josh said, able to tell Grace this as he could tell nobody else.

"Then ask him to come help," Grace implored. "Come on, Josh." Not "Cancer boy" or "Recovery boy" or "idiot." Josh. "You love the stupid Interpol cop guy—you think this is a secret?"

"No!" Josh felt peevish and scared and whiny, and he couldn't help it. "Don't you get it? He comes back now and sees me like—" He indicated himself, healthier than he had been six months ago but still *recovering.* Too thin, too tired, too unsure of things he'd been sure about for years. "Like this—and that's all I'm ever going to be to him. Some sick, pathetic *thing* he spent three weeks of his vacation comforting when he could have been out playing Pirates of the Caribbean."

Grace snorted. "I hate to break this to you, moron, but he was just as happy to be trapped in that berth as you were! God, Josh, I've never seen somebody so… so ready to step up and be Captain America, but just for one boy. You are the country of Josh, and Liam wants to be Captain of Josh. The least you could do is call him so he'll come be Captain of Josh for, you know, *Josh.*"

Josh squinted at him. "You," he said after a moment, "are making even less sense than usual. Can we just… I don't know, set up our equipment and zoom down to that balcony three floors below? Jesus. Captain of Josh. Just because you've got a Captain of Grace ready to fly in and rescue you—"

"Captain of Grace fobbed me off on you," Grace muttered, pulling out his paracord and carabiners.

Josh sighed and started getting his own equipment ready. It had been a while, but God, he and Grace used to do this sort of thing every weekend.

"Only because I hadn't gotten around to begging yet," he told Grace.

Grace gave him one of those brilliant smiles before—without warning or lining up his descent or even measuring out paracord—he jumped off the twenty-third floor balcony of a building currently being renovated in downtown Chicago.

"Grace!" Josh cried, furiously rigging his own setup so he could jump off and follow Grace down. Below him he heard the crash of a window—which was *not* in the plan—and the surprised yelp of the construction men on the floor *four* stories below, and it took Josh fifteen seconds to jump off the edge of the balcony to chase Grace through the construction site, out another window, and over one more ledge.

This time all the way to the bottom.

They came to a rest on the other side of the building from where they started, three blocks away from their car, looking around the corner to see if the construction guys had managed to follow them here.

"You asshole," Josh panted, spots swimming in front of his eyes. "That wasn't the plan at all."

Grace grinned at him, turning his face up to the tiny bit of sky visible beyond the top of the building. "So," he said, closing his eyes in the beam of imaginary sunshine, "how's those jitters?"

"Fuck you," Josh panted.

Grace cackled. "I don't see anybody—let's go!"

And then he took off, Josh after him, both of them sprinting like they hadn't done in a year. Grace won, of course, which meant he was behind the wheel, Josh's purloined keys in the ignition before Josh was three steps away—but Josh *was* three steps away.

And as Grace was zipping through the Chicago streets, shouting, "Wanna see what Chuck taught me last week?" Josh had to admit it.

His bone-deep yearning for Interpol Officer Liam Craig hadn't gone anywhere.

But his jitters were nowhere in sight.

Keep Reading
for an excerpt from
Assassin Fish
Book 8.5 in the Fish Out of Water series
by Amy Lane

Unwelcome

BRADY CARNEGIE wrinkled his nose, clutching the plastic bag with the cell phone in it to his chest almost like a child.

Well, children's pictures had been *on* the cell phone, but not the good kind. The terrible kind, imprinted in Brady's unwilling gray matter, burned behind his eyeballs for the rest of his life, those sweet, innocent babies and the preacher of the revival tent church nearly forty miles away.

And of the man whose skeleton was currently charred beyond recognition in the burned-out carcass of his police SUV.

The phone, relatively unscathed, had been unlocked, and somebody had made the homemade pornography the phone's wallpaper.

Deputy Roy Kuntz showed up in some of those pictures, but most of them featured his brother, Preacher Donnie Ray Kuntz as the star.

Brady had lived in the area for about a year and some change. He'd heard of Preacher Donnie Ray, who worked under the big revival tent about a parking lot away from a *really* big recently refurbished house.

And he'd worked with Roy. Hadn't *liked* Roy. Had done *backflips* and double shifts and worked holidays to avoid being partnered with him. Had *never* thought the man had his back.

But they'd been coworkers nonetheless, and these… these *abominations* on the phone by Roy's barbecued vehicle were blood-freezing and awful.

The sheriff, Arlen Cuthbert, didn't seem as disturbed as Brady.

A big man, much of his high school football weight sagging on his middle-aged bones and much of his gray hair reduced to a tired hula skirt around his bald scalp, Arlen Cuthbert nonetheless held some power in this weird territory in California.

East of San Diego and Los Angeles, they were also south of Meth and north of Hell—at least they were on some of the maps *Brady* had seen. On the one hand, there wasn't much out here but a whole lot of long, desolate roadways that cut through the Mojave Desert and Death Valley.

On the other hand, there were small towns strung together by hundreds of miles of two-lane freeways, towns that had banks and meth labs and mini-marts and innocent civilians and desperate people, all of whom could clash at unreasonable times.

Brady had done his research before he'd taken this job—he'd seen that the crime rate had been steadily on the decrease over the last two years before he'd transferred. He'd wanted in on that action, some police work that gave his profession a good name!

The one thing he'd realized over the last year was that whatever was affecting the crime rate, diminishing the mob presence, reducing the meth labs, getting rid of the dangerous people with guns who liked to knock over small businesses and banks—whatever the hell this force for good was, it was *not* the police force.

Not south of Meth and north of Hell, anyway.

And it sure as shit wasn't Arlen Cuthbert.

"Well, Donnie Ray and Roy, they was tight," Arlen said.

"This isn't guys at a barbecue!" Brady heard the disgust cracking his voice and wondered at his own sanity. The contents of this phone were an abomination—everything he knew about the world said that. How could Arlen be so unfazed? "This is two pedophiles and a whole bunch of kids who are never going to be the same!"

Arlen hawked and spat, the spittle landing close enough to the still smoking remains of the SUV to sizzle. "They'll be okay, I guess," he said, not meeting Brady's eyes.

Brady fought the urge to scream. "What about Roy?" he asked. "Will *he* be all right?"

Arlen stared at the blackened *thing* in the SUV for far longer than Brady'd had the stomach for. "Don't reckon it matters much now what he did when he was alive," he mused, and Brady wondered if he could be convicted for shooting his boss.

"It matters to those children!" he snapped. "It matters to their parents! My *God*, Arlen, somebody killed Roy Kuntz. Don't you even care?"

"You got anywhere to start looking for that man?" Arlen asked him.

Brady gestured helplessly to the other wreck on the road, an empty Chevy Impala that lay, crushed and useless, a good seventy-five yards away.

The car was demolished—nobody could have walked away from that disaster. And yet, nobody *had*. There were no prints in either direction of the wreck, and although Brady had searched for fifty feet in either direction of the entire collision site, he couldn't find a sign that *anybody* had been nearby when the Impala had T-boned the cop car and gone rolling off into the desert.

So… what? Was it a magic fucking Chevy Impala? It just tootled along, causing destruction and mayhem wherever it may roam? Brady loved cars—always had—but as far as he knew, his dream of a magic car that talked and made decisions of its own had gone the way of Santa Claus and the Easter Buggy… erm, Bunny.

Brady choked back a snort of laughter at that, and Sheriff Cuthbert eyed him sourly.

"What's so goddamned funny?" he asked.

"Who was driving the goddamned Impala?" Brady snapped.

"Who cares?" Arlen snapped back.

"*You should*!" Brady cried. "Arlen, whoever was driving that vehicle *murdered* a law officer!"

Arlen held out his hand and wobbled it, and Brady had to concede.

"Okay, they wreaked vengeance on a pedophile," Brady muttered, clutching the phone to his chest. "Either way, don't you want to get to the bottom of that?"

"The phone or the crispy critter there?" Arlen asked.

"Can we do both?" Brady asked.

Arlen rolled his eyes. "Son, you've got an inflated opinion of our little station house. What do I got? Eight, ten deputies? For how many square miles?"

"Then call in the CBI!" Brady told him. The California Bureau of Investigation was *made* for things like this, right?

"They'd just make a lot of fuss about that phone," Arlen said, spitting again. The spit still sizzled, so neither of them were going anywhere.

"*They should*!" Brady burst out, and Arlen's pose of annoyance gave way to absolute hostility.

"We don't need to be digging into what's already dead," he said with conviction. "Now give me that thing, and I'll put it in an evidence locker—"

"And let it rot?" Brady yanked it back from him. "No. No, Arlen. I'm taking this thing to the CBI in Sacramento if I have to drive there myself."

Arlen blinked at him slowly—not as though he was surprised, but like a rattlesnake, calculating how and when to strike.

"You think you can do that?" he asked.

Brady fought the temptation to swallow. "Yes," he said. "I'll leave as soon as I clock—"

Arlen snatched the phone from his hand, and while Brady had fast reflexes, he pulled back before he broke the older man's arm.

"What in the *fuck*?"

"You swear like a faggot," the old sheriff said. "I don't need you to do my job for me. Go write a ticket or something."

While Brady stared at the old man, he hawked back in his throat and made to spit again—on Brady's feet. Brady hopped backward, practically dancing, completely disgusted, and Arlen Cuthbert laughed.

"Go home, ya fuckin' pansy. Or go back to your desk. Or go suck dick. I don't fuckin' care. This was one of ours. We'll take care of him, and we don't need no help from *you.*"

Brady's eyebrows went up to his SCSD baseball cap, because this wasn't Texas, but he still needed something to shade his eyes. "Roy and his brother haven't been in Southern California much longer than I have," he said, stung.

"Yeah, but I grew up with their daddy. Go the fuck away, Deputy Carnegie. I don't fucking need you."

"I'll go file an accident report," he said with dignity. He didn't add, *With the CBI, asshole*! Because he didn't think Arlen knew about that.

And he was on his way to do just that, heading west toward Barstow, when he got a call on his radio. Dispatch—who apparently didn't know Arlen had lost his mind—was calling for all officers in the area to come to the residence of one Donnie Ray Kuntz.

He'd been murdered.

Brady was close enough to be the first responding officer on the scene, and as he stood in the man's study, looking in horror at the puddles—*puddles*—of blood that had drained from the man's arm as he'd sat half-naked at his desk in front of his computer, Brady listened to the screaming and sobbing of the women in the childcare wing of the house/church and had to fight off nausea.

There were pictures on that computer to match the ones on the phone near Roy's flaming corpse.

Pictures, Brady was certain, that had been taken somewhere in *this house.*

Without second-guessing himself, he pulled out his cell phone and called his local FBI contact, Missing and Exploited Children department, and told them about the murder—and the evidence.

And then he told them that they had to get their asses out to the church before Arlen Cuthbert destroyed the crime scene the same way Brady was certain he was going to destroy the phone.

They were there before any other deputies from Brady's station house arrived, and Brady turned the scene over to Jessica Chambers, a stout forty-ish woman who had competence written all over her freckled face.

"You sure you don't want to help with this?" she asked, watching as her agents started taking the women aside to interview. It was a hard slog—so many children to contend with, most of them whimpering or outright screaming with upset.

Brady raised his eyebrow. "Is that a rhetorical question?"

She turned a rueful face toward him and then registered his expression. "What aren't you telling me?" she asked.

So he told her. About the phone, about his sheriff's refusal to investigate, about Brady's threat to call the CBI—about all of it, and Jessica Chambers got a look of motherly concern that almost made Brady cry.

"Got it," she said softly. "Yeah—we'll investigate him. I'll call you when I need information. What will you do?"

He shrugged and gave his best "aw shucks, ma'am" impression. "Well, here I was when suddenly the FBI just showed up. They must have picked it up over the airwaves somehow. I have no idea how they heard."

Jessica nodded, but she didn't look appeased. "Brady, we can offer you protection here. Are you sure you don't want to take it?"

Brady thought of Arlen's cutting words—and the homophobic slur—and shuddered.

Yes, a part of him was ready to be quit of this whole scene. He'd come here to be part of some exciting new law enforcement and had found himself embroiled into the same ol' white boy corruption.

But… but… he *still* didn't know why the crime wasn't worse around here. It *should* be worse around here with Arlen Cuthbert in charge.

But it wasn't.

"There's something… odd about this area, Agent Chambers," he said thoughtfully. "And a part of me loves it a lot. I think I'll hang out for as long as possible. I've got some questions I need to answer, you know?"

"Fair, Deputy. Just… you know. Keep my number on speed dial. And let me know if any other developments in this case run by your desk, okay?"

Brady nodded his head, feeling a little like a secret agent.

At that moment, two squad cars from his department rolled up, sirens on full, humiliating blast.

"If you'll excuse me," he said, "I need to go lie to my fellow deputies."

A Pond of Sand

HIS NAME may have been Eric James Christiansen on his driver's license, passport, registration, and the deeds to three of his properties in the United States and Canada, but it wasn't the name he was born with. Sometimes he liked to think he didn't know the name he was born with—nuh-uh, couldn't remember, no such person ever existed, who were we talking about again?

But then everything in his chest and brain would become rootless, unfocused, a foggy wasteland without a point of reference.

He'd be forced to backtrack through each name, each identity, each kill in order to clear the fog, to make everything hard-edged and crystal in his mind and heart, or he'd be lost in the past and he'd forget his name *now.*

It was easier to simply keep that past on the periphery and know he could go there if he was ever forced to again.

But it wasn't his past that he was obsessing with today.

No. Today, it was whether he should put his bright and shiny name on the new, unfurnished house that he was currently pirating water, electricity, and sewage from via illegal RV hookups.

Pensively, he pondered the neighborhood as he sat on the steps of the RV itself, pushing at the six- and seven-toed kitten who kept trying to flounder his way out the door.

"No," he said, hoping his voice was firm. It was hard to be firm when you were talking to a special-needs black cat. Black cats as a whole were stompy and loud and perfect, and while this one could barely walk, he was no less stompy and loud and perfect.

"Meow, meow, meow, meow, meow…," his little friend complained, pushing his nose against Eric's back.

"I wouldn't let you out even if you had four toes," Eric told him crisply. "This isn't a special needs thing, this is a 'I don't want you to become a coyote's dinner' thing. Give it up…." He floundered for a name. He'd told people it was Oliver, but somehow that wasn't sticking right now.

"Eddie," he said, inspired. A fragment of his education—both the one he'd had in high school and the one he'd subjected himself to so he could appear cultured and well-read—drifted through his consciousness. Something about "clubbed feet."

Oedipus.

Oedipus.

Eddie. Puss.

He started cackling to himself. Finally, after a month of cohabitation, he'd found the name for his stompy, loud little friend.

"Mew." This next push against his back was a little harder. Not because the little tiger stripe was more agile, but because the tiny cart that carried her back end was so well-balanced, the kitten could *breathe* against the ground and push it half a mile.

"Katie," he said to the kitten. "Katie, my darling little girl, no, my little one. Simply no."

"Mew."

He reached behind him and smoothed her crinkled whiskers back against her crimped, tiger-striped fur. Both kittens forgot immediately about escape, and she folded her paws in front of her and leaned against his backside, while Eddie gamboled to his sister to clean her ears.

He didn't even have to look at them—he'd seen this dance before—and while his eyes had never left his new neighborhood, he sharpened his concentration on it again and tried to make his decision.

If this cul-de-sac—hell, if this block—had been placed anywhere else in the country, it would have been seen as a prime piece of real estate.

The houses were well-crafted, individual, and spacious, and their landscaping was drought friendly, which was great since they were practically *in the middle of* a place called Death Valley.

Death Valley tried to kill life forms dead—who wanted to live there?

He was lucky, he figured. He'd landed here in late February, about a month after an historic inland flood—a western hurricane, which was a once-in-a-hundred-year event—and he'd had a couple of days to figure that the high sixties was what passed as winter in a place that got to 120 regularly in the summer.

He needed to have his shit together by then, he thought, sipping his coffee appreciatively. If he was going to keep Katie and *Eddie*—most definitely Eddie—then he had to have a place that he could keep cool when he was not in it.

The RV he'd been living in for the last two months didn't qualify—although he *had* seen some beautiful scenery traveling from Northern to Southern California between December and January.

But if he wanted to stay *here*, he had to… what?

He glanced around the cul-de-sac again, remembering that one of the residents had told him that while only one person on the block kept his pool filled, they all knew each other, and were welcome to use it.

On the one hand, it sounded unbearably '70s and "let's all get naked in the disco pool," but having met all the residents, Eric had realized that while some of those men were criminals, *none* of them were "let's get naked in the disco pool" types. This was both disappointing and reassuring, really.

Reassuring because Eric had realized that his "fucking everything that moved" days needed to be left in his rearview—that sort of thing could be fun, but it wasn't good for *him*, not when he'd been craving a place to be accepted—and maybe redeemed—for the last nearly two decades of his life.

Disappointing because, well, damn. He was surrounded by *taken* gay men, not one of whom he'd kick out of bed for eating crackers.

Oh, and speaking of whom… here came one now.

Ernie—it was the only name he'd been given, and Eric knew better than to dig—was in his early to mid-twenties, willow slender, with dark curly hair and eyes so brown they were almost black. He had a narrow, almost vulpine face and an appealing, dreamy-eyed smile.

And his boyfriend was possibly one of the scariest motherfuckers Eric had ever met, in a long line of scary motherfuckers that Eric had either worked for or killed.

No, Eric would not be jumping into the disco pool with Lee Burton's boyfriend, thank you very much.

But he would accept a pastry from the plate Ernie carried, because he understood Ernie's donuts were a rite of passage and a blessing in the little community he'd found himself in.

"Oh my God," he muttered as Ernie got near and the scent wafted toward him. "Cinnamon rolls?"

Ernie gave a winsome smile. "Yes, I know," he said smugly. "Your favorite."

Eric stared at him helplessly. "I, uhm, have some milk if you'd like to sit down with me?" He'd worked with psychics before—or people who had little tiny bits of the gift strewn in with their psyches here and there.

He'd never worked or met with an Ernie before. Ernie had taken one look at him, shaken his hand, and *known* him. The good and the bad. And oh boy, did Eric Christiansen have an awful lot of bad in his soul.

But Ernie had given him a chance—given him a *vetting*—into the exclusive little club that centered on this cul-de-sac, and he could only be grateful. He seemed to recall that gratitude involved social niceties. He'd have to brush up on his etiquette.

"I'd like that," Ernie said. "Here, give me the coffee, and you can pick up the babies."

"Thanks," Eric told him, and he really *was* grateful. He scooped up the sleeping kittens and placed them gently in their top-loading crate. The inside of the crate featured a thick, soft bed, and if he was careful and timed it right—no more than two hours of napping in the crate—he could manage to get both kittens to their litter box before anything untoward happened.

Right now, it kept them from being underfoot, which, given that the RV was not exactly *spacious*, was what he wanted.

"Have you decided yet?" Ernie asked when they were situated with a glass of milk each and the *amazing* cinnamon rolls between them on the RV kitchenette table.

"Decided what?"

Eric was inhaling his pastry reverently, breathing softly in.

"Whether to move into the house," Ernie said patiently, and Eric nodded in acknowledgment before pulling off a piece and dipping it in milk.

He took a bite that was like an explosion of innocence and lust on his palate and made sounds he would have been ashamed to make in bed.

Swallowing almost left him drained.

After another deep breath—and a tentative bite of the pastry to see if it was just as good as the first (it was)—he relaxed a little and met Ernie's patient gaze.

"Was this to talk me into it?" he asked.

Ernie shrugged. "You made an impression at the barbecue. Sonny is already asking if he can visit the kittens, and while he's a grown man and can take disappointment, I like to cushion the blow a little."

Eric blinked. Sonny Daye, *definitely* not his real name, had been… interesting. Eric knew that there was something fundamentally broken in himself, something that made killing no big deal, that left him absolutely oblivious to the suffering of his fellow human beings once they'd passed a certain line in the sand.

Sonny *should* have been on the other side of that line, except Sonny had never killed another human being outside of battle.

Ever. His lover and protector, Ace (also not his real name), had shielded him from that choice.

Sonny was, for all intents and purposes, an innocent psychopath.

Eric rather enjoyed the little man's company. He was like a small, misbehaving dog. He was a good dog at heart, but he had… intrusive thoughts. Eric rather desperately wanted the good dog to win out. That meant there was hope for *him* as well.

And Sonny really loved the kittens.

"What would I have to do?" Eric asked, not even sure he knew who to contact to buy the house he was currently squatting next to. Hell, he had no idea how this entire cul-de-sac functioned—there was power, water, even trash services, but to quote a movie, they were *out in the middle of the fucking desert*! How did you apply for a lease on a house in a cul-de-sac in the middle of the fucking desert?

"Tell Burton and Jason," Ernie said, seemingly oblivious to Eric's grimace.

If Burton was one of the scariest motherfuckers Eric had ever met, Jason Constance had *trained* that man, and he was *also* a scary motherfucker. Both of them were military, Eric was *positive*. Some sort of special operation. But also both gay and living out here with their boyfriends.

He should have been looking for munchkins and a field of poppies while he was here.

"They both own this place?" he asked uncertainly.

"Well, Burton bought our house from a real-estate company that probably fainted, and then Jason supplied power and water and got services running, and then they both pooled their resources—don't ask. I'm sure you don't want me to know about your money. Same. But this place is theirs. So you ask, you pay them whatever they think is fair, and, you know, maybe don't fill in your pool. Or if you do, make it available, but seriously…." He grimaced. "Jason keeps his full, and since he and Cotton are only here for the weekends—"

"Anybody can use it," Eric said, nodding. "You told me that. Does it get used a lot?"

Ernie snorted softly. "Yes. We *all* use it. Even Sonny and Ace, on their day off."

They ran a garage across the highway from a filling station/Subway/mini-mart. They had a little house on the same property, and a tiny little dog—which is probably where Eric had gotten the analogy—and Eric got the impression that they'd started this little gathering in the desert and were quite surprised to find they were now surrounded by/responsible for other people.

They seemed to have just wanted to run their little garage and live their little lives, but Ace was meant for more than that, and he couldn't seem to squelch that sense of responsibility, of leadership, in himself.

Of all the people Eric had met in this little corner of the desert, it wasn't the scary military motherfuckers that Eric was afraid of dealing with. It was Ace.

"So their day off is…." he said, not sure if he'd be at the pool because of Sonny or not at the pool because of Ace.

And of course, he'd forgotten he was dealing with a psychic.

"Ace isn't going to kill you in the pool," Ernie said, obviously amused. "If he didn't like you, he would have told you to move on and left it at that."

Eric grimaced. Sure, Ace would have done that. But given that he'd seen the results of Ace's work the day he'd arrived here, he was still a little wary.

Ernie let out a sigh. "Look, I can see that you still don't quite get us. But please believe me when I say you have to be a *real* scumbag to have to worry about one of us offing you. I mean, I'm all-but-married to a government assassin. I was *supposed* to be a *hit.*"

"He couldn't do it?" Eric asked, surprised. After meeting Burton, he didn't think *anything* could interfere with the man's agenda.

"Well, he was studying me as a hit, and he realized that it wasn't that I was dangerous to the population, but what I knew was *very* dangerous to the man who'd tried to train me to help create assassins."

"Oh! Karl Lacey?" Eric's old unit, Corduroy, had been going to hook up with Admiral Lacey's little psychosocial experiment—with an emphasis on *psycho*. He saw the expression on Ernie's face and said, "God rot his soul in hell."

Ernie nodded. "Yup. That's the fucker. Burton figured out I could bring Lacey down, so he and Jason worked an undercover op to do that. We had some help, and it's not all wrapped up yet, but yeah. Burton and Jason both have a conscience—and a skill set. Same with Ace and same with Jai."

"The, uhm…."

"Giant bald Russian enforcer," Ernie said. "Yeah—hi, Jai!"

"You are here," said the giant bald Russian enforcer from Eric's doorway. "I thought so. George is at work, and I am going to the garage. You are coming?"

Ernie grunted. "Yeah. I told Ace I'd work today. I wanted to show Eric how to care for the cats so he could be—"

"You wish to indoctrinate him into our happy neighbor assassin cult," Jai said, and his broad face was so intimidating, Eric had trouble deciding if he was kidding or not. Only a twitch of his full mouth gave it away. "No need for the high pressure. You had him at cinnamon rolls."

Eric was going to protest that he wasn't that easy, but his mouth was full, and he didn't want to rush the cinnamon orgasm that was about to explode in his palate.

Ah yes. He could breathe now.

Okay, then.

He gazed at Ernie and Jai in pure bafflement and said, "If I'd known my soul could be bought so cheaply, I might have settled for petty theft and assault before graduating to full-out assassin."

Ernie guffawed like the twenty-something he appeared to be, and Jai's laughter shook the RV. From their crate, the kittens purred contentedly, and Eric decided they would be fine in the mild temperatures while he took a tour of Ernie's house.

Writer, knitter, mother, wife, award-winning author AMY LANE shows her love in knit wear, is frequently seen in the company of tiny homicidal dogs, and can't believe all the kids haven't left the house yet. She lives in a crumbling crapmansion in the least romantic area of California, has a long-winded explanation for everything, and writes to silence the voices in her head. There are alot of voices—she's written over 120 books.

Website: www.greenshill.com
Blog: www.writerslane.blogspot.com
Email: amylane@greenshill.com
Facebook: www.facebook.com/amy.lane.167
Twitter: @amymaclane
Patreon:https://www.patreon.com/AmyHEALane

Follow me on BookBub

A LONG CON ADVENTURE

The Mastermind

AMY LANE

"Delicious fun." – *Booklist*

Long Con Adventures: Book One

Once upon a time in Rome, Felix Salinger got caught picking his first pocket and Danny Mitchell saved his bacon. The two of them were inseparable… until they weren't.

Twenty years after that first meeting, Danny returns to Chicago, the city he shared with Felix and their perfect, secret family, to save him again. Felix's news network—the business that broke them apart—is under fire from an unscrupulous employee pointing the finger at Felix. An official investigation could topple their house of cards. The only way to prove Felix is innocent is to pull off their biggest con yet.

But though Felix still has the gift of grift, his reunion with Danny is bittersweet. Their ten-year separation left holes in their hearts that no amount of stolen property can fill. A green crew of young thieves looks to them for guidance as they negotiate old jewels and new threats to pull off the perfect heist—but the hardest job is proving that love is the only thing of value they've ever had.

Guess who's swimming in the same pond...
FISH OUT OF WATER
Amy Lane
1

Fish Out of Water: Book One

PI Jackson Rivers grew up on the mean streets of Del Paso Heights—and he doesn't trust cops, even though he was one. When the man he thinks of as his brother is accused of killing a police officer in an obviously doctored crime, Jackson will move heaven and earth to keep Kaden and his family safe.

Defense attorney Ellery Cramer grew up with the proverbial silver spoon in his mouth, but that hasn't stopped him from crushing on street-smart, swaggering Jackson Rivers for the past six years. But when Jackson asks for his help defending Kaden Cameron, Ellery is out of his depth—and not just with guarded, prickly Jackson. Kaden wasn't just framed, he was framed by crooked cops, and the conspiracy goes higher than Ellery dares reach—and deep into Jackson's troubled past.

Both men are soon enmeshed in the mystery of who killed the cop in the minimart, and engaged in a race against time to clear Kaden's name. But when the mystery is solved and the bullets stop flying, they'll have to deal with their personal complications… and an attraction that's spiraled out of control.

Scan the QR Code Below to Order!

THEIR BLOODLINE MAY NOT BE ROYAL,
BUT THE FAMILY ATTITUDE CERTAINLY IS.

Val Royal's tight family has always had his back, but they love to interfere in his life. That interference almost sends him over the edge when they arrange for Rory McCauley, security specialist, marksman, and hound-dog smartass, to ride shotgun as security on his latest run.

Hot, bossy, and sharp as a tack, Val ticks all Rory's boxes, but Val's looking for something real, and Rory's allergic to intimacy. Besides, their gig running refrigerated bull semen from Bakersfield to Austin could make or break Val's buddy's ranch, so Val's understandably pretty focused on the job. Rory still wishes Val would let him help Val, uh, *relax*.

As Val and Rory work to keep their payload safe from a couple of determined saboteurs and they get to know each other as smart, competent, fearless professionals, sparks fly, and Val starts to fall for Rory's roguish charm. But can he convince Rory their romance would be worth more than a straight shot to Austin—that it would be a love worth coming home to?

SHADES of HENRY

One bootstrap act of integrity cost Henry Worrall everything—military career, family, and the secret boyfriend who kept Henry trapped for eleven years. Desperate, Henry shows up on his brother's doorstep and is offered a place to live and a job as a handyman in a flophouse for young porn stars.

Lance Luna's past gave him reasons for being in porn, but as he continues his residency at a local hospital, they now feel more like excuses. He's got the money to move out of the flophouse and live his own life—but who needs privacy when you're taking care of a bunch of young men who think working penises make them adults?

Lance worries Henry won't fit in, but Henry's got a soft spot for lost young men and a way of helping them. Just as Lance and Henry find a rhythm as den mothers, a murder and the ghosts of Henry's abusive past intrude. Lance knows Henry's not capable of murder, but is he capable of caring for Lance's heart?

BONFIRES

Ten years ago Sheriff's Deputy Aaron George lost his wife and moved to Colton, hoping growing up in a small town would be better for his children. He's gotten to know his community, including Mr. Larkin, the bouncy, funny science teacher. But when Larx is dragged unwillingly into administration, he stops coaching the track team and starts running alone. Aaron—who thought life began and ended with his kids—is distracted by a glistening chest and a principal running on a dangerous road.

Larx has been living for his kids too—and for his students at Colton High. He's not ready to be charmed by Aaron, but when they start running together, he comes to appreciate the deputy's steadiness, humor, and complete understanding of Larx's priorities. Children first, job second, his own interests a sad last.

It only takes one kiss for two men approaching fifty to start acting like teenagers in love, even amid all the responsibilities they shoulder. Then an act of violence puts their burgeoning relationship on hold. The adult responsibilities they've embraced are now instrumental in keeping their town from exploding. When things come to a head, they realize their newly forged family might be what keeps the world from spinning out of control.

www.ingramcontent.com/pod-product-compliance
Lightning Source LLC
LaVergne TN
LVHW020526100826
845148LV00010B/1360

* 9 7 8 1 6 4 1 0 8 8 9 5 4 *